going away party

going away party

A NOVEL BY LAURA PEDERSEN

Dear Joan,
Thanks for the
invitation to speak.
All the best,
[illegible]

STORY LINE PRESS
ASHLAND, OREGON

First Printing

Published by Story Line Press, Three Oaks Farm, PO 1240, Ashland, OR 97520-0055 / www.storylinepress.com

This publication was made possible thanks in part to the generous support of Bloomsbury Books of Ashland, Oregon, the Andrew W. Mellon Foundation, the Oregon Arts Commission, and our individual contributors.

Book and cover design by Lysa McDowell
Cover photo by Charles Duncan

Library of Congress Cataloging-in-Publication Data

Pedersen, Laura.
Going away party : a novel / by Laura Pedersen.
p. cm.
ISBN 1-58654-010-6 (alk. paper)
I. Title.

PS3566.E2564 G65 2001
813'.54—dc21 00-054143

For my loving parents,
John and Ellen Pedersen,
who encouraged self-reliance.

"God likes happy children."
Sister Clementine, St. Benedict's Preschool.

"Your teddy bear fell apart in the laundry."
Joan MacGuire

Chapter 1
Home Alone
Monday Evening

Huddled over the white Formica-topped kitchen table, surrounded by reams of poorly taken calculus notes, I give serious consideration to the advice my knuckle-dragging brother Jack had yelled as the family camper pulled out of the driveway.

"Hey Sis, it's better to cheat than repeat!"

But after scanning the multitude of formulas and considering how many I might reasonably be able to ink onto my wrists, the answer is clear: Not nearly enough. Besides, I still wouldn't have a clue as to how to use the damn hieroglyphics. In any event, I am not a cheat, and I realize that even considering his stupid advice is just another excuse to stop trying.

I shove the book away from me in disgust—disgust for me, for calculus and for all the history books that say that Columbus discovered America. I mean, honestly, how the hell can you discover a place where thousands of people are already living?

Normally I'm quite talented at converting desperation into inspiration. And now is my big chance to prove to Mom and Dad that I can actually succeed at something. Something important. But I am getting absolutely nowhere.

And the silence is deafening. In fact, it's positively distracting. For the past eight weeks I've been looking forward to finally shaking the family and having the house to myself and now it suddenly seems spooky. When I lived in my apartment near college there were always roommates around to bullshit with—probably a big part of the reason I got an A in my negotiation seminar and then flunked calculus. At least when the kinfolk are in residence there is always someone around to fight with. I thought I'd be really happy after they all took off. But it's awfully quiet now. Too quiet.

A few minutes pass and I hear the welcome sound of raindrops plunking against the roof. I shift my gaze from the calculus book and out to the safety of my own backyard and intently study the chubby droplets as they ricochet off the vaulted ceiling of our slightly mold-stained St. Peter's Basilica birdfeeder. Good. It's been so fucking hot. Maybe the rain shower will help. This scorching summer has broken every high temperature and humidity record, and it's not over.

The phone rings and I glance at the clock—right on time.

"Calculus gulag. Hello warden."

"That's not funny Jessica! And how did you know it was me?" my mother inquires in her perpetually surprised-sounding soprano voice. "It could have been Aunt Iris, or heaven forbid, someone from your father's office."

"It's exactly 6:30 PM on Monday night. It's National Park pilgrimage protocol," I explain. "You always call right after you eat on the day you've left for vacation. And you always stop for a picnic dinner at exactly 5:45 PM. Then you use the payphone to remind whoever is taking care of the house to water the plants or something that you've told them to do but are afraid they'll forget. In the meantime, Dad gets gas and scrapes bird shit off the windshield."

"Watch your language Jessica! I suppose I do, but I just never thought of myself as being quite so predictable." Mom acknowledges my observation rather good-naturedly. "And the correct English, by the way, is whomsoever. I just wanted to make sure that everything is all right and that you remembered to close the garage door and to turn on the porch lights."

"Mom, now you know I'd sooner be struck by lightning than forget about the porch lights," I cheerfully lie. Cheerfulness is the key to committing successful perjury. Glum children make my mother immediately suspicious.

"And be sure to close the windows if it starts to rain." Joan diligently continues through her checklist. "It's already sprinkling here and your father says that there's a storm headed in your direction."

"Right. Windows!" I try to answer in a brisk and efficient tone of voice, which I hope will make it sound as if I've already completed this task as well. However, glancing through to the family room I can see a legion of hearty raindrops plopping through the mesh screen, collecting in small pools on the maple windowsills and then running down the wood-paneled wall towards the light sockets.

"Are you studying, Sweetie?"

"No Mom. I'm trying to figure out why the caged bird sings."

"Don't be a smarty-pants, Jessica."

"Of course I'm studying," I say in an exasperated tone, more out of habit than anything else. "I know you and Dad may find this hard to believe, but I didn't fail math on purpose—as if I'm trying to get into the *Guinness Book of World Records* for how many times I can repeat calculus."

"I suppose that's all then," Mom says hurriedly. Though time is running out and I know she doesn't wish to feed more money into the telephone I sense there is another round to come when I hear the kerchink of another coin dropping in. "And what did I tell you about watering the garden?"

"I can't believe you don't remember. You only said it, like, five hundred times."

"And you wonder why you can't find a job, with a sarcastic mouth like that?"

"Mom, seriously, right before you left you told me at least ten times to water the garden on Wednesday morning."

"Well don't forget, then. Are you sure that you'll be all right staying at home by yourself this week? You can still go to Grandma's. I know that she'd love the company."

"Mother, *please*," I groan into the receiver. "I've lived in a dorm or an apartment since my freshman year of college."

In the background I hear my father's Irish tenor voice complaining about the exorbitant cost of fuel on the highway, poor gas mileage due to the overloaded roof rack and falling behind schedule. He's been agitated about the schedule all week, muttering that the extreme heat is sure to draw wild animals in search of water out onto the interstate and increase the amount of roadkill, thereby causing more accidents and generally slowing traffic.

"All right then. Just don't forget to water the garden, Jessica. And don't eat pizza every night. There are lots of leftovers in the refrigerator. I left some good chicken breast in there for you and some nice meat loaf. And fresh fruit for snacks." I've often noticed that Mom cherishes the adjectives *nice* and *good* when it comes to describing remaindered food items.

"Come along Mother!" I can hear Dad closing in. "Let's hit the trail!"

It was almost a decade ago that my father had fallen into the married, over-forty trap of referring to Joan as *Mother*. Unless they are at a bank function and then he jokingly says that she is his family co-CEO. Cringe. Lawn widow is more like it. My folks are probably about three years away from exchanging their double bed for two singles, sharing reading glasses, never allowing the gas gauge to dip below three-quarters and arriving at parties a full hour early.

"Jess dear, Daddy says hello. Bye-bye honey. I have to go. We miss you. See you on Sunday night then."

"I miss you too," I recite automatically.

The rain lets up and in the backyard a harsh sizzle emanates from the bright blue neon coil of death which is at the epicenter of Dad's deluxe electric bug zapper, fracturing the otherwise still evening. I jump more than slightly. I don't know why. Just edgy, I guess. After all, it's only the sound of nature taking its course in galvanized suburbia—

the familiar hiss announcing the demise of another one of God's smaller and more irksome creatures. I suppose it should be a comfort to know that I'm not the only one fighting for my life, and losing.

Once again the silence hangs so heavily inside the house that I decide math will just have to wait a few more minutes. Besides, a girl can't be expected to endure a phone call from her mother and then immediately plunge back into everyday life without some sort of a buffer zone in-between. I absentmindedly page through some mail-order catalogs that are stacked in an orderly pile on the kitchen counter and wonder aloud who the fuck is ordering stainless steel cookie cutters and liquid soap dispensers in the shape of orca whales.

The calculus book seems to be taunting me, appearing in the corner of my eye every ten seconds or so, challenging me from its place on the table. It doesn't take a genius to figure out that it is for sure demonically possessed, like one of those spooky portraits of pasty old men in charcoal suits with dark beady eyes that follow you around the stacks in musty old libraries.

When I begin to study again it's out of sheer panic. Abject terror begotten from the knowledge that if I don't manage to graduate from college the following week, I will be living out my days at home with my parents eating *good* tuna salad with *nice* chopped scallions and being perpetually advised to put a barrette in my hair.

I chew on a stale Power Bar in an effort to achieve tri-harmony—mind, body, and spirit all working together in one Herculean push to grasp and absorb differential and integral calculus. The only thing I'm missing in large doses is spirit, although the mind is in desperate need of a tune-up and if the body was totally replaced I would not exactly complain or anything.

But positive thinking isn't getting me where I need to be and so I decide that it's time for a fructose corn syrup jolt. This heat has been making me thirsty all the time. Lately I've been fantasizing about sticking an IV of pink lemonade into my arm. Removing a tall glass from the cupboard I accidentally knock over my sister Katie's favorite plastic Wonder Woman mug. At least it was Katie's favorite mug when she was eleven—back then she would have held her breath until she passed out before so much as touching any other cup to her lips. But now she's fourteen and cares a lot more about boys than a cartoon character who flies around in an invisible plane wearing a silly looking bathing suit. Picking up that old mug, now all chipped and faded, and putting it back in its place makes me think that I wouldn't mind so much if Katie had stayed here at home with me. Sure, she's still a kid and all, but we can talk about stuff or at least go shopping together. And she's not bad company. In fact, she's even got a boyfriend and so we could talk about what jerks guys are.

When she was younger Katie used to sort of idolize me—follow me around wanting to do everything that I did. Little sister shit. It annoyed the hell out of me back then and I'd try to ditch her or threaten to paste her or else complain to Mom. In retrospect, it was kind of cute, I guess. And for sure it's not like anyone is following me around in a state of total admiration nowadays. Not that they should, since lately I've been a total puke. Even I'll admit that. And of course, Katie's a teenager now and doesn't feel that way anymore. Earlier this afternoon, when I was looking for an eraser, I came across this little square of construction paper in her top desk drawer on which she'd mapped out how she's going to rearrange our room after I move and get all my shit out of there. I'm not mad about it or anything. I mean, it's not as if she's being presumptuous, because the fact of the matter is, I threaten to move out every day. All I need is this stupid degree and a stupid job and I'm going to do it too.

I pour a tall glass of cola, none of that diet shit, and dump in six packets of sugar just for good measure. After a big gulp I place fingers to temples and psyche myself up. *You can do this!* I silently scream.

Chapter 6. Introduction: Synthetic division is a short way of dividing a polynomial by a binomial of the form x-b.

I read it again. And then again, highlighting a few lines with an electric pink marker. Now, with all this information seeping into my brain,

I feel in control. I can do this. It's just a bunch of stupid numbers, excuse me, integers, and all I need to remember is that there are different tricks for putting each heap of them together. That's all. In other words, the entire calculus course is just another conspiracy against me.

And it might actually help if I could see the numbers. If I can just get this fucking hair out of my eyes once and for all. If only Mom would stop insisting that I use barrettes to clip it back then I believe I might actually consider doing just that.

The excessive humidity commingles with the bright orange pizza grease and makes my book pages stained and gluey so that they stick to one another. The air in the kitchen is moist and stagnant. So much so that I wonder whether I might be able to carve my initials in the watery haze with my index finger.

To make synthetic division shorter we leave out all the x's and just write the coefficients.

What is a coefficient again? And who does the author think he is saying *we*, as if we are all in this mess together.

After half an hour I finally get up the courage to tackle the sample problems that are housed at the end of every chapter in a light gray shaded box. Everyone knows that being able to complete the sample problems is what separates the future mall clerks from tomorrow's bank managers. And I certainly wouldn't mind being among the latter.

Unfortunately, they make absolutely no sense to me. Is it possible the printer made a mistake in my copy? How am I ever going to get through this stupid exam? I purposely crush my pencil tip into the tabletop, drop my head down on top of the page and try to cry. But I am barren and if I cannot produce the answers to differential equations how can I possibly yield tears?

A natural logarithm of a positive number x is the logarithm of x to the base e, where e = 2.71828 . . .

Surely, they must be joking. My degree is in marketing, for Chrissakes. Selling! Shopping! Giving the professor a blowjob is probably out of the question. He keeps referring to a wife and six-pack of kids back in Bangladesh.

Somehow I force myself to solve problems for almost an hour and a half. I feel slightly relieved. Like some days calculus wins, maybe even most days, but some days Jess wins. Although I'm not anywhere near being able to pass that stupid final exam on Friday.

The doorbell rings. Hallelujah! Study break! I prepare to buy whatever they're selling, sign all petitions, and donate to whatever cause—anything to escape natural logarithms for even five minutes. The bright green numbers on the microwave oven clock flash 8:41 PM. Surely it's too late for the proselytizing of the Jehovah's Witnesses. Too bad. That could have easily killed an hour, arguing about imminent destruction and the world's wickedness.

More than likely it is not a representative of a religious order, but a member of Jack's not very highly-evolved rat pack of eighteen-year-olds who have probably not received word of the annual MacGuire family camping trip. If this crew were any dumber they would need to be watered and pruned twice a week. Personally, I am of the opinion that Jack enforces a strict *zero intelligence* policy when it comes to choosing his cronies.

Before swinging open the heavy oak front door I peer through the little side faux-stained glass window to check who's there, more out of habit than anything else. But it's already too dark. Damn. Serves me right for lying to Mom about turning the lights on. One point for you, God.

I hate to switch on that eerie urine-colored bulb once a visitor is already standing at the front door. It's such a blatant act of suspicion and always seems so rude when the tables are turned and I'm the illumination victim. Nevertheless, I flick the switch in the front hall as I've been taught to do and once again peer out the narrow window.

There stands a middle-aged man I've never seen before, apparently startled by the sudden bath of garish yellow light, as if he wasn't really expecting the door to be answered in the first place. He looks to be late forty-something, of average height with salt and pepper hair and owlish glasses that make his blue eyes appear slightly lampy. Under an open black windbreaker he has on a faded, forest green LaCoste polo shirt, an obvious late-'80s purchase, the *de rigueur* tan pants of the suburban male, and on his feet are the standard I-work-in-an-office-but-they-sometimes-set-me-free-on-Sunday Docksiders. It's definitely not the uniform of the meter reader from the local gas company. Though he looks like the kind of guy who carries one of those Swiss Army knives in his pocket.

He glances up as if to confirm that the source of the gaudy glare is indeed the overhead fixture and then hastily turns and retreats down the driveway.

I pull open the front door and speak at the retreating windbreaker, "Excuse me mister, can I help you?"

The man spins around and squints at me curiously. He deliberately hikes back up to the porch, towards me, and stops directly underneath the light. By now a few triangular white moths have begun dive-bombing the frosted glass fixture. "I'm sorry," the mysterious stranger says. "I—I didn't think that anyone was home."

"Oh," I remark curiously and can't help but wonder why a person would ring a doorbell if he doesn't think that anyone is home.

"Well there nearly wasn't, I mean I almost didn't open the door but then I decided you don't exactly look like the murdering kind. In fact, you sort of resemble an encyclopedia salesman, though you aren't carrying any books or a briefcase. Actually I've only seen door-to-door salesmen in the old movies that my parents like to watch, but you're how I picture a modern one might look. So what can I do for you?"

It takes the guy a minute to recover from my blast. In situations where I'm not sure what to say I have a habit of rambling. Besides, prattling out a pile of garbage gives me time to think and basically confuses the hell out of the person who is causing my consternation.

The man eventually revives. "I—uh, I used to live here," he explains. "I was just sort of reminiscing." He casts his gaze up at my two-story white clapboard house and then over to the garage as if to prove his point.

"Oh," I say. Well at least this is now starting to make some sense, since I'm aware that people occasionally embark on tours of their past. Though not usually at nine o'clock at night. It's just like calling up old loser boyfriends on a Saturday night when you're alone and miserable. We're all guilty.

"I guess it's rather late," he says as he glances down at his watch, as if he has read my mind. "I'm sorry that I bothered you." Again he starts turning away.

No way baby. I need some company around this cracker box and there's no one else in the frame. And suddenly I get a little help from old Mother Nature as a cloud bursts directly overhead and the rain pounding on the aluminum overhang makes it difficult to hear anything.

"Why don't you come in and dry off and wait for this to stop?" I shout above the din. "Besides, my folks would never forgive me if I didn't give you a chance to look around your old home." And who knows, maybe the guy is a whiz at calculus.

He looks past me and inside the house, as if he is going to make his decision based on the color scheme that my mother has selected for the front hallway rather than the weather. "Yeah, okay, sure," he replies uncertainly and follows me inside.

"If you're honest and fair then things will always work out."
Miss Kendall to the first grade at Stuttaford Elementary School.

"Fairies are real. And when you say you don't believe in them, one dies just a little bit."
Grandma Maggie on the Tooth Fairy.

Chapter 2
Suicide in Stuttaford is Redundant
Monday Night

No sooner are we inside the house than it strikes me that maybe he really is some sort of a criminal. There had been a spree of break-ins over the summer. Perhaps a maniac? No, too brand conscious for that.

But I'm relieved of my anxieties when I see how carefully he dries the soles of his Docksiders on the thick burlap mat lying on the floor in front of the door. And it's also at this moment that I realize I've seen him before and it definitely wasn't on a black-and-white poster down at the post office. Maybe some of his kids went to my school.

"I'm sorry for not introducing myself, by the way." He smiles pleasantly at me. "My name is Denis Sinclair." He steps off the doormat and politely extends his right hand.

"My name is Jess MacGuire," I say and shake his hand, only to screw it up. I can never figure out how many times you're supposed to pump before letting the other person's hand go and my worst nightmare is to shake for that extra few seconds like Father O'Flaherty does, and so I tend to release too early. This always gives the person whose hand I'm shaking the sense that I'm trying to escape them or that I fear they have influenza. But Mr. Sinclair doesn't seem to notice.

"Um, do you mind if I take this off?" He asks hesitantly and nods toward the dripping sleeves of his wet windbreaker. "I wouldn't want to get water all over your floor."

Stupid. Stupid. Stupid. I quickly go back to the business of berating myself. *May I take your coat, please*, was the first full sentence Mom had taught me. I take the rain-soaked garment from him and hang it on the closet doorknob in the front hall.

"Why don't we go into the kitchen and I'll make some coffee?" I suggest.

"Sure, thanks, that would be fine," he says.

However, Mr. Sinclair seems more interested in examining his new surroundings than having a coffee klatch. Not surprising, I suppose. After all, he used to live here. He probably just wants to see what kind of changes my parents have made.

"Or I can show you around if you like," I offer. "You know, kind of like a memory tour. Once my mom drove my little sister Katie and me on a trip to her hometown of Columbia, Missouri, just to show us the farmhouse where she was raised. The hidden agenda was of course to prove that life was much more difficult when she was growing up—to verify that she and her sister did chores every morning for an hour before climbing on board the school bus."

"No, no that's okay." He declines with a polite wave of his hand.

"I don't blame you. We didn't end up staying very long with Velma."

"Velma?" He asks.

"The old lady who purchased my mother's birthplace. She'd covered every inch of the farmhouse with this tea rose wallpaper that was positively whirling with tiny flowers, stems and buds, and which, when combined with some horrific lavender toilet water that she must have used to clean the floors, made us all feel like we were in the ladies room of a funeral parlor and frankly, it made us all want to chuck our lunches."

Mr. Sinclair makes no response so I head towards the kitchen. But he lags behind, pausing to inspect everything. First he surveys the living room and glances up the stairs towards the second floor, but it's dark and he can't see anything and so he starts to follow me again, then makes a brief stop to peer into the family room. For a long moment he studies a recent family photo mounted on the wall across from the two steps that lead up to the kitchen area.

He doesn't say anything and I keep checking his face for a sign of approval or disapproval—nothing. But I guess that's about right. Our home looks pretty much the same as most of my friends' houses. Mom has opted for the standard Sears department store Colonial decor. There are brass-plated American eagles in prominent places, patchwork quilts neatly folded atop solid pine furniture, and on the mantelpiece stand two thick silver candlestick holders. Adorning the walls are a few of those brightly colored farm scenes that make the cows and barns appear to be very flat and one-dimensional. In fact, if Paul Revere were to suddenly gallop up he'd be right at home here—that is as long as he said *please* and *thank you* and was partial to iced tea.

Nestea lemon-flavored iced tea is the Joan MacGuire miracle cure for anything from a migraine headache to a bad hair day. And unlike wine or seasonal drinks such as eggnog or apple cider, Joan insists that iced tea is a versatile year round refreshment which goes well with fish, meat or poultry. And if the suits at the Lipton tea headquarters ever discover her unbridled enthusiasm for their product, I think Mom could perhaps popularize their beverage on a par with the marketing miracle June Allyson performed as spokeswoman for Depends adult diapers.

"Do you mind if I dry off a little bit and wash my hands?" Mr. Sinclair cordially asks.

"Sure, I mean, no. I mean, go right ahead. There's a bathroom right there." I point to the door right before the one that leads to the basement. "The towel hanging over the mirror is clean." Did I just hear myself say *clean towel?* Surely it isn't long before *nice* and *good* enter my permanent vocabulary. Maybe I'll start carrying a couple cyanide capsules around in my backpack just in case I do it again.

While Mr. Sinclair is in the bathroom I hit upon the ideal fail-safe adult topic: the weather. Grown-ups can never get enough weather talk. I practice a few ideas in my head while disposing of the grease-drenched pizza box and attempt to wipe all the crumbs and cola rings off the table and counters. How did I manage to make such a total mess in the five short hours since they'd all departed?

When Mr. Sinclair returns to the kitchen I immediately launch into my prepared dialogue. "So, hopefully this rain will give us a break from the awful humidity we've been having." I am really pleased with this opener and think that I sounded pretty damn cheery and engaging. I grade it—ten out of ten for content and eight and a half out of ten for delivery. I shave off a point and a half since I couldn't look at him while I said it. But I believe Mom would have been proud.

"Don't count on it," Mr. Sinclair distractedly replies and shifts his gaze around the kitchen, as if he's wondering if maybe he left his wallet or keys on our countertop. "It's not likely to break until Friday when this high pressure system from Canada moves in. What we really need is a good, strong cold front."

Okay, something sounds very familiar and then suddenly it clicks. I stop what I'm doing and blurt out: "You're the weatherman!"

He takes my astonishment in stride, as if this has happened before.

"Not very often. Just when Reed Donner has an emergency. I haven't done it in awhile." He says all this in a monotone, as if being on television is not a big deal and he couldn't care less about it—like it's actually a big drag just to get out of bed and drive all the way to the studio and point at the satellite map.

"Well, why didn't you say so? I knew that I recognized you from somewhere!"

"I don't know. I guess it's kind of embarrassing. And anyway, it's not my real job. In fact, they hardly pay me anything for doing it."

His modesty appears genuine, which appeals to me. If I were on television I'd tell everyone I met.

"And here I was thinking that maybe you had kids who went to Stuttaford and that I'd seen you at a basketball game or a school play or something like that."

"No. Garrison. I have three girls that went to Garrison High School. But my wife worked at Stuttaford Middle School."

Suddenly I recognize his last name. "Hey, isn't your wife the guidance counselor for last names O thru Z?" I ask. At first I wonder if he's giving me a weird look because of my decidedly juvenile and parochial star-struck deportment but then I want to scream *Oh shit!* The story had been all over the television and newspapers in July—a tractor-trailer jackknifed on Highway 27 during a torrential downpour and killed the driver of an oncoming car.

"Yes. Sarah was my wife," Mr. Sinclair somberly acknowledges. "She died in an automobile accident several weeks ago," and then adds a very weak *but it's not your fault* sort of smile.

"I know. I mean, I'm sorry. I knew that. I didn't uh, I just didn't make the connection right away."

"That's okay." He sighs and the very weak smile disappears and he looks forlorn and sad.

Dammit, I feel like such a jerk for saying something so incredibly stupid. It's just like my mother is always warning me, that the lint trap between my brain and my mouth is frequently missing in action. She tends to criticize everything in laundry or cleaning terminology. There could be no real recovery from here. My rule of thumb is that when you get conversationally jammed up like this it's best just to continue on in a hurry. In life one should always keep moving forward and toward the door. But I can't think of anything. I'm desperate to cover the stain of this last fuck up with some words, any old syllables, much like my mother is forever putting place mats over the gouge marks in the dining room table, even though we all know perfectly well that they are there.

As the silence starts to suck the oxygen out of the room I feel a monumental panic rising within me. However mawkish, I know that some condolences are in order. I mean, you don't just get notified of a death, even a death you already knew about, and then sail right on to the next subject. His wife couldn't have been any older than my parents. And what an awful way to die.

But what to say? How would Joan handle this? So many times I've been with her in the supermarket or at a Little League baseball game where she walks directly over to the person who has just experienced a major tragedy—breast cancer, miscarriage, house burned to the ground, whatever—and expresses the perfect sentiment in the right words, accompanied by the appropriate gestures of friendship and concern. A human Hallmark card. Why hadn't I paid more attention or at the very least kept a notebook?

Out of nervousness I start to pick at the fresh scab on my forehead. It was from one of those awful zits that give you a headache whenever you bend over and so this morning I'd finally squeezed it.

"I was . . . uh, really sorry to hear that your wife, uh, died," I finally manage to say and then exhale. While scrupulously studying the linoleum flooring underneath my feet. I had never before noticed that there is a tan and cream colored crisscross pattern etched into it. But I feel awkward the minute these words are out of my mouth and regret not having said, *passed away.* Damn. Everyone knows you're not supposed to say *died.* This was quickly escalating into one of those impossibly uncomfortable moments like the time I met my friend Brenda's father and he had a limp and I asked, *So how'd you hurt your leg?* and he smiled and graciously replied, *I had polio as a child.*

"Uh, thanks." Mr. Sinclair also looks down for a moment and shuffles his feet and I wonder if maybe he too is admiring the crisscross pattern on the flooring. "It was a shock, a shock to everyone," he adds.

I regret inviting him in. Maybe being alone wasn't so bad after all. I feel totally out of my league.

Trying to envision Mom with her constant composure and even tone of voice I take a deep breath and ask, "Would you care for some coffee?" But I panic again, scrape my fingernails across my forehead in an effort to sweep my bangs from my eyes once and for all and accidentally tear the loose scab off my pimple. Now I imagine that a stream of blood is pouring out of my head. Plus I had sounded perky—much too perky. In striving for a tone that reflected concern and reassurance I had instead come off like a morning talk show hostess exclaiming over a new recipe during a cooking segment, or else as if I was auditioning for a Folger's coffee commercial.

When I finally gain the courage to glance up from the linoleum, if for no other reason than to keep the possible flow of blood from trickling down my face, it appears that Mr. Sinclair hasn't registered any of my anxieties.

He eventually slides into a chair at the kitchen table and eyes the cover of my math book. I realize I probably should have offered him a seat.

"Ah, calculus. This yours?" He reaches out his hand and lightly passes his fingertips over the cover of the toxic tome.

I relax a little. "Unfortunately. Through some bizarre twist of fate, after fifteen years of full-time education, of consuming useless barrels of drivel and vomiting it back up again upon command like a trained sea lion, my future has somehow become inextricably linked to the results of a calculus exam this Friday. No tickee, no washee—no pass, no degree, no job, no money, no life."

"That bad. A defining moment?"

"Worse. A death-defying moment." Did I just say *death*? I automatically glance disdainfully at the evil calculus book that has recently consumed my life and now holds all the cards to my future. For a dead tree and a dollar's worth of printer's ink it is certainly wielding an inordinate amount of power.

"Coffee's almost ready. Do you want something to eat?" I feel as if I'm entertaining a celebrity and wish that I had something really good to offer him. I've never met anyone who is on television, except for neighbors who have participated in those idiotic local human-interest stories about growing the largest pumpkin or winning the annual kite-flying contest. "Maybe some salad or, or a peanut butter sandwich?" Am I a complete and total moron? My I.Q. has just plummeted to my age or possibly even my shoe size. Peanut fucking butter! People in their forties don't eat peanut butter, and particularly not chunky peanut butter. Maybe I'm just dehydrated. Perhaps I should swallow some salt tablets.

"Eat? No thank you. I'm not really hungry," he politely declines.

I'm surprised because he looks sort of hungry, like a sandwich might be just the thing, but then it's none of my business.

Carrying the scorching black sludge to the table is when it occurs to me that it is entirely too hot to be drinking coffee and that I should have offered Mr. Sinclair something cold to drink. Oh well. It's too late now.

I place a half-gallon cardboard carton labeled chocolate milk on the table in front of him. "Contrary to what the label says, this is regular milk," I explain. "My dad had a heart attack a few months ago and so my mother puts the whole milk in this chocolate milk carton and the fat-free milk in the whole milk container. I know," I say before he has a chance to comment, "it's all incredibly stupid. But it's because he's not supposed to have regular milk anymore. The doctor ordered him to lose twenty pounds by yesterday."

"Oh. I'm sorry to hear that your dad was ill. But doesn't he figure this milk scheme out when he sees that after pouring from the chocolate milk container you're indeed drinking regular white milk and not chocolate milk?"

"My mother only puts the whole milk container out on the table at dinner time, which is of course the one with the fat-free milk. If we want anything else we have to go and get it in the kitchen. My mother basically serves him everything. Dad never goes near the kitchen."

"Ah, very clever. The old pour and switch routine."

I set the mug of coffee down in front of him and Mr. Sinclair gingerly cradles it between his palms and glances up at me. I wonder what he is thinking. For some reason I specifically wonder what he thinks of me and I suddenly wish that I didn't look like such a slob, or had at least brushed my hair or tucked in my shirt. Mom is always saying that I'm too old to hang around *looking unkempt* because *you never know when or where you're going to meet your future husband.* She read in *People Magazine* that Mary Tyler Moore met her husband while taking her mother to the doctor. He was the doctor. Obviously this story appeals to Mom on more than one level; devoted daughter caring for ailing mother, romance ensues and appropriately results in marriage and furthermore, being in the medical profession, spouse registers an out-of-the-ballpark homerun on the career-o-meter.

I think that Mr. Sinclair is going to say something but he doesn't and so the silence again starts making me anxious. Unfortunately, I'm now completely out of ideas. I'm convinced that I did as much as I possibly could with the weather. Ultimately I panic and go into repeat mode. "Are you sure I can't give you a tour of the old homestead?"

He looks hesitant, as if he doesn't want to appear rude by declining. "No, I don't want to be a bother. Everything looks just great." Mr. Sinclair smiles approvingly at the kitchen cabinetry.

"I've never understood why people want to go back to where they grew up anyway. Or at least if they grew up here I can't imagine why they'd want to come back."

"Why do you say that?" he inquires.

"Please. The people in this neighborhood are all a bunch of nosy middle-class republicans whose only concerns are that other homeowners aren't properly caring for their lawns or that their property values are under siege from higher taxes, the local zoning board, and morally depraved teenagers running rampant during summer vacations. When the neighbors gather at block parties the talk eventually turns to marauding minors and graffiti-covered traffic signs. It's never long before some old fart chimes in with, 'You know, over in Japan the kids attend school almost all year round. And just look at those math scores!' Besides, I hate it here. All my friends have gone on to greener pastures, or at least had the good sense to join the Army or become autoworkers in Detroit. Ones with paid vacations I might add. Even my best friend Wendy, voted mostly likely to live and die in Stuttaford, got worn down by the static quo and packed off to Menlo Park, California. She said that if she was going to waste her life as a secretary it may as well be one with stock options in a start-up software company in Silicon Valley." Uh-oh, I was rambling again. Possibly

I was going into a full manic episode, like the time my folks forgot that the insurance salesman was coming over and I had to entertain him for a full hour while waiting for them to return home.

"I see." He purposefully moves his coffee mug to another spot three inches to the left without taking a sip. "Can I ask you something?" He doesn't wait for me to answer. "Is your family sitting shivah?"

"No. They're camping at Sleeping Bear Dunes National Lakeshore," I reply matter-of-factly. "Where's Shivah?"

A smile briefly curves the corners of his mouth upward and makes his face look much less somber and I decide that I'm happy to have invited him in after all.

"Shivah is . . . you sit shivah when someone dies," he explains in a tone that borders on a chuckle. "I just assumed that with all the mirrors covered and you dressed in black in the middle of the summer . . ."

"Oh, the mirrors. I just prefer to make an appointment to see my reflection rather than have it suddenly pop up in unexpected places. You know, 'Mirror mirror on the wall, I am my mother after all.'" Earlier that day, after waving the family off on their trip, I caught my reflection in the front hall mirror and immediately wanted to throw up or, at the very least, develop one hell of an eating disorder. The gangly body, blotchy skin, the straight oily hair, the pimple—a beacon on my forehead, all leered at me from the looking glass in my own mud hall. Why be tortured all week in the comfort of my own home I had asked myself. As soon as the taillights of the family Towlight camper disappeared down the block I seized almost every towel in the laundry room, clean or dirty, and frantically ran from room to room draping them over my reflection wherever I happened to find it. But I certainly wasn't going to tell him that.

"It's so hot that I covered them all with towels," I state. I've often found that the key to success in evading a truthful answer is to say something brief and totally idiotic, but to say it seriously and then move on fast. "And I almost always wear black. I like to think of it as serial killer chic, you know, it keeps away anyone considering unnecessary casual contact or conversation. So I guess the answer is no, nobody died." Whoops, death once again, the totally wrong thing to say. "I meant that, uh, no one died here. At least, not that I know of." How is it that the D word keeps popping up? It might be a good idea to change the subject. "So, uh, Mr. Sinclair . . . "

"Please call me Denny," he offers and smiles at me.

"Wow, that's really cool. A certified Other actually requesting that I use his first name." Another dumb thing to say.

"What's an Other? Is that like a UFO?"

"No, no. It's stupid." Why did I tell him that? "It's just, well, it's how I refer to people who have real jobs and cars and stuff. Just inside my head, you know."

"I see," he says. "A code word. Sort of like *you* versus *us*, the *shirts* against the *skins*."

"Yeah, sort of." I'm so used to calling all my neighbors, parents' friends, and professors by Mr. and Mrs. that I'm suddenly anxious to try this first name thing out right away, in case there is never another chance. Like, maybe his first name will just get stuck in my throat. And if I fail calculus, I'm quite sure that there will never be another chance—largely because I will run away to Mexico and support myself by addressing the general population as Señor and Señorita as I inquire whether they'd like fries with their Felicidad Meals at the Golden Arches in Guadalajara.

"So, uh, Denny," I pause after saying his first name and look up to see if possibly he has changed his mind about the offer, but he doesn't seem to notice I'm running such a test. I briefly savor the words and picture myself at a cocktail party, snacking on dainty *hors d'oeuvres* that require wooden toothpicks with brightly colored plastic cellophane curls and small white paper cocktail napkins underneath—not the pigs-in-a-blanket that are always served at the annual Volunteer Fireman's Potluck Supper. "You must have lived here quite awhile ago because I was born in this house. Well, not exactly in the house, you know, in the hospital. But we lived here then and that was almost twenty-one years ago. So, uh, what was my house like when you lived here?" What a dumb thing to ask. It's the same house with different furniture and different pictures on the walls. Was I thinking that my parents had purchased it and then perhaps rotated the foundation thirty degrees to the east in order to receive maximum exposure to the morning sun?

"When I was here it was uh, very different, uh let me see," Denny says slowly.

"Are you sure I can't give you the Grand Tour?" I excitedly ask and jump up. "My dad has put up a lot of shelving in the basement and the garage which I'm sure you'd like to see."

He doesn't get up. "Uh, that's okay. Really." Then he stops talking and looks directly into my eyes. For a second I wonder if maybe he's a Pentecostal minister in disguise who has come to convert me and I've just given him the necessary cue to start his spiel. "I was lying. I never lived here, okay," Denny says solemnly.

At first I must appear worried, as if my initial fears about inviting a total stranger into the house may have been justified after all. I know I must look confused because that is how I feel. What is with this guy?

"I . . . I've run away from home!" This next line tumbles out like a defiant child offering up a lame excuse and he resembles one of my brothers trying to explain some dumb screw-up.

But searching Denny's earnest face makes me relax again. In fact, I almost laugh right out loud. And if he hadn't said this so seriously I know that I would have. It's just about the most ridiculous thing I have ever heard of, that is, after the concept of one-size fits all in women's bathing suits. Here is a grown man who occasionally does the weather on television, a total adult—who now sounds about twelve-years-old.

"You've run away," I repeat.

"That's right," he says seriously. "I'm on the lam."

He says this so seriously that I'm having second thoughts. Maybe he's a psycho after all. "Well then why did you say that you used to live here?" I demand.

But then his face relaxes and he leans back in his chair again and grins at me. "I didn't think you'd believe me if I said that I was looking for a fourth for bridge," he jokes halfheartedly. "Actually, I have a friend who lives on this street, Walt Sutherland. And I thought—"

"I know Mr. Sutherland!" Finally, something sensible to grab onto. "He lives three houses down on the left, this side of the street, and has practically the exact same landscaping." Walt Sutherland is a friend of my dad's. Every spring they split a big topsoil delivery from the Stop & Grow Garden Center and then spend hours masterminding how they're going to prevent the gophers from ravaging their lawns.

"Mr. Sutherland actually drives me crazy because he's always referring to himself in the third person. For instance, I'll be walking by his house and he'll announce, 'Walt's just finished reseeding his backyard,' or 'You can bet your bottom dollar that it's going to rain when you see Walt putting a tarpaulin on his grass seed.' It's either positively frightening or you just have to view Mr. Sutherland as an interesting contrast to the real world. Neighbors consider themselves just plain lucky if they can get past the Sutherland house with only a wave and a *howdy* and not have him start calling out his stupid gardener's daily meditations like, 'The best fertilizer for the soil is the owner's own footprints.'"

"One and the same," Denny says and smiles somewhat conspiratorially.

And for some reason I suddenly feel as if we've bonded over Mr. Sutherland's wackiness—like Denny completely understands how goofy the guy is. Whereas my dad just does not grasp that hanging out with Walt Sutherland should be viewed as a total embarrassment.

"Well he's a bachelor, at least sort of, last I heard anyway, and so I thought that maybe I'd just hide out over there for a few days. Only I couldn't figure out which house was his. I haven't been over this way for awhile and in the dark they all looked alike."

"I'm not surprised. They all look alike in the daytime too," I say.

"I accidentally mistook your house for Walt's. But then when I realized I was wrong, I thought I'd just ask for directions or see if I might use the phone," he explains.

"It's an easy mistake to make. The Sutherlands have almost the exact same two-story white aluminum-sided house with green shutters and a bronze eagle tacked above their garage door. Dad and Mr.

Sutherland bid on those buzzards together at an auction last summer."

"I'm sorry," Denny mutters.

"Oh they're not that bad. I mean people around here don't realize how ridiculous they are."

"No, I mean I'm sorry about bothering you and saying that I used to live here and all that. I didn't mean the birds."

"Oh, well, no problem. But I don't understand why you didn't just say that you were looking for the Sutherland's house in the first place."

"I don't know either, it was stupid of me."

Denny looks agitated or confused. I can't decide which one. He reminds me of my roommate Kim when she took almost a whole container of diet pills the morning of the philosophy final exam—dissipated yet energetic. "Are you okay?" I ask.

"I'm fine. It's just that you remind me of someone and it kind of threw me off. That's all."

This could be good or bad. Do I take the bait? I'm a sucker. I still pick up lucky pennies, buy lottery tickets and fill out all the sweepstakes entries that arrive in the mail. But just as I'm about to ask who it is that I resemble, I finally smarten up and deduce that it must be his dead wife. Why else would he be acting so peculiar? And I'm certainly not about to get into that discussion again. I vaguely remember Mrs. Sinclair. She also had shoulder length hair and similar coloring to mine, but beyond that I believe the similarities end. So I say nothing and let him carry on.

"It's just been so crazy since Sarah died," Denny says by way of explanation. "No one expected it. I mean, I guess you never expect anything like that to happen. The coroner said that she probably didn't feel a thing."

From reading the newspaper I happen to know that his wife was only forty-five. And also that a memorial has been funded by the faculty and parents of the students at the Stuttaford Middle School, which is to be erected on the median of the highway where Sarah Sinclair died. But I decide not to let on that I know anything.

"People just keep coming over to our house," Denny continues.

"Some I haven't seen for twenty or thirty years; relatives, Sarah's friends from college, some of whom I've never even met before. It's totally exhausting. Lately I've been feeling like I'm a display in Madame Tussaud's wax museum. It's all getting very surreal. First they talk about the weather for half an hour and then somehow manage to segue from high humidity into the fatal car accident. And they keep bringing food." He puts his hand up to his forehead and appears to be exasperated just thinking about it. "I've never seen so many pies and pound cakes in all my life. The kitchen is covered with hot dishes, cold dishes, cookies and Jell-O molds. There's no place to put down a glass anymore. The counters are loaded with unclaimed Tupperware containers, casserole dishes, rotting baskets of fruit and wilted flowers. I must have three pot roasts in the fridge and a kugel . . . "

"A what?" I ask.

"It's a noodle pudding type thing, Sarah's parents were Jewish," Denny explains. "By the look of things over at my place you'd think that we had called a caterer instead of an undertaker."

And as he is busy talking and absentmindedly examining the handle of his coffee mug, I examine him. Denny is rather attractive with his graying hair and professorial glasses. But reality bites back hard. God, if Mrs. Sinclair was forty-five then he must be about the same age. Am I losing my mind? Have I been overexposed to fertilizer this spring? Or maybe it's the calculus driving me towards matrix multiplication madness. Algorithm overdose. Either way, I decide that the summer has been way too long and sweltering and it is definitely time to get out of Dodge City.

"Would you like something else to drink," I offer. Although I don't think he's touched the coffee and even I must admit, it tastes like shit.

"Uh, no thanks," Denny replies, unaware of my impure thoughts.

But it doesn't take long for him to continue his saga about fleeing the homeland. "Then there are the kids. Zoë, daughter number two, works as a veterinary assistant in Kalamazoo and she's been driving home on weekends. Katrina's eighteen and still lives at home. She was supposed to spend July and August working at a cheerleading camp in

Texas but of course that was jettisoned.

And then Lori, she's the eldest. Lori brings our grandson Timmy over almost every day. They only live a few minutes drive from us and we have a swimming pool—and it's been so unbearably hot this summer. But I guess I don't have to tell you that."

Denny suddenly looks up, probably to check if he is boring me. But I doubt he can tell anything by my expression. So I purposely catch his eye and bounce my chin up and down just slightly to affirm that I am indeed paying attention, and thereby issue an invitation for him to continue talking, if that is what he wants to do. In fact, I really don't want him to stop. I'm thoroughly enjoying this diversion. It's turning out to be better than that show *Real World* on MTV and certainly more interesting than any of the best gossip I'd ever heard through eavesdropping on Mom and my Aunt Iris when they thought they were alone in the kitchen and got down and dirty picking over the family tree while preparing Sunday dinner. Maybe there is even the seed for a sociology term paper here, if I ever decide to attempt graduate school. I could call it: *A Survey of Grieving Patterns in the Bland Belt and What to Bake.*

"At first it was good to have them all around," Denny says, accepting my silent proposal to carry on. "Especially since there were so many arrangements to make and the phone kept ringing and I really didn't want to speak to anyone. This probably sounds terrible, but after five weeks of the grieving drill, I've really started to get antsy these past few days. Everyone is giving me sideways glances and then looking away when I catch them. Or else I've become totally paranoid, which isn't completely out of the question. The other household pastime is trying to make me something to eat. They keep asking *'Dad are you okay? How about a hamburger? Can't we clean the upstairs? Are you drinking too much? Why don't you change your clothes?'* And if Katrina goes out for even an hour she calls me the entire time. Gosh how I wish portable phones had never been invented. They're like casual day at work. They sound like a productivity-enhancing concept, but then the convenience ends up making your life even more complicated."

I nod and picture my mother standing out in the driveway almost every Friday morning, the dreaded casual day at the bank, attempting to sartorially sort Dad out and get him to change his belt or his socks and shoes. By the time he finally reaches the accessories stage he's always late for work, missed his breakfast, in a foul mood and going through the early stages of withdrawal from his neatly pressed white Oxford pinpoint cotton shirt and single-breasted navy blue suit.

"'*How did I sleep? Did I get the mail? Do I need a shrink?*' Then to top it off there's Helene, my mother! She's been over every single day since the accident." Denny becomes very animated talking about Helene. "If the truth be told, she's the one who's really driving me nuts. I could probably deal with the twenty-somethings, but Helene is a force to be reckoned with. I honestly believe she should have her own element on the periodic table," he says half-seriously. "Right there between Hafnium and Helium. Although it's probably more scientifically accurate to put her picture adjacent to something combustible such as Hydrogen or Nitrogen," he muses aloud. "Some communities have drive-by shootings. Well, I have drive-by naggings."

"Join the club," I offer. Although I try not to let on how astounded I am that someone of Denny's advanced age is bitching about his mom. I had thought that you get over that when you finally turn twenty-one. After all, he has a job and his own house. He could just lock his mother out or move or change his phone number. Me, on the other hand, I'm stuck here.

"Mother wants me to pack up Sarah's clothes and donate them to the white elephant sale at her church. Then she insists that with the girls all adults now that it's time to think about moving into a smaller place—maybe a condo or a townhouse. But I'm just not ready to do anything yet." Denny pauses for a moment and once again starts shifting his coffee mug from place to place as if he's playing an imaginary game of checkers. "She just won't let up. It's as if I'm a child again."

"Are you sure I can't get you some iced tea or something?" I repeat my beverage replacement offer.

"No. No thanks," Denny says.

"So this is why you've run away from home?" I say in an effort to get him back on track. I don't want him to lose his place in the soap opera. "Because everyone is driving you nuts, right?"

"Right."

"Makes perfect sense to me." And it does. More than I could ever tell him.

"It does?"

"Sure. I've always felt that our society puts a negative emphasis on running away from your problems, especially when it's often the best option available."

"I guess because it's considered cowardly."

"I prefer to think of desertion as a temporary tactical retreat," I say. "Better known as ducking."

Denny looks down at his coffee and gently swirls it around in the ceramic mug.

"Is there something wrong with the coffee?" I politely inquire, though it's obvious to us both that during a week of ninety-five degree plus days coffee was perhaps not the finest beverage choice in the first place. "I think it's a little hot for coffee," I finally say.

"I guess so. I'm sorry that you went to all that trouble."

"It was no trouble. Can I get you a cola or a glass of water?" Then I remember I'm not entertaining a teenager and change gears. "Maybe you'd like a beer or a glass of wine?"

"A glass of wine might be nice. I mean, if it's not an inconvenience. It's just that my nerves are kind of shot, you know, with the weather and all."

I realize that one can actually blame almost anything on the weather; malnutrition, temporary insanity, memory loss, the South turning republican, the difficulty in finding the Northwest Passage and even the decline of Western civilization.

"Sure. I think that there's a bottle of white wine in the fridge. Is that okay?" I grab a three-quarters full bottle of Chardonnay from the inside door of the refrigerator and hold it up for his approval. Denny nods appreciatively and so I fetch two goblets from the cabinet and pour us each a generous glass of wine.

"Thanks," he says gratefully and puts the glass to his lips and takes a long, leisurely sip and then appears to relax again having worked the Helene jeremiad out of his system. Denny slouches into his chair, exhales, and then looks up and gives me a weak but friendly smile. "Are you sure that your parents won't mind? I wouldn't want to get you into any trouble."

"No problem. I'm allowed to drink," I lie slightly. I decide it's not necessary to elaborate that as far as my parents are concerned, I'm permitted to have one glass of wine at Easter, Thanksgiving, Christmas and on the occasional anniversary celebration.

Gingerly taking a sip of the chilled Fetzer I must admit that it is considerably more refreshing than hot coffee.

"I'm going to buy some bait early tomorrow morning and head out to Lake Agnes for some serious fishing," Denny explains unenthusiastically. He may as well be describing an upcoming hip replacement operation.

"Won't they come looking for you?" I ask.

"Hopefully not. I left a very comprehensive note explaining that I'm of sound mind and body and that I didn't go off to commit suicide in some tawdry motel room and that I'll be back in time to start work next Tuesday. I even took the garbage out before I left and then typed the note on the word processor so that it all looks very businesslike. People don't normally type suicide notes, do they? Lori will definitely call around so I think I'll steer clear of local motels. But the violin will reassure them."

"The violin? You left the note in a violin?" It was all starting to sound like an episode of *Murder, She Wrote.*

"No, no. I took the violin. I mean, it's my violin. You see, if I had left the violin then they would fret because they know I'd only leave it behind if I was going off to drown myself."

"But what if they think you're trying to trick them by taking the violin because you know that if you left it behind then they would have reason to be worried?"

"Huh?" Denny suddenly appears anxious and begins drumming the fingers of his left hand on the table. "I never thought of that. Do you think that that's what they'll think?"

"No."

"Why not? That's what you just said."

"It's obvious that if you weren't tricky enough to have considered outsmarting them like that in the first place then they probably won't think you're capable of such a ruse."

"Ruse is a good word," Denny politely interjects. "You never hear it anymore."

"Thank you. I learned it for the SAT but don't have a chance to use it very often. I'm single-handedly trying to get it back in circulation. Normally it's a thankless job . . . "

"But somebody's got to do it," he finishes for me. "Anyway, I'm not sure if I should be insulted. I mean, you apparently don't think I'm very clever since I didn't consider the possibility of the violin backfiring."

"I didn't say that. The word I used was *tricky*. Tricky is different than clever."

"What's the difference?" he asks curiously.

This was becoming absurd but it was the first time I'd had any fun in a long time. Watching *Jeopardy* every weekday was starting to wear me down. Especially since in the summer they're all repeats and I knew I had heard the answers before but still couldn't remember them. And here was a grown-up in my very own kitchen who was actually treating me as an equal.

"Okay," I begin to explain. "You're either born clever or not clever. And then there are a few who are born clever but get dropped on their heads at a young age—like my brother Jack, for instance, our resident oxygen thief. But tricky is something you become, like according to Darwin's Theory of Acquired Characteristics. For instance, we have seven people in this house and only one shower stall for us five kids to share. Therefore, one must master the art of being tricky in order to get into the shower. See, now let's say that Jack's in the shower and I want to use it. Instead of banging on the door for him to get out, which I know will only tick him off and make him stay in there longer and purposely use up all the hot water, I'll go down to the basement and shut off the hot water so he thinks we've run out. Then after I hear him holler, I wait for a full minute, turn it back on, and go up and take a nice hot shower."

He looks at me as if I'm slightly clever or slightly crazy. "You know, I believe you're right. They won't think that I took the violin to try and deceive them." He pauses and says quite seriously, "You probably think I'm nuts, huh?"

"A little. I mean, if I were you I would just order them to get out and leave me alone. It is your house, after all. But I do understand wanting to get away from everyone. Family can be a real drag."

"Oh, Jess, if it were only that simple." He puts his hand on my arm for a few seconds in a way that seems sort of natural, like part of the conversation, not like anything perverted. It's really weird and all, but I decide that I don't mind, even though normally I don't appreciate anyone tossing grandmotherly gestures in my direction. But then he removes his hand without seeming to notice that I was even obsessing about the casual contact. "You don't understand," he continues. "I could never ask them to leave. I'd feel awful. And the girls are hurting too. After all, their mother died. But I just need a break from everything. So I decided that it would be much easier to escape from four women rather than to try and evict them."

"You're probably right about that."

"It's not even them so much as the house. I mean, I think it's probably okay for women to spend the day at home but it's unnatural for a middle-aged man to be in the house all day long."

I automatically raise an eyebrow and wonder if he is one of these guys who believe that women belong barefoot and pregnant and preparing hot cross buns in the kitchen. Maybe Denny Sinclair is partially responsible for the wage gap, women earning only eighty cents to a man's dollar.

But Denny catches my look and immediately amends his statement. "Oh, I don't mean to say that women shouldn't be out working and getting equal pay and all that. It's just that, well, when I think back to ancient times—in the mornings the men left with their spears to go out hunting and the women gathered berries and organized the cave. I mean, you don't see any cave paintings depicting men taking the afternoon off to hang around and choose window treatments or sew slipcovers." But the logic eventually flounders and when it does I actually feel relieved that I'm not the only one who has put my foot in my mouth tonight.

"I don't know," he continues. "I didn't mind staying home when the girls were little or if I had a day off. It's just that I probably should have gone back to work last week. Only I was afraid it wouldn't look right. I just want to return to my job and try and get my mind off of everything else. Being in that house all the time is depressing me. Besides, it's not like sitting there and organizing fruit baskets by height and opening condolence cards can bring Sarah back."

I'd be lying if I said that I didn't understand the point Denny was trying to make about hanging around home and hearth. My own mother is none too happy when Dad decides to take a week of vacation to *putter around the house.* Translate: get in Mom's way. And I thought they were going to kill each other when Gene was home for three weeks (the doctor ordered six) recovering from his heart attack.

"So what are you going to do now?" I ask as I twist a chunk of my lank hair around my index finger, which I always do when I'm tense. I can't figure out why he is suddenly making me nervous, but he is. I guess I'm worried that he will leave. And yet I'm also worried that he will stay.

"I'm going to see if I can spend the night at Walt's house. Do you happen to know if his wife ever came back?"

"She didn't. Mr. Sutherland claims that Mrs. Sutherland's mother is sick in Fergus Falls but my mother said that Mrs. Sutherland's mother died of the German Measles when she was twenty and that what really happened is that Mrs. Sutherland attended her high school reunion two years ago, hooked up with her old sweetheart and just never came back. He's a night watchman there, which drives Mr. Sutherland crazy because he insists that Mrs. Sutherland is a morning person, just like he is. But my mother says that we should be polite to Mr. Sutherland and always inquire as to how his mother-in-law is getting along."

"I heard something bizarre like that. It sounds like old Essie isn't coming back. Would it be all right if I use your phone to call him?"

"Help yourself." Yet I find myself hoping that Mr. Sutherland does not answer.

Denny pulls a crumpled piece of paper out of his pocket and punches Walt's number into the cordless phone. Obviously the answering machine picks up since after listening for a minute he hangs up.

"Must be his poker night," I say.

"Is Monday his poker night?"

"I think that these days every night is poker night." I can't help but giggle. "My mother claims that all the women on the street are angry because Mr. Sutherland's home has become a sort of neighborhood sports bar and casino since he's been returned to bachelorhood. The wives call it Sutherland's Hideaway."

"Oh. I haven't seen Walt in awhile. I didn't realize he'd become so committed to the game."

"Try back in a little while," I suggest. What I don't tell him, what I should tell him, is that Mr. Sutherland has moved all the family room furniture, including the big screen TV, and a mini fridge that his son had used in college, out into the backyard and that there are probably a bunch of Budweiser-soaked guys out there right now playing five-card draw and watching a South Africa versus New Zealand rugby match via satellite dish. "How about another glass of wine?" I offer.

"Okay. Thanks." Denny smiles at me.

I get another bottle of wine out of the fridge. "So, what do you do?" I inquire as I uncork the Chardonnay. From making conversation with grown-ups in church I happen to know that this is always a good question. Although it occasionally leads to volunteering for something which I don't want to do, like working at the St. Augustine's car wash fund-raiser. "You must be a—what do you call it—a meteorologist."

"No. Actually I'm an atmospheric chemist."

"That's cool. That was my next guess. Not!"

"At least I *was* an atmospheric chemist. Now I'm in management. I work with a big environmental consulting firm over in Mannenberg. We do impact studies, operational forecasting and stuff like that." He explains this like a man accustomed to explaining what he does for a living and then concludes by waving his hand to indicate the general direction of the town of Mannenberg.

"So how come you sometimes do the weather?"

"The station manager is an old college buddy of mine. Once, about seven years ago, when the regular guy—this was before Reed—slipped a disc thirty minutes before the broadcast, he called and asked me to fill in. So now whenever they're stuck and I'm around, I do the weather. It's kind of fun."

"I've always wondered how come you guys never mention the nights when it's possible to see the aurora borealis. Why is that?"

"Because the aurora borealis appears north of Scandinavia, south of Greenland and in parts of Alaska." He looks at me quizzically. "Why would anyone around here care about the Northern Lights if they can't observe it?"

"That's totally not true! I see it out the living room window almost once a month, and if it's really clear out, sometimes even more."

"Let me see," Denny says and his eyes dart around the room as if he has a global positioning system attached to his forehead, "What direction does your house face?"

"East," I answer. "Or maybe it's North. I forget."

"No, you're right. It faces Northeast. Jess, I hate to be the one to tell you this but I believe you're seeing planes landing at Madigan airport. That's where all the mail arrives."

"No way! It's the aurora borealis. I've been spotting it for years."

"Well, I'm not saying that it's completely impossible," Denny says in a tone of voice meaning that it is indeed impossible. "I mean, occasionally amateur astronomers in Boston report observing a little auroral activity. But to actually view the aurora borealis you would need to be at a higher latitude than we're at in Michigan."

"This is so awful!" I say. I have a flashback to a particularly horrendous day in elementary school when for Show & Tell the twins Eddie and Teddy Burke brought in secretly videotaped footage of their parents wrapping all of their Christmas presents and putting them under the tree and then, as the entire third grade gasped in horror, eating Santa's cinnamon graham cracker snack and then kissing, as if exhilarated by their own deceit. "You don't understand. Every time I've seen those lights over the past decade I've been convinced that they would bring me good luck. I've even made wishes on them. I just can't believe this." Santa Claus is murdered again.

"Listen, I don't want to ruin your fun, but let me just ask you this: have you ever seen the lights after 10:30 PM?"

I think about this for a moment and finally have to answer, "No, I don't believe so."

"Well, the airport is near a residential area and that's what time it has to close."

"Shit." I say. Why don't I just go upstairs and throw my favorite blanket in the trash? Because that's how bad I now feel.

"So what about you?" He asks.

"What about me?"

"What do you do?"

"Do? I'm a nothing," I answer.

"Everybody's something," Denny corrects me.

As evidence I pull out a nearby box of resumes and hand him a copy. "Here." I shove it into his hands. "Twenty years summed up in standard targeted reverse-chronological format and printed in Times New Roman typeface on a single page of ecru Crane's Crest paper.

Read it. I'm a nothing. And I can't even get a Mcfrigging job."

He glances down at the resume and then nods towards the calculus book that has been relocated to the opposite end of the table. "So then you're a student," he surmises.

"It depends on who you talk to. This spring I finished four years of college in Wisconsin only to discover that I failed calculus and would have to repeat the class over the summer in order to receive my degree. Too many parties and not enough parametric equations."

"So are you going to go back?"

"No. Too expensive. The school allowed me to attend graduation with the understanding that after shaking hands with the President of the College, I'd receive an empty vinyl diploma folder to be filled in if, and only if, my local Community College sends a transcript, at some point within the next ten years, saying that I've passed calculus with a grade of C or higher."

"It's nice that they give you a lot of time," he replies seriously. "No rush then."

"Yeah, it shows that they have a lot of confidence in me," I flippantly retort.

"So you just have to finish this one class, right?"

"Easier said than done."

"When is it over?"

"Hopefully at the end of this week." I dig some cigarettes out of my backpack. Career talk always makes me agitated and job interviews actually cause me to break out in hives. "At first I didn't really care about having to retake the class during the summer. I mean, the job hunt was going really badly and so I just figured that I could use the additional time to, you know, shape up my resume, write some decent cover letters, comb the Milwaukee and Chicago classified ads and search the Internet for job postings."

"That sounds like a sensible strategy."

"Yeah, well it's been three months, a couple hundred resumes, over two dozen interviews, a hundred bucks in dry cleaning bills, complete humiliation and no paycheck in sight."

"So, you still count as a student until you finish your degree."

"I think that *academic refugee* is probably a more accurate description right now, if it's all the same to you."

"Maybe I can help," he says politely. "I took a lot of math in college. Do you mind if I look at your book?"

I slide the calculus book across the table. "Be my guest." If this guy can help me it would be a Miracle of Grace. I'll say a novena every single day for the rest of my life and wear out a rosary every month.

After flipping through the chapters and studying some of the problems Denny appears both startled and confused. "This is what they're calling calculus these days, huh?"

"That would be the title of the class," I reply.

"I'm sorry but I think I hear the Smithsonian calling for my slide rule. I guess it was a while ago. I don't even recognize anything in the table of contents."

"Thanks anyway. I've got this guy at the math clinic tutoring me. And if only I'd stop oversleeping it would probably do some good."

"Oh that's—"

A thunderclap interrupts our conversation and the kitchen light flickers but then apparently decides to stay the course.

Denny glances at his wristwatch. "It's almost ten thirty. Maybe I should just go home. This is rather inane. I'm hiding from my own family."

"Well, wait a minute. There's something to be said for that. Although you're definitely the oldest guy I know who has run away from home."

"At least with the mortgage and property taxes paid up," Denny adds wryly.

"Your family should be pleased that you're not one of those deadbeat dads who takes off owing a lot of back child support." I say this to buy some time. If I'm going to invite him to stay it seems as if the moment of truth has arrived. But I chicken out. "Maybe you can go home tonight and then run away tomorrow. You know, get a fresh start," I suggest.

"No, no. That would never do. They'd circle the wagons and put me under house arrest. Then they'd tie me down and feed me."

Denny looks at me for a reaction after he makes his little joke. I feel encouraged, but then he shakes his head from side to side and grumbles, "No. I'll just have to find a motel."

Don't go, Denny Sinclair. It's such fun talking to another human being. Especially one who knows absolutely nothing about me. It's been an opportunity to escape the misery of my life and to be somebody else for a while. To shake the feeling that there is a conspiracy mounting against me—that everyone, all the Others, are scheming to help me, but in all the wrong ways and for all the wrong reasons. And calculus is such a total bore. Why won't he just ask to stay overnight? And I could act as if I was mulling it over and then finally say okay. But he wouldn't, of course, ever suggest anything so outrageous as that. And I can't bring myself to do so either.

"It is the nightly custom of every good mother after her children are asleep to rummage in their minds and put things straight for the next morning, repacking into their proper places the many articles that had wandered during the day."
Joan MacGuire's favorite line in *Peter Pan*.

"You'll look better when your bangs are trimmed."
Aunt Ida, scrutinizing the annual family Christmas photo greeting card.

Chapter 3
Hide In Plain Sight
Late Monday Night

"It's obvious that you know nothing about running away," I say. It's more of a smoke screen sentence that I utilize in order to quickly lean over and refill Denny's glass.

"What do you mean?" He takes a sip of wine and suddenly doesn't seem to be in as big a hurry to leave and go and get his fishing gear organized.

"For starters, you don't have a very good game plan. You should have called Mr. Sutherland days ago and gotten a key or made some sort of arrangements to stay there."

"But I didn't decide to leave until seven o'clock this evening!" he argues defensively. "Mother came around with a whole pile of packing containers and strapping tape and I just couldn't deal with it one more minute! It was either box up Mom and put her in the attic or just get the hell out of the house." He shakes his head from side to side.

I pretend to ignore his excuses, though it's actually sweet music to my ears to hear someone else griping about their mother and I could probably listen to that sort of thing for a very long while. "Second, you started too late. Every third grader knows that you have to run away early in the morning. That way you get a twelve-hour head start. No one ever reports a missing person until after sundown or when the mall closes at half past nine. Apparently there's a fine line between missing and shopping. And third, you must either steal a car and put mud over the plates or travel by bus or plane and pay with cash. My God, haven't you seen any John Grisham movies? I sure hope that isn't your own car out front."

"Of course it's my car. Why wouldn't it be my car?"

"The police are probably out there right this very minute holding a flashlight to your license plate and radioing your mom back at HQ." I guess this could be considered unnecessary cruelty but I can't resist.

Denny dashes to the phone and pushes the redial button. And I know what he's thinking—that the Sutherlands have a two-car garage. And I'm thinking so do I. He hits the speakerphone button. The Sutherland's answering machine picks up after four rings. A woman's voice says: "Greetings, this is Walt and Essendine, we're not here to take your call right now . . . "

He again clicks off the phone.

"If you, um, want," I hear myself saying, "I mean, you're probably a murderer or something." God, have I completely lost my mind? What am I doing? Taking candy from strangers is one thing, however inviting them to sleep over is insane. But surely he's harmless. They wouldn't let him do the weather if he was a maniac. Would they? No. No one ever talked about weather reporters going berserk and impaling engineers down at the station on that pointer they use to track tornadoes up the Gulf Coast. It wasn't like the post office, where an average day included a couple rounds of machine gun fire.

Denny glances up and now we're staring at each other. Can he possibly be anticipating what I might say next? And be preparing to reject me? I wish I had ESP like my mother. But she says you only get it after experiencing the pain of childbirth. I decide it may come as a surprise to Denny but I say it anyway.

"I mean, if you want to, you can stay here tonight. Also, we have a garage. So you can hide the getaway car in there. And besides, my family is on vacation." I gaze out of the window so I can pretend that I've actually been talking to myself or possibly to an imaginary friend. Outside it is still drizzling.

From the corner of my eye I can see that Denny is not looking at me either but staring blankly at the calendar on the wall. Seconds tick by that take forever.

"I should probably just go to a motel."

He sounds so dejected that I really wish he would stay, but not so much for me anymore. I suddenly can't stand to picture him walking out into this rainy night and checking into some roadside motel with paper bath mats and plastic drinking cups.

"It's kind of you to offer, but I'm not sure."

For a second I actually have an unmistakable urge to comfort him. It's a dangerous surge of maternal instinct that I never even knew I had. Or else I'm coming down with a virus.

I quell this crazy impulse by moving into bossy mode. "What's not to know? Besides, you'll never get a room this late, I know that. Everyone is here for the last week of summer vacation. Monday is Labor Day and then it's all over. You can't sleep in your car or you'll get arrested for vagrancy. And if you go home now it'll be worse than ever. So you're spending the night here and that's all there is to it."

"Okay," he acquiesces, still sounding uncertain. "I guess that would be okay. But it would just be for tonight. I won't be any trouble. I'll sleep on the porch." Now he is taking politeness to the extreme. But I've lived in the Midwest all my life and can match his demure and even raise him a hostess gift if need be.

"Oh no, it's way too damp out there," I say. "Even the silverfish have packed up and moved into the family room. Besides, I think my little brothers are operating some sort of a night crawler farm out there. I mean, small dogs enter the back porch and are never seen again. Anyway, if you were a murderer, with body parts in the freezer, I'd probably know by now. After all, your wife worked at my school. It would have made the *Stuttaford Scene* student newspaper."

"Was my wife your guidance counselor?" he asks with a sudden surge of excitement in his voice.

"No. Last names A thru N went to Mr. Dorsey." I'm not sure if this is good or bad. This is the thing you can say about almost all queries by grown-ups, there's normally a right answer and a wrong answer, and it's part of the game to try and figure out which is which before deciding upon your answer. Maybe he's hoping I'll share some memories about Mrs. Sinclair—like that I was feeling a lot of peer pressure one day and went down to the guidance offices and Mrs. Sinclair convinced me to *just be myself* and my emotional health was immediately restored. Or that she inspired me to run for student government.

"Would you like to see some sort of identification? I could show you my driver's license."

"That's okay. I've seen you on TV."

"Yeah, well O. J. Simpson was on TV. And I've been down at the station after those serial killers are apprehended and right on camera their astonished neighbors always insist: 'He was a quiet guy and nice to children. He always bought lots of Girl Scout cookies and on Halloween he handed out real silver dollars for UNICEF.'"

Denny looks and sounds so earnest and yet the situation is so bizarre that I laugh. It must have been the right thing to do because he smiles a big, silly grin and I feel that we finally make a real connection. Having him in my kitchen no longer seems awkward. Up until now it felt more like he was one of my parents' friends who happened to stop by.

"Yeah. Well for some reason I don't think I'll need to count the spoons after you leave. There are three empty bedrooms upstairs. Do you like the Mighty Morphin Power Rangers? My little brothers have their room covered in that crap."

"Can't say that I've heard of them," Denny shrugs.

"Well, across the hall from that there's some leftover Batman decor.

But it's probably a pigsty. That's Jack's cell. He just turned eighteen so, well, you can only imagine."

"Batman sounds great. You know, I had the first Batman comic books that were issued!"

"No kidding!" I deadpan. But the look on his face tells me that enthusiasm would have been better than sarcasm here.

"It would be like owning the first Barbie doll," Denny explains earnestly.

"Really?" I reply. "I've never found much use for Barbie beyond volunteering her for occasional home scientific experiments. Besides, by the time Jack was six he had lobbed off the heads of both Barbie and Ken and frozen them into Kool-Aid ice pops. Mattel might want to try selling a Cryogenic Barbie, germfree and easy to store."

But Denny doesn't seem to hear me. Batman has apparently sent him reeling back in time. "After I left for college my mother cleaned out my room and threw all of my Batman comic books away. They'd sure be worth a lot of money today."

"She probably thought that the date on the cover was an expiration code," I suggest. "Mothers automatically throw away anything after three months. Except tissues. They keep those up their sleeves and in their purses for decades, right along with the worst photo ever taken of you during the ugly duckling years."

"I suppose so."

The brief connection we had seems to have faded, leaving two strangers sitting opposite each other, talking but not hearing. But in an odd sort of way, that's the good thing about strangers—you can say whatever you like. Be honest even. I decide to give it a try.

"I hate staying in this house by myself. It's so big compared to the apartment where I lived when I was at college," I explain. "At night it creaks in weird places."

"Didn't you have a spate of robberies in this part of town in July? I remember Walt telling me his leaf blower was stolen."

Denny ignores my invitation to a conversation that might tell him a bit more about the real me. But then why would he care to hear a twenty-year-old's view on living conditions in the modern age, whether it be about overcrowded apartments or haunted houses.

"Yeah, there were some robberies, but it's more likely that Mr. Sutherland's leaf blower was a mercy theft by an annoyed neighbor. That contraption was older than the first Earth Day and it made more noise than six snowblowers. And the fact that he cranked it up at six in the morning didn't help matters. Besides, the thieves mostly took bicycles out of garages and stuff like that. I don't know what they'd want with an antique leaf blower. They broke into houses of families on vacation and stole some jewelry and watches and I think a computer."

"Really?"

"Yeah. It surprised everyone. Who ever heard of robberies in Stuttaford? I mean, whoops, there goes the neighborhood." Though I remember being shocked for a completely different reason. I was so busy trying to break out of here that it had never occurred to me that anyone would want to voluntarily enter my house.

"I can guarantee you that this block never lost anything. Probably because the old lady across from us is always out front hunting rats with her B-B gun. There's an empty lot next to her house that people seem to think is the town dump and so it attracts rodents that tunnel into her basement. And let me just warn you right now, her aim is about as good as my ability to solve trigonometric equations."

"Ah, I think I read about her in the paper, the notorious Stuttaford Sniper?"

"Bernice Butler. One and the same."

"Didn't she start mailing dead rats to the health department?"

"Indeed she did. And Clyde, the UPS man, told me that she even splurged for the extra seventy-five cents so that she could track the packages."

We both smile again. He looks at me appreciatively. Wow, it suddenly hits me, I'm actually having a real conversation with him.

While we're experiencing this shared moment, I decide that Denny reminds me of Dr. Edgar Bennett, the Professor who taught my Classics course during freshman year of college. Dr. Bennett was one of those stereotypical brilliant-but-distracted professors famous for not wearing matching socks or an overcoat, even in the middle of winter. With his shirt tucked in on only one side and perpetually windblown hair, Dr. Bennett was handsome in a rumpled sort of way. However, he transmogrified into a Shakespearean actor when reciting to the class from *I, Claudius*. By the time we got to *Madame Bovary*, most of the female students, myself included, had developed a huge crush on him, to which he was completely oblivious. Dr. Bennett was oblivious to most everything.

"Why are you staring at me?" Denny asks.

"Was I?" Denny jolts me back to the here and now. For a moment I think I'm going to blush. Fortunately I don't. "I was just thinking that you look like someone I know." Two can play the you-remind-me-of-someone-game.

"As long as it isn't someone you saw on *America's Most Wanted*," he smiles.

Denny is getting comfortable now, I decide, with his third glass of wine and his wry little comments. "No. A Professor at college," I say. "You're both rumpled."

"Rumpled? I guess that's okay. No one ever died of rumpledness. Rumpled and tired." Denny yawns and slowly rises from the table, as befitting a person suffering from a deep physical exhaustion. "I'd like to try and get some sleep if that's okay with you. I want to be down at the lake by six in the morning complete with my fishing pole, a spicy Bloody Mary and a can of grubs."

"Sure, whatever. C'mon, I'll show you the room selection."

"No, no. You get back to your books. I'll find it. The Batcave can't be that difficult to locate."

"Okay. There's soap and toothpaste and all that kind of stuff in the bathroom at the end of the hallway. Help yourself. And if you want pajamas or a T-shirt just grab something out of my dad's closet. It's on the left in the master bedroom. And feel free to change rooms. When no one is home I usually sleep down here on the couch, so the upstairs is all yours."

"Okay, thanks a lot," he replies and leaves.

The good thing about preparing to study again after a long break is that there is a requisite amount of procrastination necessary before one can legitimately expect to be back in the saddle; organizing pencils by sharpness and reshuffling notes, going to the bathroom even if you don't have to, and pouring something to drink. When I finally turn my attention back to the page where I left off, it sinks in that I have a house guest and suddenly binomial distribution doesn't seem quite so bad, and I can actually finish some of the problems.

Just as I'm beginning to set up a really complex equation Denny reappears in the entrance to the kitchen. I assume he's changed his mind and I am overwhelmed with such a sense of dread that it shocks me. I don't quite understand why I feel that I need him here. It isn't as if we were going to hook up or anything like that. If I analyze it, I guess part of Denny's appeal lies in the fact that not only is he nice and sort of humorous, but he's not too busy. It seems as if everyone is always so busy these days. No one has time for other people anymore—to actually sit down and find out what is going on in another person's life. And I guess this is the closest I have ever been to finding what really goes on in the minds of grown-ups—what makes them tick.

I pretend to concentrate hard, as if I'm right on the brink of decoding a theorem which will not only guarantee an A on the exam, but put me right up there in the company of Fermat and Fibonacci. Anything to postpone hearing that Denny is leaving, if that is what he has returned to announce, as I'm pretty sure it is. He patiently stands in the hallway and waits for me to glance up from my book.

With the threat of abandonment looming large, it dawns on me that I've felt incredibly lonely the past few weeks. Of course, this is entirely my own fault, which my mother has not hesitated to point out, whenever she gets the chance, by reminding me that I've been purposely going out of my way to alienate every member of the family. Her exact words were: "I'm worried that you want to live in a house by the side of the road and torture your fellow man." This was either a malignant twist on Homer's *Iliad* or else the Good Samaritan parable in the *Bible*. Mom was raised Protestant and likes to hurl chestnuts from the classics and *Bible* verse around like wet slush, to make you feel cold and bad. In a small cedar box on her dresser she keeps a selection of gilt-edged leather bookmarks that she had earned as prizes for memorizing and reciting scripture as a girl in Sunday school. And though she has use for only so many bookmarks, Joan doesn't let her declamation gifts go to waste, especially when she believes that her offspring may be in need of a little divine inspiration, or castigation, such as the case may be. And it just so happened that the New Testament was Joan's idea of the perfect self-help manual.

And Mom is right. I have felt a kind of steady, low-level anger smoldering inside me for almost a year. I've become a regular purveyor of random acts of unkindness and senseless ugliness. Lately, everyone's head has looked like an invitation to batting practice. Maybe Denny leaving is payback for all my recent unpleasantness.

I finally look up from my book.

"Sorry, I didn't mean to bother you," Denny says, probably because I'm wearing a look of resignation that he could easily have mistaken for annoyance. I know that any further persuading him to stay is inappropriate. So why end on a desperate sounding note? It had been a nice evening all the same.

"It's uh, it's just that we forgot to put my car in the garage. Could you tell me if there's an electric opener?"

Of course. The Batmobile! I'm flooded with a mixture of relief and frustration with myself for getting worked up over something so stupid. "Yeah, there's a button right inside the door. I'll show you."

"No, no. I'll find it."

I feel exhausted by this whole day, this entire sweaty summer.

Though it has finally stopped raining, I can hear a steady stream of water rushing down from the gutters. After a few minutes Denny returns carrying a worn and peeling black leather case that looks like it houses an Uzi. Or else it's all the rage in fishing tackle boxes. I stare at it.

"My violin," he says rather sheepishly. "I, uh, I don't think it's a good idea to leave it in the car—temperature fluctuations and all that."

"Oh right. You can put it in the living room if you want."

"I'll take it upstairs. Maybe I'll tune it."

"Whatever." It crosses my mind that it's probably a good thing he doesn't play the trumpet. "Goodnight," I say. But he has already gone and I am alone with my pile of unsolved calculus problems.

"With handwriting like that I wouldn't be

surprised if you became a doctor."
Miss Carp, 5th grade teacher.

"Pulling out weeds is good exercise."
Gene MacGuire to family, every summer.

Chapter 4
Denny: Role Model or Cautionary Tale?
Tuesday Morning

The following morning I rise at eight in order to make my nine o'clock class. I assume that Denny has left to go fishing hours ago and that maybe he's left a note. More than a note, I'm anxious to see if he's left his violin, indicating that he will return.

When I can't find a note downstairs, I go and look in Jack's room. There's no note there either, just Denny fast asleep under the covers in Jack's twin bed. So much for fish and worms and tangy Bloody Marys. Men are such talk sometimes. I dash back downstairs and hastily scribble on a piece of geometry graph paper with a red crayon and tuck it through the handle of the coffeepot:

D, Went to class. Back around noon. Help yourself. J.

* * *

When I arrive home Denny is standing in the kitchen and pouring a cup of coffee. I feel an irrational sense of delight that he has not yet departed. "Hakuna Matata!" I shout. This apparently startles him a little too much, as he drops the mug he's holding and it breaks, splashing coffee all over the countertop and onto the linoleum floor. "Damn," he mutters and reaches for some paper towels.

"Hi there," I say.

He gives me a weak smile.

"Sorry about the oil slick," I apologize. "My fault."

After I help him clean up the mess, Denny goes to select another mug from the fifty or so that are hanging from wooden pegs on the wall next to the refrigerator. A repository of Mother's and Father's Day gifts gone by. Most have cutesy cartoons or sayings on them. And then a few are those red and white ceramic faux Campbell's soup can mugs which Dad had acquired at flea markets or as free gifts. Without seeming to give the choice much consideration, Denny chooses the one with "Dad" printed on it in green and blue plaid block letters.

"So how was school?"

"Oh great," I lie. "I've got a really good tutor," which isn't a lie, but it also isn't going to help me any unless I buckle down and really concentrate. What I didn't want to say was that I'd wasted the better part of the morning staring out the window and wondering whether Denny would still be here when I returned. Or would I find an empty house, a *gone fishing* bumper sticker and a thank-you note.

"Learning anything good?" he asks.

"We reviewed how to graph derivative functions." Only I'd spent most of the two hours seeing how many phrases I could come up with that contained the word derive; *this class is deriving me crazy*, *don't drink and derive*, *to hit a line derive*, and of course, *an overactive sex derive*.

While waiting for another pot of coffee to finish brewing Denny examines the family photos which are stuck to the refrigerator door with plastic magnets, most in the form of three-dimensional glazed vegetables. "Jack must be the redhead," Denny eventually observes aloud. "And your little sister, she looks a lot like your dad, dark Irish."

"Yeah, I guess she does," I agree as I unpack my knapsack.

"How'd you know my dad is Irish?" I ask.

"Uh, you know, MacGuire—good Irish name."

"Oh yeah, I forgot about that. I guess it's a giveaway. Actually, Katie looks just like Dad's Mom, Grandma Maggie, especially if you look at old photos of Grandma when she was a girl."

"If your hair is only tinted maroon, as I'm guessing it is, and without all those necklaces and earrings, you're a dead ringer for your mother; same high cheekbones, fair skin and eyes the shade of dark Jade mixed with just a touch of gray."

I look at him quizzically for a second. I hadn't realized that the Polaroids on the refrigerator were quite so revealing, or in focus. "So they tell me," I say with resignation.

I open the refrigerator door and search for something to quench my thirst but can't decide what exactly it is that I want and stare at the contents. The cool air feels good and it's a treat to have a lengthy look without hearing my mother's unopen-door policy refrain: *Are they showing a movie in there?* or Dad's, *Do you think I'm made of money?*

"So what was that?" I ask. "A little fourteen hour nap? Fishing at six in the morning my ass!"

"I know. I can't believe I slept so long. Christ, you'd think I was bitten by a tsetse fly."

"Quick, who's President?" I quip.

According to the microwave oven the time is now 11:56 A.M. "Are you sure that this clock is right?" he asks. "Is it really almost noon?"

I check my watch. "Sorry, but it's actually five minutes slow. It *is* noon."

"I spent half the night dreaming that I couldn't sleep," Denny complains.

"Yeah, I know the feeling. That happens to me when I mix Pepsi with NyQuil and cherry PEZ." I finally choose a peach wine cooler and close the refrigerator door.

So far we could be talking to ourselves, intersecting monologues, but that doesn't seem to matter. It's comfortable.

Denny carefully pours another cup of coffee, this time not spilling any, and slumps down in Dad's head-of-the-household La-Z-Boy recliner in the family room. Since the two rooms are only separated by a few small steps and a low wrought iron divider, I can still see the back of his head. How odd to have this man sitting in my living room and wearing my father's khaki shorts.

"The girls, you know, they watch me sleep," he says. "I'm serious—I can't figure out if they're trying to make sure I'm not dead or just hoping that I get some rest."

I swig down the wine cooler in a matter of minutes. "It's hot as hell out," I say as a way of justifying taking another one out of the fridge. Then I go to the pantry and bring out a plastic container of Flintstones vitamins. Sitting down on the couch across from Denny I empty the contents onto the coffee table so that a rainbow of forty or so Lilliputian Stone Age people are spread out in front of us.

"I used to sleep so soundly," Denny remarks. "But lately I've had insomnia. I didn't think that I'd ever sleep again. I was going to put up a satellite dish so that I could at least watch the Fishing Channel all night long."

"Yeah, well I knew a guy who was dyslexic, agnostic and insomniac," I tell him as I sort through the orange, pink and violet pills.

"What?" Denny asks.

"He stayed up all night wondering if there was a dog. Get it?"

Denny thinks for a few seconds and then chuckles. "That's actually pretty funny," he finally says. "Uh, what are you doing now?" He watches me pick through the tablets and methodically sort them by character.

"Vitamins—smart drugs," I reply. "I'm looking for three Wilmas or possibly four Dinos. I've always believed that you shouldn't mix your cartoon characters."

"Wilmas?" asks Denny.

"Yeah, the Flintstones," I reply and hold up the bottle for his inspection. "You know—Bedrock. Yabadabadoo."

"Sure. Of course I know the Flintstones."

"Yeah? Then name 'em."

"No. I don't want to. Listen, are you old enough, I mean . . . " Denny sounds concerned and perhaps embarrassed. He rises and walks over towards the big bay window that overlooks the backyard.

"These are children's chewable vitamins. Very safe—even after I double the recommended dosage. Complete with 12 vitamins and 7 minerals, including vitamin C, iron and calcium," I recite like a commercial announcer.

"What I meant was, are you old enough to drink?"

"Duh. I know what you meant. Actually, I'm two hundred and fifty-one months old, four weeks shy of the drinking age, which is two hundred and fifty-two months, in case you don't feel like doing the math. But I'm lactose intolerant so liquor is really the only way to go. You know, purely for health reasons."

Denny looks at me skeptically but I keep a straight face. "Almost twenty-one? Wow. Are you sure?" he asks incredulously.

This comment really makes me laugh. "I mean, I may be bad at calculus but I think that I at least know how old I am."

"Of course. I don't know why I said that. I just thought you were, maybe eighteen."

"I was eighteen. I was seventeen too. Only it was a couple years ago." There is more than a twinge of hostility in my voice. Why do people always think I'm younger than my age? Couldn't someone just once say, *You're only twenty, my God, I thought that you were at least twenty-four!* What is the point of finally getting those God-awful teen years safely behind you just to have people still think of you and treat you as a stupid adolescent?

"Sorry," Denny says apologetically, "Did I say something wrong?"

I pout and forcefully push my bangs back behind my ears but it's a useless gesture since they won't stay anchored there. The bangs situation is completely out of control. It is now to the point where I can no longer even use both of my hands at the same time and still see what I'm doing. I need one hand to keep scooping hair out of my eyes.

"It's just that why does everyone always think that I look like a dumb teenager?" I complain. "I'm so sick of being carded every time I go into a bar or to buy cigarettes and being made to sit at the kids' table at every family function. I can't wait until I'm thirty."

"I didn't mean it as an insult. I'm sorry. Perhaps what I meant was, isn't it kind of early to be having a drink?" He glances at my wine cooler.

"Are you sure that my parents didn't pay you to come and spy on me? I mean, really, I'm the lady of the house and you're just a fugitive meteorologist who I've taken under my wing because I believe that you can be rehabilitated, gainfully employed and eventually returned to polite society."

"You're right. It's none of my business," Denny contritely acknowledges my point. "Sorry. Don't be mad."

"It's just a wine cooler," I explain. "The more wine I drink, the cooler I become! And anyway, it's more like research. I'm thinking of working part-time as a designated driver, you know, the person whose job it is to find the car. Or as a decoy, the party-goer who distracts the police by swerving all over the road in order to give all the intoxicatees a chance to sneak home. Maybe I'll even go to bartender school. They must make more than six dollars an hour if you include tips."

Denny goes back into the kitchen and pours another cup of coffee.

"Help yourself to some breakfast," I call after him. "Or lunch. Or whatever."

He opens the fridge and pokes through the shelves and I hear a few of the plastic bins open and close. From one he pulls out a bundle of spinach that has wilted and turned brown. "I'm going to toss this, okay?" He comes out from behind the door and holds it up for review.

I glance over at the decayed pile of greens. "Whoops, Mom missed that one. You can tell she was discombobulated. I can't understand why they call that bin a crisper when all it does is rot stuff. They should just call it a rotter. English is a very dishonest language. I was in the mall last week applying for a job and now they're calling bathing suits *swim systems*. Anyway, I think that will be my claim to fame, getting the name of that drawer changed. You know, my *raison d'étre.*"

"Hey, you know, you have a good sense of humor. Where do you get this stuff?" Denny looks up from the garbage can after retiring the spinach. "Is your father funny?"

"Oh, I'd have to say that both of my parents are very funny, although they aren't aware of it. But don't be fooled by my sarcasm. It's only the defense mechanism of a weak individual at work. Underneath I'm just a confused child crying out for a trust fund. Listen, why don't we just go to the diner and order some grilled hash? I'm a Starvin' Marvin."

"I suppose we can do that. I have about twenty dollars. But I could go to the cash machine."

"Twenty bucks? You ran away with twenty dollars in your pocket! You can't go to a cash machine. Your family probably reported to the bank that your card has been stolen so that any transactions you make will be traced. At least that's the first thing I'd do if my dad ran away from home." Then I laugh at how ridiculous that sounds. Dads didn't run away from home. But Denny had.

"Hmm. I didn't think of that."

"Obviously you know a lot about science and weather and probably even homeowners insurance, but you are awfully naïve when it comes to living on the run, fugitive style."

"Are you sure that you're not studying to be a detective?" he asks.

"It's a backup. But don't worry, my parents left me some money. I mean, not an inheritance. Just a couple of bucks for food and to put air in my bike tires."

"What if someone sees me?" Denny asks.

Now he's being paranoid. "Well, as my dad would say, you've certainly chosen to be a part of the problem and not the solution."

"How about I cook something for us here instead?"

"Sure. I don't mind if you don't mind. You aren't going to give me Legionnaire's Disease or anything like that, are you?"

"Legionnaire's Disease? What are you talking about? You get that from bacterium in commercial air-conditioners. Speaking of which, does your air-conditioner work? It's stifling in here."

"Since the moment my parents walked out that door with half a dozen cans of bug spray under each arm I have not been able to get that stupid thing to blow anything but warm air. I swear to God I think that this past summer finished it off, that the old A/C unit just finally gave up the ghost as soon as it saw my dad pack the roof rack for vacation. We've had it for ages and it's probably been running full tilt every day for the past two months. In fact, last month's electric bill almost gave my dad a second coronary. Maybe he sabotaged it in order to save money, an inside job. C'mon and I'll show you where most of the food is stored." I motion for him to follow me to the cellar door. "I'll give you a tour of bulk heaven. Besides, it's cooler down there."

"What's bulk heaven?"

"The bomb shelter." I flip a light switch and lead the way down the steep stairs to the basement. "Actually it's more like bulk hell since it's in the basement, but you're not allowed to say the H word around my house." Denny watches in amazement as I proceed to open the doors of a large Jerry-rigged pantry, thereby displaying row upon row of canned foods, paper products and cardboard flats of almost every imaginable nonperishable consumer product known to shoppers.

"Holy Moly!" Denny appears awestruck.

"Holy Moly, huh?" I light a cigarette and exhale. "I guess you weren't kidding about Batman."

"I've never seen so many, uh, so many provisions in one place outside of the grocery store."

"Yeah, well it's kind of my dad's hobby."

"Is he a survivalist like those people in Montana preparing for Doomsday?"

"Hardly. He works as the manager of a trading department, or something like that, at Erie-Michigan bank and it has severely affected his private life." But Denny only appears to be further confused by my explanation.

I open a restaurant-size freezer and display the raw animal flesh section. "Gene, my dad, insists on buying our groceries in bulk. He calls it *consumer arbitrage* because he gets a good deal on products which he could then resell for a profit," I explain.

"He sells this stuff?" Denny sounds incredulous.

"Oh, no. He only uses the argument that he *could*, and at a profit, to justify purchasing it all in the first place. Actually, Dad just keeps on loading up and insisting that he's actually making money because he never pays full price. If anything, I guess it's a leftover habit from the Cold War, only now cold means stocking the freezer. If we're ever attacked I can shell the enemy with Birdseye frozen peas or launch a box of Mrs. Paul's Frozen Fishsticks at them."

"But at the bank he works with mortgages, not food, right?" Denny confirms.

"Yeah. At least I think so. He's one of those dads no one is quite certain what he really does at the office. He goes off in a dark suit early every morning carrying a briefcase that could easily hold a medium-sized dead body and comes home late at night looking tired and frazzled. All I know is that it's very stressful, there's lots of talk about Eurodollars, the Federal Reserve and the prime rate of interest. Oh, and my mother doesn't like us kids to make a lot of noise when he gets home."

"I see."

"So use whatever you want. I've got to do some homework. The countdown has begun." I hold up three fingers to indicate the number of days left until the final exam. "Friday is D-Day."

I watch for a second as Denny opens another cupboard that turns out to be overflowing with canned carrots, jars of jam, box upon box of long-grained wild rice and a case of instant hot cocoa mix. "Are you sure it's okay to use this stuff?" he asks.

"Sure," I reply. "Gene loves it when stock is depleted. Then he can organize a seek and stock-up mission to replenish his hoard. Imagine how popular I was when I rolled up at college with enough liquid soap, Bounce dryer sheets and microwave oven popcorn for an entire dormitory. Dad can't shop small. He was a supply guru in the Vietnam War, you know, what do you call it? Logjams. One of those guys who figures out how to send potatoes and combat boots and stuff for, like, six hundred million people."

"Logicians."

"That's it."

"Is this hamster food?" Denny inquires and points to some large sacks of grain on the floor.

I look at the five industrial-sized bags of bark-like cereal. "No, that's colon blow for a nation. You know, granola, nature's broom. Gene's become macroneurotic since his post-heart attack cardiac care classes and so our house was recently declared a whole grain zone. We're now officially a high fiber family."

I head back upstairs to quickly make a peanut butter sandwich and then hit the books, leaving Denny to peruse the overflowing larder.

He spends the afternoon poking around the kitchen and muttering to himself over one of my mother's recipe books while I grind away at adding all my little x's and y's together and wonder why mathematicians are obsessed with adding up letters. It's so stupid, it would be like people deciding to speak using numbers instead of words.

"Life is always a rich and steady time when you are waiting

for something to happen or to hatch."
Mrs. Farley, reading to the class from *Charlotte's Web*.

"Renewal is the principle—and the process—that empowers us to move in an upward spiral of growth and change, of continuous improvement."
Gene MacGuire, quoting *The 7 Habits of Highly Effective People*, explaining to Jess why she is being forced to attend St. Jude's Summer Camp.

Chapter 5
When the Going Seems Easy, You're Going Downhill
Tuesday Evening

The afternoon slips by in a haze of parabolic equations punctuated by the sound of Denny slicing and dicing, running water and rattling pans in the kitchen. I actually don't mind the bit of background noise, especially when he sings snatches of *Bye Bye Blackbird* and then the sound of the double boiler crashing into the sink is followed by muttered curses. Denny could star in a musical cable TV cooking show called *Stove Rage*.

"Are you sure you don't want some help?" I offer. That's how bad this calculus thing is. I'm actually wanting to help in the kitchen. If I was a guy I would be hoping for a war and then be the first one on the bus to Detroit to go and enlist. Although I am getting through the work faster than I thought I would—which is a pleasant surprise.

"No. No. Everything's under control. Too many chefs spoil the broth and all that."

After singing *What Are You Doing New Year's Eve?*, Denny finally calls me to the table. For a minute I think I'm at a restaurant. He's put out white linen napkins, wine goblets, soup spoons and even a little vase of freshly picked wildflowers. I look over at him as he stands with his back to me, making some last minute adjustment to a lemon wedge. "Denny, this is fantastic! I feel terrible. I should have helped."

"Forget it," he calls back, without turning, obviously at a critical paring knife moment. "It's been a treat to have a kitchen to myself again after the invasion at home. I enjoyed it."

We sit down at the table and Denny presides over pouring the wine and serving the food as if he's headwaiter at an elegant restaurant. Whatever it is that I'm eating is delicious.

"This is really great," I say between mouthfuls. "Where did you ever learn to cook like this?"

"Oh, thanks. This is nothing—just a casserole of egg noodles mixed with diced chicken breast and vegetables. Sometimes you can even make it out of leftovers. And it's even easier with all of the provisions that you have stockpiled in the basement. This way you don't have to plan everything ahead of time. Shopping and chopping is what takes the most time. The rest is just about measuring and then applying heat."

"Do you cook a lot?" I am definitely intrigued.

"Oh, all the time. I've almost always done the cooking at home. I really enjoy it," he adds with sincere eagerness. "To me, it's just like science. You know, if you follow a reliable recipe it usually works out and you get the desired results," Denny explains and gesticulates enthusiastically with his hands. "It's not foolproof. I mean, you have to be careful. For instance, some recipes leave out a lot of key directions and then it's more difficult. And some cookbooks are very pretentious and just assume that you know more than you do, like you've been macerating, leavening and deglazing your entire adult life, and so you just have to throw those books away because they're ridiculous. But over the years I have found quite a few very sensible cookbooks containing recipes that absolutely anyone can follow, even a latchkey kid. And that's the secret to edible cooking as far as I'm concerned, a comprehensive recipe. That and getting everything to come out at the correct time. Synchronizing the appearance of the food on the table takes a little more practice. When I first began cooking I had a tendency to start baking the potatoes and blanching the asparagus at the same time."

"Very interesting, weatherman and galloping gourmet. Who would have guessed?" This is particularly newsworthy since I live in a suburb where married men don't cook or do laundry, even if they own a restaurant and a laundry.

"Well, with all the kids and everything, I've had to help Sarah out." He straightens up at the head of the table as he says this, as if to confirm his manhood. "She's worked an outside job for all but five years of our marriage," he proudly states.

"Well, I think it's cool. Actually, it's really nice. Even though my dad loves to purchase food, he wouldn't be caught dead actually preparing it. He won't even scramble an egg. In fact, I wonder why my mother even agrees to go on these stupid camping trips. Her every waking moment is consumed with preparing meals, procuring water and scrubbing out pots and pans."

"Why does your family always go on camping vacations?" Denny inquires. "Don't you ever go skiing or to Disneyland or places like that?"

"No. The only roller coaster ride we ever get is driving up and down craggy gravel paths in the minivan, dragging the pop-up camper and hunting for our assigned electrical hookup. Gene regards it as ludicrous to waste money on flying and luxuriating in Holiday Inns when the family can just as easily be ambling down America's highways and byways and staying at the campgrounds of our country's fifty-four National Parks. His words, not mine."

"Do they always drive?"

"Gene insists that with coast-to-coast passenger railroads gone the way of the Stegosaurus, driving is the only way to really see this great land from sea to shining sea, and at a quarter of the price."

"Camping does sound like fun," Denny concedes. "Especially if you have a big family. Vacations are, after all, rather expensive these days."

"As far as I'm concerned the only reason to go camping is if you're one of those unfortunate homeless families that occasionally wind up as features in the metro section of the *Detroit Free Press* around Christmas time. Seriously Denny, why anyone who owns a home with central heating and air-conditioning, hot showers, an all-electric kitchen, including a Cuisinart and a Melitta coffeemaker, would voluntarily forego all that for a week of roughing it—and have to pay Uncle Sam for the privilege, is a mystery to me. I think that if I'm ever so financially secure as to be able to afford my own place, I would never leave it for a vacation that required packing sleeping bags, two dozen frigging cans of Sterno, electric socks and a jackknife. And certainly not for the excitement of treating raw sewage and sleeping in a trailer half the size of our two-car garage. Sleeps seven! Yeah, right? Seven what? The seven dwarfs, maybe."

I rise from the table and start stacking the dishes in the sink.

"You don't realize it now but when you're older you'll look back on all those trips as the best times of your life," Denny remarks philosophically. "And you'll have some lovely memories."

"You've got to be kidding me! Right now my biggest fear is that I won't be able to forget those God-awful trips and that I'll have to go for reverse-repressed memory therapy just to get rid of the chronic nightmares. Because if I think back on them with anything but abject horror, I promise to kill myself immediately." Oh shit! I just did it again. It is amazing how difficult it is to have a conversation with someone whose wife has just died and not keep broaching the subject of death in one way or another. It's like accidentally saying *Don't you see?* over and over to a blind person. It just keeps popping out.

Denny either doesn't notice the remark or politely chooses to ignore it.

"Tell me Mr. Sin—I mean Denny, is that your idea of a good time? Pup tents, picnics, Coleman stoves, mess kits, boring scenery, ten hours of your brothers fighting over the window seat, the hump seat and the backseat, followed by eight hours of the mind-numbing license plate game? Puh-leeze! Do you take your family camping?"

"No one in my family has ever expressed a strong interest in roughing it. The girls' idea of a holiday is burning their skins to a crisp on some white sand beach in the Caribbean and then slathering on Noxzema and going shopping. So I would always just ask the travel agent to try and find a place like that where I could at least get in some ocean fishing."

"I rest my case. Camping is no picnic."

I dish up big bowls of Neapolitan ice cream that we take into the living room. I can't actually ever remember sitting in my family room and eating a bowl of ice cream without the television blaring in the background. I decide that it's kind of fun to just sit around and talk. At least, it's neat talking to Denny. When my little brothers are around it's an endless stream of fart stories, knock-knock jokes and reports of recent bogeyman sightings.

"Not to change the subject, but why do you sometimes refer to your parents by their first names? I'm assuming you're not adopted or the child of a previous marriage."

"If I was adopted I think it's safe to assume that the people returned me in a hurry, and that my parents were forced to raise me against their will. I don't mean to insult the office of parenthood itself. It's just that I'm so sick of living at home with my mom and dad ruining my life—did I say ruining? I meant running—that I've been trying to distance myself from them mentally and emotionally. To distance myself physically would be first prize, of course, but that doesn't seem to be in the stars at the present time."

"And they don't mind?"

"Are you kidding me? They don't know. I mean, I don't do it to their faces. They'd kill me." I finish my ice cream by drinking the remaining lava of pinkish-brown melted goo directly from the bowl. "Do you want a beer or something?" I offer.

"Are you going to have one?" Denny looks up at me expectantly from his seat on the couch.

Since it's already almost nine o'clock I had rather meant this question to be a euphemism for *Do you want to sleep over tonight?* If he stays for another drink I decide that it must mean he's planning to hang around for the night.

"Hmm," I go into the kitchen and scan the shelves of the fridge. "No. What I'd really like is a drink, a sloe gin fizz, I think." I reach for an unopened two-liter jug of 7-Up that is in the very back of the refrigerator, behind Joan's light blue-tinted plastic celery container/freshener.

"Yuck! I haven't had one of those since college. You'll get a cavity before you get tight."

I feel embarrassed by my choice. Why didn't I ask for a mature drink like a martini or a Manhattan or a pink lady? No, those would have sounded stupid, too. "I'm going to have a rum and Coke instead," I finally say. "Do me a favor and get the rum out of the liquor cabinet, please. It's right there in the family room. And help yourself to whatever you want."

From the cupboard I select two glass tumblers, long since dulled from having endured too many dishwasher cycles with the dial set on Pots and Pans/Heavy Scrub. Along with a jug of generic cola I carry them to the family room, or the rumpus room, as Joan likes to call it, and arrange everything on top of Gene's homemade wet bar. So far it is the only project that he has completed with his five-year-old, $1,200 worth of power tools from Montgomery Ward—thick metal instruments that he religiously dusts once every six weeks with his handheld air compressor.

The wooden doors with the faux brass mesh-covered windows are swollen from the heat and not easily opened. Denny has to yank quite hard in order to coerce them out of their narrow slots. "Wow, I've never seen such a well-stocked liquor cabinet!" he exclaims. Next to the array of bottles are three neat rows of shimmering shot, highball and cordial glasses, all arranged with mathematical precision. Two Waterford decanters filled with different hues of copperish-colored liquid stand against the back wall of the cabinet like the king and queen on a chessboard.

"At least it makes more sense than hoarding food. I mean, booze lasts for decades. Think about it, a douche is only going to hold out for a few years on the shelf until it becomes chemically altered into cough syrup or something equally icky. But a bottle of Jack is forever."

"You're crazy," Denny says to me.

"No. My dad's crazy," I correct him. "I'm just bored. Get this," I say to prove my point, "Last year he used his frequent flyer miles to take the entire family to Europe for two weeks, camping, of course, and made us all bring old clothes so that we could throw them away as we went along."

"No way!"

"Way! Even underwear. My mother was petrified that we'd all be in an accident on the Autobahn or some type of international incident and be seen in ratty, worn-out clothes on *World News Tonight with Peter Jennings*."

"Old clothes for the Old World," Denny jokes. "Your dad certainly is efficient."

I lazily mix the rum and Coke with my index finger and fancy that I look a bit like Madonna in her movie *Truth or Dare* while Denny pours a gin with a splash of tonic for himself. And now that I think of it, Madonna is a good example of a girl who got the hell out of Michigan and made something of herself. I would change places with Madonna in a heartbeat. I wouldn't mind being a Material Girl.

"When that book, you know, *The Seven Habits of Highly Efficient People* came out, that was a bad day for this family," I explain.

"Actually, I believe that it's *effective* people," Denny amiably corrects me.

"Yeah, whatever. Anyway, my dad decided that, just like a business person or a cutting edge corporation, we could become a more effective family if we set goals. So he started basing all of our allowances on the completion of assigned tasks and the achievement of personal objectives. Didn't you notice the duty roster on the basement door?"

Denny nods his head to indicate that indeed he had.

"Poor Brendan was in kindergarten when the program was started, or rather *initiated.* My dad of course had to have a *launch party* and Brendan had to write down stuff like *remember milk money* and *try not to eat paste* on his contract in an effort to fulfill his interdependence paradigm. It's no wonder he eventually cracked up and took refuge in *The Cat In the Hat*. I mean, who wouldn't have?"

"What does his allowance have to do with *The Cat In the Hat*?" Denny asks.

"You don't want to know, it's really bizarre." But of course I tell him anyway.

"Brendan is the youngest. He's seven-years-old and has this quirk of answering in Dr. Seuss syntax whenever possible. Sometimes he'll only speak in Dr. Seuss."

"What do you mean 'speak in Dr. Seuss'?" Denny asks.

"Okay, let's say you're having dinner at my house and you ask Brendan if he wants more carrots. He'd probably launch into that bit from *Green Eggs and Ham*—you know: '*I will not eat them in the rain. I will not eat them on a train.*' Only he goes on and on and on and we can't shut him up."

"That's kind of cute," replies Denny. "But how does he remember it all?"

"Good question. At a meeting with Brendan's teacher and the school psychiatrist, Gene and Joan were told that he is probably just trying to 'demonstrate his scholastic prowess as a modus for competing with the accomplishments of his four older brothers and sisters.' This is supposedly quite normal, they were reassured by Brendan's teacher, Mr. Benzinger." I use an academic-sounding tone of voice in an effort to mimic the experts: "The youngest child is often anxious to keep up with his or her more academically mature siblings. Mr. Benzinger estimated that Brendan has committed twenty-six Dr. Seuss books to memory and that he can liberally recite from the remaining eighteen, no small feat for a second-grader. Mr. Benzinger claims that Brendan's headed straight for the gifted and talented track. *I'm sure*, as if Einstein and F.D.R. also perpetually declaimed from *Horton Hears A Who* and *McElligot's Pool* in their formative years."

"Maybe he's one of those geniuses, an idiot savant or something like that," Denny helpfully suggests.

"I'm certain that you've got the idiot part right. But for the rest I think the problem is more like Jack and Roger are always beating the shit out of him when my parents aren't home and the remainder of the time he gets clobbered by his classmates on the playground."

"So how would that make him recite Dr. Suess?"

"Simple, I mean, you don't have to be B.F. Skinner to figure out that in Dr. Seuss books the underdog always wins. I think that my parents should quit reading manuals like *How to Educate Your Gifted Child* and instead spring for some martial arts lessons, or at the very least, a bodyguard for the little twerp. But then I'm no school shrink. And I have to admit that I find it annoying how all the guys in my family are treated with kid gloves while I'm not allowed to have any problems."

"What do you mean you're not allowed to have problems? Everyone has problems at one time or another. It's part of growing up, part of life."

"It just seems that whenever I express any worries about not having any friends to do stuff with around here anymore or something, absolutely anything, I'm told that I'm being silly, selfish and unreasonable or feeling sorry for myself and I am advised that it's nothing that a good night's sleep can't fix. Meanwhile, the boys are allowed to have growing pains, out of control hormones, errors in judgment, peer pressure and all sorts of other crap. Whenever I vie for a little sympathy or pop psychology in this house I'm quickly reminded that I'm the oldest and therefore should be more concerned with setting a good example for my siblings. And that I should start acting my age and not complain all of the time. Everyone just thinks Brendan is so cute and clever. Well I can tell you that if I had pulled just half of the shit that my brothers have gotten away with, I would have been grounded until the middle of twenty-first century. But on them it's just precious or precocious or they're 'going through a phase' or a friend made them perform some evil deed."

Denny doesn't dispute my statements. But then how could he? He only started living here last night. Instead he checks the mantel clock, which reads 10:40 PM, and rises from his chair, as if preparing to make his final exit. "Well, it's been a pleasure but I'm sure you have to study and I guess I had better get going."

I understand that he has to say this so I make the appropriate noises. "What do you mean? Did you get in touch with Mr. Sutherland today?"

However, by the way he starts to carry his empty glass to the kitchen I suddenly realize that he is serious about leaving. But why? I'm probably boring him to death for one thing. And besides, the beleaguered man is trying to get some relief from women in their twenties and now he is right back where he started. Only I have this nagging feeling that if he will only stay here with me, I can get through the entire calculus thing—and that otherwise, I am losing it, cracking up. In Denny Sinclair I've found the voice of reason and yet at the same time he isn't judging me, correcting my behavior, or telling me to change into someone else, like all the rest of the grown-ups. He even has a car and a real job with benefits. And best of all, he isn't saying how attractive I'd be if only I would put a clip in my hair.

Maybe he's my guardian angel? Can a person be another person's guardian angel? I wonder. Joan would know. Joan is a big believer in angels. A few years ago, right after Jack recovered from a burst appendix, which almost killed him, she had installed a plaque in the upstairs hallway quoting Psalms 91:11-12: *For he will give his angels charge of you to guard you in all your ways. On their hands they shall bear you up, lest you dash your foot against a stone.* And following my car accident last spring, after which I'd astounded everybody by walking away unscathed, Mom had insisted that just the day before she'd experienced a presentiment that I was about to receive a message from an angel, though I doubt she knew it was going to be in the form of a black two-door Dodge Omni, and she quoted Luke: *'The angel went to her and said, Greetings, you who are highly favored! The Lord is with you.'* I'd actually felt sort of funny for a few days after the accident, like I'd had too much herbal tea to drink and then smoked some not-so-great pot and so I'd finally asked what she thought the message meant. Mom said she was pretty sure that the angel was saying that I should slow down and study more.

"I didn't quite manage to round old Walt up," Denny says. "I just think that I'd better be moving on. No offense, but what if your parents find out I'm here? I mean, it doesn't look right. And what if the neighbors see us?"

My mind reels with all the reasons that he should stay but I can't articulate most of them. "I'll just tell them that there was a prowler and that I was scared and you happened to be driving by looking for Mr. Sutherland—oh the hell with it! We don't need an excuse. Nothing's wrong with it. And fuck the neighbors."

"Jessica!"

"Sorry, screw the neighbors."

"That is exactly what they'll think we're doing."

"And don't call me Jessica. I hate that name! My mother always calls me Jessica. Unless she's mad. Then it's Jessica Anne, as if there are three Jessicas living at 42 Ferndale Drive."

"When did you say your family was coming back?"

"Sunday. Sunday night."

He appears doubtful and unconsciously smooths his right eyebrow with his fingertip. "I mean, I can't just live here until then." But then he rises up and refills our drinks anyway, as if *then* is still a long way off. "Where did you say that they went camping?" he asks.

"I can't even remember. Some stupid National Seashore or someplace like that. Put it this way, I'm sure they had to drive past several khaki-clad Park Rangers to get to wherever they went. It's at least a couple hundred miles from here—took them half a day just to get there." I relax a little. Denny has a fresh drink in his hand and no longer seems to be in a hurry. Maybe that's my answer—cocktail nation. He has to be getting fairly well-oiled by now. If he has a few drinks every night then surely he won't be able to drive. I quickly go to the kitchen and bring out two of the biggest bags of the saltiest snacks I can find and dump them into gigantic wooden bowls. "The best thing I can say about this trip is that they at least decided to stay in the state of Michigan. Last year Gene dragged our sorry asses all the way to the South Dakota Badlands National Park—twenty-two hours of frigging highway bingo just to see a bunch of dirt and rocks."

"You drove all the way to South Dakota?"

"Yeah. And not just South Dakota. Western South Dakota." I light up another cigarette. "Is there a plain Dakota? I mean, why do we have South Dakota and North Dakota but no Dakota?"

"Uh, I really don't know. Do you mind if I switch on the eleven o'clock news?"

"Not at all. Here I'll do it." I search for the channel changer and then flick to the news. "Let's see who was fatally killed today." Denny winces.

Shit. I did it again.

The normal anchorperson is on vacation and another man is taking his place. "Jesus, it's so stupid when they say, 'I'm filling in for Jim who's got the night off.' I mean, who cares? Does the guy at the convenience store declare, 'Herb is out today so I'll be getting your cigarettes'? Christ, these people read the news, that's all. They don't make it and I'll bet you anything that most of them probably don't even write it."

"It's so you'll trust them. They want to make you feel as if they're your friends," Denny explains distractedly and stares at the TV set.

It is at moments like this that I am convinced the entire world is purposely trying to annoy me in all sorts of micro ways. Because someone up there knows that I'll reach my breaking point and one day I'll finally snap because of something mundane like a payphone eating my last coin. And I'll go totally berserk and chop down the phone booth with a nearby fire ax. And the police and the psychiatrists won't understand that losing the money was just the final straw after enduring a lifetime of annoyances, like *Baby On Board* yellow triangles hanging in car windows and convenience stores that sell hotdogs in packs of eight next to buns in packages of six. The police will report to the psychiatrist only that I lost my phone money and then lost my mind and it will make the evening news and PMS drug manufacturers from all over the world will try and get a statement from me in order to bolster their research and sales. The judge will sentence me to six months of anger therapy and give me a choice between a mental hospital or the kind of house arrest during which I must wear a parole ankle bracelet and live like a suburban dog behind an electric fence, supervised by my parents. But I'll shock everybody and chose the mental institution over being at home and even though the booby hatch will have neatly trimmed grounds, the decision will devastate my parents. And from that day on whenever I ask, "Excuse me, but does anyone have some change I can borrow to make a phone call?" people will get incredibly nervous.

What will I say when the social worker asks me what went awry? Possibly that it was the unflattering cut of my Girl Scout pantsuit, which led the roadie at the amusement park to mistake me for a boy and shout across the entire length of the Tilt-A-Whirl, "Pull the bar down tight there Sonny! We wouldn't want to lose anyone now, would we?"

From then on, over badminton games and mint juleps the nosy neighbors will whisper, "That Jessica MacGuire had so much potential but then everything suddenly unraveled after her senior year of college." And for many years to come, as they patiently wait in line at the butcher shop or sit getting manicures in the beauty parlor, townsfolk will speculate as to what went wrong with my life.

Me? I'll end up spending the rest of my days in the family room, a ne'er-do-well busily constructing ashtrays out of maple leaves, watching infomercials for hair extensions and listening to self-help books-on-tape.

I click off the TV when the business news and the weather wind up and the program ends. "I don't understand why our financial institutions lend these stupid South American countries money," I say. "When Brazil can't repay the money they owe us they just walk away and leave all of our banks in hot water."

"That's because our banks can command higher interest rates on riskier loans," Denny carefully explains. "In the environmental consulting business the first thing you learn is that the price of everything is driven entirely by supply and demand. It's the same thing with lending money. If a bank wants to earn more interest then it must make less desirable loans."

"Yeah, but the countries get off scot-free and then just go off and borrow more money somewhere else. It's not fair! The foreign banker just says 'we don't have the money' and our banker says 'okay, don't worry about it, we'll just charge Jess MacGuire a higher interest rate on her student credit card.'"

"Well, they're emerging markets and partly Third World countries and so they don't have anything valuable to put up as collateral. One just has to bet on the synergy of their economy and any available resources."

"Sure they have collateral. A lot of them have great beaches."

"So you think we should get the beaches in return?" Denny asks and laughs at the absurdity of such a notion.

"Damned right I do," I say.

"I'll bring it up at my World Bank meeting in the morning. But just so I've got the facts straight, do you think they should ship the beaches up here or just annex them on behalf of the US and we'll fly down there to use them?"

"Definitely bring them here. Flights are much too expensive."

He takes a handful of pretzels and continues to chuckle. I can't decide if he's laughing with me or at me. "Cut it out. It's not that funny."

"Yes, it is."

"Quit laughing at me." I suddenly feel simultaneously foolish and sheepish. Why did I even attempt to have a serious conversation about banking, a subject that I know absolutely nothing about, aside from a skimmed chapter in a finance class textbook. I have a strong desire to try and redeem myself in his eyes. "All I was trying to say is that we've got to start running this country like a business, not a charity."

"In that case," Denny remarks dryly, "We should probably just burn it down and collect the insurance."

"Now there's an idea with some potential!" I pretend to turn the concept over in my mind but I'm actually thinking about how hot the room is. I'm sweating even though I'm only wearing shorts and a tank top and so I get up and once again crank the knob that controls the air-conditioning. More hot air. "It's so humid in here that I feel as if I could take a breath and get a drink of water at the same time. I'm almost positive I'm getting building sickness syndrome. Maybe I can sue my parents for endangering the health of a minor."

"Believe me, you don't have sick building syndrome. You would need to have been exposed to uncovered asbestos for the past ten years, not sheet rock and wood paneling and early American patchwork quilts. It's still about ninety degrees outside. You may as well get used to these heat waves. Environmental terrorism is going to be the next big problem in this country—radicals getting hold of the technology and machinery necessary to control the atmosphere. Then it's all over. They'll own us. Most people are shocked when I explain to them that weather terrorism is just around the corner. The media does not seem to grasp the magnitude of this threat. There is technology in the pipeline right now that will confer upon humans the capability to destroy mankind through altering the temperature by sixty or seventy degrees. I mean, forget about the plastic explosives being used to bomb airplanes—amateur stuff. And it was all foreshadowed through the Lex Luthor character in the Superman comic books back in the late 1940s—Luthor was always threatening global ruination by interfering with the weather. And then there was Kurt Vonnegut's book *Cat's Cradle* that, though it was sardonic, arrived at the right place—destruction of the earth from a substance called ice nine, which could freeze all of the oceans. The only difference is that now we really have the scientific capabilities—it's not just bestselling science fiction anymore."

"Can someone really destroy the entire Earth if they change the weather?" I ask incredulously.

"Sure. It's already possible to chemically seed clouds, prevent bodies of water from freezing and grow food independent of external forces. It may be feasible to temporarily isolate a particular city or a country from such a cataclysm, but eventually someone will hit the wrong button and we'll all get it. Or maybe it's the right button, if that's what they're trying to do. The press should stop obsessing about germ warfare, computer glitches, nuclear radiation and Armageddon because I can guarantee you that we're all going in a gigantic freeze or a tremendous heat wave. It's no mystery. Humans can only survive in a very narrow band of temperature."

"Is that why we've had such extreme heat this summer? Are the Iraqis controlling our weather?"

"You never know," Denny replies matter-of-factly. "Like I said, it's just a matter of time. Though it has been unusually hot this year. In fact, I wish that I were fishing for Sockeye Salmon off the coast of Ketchikan, Alaska, right now. That's where Sarah and I were supposed to go on vacation this month," Denny wistfully remarks and then walks to the freezer to get some more ice. "Uh, Jess," he says as he passes me, "You've got something stuck between your teeth."

"Oh God, I hate that!" I move my tongue across the front of my mouth and then scrape in-between my front teeth with my thumbnail. "Is it gone now?"

"No." Denny stands in front of me and points to the same spot in his mouth in an effort to help me locate the offending foreign object. "Over here."

I try again. "My teeth are like boxcars with cowcatchers. I can't believe that you waited until now to tell me about this. We ate dinner almost three hours ago. Do I also have toilet paper hanging out of the back of my shorts?"

"I'm sorry. I thought it would sort itself out."

"How embarrassing. It's green isn't it? Those things are always green."

"Yellow. Probably corn. Maybe squash."

"Is it gone now?" I smile at him again.

"No. Here let me try." Denny reaches over and then, apparently having second thoughts, stops short. "No, it's really wedged in there. You'd better go and brush."

"Brush? You're definitely in cahoots with my mother. This whole thing is a set up, a trap so I that eat properly, study hard and brush my teeth." I go to the front hall mirror and push aside the fluffy taupe Fieldcrest shroud and pluck the small chunk of yellow squash out from between my two front teeth. I wonder how it is possible that I have the chapped lips of a seven-year-old. Then I carefully scrutinize my face for any new pimples or other outward signs of lingering youth. "This chocolate, stress, acne thing is a vicious circle," I say loudly enough so that Denny can hear me in the next room.

"I read that chocolate doesn't cause pimples," he shouts back from the family room.

"Yeah, but when I'm stressed out I eat a lot of chocolate. Then come the zits." I examine the forehead pimple Chernobyl disaster site and decide that it will take another two or three days for that to heal. The bangs are certainly a dilemma, I conclude. I had cut them myself in order to hide some pimples on my forehead, but then I had discovered that having clumps of oily hair rubbing against my skin the whole time was just making my skin break out even more. "When I look at myself all I see is one big pimple."

"Your skin looks fine to me."

Still standing in front of the mirror I pull my shirt tight around the front and scrutinize my chest in the mirror. Then I turn to examine the slim outline that my breasts make. Ping-Pong balls. What had God been thinking? Scarecrow, obviously.

When I reenter the family room Denny is skimming a recent copy of *Corporate Executive* magazine that had been lying on the coffee table, atop a pile of business periodicals and lawn care catalogues. I set about making us both another drink, even though Denny's hasn't quite finished his last one. However I'm carrying out my plan to keep this guardian angel in a liquid rather than a solid state, which he apparently doesn't seem to mind very much.

"Denny, I want you to tell me the truth about something. And besides, I figure you owe me one since I could have called the Children's Aid Society on you for running away and abandoning your kids."

"I'll tell you anything as you long as you promise not to call my mother and tell her I'm here. Why do you think I wanted to watch the news?" Denny replies seriously. "It was to make sure that she didn't somehow force them to display my picture." Denny takes a sip of gin, looks up from the magazine and acknowledges the fresh drink that I put down in front of him with an unusual expression—one more of surprise than thank you. "So name it. What do you want to know? Want me to explain the Doppler effect? It's very interesting. When the frequency of a sound, light or microwave energy—"

"Definitely not. It sounds vaguely related to calculus."

Dropping down in the cherry-red beanbag chair with the big frog on the front, one of Joan's leftover craft projects from the late eighties, I ask, "What I need to know is what do men really think about womens' breasts?"

"Beg your pardon?" Denny coughs and then chokes before achieving a general state of spluttering and sweating. "Excuse me but is this for school?"

"No, of course not. It's just so confusing." In the back of my mind is the fact that my boyfriend has been in possession of a roving eye of late and I am beginning to wonder if men and big tits are just predestined to randomly bounce around in the universe until they eventually find one another. "Everyone says that your personality is what really matters and then all of these women get implants or wear push-up bras and all the beer commercials and billboards feature Playboy bunnies exploding out of their bikinis. Though it starts even earlier. At the age of five they give little girls anatomically incorrect Barbie dolls to play with. You're a guy so I just thought you could perhaps solve the mystery. Do men desire women with big breasts? I just want to know, that's all," I ask matter-of-factly.

"No, of course not," Denny hastily replies. "It depends really. Actually, I'm not the right person to ask. I'm a father." His face turns scarlet and he resumes looking down at the magazine, quickly flipping the pages.

"No, don't you see? You're the perfect person to ask because you can be objective. So what if you're a father—I mean, you're still a man." I take a drag on my cigarette, exhale quickly and wave the tobacco stick in the air like a sparkler on the fourth of July. It's just like men and fighting. In school they teach kids not to solve problems by punching one another in the face but then people openly admire men who start fights, go to war or play professional football. If hockey players didn't try to rip each other's faces off then no one would bother going to the games."

Denny seems to be completely discomposed now. "Okay, let me see—" He glances up and accidentally looks directly at my chest, catches himself and quickly casts his eyes downward. "I mean, let me think for a moment."

It started out as a semi-serious question but now it is fun in a weird sort of way. Like a scary ride at an amusement park. Being able to embarrass Denny—me tormenting a grown-up.

"C'mon. You *know* what you think. Just be honest and say it. Say what you think. If you can't ask a complete stranger a question like this, whom can you turn to? The school nurse? I don't care if the truth hurts. I honestly don't. It's just that someone should have the courage to say it once and for all so that the American people can breath a collective sigh of relief and get down to the business of studying the trade-offs between implants and padded bras. Maybe the IRS can even start incorporating rebates into the tax code for these amenities."

Denny drains his almost-empty glass and takes another swing at it. "Let's try taking a scientific approach. When we're born that's one of the first things we need. And then you forget about them for ten years or so and well, then women get their own and so where does that leave the men?"

"Denny, it's a simple question. Do-you-like-women-with-large-breasts?" I enunciate the words clearly as if I'm teaching the English as a second language course at the Community Center.

"Well certainly not the ones in *Penthouse*, if that's what you mean." Denny picks up the fresh drink that I have left for him and thoughtfully gazes into the glass as he slowly swirls the contents. "But I guess that, uh, like most men, I notice a woman's proportions."

"Oh, well. That's what I thought. After all, at over a million dollars per minute, Superbowl commercials don't lie, only the spokespeople do."

Denny retrieves the magazine from his lap. He thumbs through it so haphazardly that I know he can't possibly be seeing anything. While skimming the pages from back to front he says, "Uh Jess, if this is about you, I uh, I think that you're an attractive and well-proportioned young woman." Having said this he exhales and pokes at a lone ice cube floating in his glass with his fingertip.

"Thanks. But I'm wearing a Wonderbra. You know—you pick a guy up at a club, take him home and he wonders where your tits went."

"Jess!"

"Language. Language please!" I mimic the favorite expression of Mrs. Watson, my second grade Sunday school teacher.

"In an interdependent situation, synergy is particularly powerful in dealing with negative forces that work against growth and change."
Gene MacGuire, quoting *The 7 Habits of Highly Effective People*, explaining to his children why they should do their homework together instead of getting into fistfights.

"You cannot graduate without knowing your multiplication tables."
Miss Buchanan to the third grade.

Chapter 6

Take This Test and Shove It

Tuesday Night

As the hour rolls past midnight it occurs to me that I should probably go to bed. If for no other reason than my father insists that when you are trying to solve a problem, your subconscious will continue to work on it while you're asleep. Then BINGO, you wake up in the morning with all the answers, a regular Rhodes scholar. And Lord knows, I'm trying to solve all kinds of problems, not just calculus. If Dad is right I should try and pass out for a year or two, nothing short of a coma.

But I don't go to bed. Nor does Denny seem interested in heading off to bed. He doesn't talk about fishing much anymore either. Or if he does, it's in the abstract sense—he no longer implies that he might actually go fishing, personally, that is. Not this week, anyway.

We are content with baby-sitting the night. By two o'clock in the morning Denny and I are slouched on opposite sides of the coffee table making a feeble attempt to play a game of Tiddledy Winks.

After Denny had suggested that we play chess I was forced to explain that not only do I not know how to play chess, but that my younger brothers had glued all the pieces to the chessboard. Or at least they are the number one and two suspects after Gene's attempts to teach them what he considers to be a gentleman's game met with great resistance. A bunch of carved wooden figures that have to be pushed around by hand can't exactly compete with slaying dragons and saving Princesses on a computer complete with joysticks and multimedia speakers.

I've placed an ashtray on the floor next to my right knee that, as the night progresses, has become overloaded with the crunched butts of about twenty Marlboro Lights. "You know the difference between being poor and being broke?" I ask rhetorically. "Poor means I can still afford the $3.80 for cigarettes, even if I do have to borrow it from the drawer where Joan keeps the lunch money. But at least I haven't been dipping into the offering plate at church like Jack does, or skimming pennies from the mall fountain a la my grifting little brothers."

"Okay, it's your turn," Denny says after flipping a kelly green Tiddledy Wink right off the board and onto the maple border of the glass coffee table.

I hopelessly flip a bright blue Tiddledy Wink straight over the coffee table and onto the carpet. "This is a really hard game," I remark. "I don't remember it being this difficult when I was a kid. It's your turn."

"Yeah, I think fifty is too old for Tiddledy Winks. No reflexes left. It's like playing Frisbee with your grandfather."

He's fifty! Christ, I thought he was, like, mid-forties, or at least still middle-aged. I immediately begin to pray that he doesn't have a stroke or some kind of angina thing from this heat wave. "Want me to get the fan out of the basement?" I suddenly interrupt him.

Denny looks up slightly perplexed but politely answers the question that came out of left field. "No, uh, it won't do any good anyway—just blow the hot air around."

"Oh. I guess you're right."

"So," Denny continues but then hesitantly glances up as if to see if I have any more *non sequitur* outbursts waiting in the wings. "Tell me why your dad stockpiles all that detergent. I mean, food I can sort of understand. Not that it doesn't make sense, in a way. Sarah is always running out of stuff and having to go to the drugstore at ten o'clock at night."

I notice that Denny still hasn't gotten into the habit of referring to his wife in the past tense. It reminds me of my great Uncle P. J. who still talks about Adele, his late wife, who has been dead for almost fifteen years now, in the present tense. Uncle P. J. actually says things like: "Adele and I have been thinking that we may spend the rest of the summer on the Upper Peninsula. Lots of fresh air and moose hunting up there." My mother says that Uncle P. J. is "not quite right." That is Joan's favorite catchall euphemism for anything from kleptomania, mild retardation or just a few harmless eccentricities like those of cousin Melanie, who will only drive herself places if she can make all right-hand turns in order to get there. Melanie can actually go a lot more places than one might think since she's very good at planning right-turn-only routes. It's just that sometimes it takes her five minutes to get to the mall but a half an hour to get back home. For more extreme or complicated degrees of mental illness, Joan prefers the designation "touched."

"I don't take Gene's obsessive-compulsive behavioral quirks very seriously. I mean, we're talking about a guy who will actually say 'The hurrier I go, the behinder I get,' to complete strangers in the supermarket if they drop something or bump carts. When he finds stuff on sale and he has a triple coupon he just loads up. What can I tell you? The Masai Warriors demonstrated their wealth by accumulating cattle. The MacGuires have a lot of Tide laundry detergent." I shoot another Tiddledy Wink over the edge of the coffee table. This one lands in Denny's lap.

"I didn't notice any powder, just liquid." Denny says.

"Liquid dissolves better."

"But I still don't think I comprehend the underlying principle," he muses aloud.

Denny is unable to get his next Tiddledy Wink airborne. His fingers are sweaty and his thumb keeps slipping off the round shooter. He finally surrenders and shoves the plastic board across the coffee table in the manner of a petulant child. "I can't play this stupid game. I think you have to be under ten."

"We should have played Twister. Want another gin and tonic?"

"Sure, what the hell. I don't have to drive. Only go easy on the tonic—just a swash."

"A swash, huh? Okay Beefeater boy. One gin with a gin chaser coming up." I go to the bar and mix two more drinks.

"If you don't mind me being honest, I'm getting drunk Jess. Aren't you?"

"I've been feeling kind of soggy inside my head for the past two hours but I can't decide whether I'm going to pass out or puke and so I think it's best to keep going until I come to a conclusion."

"Good. I was starting to worry that you have a hollow leg."

"Actually, I'm a little disappointed that this excessive drinking hasn't had the desired effect of making me want to try and balance a lampshade on my head and dance across the furniture without touching the ground. At least that's what it did for most of my roommates at college."

"Yes, I recall a few fraternity parties like that. I guess some things never change."

"Recently I've taken to getting totally polluted at every opportunity as an experiment to see if perhaps there is another person underneath, a sweet inner child, someone who is more fun and less inhospitable, a woman who will eventually be in the million dollar roundtable of her organization as a direct result of sophisticated and refined social skills. Boy how my dad can work a room; lots of jokes, patting people on the back, trading business cards and then promising to shave a point or so off their mortgages if they come in to refinance within the next few days. Wink, wink. Nod, nod."

"Well if we need to give personal testimony in order to keep the booze flowing, if you're trying to find more of yourself, then I'm trying to get rid of most of myself."

"Oh goody gumdrops. Maybe we'll be able to work out a trade."

"I doubt you'd want any of the cards I'm looking to toss in," he replies.

"Actually, if you're tossing in a job I'd be very interested."

There is a long silence and I now feel depressed and he looks depressed and we both stare at one another and then at the dark empty fireplace. Denny finally sighs and closes his eyes for a few seconds.

"Don't get me wrong," he finally says, "Because I'd never do it. But I can see why people commit suicide. Right now it seems that my life couldn't possibly get any worse. Nor any better, for that matter. I feel as if I'm floating. How am I going to return to work next week when it's all so meaningless? How can I possibly pretend to care about installing solar panels or that our Dallas office is once again over budget?"

"Honestly Denny, I think you need a shrink or some tranquilizers. You drink too much. It's not healthy."

"Thanks for the advice but I don't drink," Denny replies. "I sip. Big difference. And even if I do occasionally overimbibe, you should know that for a man of my age and position, being a hootch hound is considered to be an excellent occupational strategy. Look at President Ulysses S. Grant, he did all his best work completely crocked. And all those Nobel prize-winning writers: Hemingway, Faulkner and Steinbeck. And what about Noah?"

"Noah who?"

"You know, Noah's ark."

"Noah wasn't a drunkard."

"Sure he was! It says so right there in the Bible. Shit-faced all the time. Probably couldn't have counted much past two. It's a miracle he ever got that barge out of the shallows."

"Well I still say that there are better ways of dealing with life than drinking too much."

"My wife died," he replies caustically.

It's the first time I've seen him act anything but affable, and this is despite my tirades.

"What's your excuse?" he continues pointedly. "At the rate you're going, you'll need to graduate college and a twelve-step program before landing a job."

I hadn't meant to make him angry. Or maybe I had. Either way, I don't really care anymore. Lately I've had this weird idea that maybe somewhere a grown-up needed to be sacrificed in order that I could enter their world. Possibly a kind of substitution theory or some obscure pagan ritual. Or maybe like a hospital—old people dying in some rooms while replacement babies are being born on the floor below.

"Not a bad idea," I reply sarcastically and casually take a sip of my drink. "Maybe I'll get a B.S., A.A," I say with mock thoughtfulness. "That actually works out fine since it just so happens that I'm majoring in marketing and minoring in alcohol appreciation."

"So tell me," he inquires seriously, apparently recovered from his burst of self-defense, "Why are you so hostile? You're young, you're smart, you're attractive and you have your whole life ahead of you."

"That's exactly the problem! Don't you see? I'm young and I have no life ahead of me," I sigh dramatically. "I've been pessimistic about my future ever since I received a check from the tooth fairy when I was eight and it bounced. Second, I'm part of Generation X—the first in thirteen generations to have less than their parents—so, unless you're a silicon valley whiz kid, a breakfast cereal heiress or a lesbian folk rock star, you've got no future and nothing to look forward to. Except maybe to being the oldest papergirl here in Stuttaford and paying for your social security checks—if the program lasts even that long. That's the latest good news, didn't you hear? Anyone retiring after 2025 is shit out of luck. Maybe if I'm really fortunate I'll become a Publisher's Clearinghouse Sweepstakes finalist. And third, I'd rather be lucky than smart, any day of the week."

"So why are you going to summer school if it's all such a lost cause?" he scoffs.

"After four years of all these bullshit pop quizzes and group projects I at least want to get my degree. In retrospect I think maybe I flunked calculus because I was taking too many credits. I mean, I also flunked because I can't do it, but I changed majors in my junior year so I had to squeeze in a lot of extra classes. In fact, I almost had to go for a victory lap."

"Why did you change your major?"

"I was studying English Literature and eventually realized that I'd never make any money. And so I decided that a life of intellectual fulfillment and poverty might not be very appealing in the long run. I mean, English Literature? Give me a break. As far as the job market goes, I may as well have been studying interpretive dance or paint-by-numbers."

"So you decided that you wanted to print some money?"

"Not money specifically so much as to have my own apartment—one which I don't have to share with any members of my immediate family or four other roommates, for that matter. I also wouldn't mind having the freedom a car could give me. It's such a drama to ask my parents to borrow one of theirs and then do all the scheduling of the kids' carpools and baseball practices. I don't even bother anymore. Any old secondhand junker would do. Even the Tom Joad dustbowl jalopy is looking good at this point, especially when compared to my Jess-powered ten-speed. If I had a car I'd put a plastic St. Christopher statue on the dashboard and cover the rust and dents with bumper stickers that say *Will Work For Food* and *Don't Tailgate Or I'll Flick a Booger on Your Windshield*."

"Did you get those directly from Martin Luther King Jr.'s *I Have A Dream* speech?" he inquires.

"Seriously Denny, greed is not an easy thing to admit to. The realization that I crave upward mobility disgusts me. The urge to rise above the level of starving student and a bohemian packing-crate-for-furniture existence just hit me like a ton of bricks during my junior year of college. I was sitting on the toilet in this tiny apartment which

I shared with three other students and a constant stream of their boyfriends and visitors."

"You were sitting on the toilet?" Denny asks as if he wants to make sure that he heard me correctly.

"Yes. It just so happened that the day before my epiphany I had purchased two rolls of toilet paper and suddenly they were both gone. I was just totally drained by the relaxed, non-replacement attitude of these roommates when it came to the consumption of everyday personal hygiene items such as shampoo, soap and particularly toilet tissue. There was this voracious paper products food chain at work. When the napkins ran out everyone began substituting with paper towels. Under the added pressure the paper towels surrendered without a fight and so the masses quickly migrated to the Kleenex box. By the time that supply was exhausted my roommates were using wads of toilet paper to do everything from scrub pots to clean out their crusty carburetors."

"Yes. I recall we had a similar system at my fraternity house. I remember on one occasion using the soap off a Brillo pad to wash my hair."

"So I switched to marketing," I conclude. "Despite the fact that all the career tests indicated that my personality type is best-suited to becoming a lighthouse keeper."

"Marketing is a very respectable major. In fact, we're losing lots of good minds in the sciences because students all seem to want MBAs these days. I can't disagree with you in that the road to Yuppiedom is paved with business degrees."

"I sold out. As they say, love comes and goes, but a business . . . "

"That's not necessarily true," Denny says diplomatically. "People change careers all the time. So you want a cubicle with an air fern. What's so awful about that?"

"No, Denny. It really is odious. I've decided to become everything I've always despised," I state acidly. "Let's face it, it's impossible to graduate from college these days and enjoy all the things that you and Sarah and my parents had on the salary of an English major or on the wages of almost any undergraduate liberal arts degree—unless maybe you went to Harvard or have some sort of a family fortune. I'd probably never even own a house without at least getting a Ph.D. in English. And even then, if I was really lucky, I'd end up with a lousy teaching job at a Community College in some shitsville backwater town like this in the farm belt and have peeling white wicker furniture creaking in my living room."

"So if this is such a terrible place why do you return at all?" Denny asks sounding defensive.

I lean my chair back on two legs, cackle like the Joker in *Batman* and look at him disdainfully. "Why do I come back? I'll tell you why I came back this summer. I was looking for a parking spot in Detroit and this was as close as I could get." My voice is dripping with sarcasm. "I'm broke Denny. B-R-O-K-E, rhymes with JOKE. What did you think? That I was in the AAA Gold program? Not only am I insolvent and jobless but I drive a '98 Raleigh, a bicycle." I'm on a roll now and I don't care. "Why do you think I'm here? Possibly for an open house? Not to mention that I've recently decided that it's much better to get than to give."

"Okay, okay. I'm sorry I asked." Denny rises slowly as if it's difficult to completely straighten up and refreshes our drinks. "Is that where you want to go, Detroit?" he asks.

"Where I'd really love to go is Paris," I reply dreamily. "I'd love to live in the Latin Quarter, go for long walks on the Left Bank, ski in the Swiss Alps and have love affairs with lots of Eurotrash guys who use great smelling hair gel. You know why they call this the Heartland?" I ask rhetorically. "Because there aren't any brains here."

"Paris? Yuck. Have you ever been there? It's loaded with dog crap—everywhere you look. I worked on a consulting project in France for three weeks and I spent the entire time stepping over dog shit or, worse, scraping it off the soles of my shoes. The Boulevard St. Germain, the Rue du Faubourg St. Honoré, in front of the Arc de Triomphe. All covered in crap. The City of Light my ass. It's the City of Dog Shit."

"I'm sure it's not that bad." I say this with mild disgust. I mean, we're talking about Paris now; the city of high fashion, perfume, romance, artists and literary salons. I silently chastise myself for sharing this closely held fantasy with a stranger, mistakenly believing he was on my side. When in reality he is just another corporate stiff whose dreams have evaporated and so he doesn't dream anymore, and doesn't even believe in them and is therefore busily occupied in bulldozing everyone else's castles in the air, just for revenge.

"But I have no chance of ever living there anyway so what's the difference," I say. "On a more realistic note, I was sending out resumes and interviewing for jobs in Chicago, Milwaukee and Detroit before I eventually gave up and resigned myself to a mall job."

"Hey, I grew up there—on the West Side of Chicago."

"So why did you ever move here?" This just proves that he's nuts.

"Usual reasons. I was offered a good job. Sarah and I had recently married and we wanted to start a family. This whole area is a fantastic place to raise kids."

"Yeah right. Unless, that is, you happen to be a kid," I add wryly. Mecca or a mirage? That's the real question here. But I decide to save it for my encounter group, if I can ever afford an encounter group.

"And we enjoy a much better quality of life in Garrison than we would have had anywhere near Chicago. In fact, after my dad retired he and my mother even moved out here."

"Why'd they do that?"

"They wanted to be closer to the grandchildren. Besides, they had to move, the neighborhood where I grew up really went downhill. Gone are the days of stickball and kick-the-can. Last time I drove through there kids were busy playing get-the-vial-from-the-junkie and dodgebullet instead of dodgeball. Although my brother still lives not too far from there, in fact, just a couple of blocks from our old house. It's only a thirty-minute train ride to downtown Chicago, which is where he works as a podiatrist."

"But I thought you just said that it isn't safe anymore?"

"He's divorced and well, I guess it depends on how fast you can run."

"I still think someone would have to be crazy to purposely move to Stuttaford." I cynically shake my head from side to side. "The first move after college is really key—it's, like, your geographic destiny. Hopefully someday I'll start a career in a place far away from here and maybe even meet my future husband there. Or who knows, maybe a bus will hit me. I don't care just so long as it's not here. I hate living at home. It's the worst. I'm so totally over Stuttaford that I don't even want to be buried here. It's the most boring place in the whole universe. And every time I try and objectively point out the monotony, I'm sick to death of hearing my mother say that 'You have to make your own fun' and how lucky I am just to have a good home and that I should be busy counting my blessings."

"Chicago? Why anyone would want to leave a place with a high suicide rate for one with a high homicide rate is a mystery to me," Denny says thoughtfully. "And what's so bad about living at home? At least it's free."

"Why don't you tell me? I don't see you exactly rushing to get back to your house." Ha! I got him good with that one.

"That's different." Denny fumbles for a reason but doesn't seem able to produce anything within the regulation conversation response time.

"Yeah, right." I'm thoroughly amused by this double standard. Although now that I have him cornered I begin to feel guilty about my previous tantrums. If I ever went off on my parents with a tirade like that my father would take me out to the tool shed along with his leather belt.

"I guess I'm just angry about my life." I finally fill the silence. And it's true. "I hate myself for wanting a house, a car and a VCR and for studying subjects that I'm not really passionate about."

"I think it's safe to say that most people aren't calculus enthusiasts," Denny theorizes aloud. "It's just a building block."

"Calculus? I can't do any math. I failed algebra. They asked me 'What's two A plus two B?' and I answered ABBA."

"Isn't that a Swedish rock group?"

"I dunno. Before my time. I mean, you show up in kindergarten and it's bad enough that they want you to make words out of letters. But adding them together? That's where I get off. Besides, I'm going to make a million by the time I'm thirty and then work as an animal rescuer, volunteer at the Salvation Army and maybe write poetry in French."

"I was in the Peace Corps after college," Denny volunteers. "I taught farming in Africa."

"That's cool! You know I'd love to do something like that, join Teach for America or the Peace Corps. But it just isn't viable anymore."

"What do you mean it's not viable? I know they don't pay much, but it's an incredible experience. And you'd be accepted in a minute."

"You don't understand. These days if you drop out of life for two years and then come back and try and find a job you're completely screwed, you know, out of the market. It's not like when you graduated Denny. When I was a freshman in college I had this boyfriend, Felix, who went and did disaster relief in India for two years, you know, because it was something he really believed in. His parents were missionaries and he was raised to think about the downtrodden and spiritual stuff like that. But then when he came back he couldn't land a job. At least not any kind of decent paying job. All the employers wanted someone with recent work experience, which did not include sandbagging the fucking Ganges River. Otherwise, they may as well hire some freshly-minted college student who can operate Microsoft Winblows 2010 and whatever the latest computer languages and programs are and has just finished, like, twenty-five internships for corporations with recognizable logos."

"It's that bad, huh? So at least tell me how you're going to make a million. Do you have an idea for some new computer chip or digitally enhanced genetic coding device or something along those lines?"

"Me? Science and technology? No way. Although Moviephone, you know that service in big cities where they give you the times for all the shows, that was my idea Sophomore year in college. That guy made millions with my idea. It really was, just ask Carl," I say and feel more than a certain amount of regret in my voice. Am I mourning Carl or Moviephone?

"Anyway, I'm going to be an entrepreneur. I already have an entire business all figured out. One that's going to make me fantastically rich—all I need is some start-up money."

"Really?" Denny replies as if he isn't sure whether this is another one of my jokes. He takes another sip of coffee. "Uh, do you mind if I ask what it is?"

"Sure. But you have to promise not to tell anyone?"

"Of course not. I'll sign a non-compete agreement if you want."

"What's that?"

"It's a document basically stating that after explaining your concept I won't steal it."

"I don't think we need to go that far. Can you keep a secret?"

"Actually, that's one of my problems—I'm too good at keeping secrets," he answers cryptically.

But I'm too excited to ask about any hidden meanings in his answer. "All right then." I can barely hide the excitement in my voice as I unveil my idea. "I'm working on a line of greeting cards for dysfunctional families!"

"Really?" Denny sounds skeptical.

"Yeah. Don't you think it's a great idea? Nobody is doing it."

"Makes you wonder why not. What exactly would they say?"

"Let's see, I have about twelve so far. Get well cards for nervous breakdowns and drug and alcohol rehabilitation. And 'Congratulations on your face lift,' very big on the Coasts I would imagine. Then there are invitations for coming out parties and announcements for grown children leaving home. And, of course, sympathy cards for grown children moving back in. Get well cards for rollerblading accidents and the end of bad relationships. Then I have congratulations for weight loss, liposuction, collagen treatments, 'Hope your fertility treatments work this time' and 'Good luck with the divorce/remarriage.' You get two cards for the price of one with that."

Denny winces when he hears the last one. I know that some people are funny about not waiting a year before getting married again and I chalk his expression up to this.

"As far as the idea itself goes, it actually sounds plausible," he says. "Those topics are all the rage on the daytime talk shows and in the supermarket tabloids. But do you think that enough people would buy them?" he asks seriously.

"Sure. I mean, if a family has more than one person then it's probably dysfunctional, right?" I analyze. "See, I'm going to call them dysFUNctional with the word 'fun' capitalized. I'm also working on a separate line for pets, you know for birthdays and get well cards in case Fifi gets hit by a car. And owner condolence cards for when pets have to be put to sleep. Also, congratulations on puppies or kittens. But I think somebody may already be doing that."

Denny nods his head as if either this all sounds very interesting or he thinks I'm completely off my rocker. Time for a change of subject.

"So, do you have a picture of your grandson?" This is the only thing I can think of to say. But wouldn't Joan be pleased? You can never go wrong asking people to see photos of their grandchildren or if they are planning a vacation. That's the kind of cheerful talk that just swirls like a PCP crop dusting around the room at the Saint Mary's Star-By-the-Lake Church annual all-parish pancake breakfast, which raises money for the Catholic housebound elderly.

"Yes." Denny digs into his pants pocket and pulls out a two-by-three inch photo in a clear plastic frame that is attached to his key ring with a thin metal chain.

I carefully study the picture of Sarah holding Timmy and posing in front of an overly decorated Christmas tree and I am rather startled to see what must be a fairly recent photo of his wife. "Uh, he's really cute."

Denny seems to sense that I'm fixating on Sarah. "She looks great, right?"

"Uh-huh," I say softly. It's kind of creepy to see a photo of a person recently deceased. Especially one who doesn't appear at all as if she is about to give up the ghost. For a second I imagine that it could have just as easily been my dad. If Gene had died after his heart attack I might be sitting here and staring at a photograph of my own father instead of Denny's wife. But fortunately there had been a clerk in aisle four, one aisle over from where Gene was shopping in Sam's Club. And the clerk had heard the industrial-size jar of gherkin pickles crash to the floor and when he saw Gene slumped over the shopping cart he immediately called 911, without so much as first taking Dad's pulse or going to get a mop. Mom said it was a good thing that Gene hadn't dropped a twelve-pack of toilet tissue or something else that wouldn't have made such a loud crash because Gene may have lain there until the store closed, and that it was his guardian angel who made him go for those gherkin pickles and not the triple roll of Bounty. But it's funny, because even though the gherkins saved him, Gene won't eat pickles anymore, not any pickles; gherkins, Kosher dill or even those fancy little sweet ones. He considers all pickles to be bad luck now, just like aisle three.

"She is really attractive Denny." I purposely stick with the present tense, as I now know from experience that he prefers it. "I never really noticed that in Middle School."

"Yes, and you know, I think that she looked even better as she grew older. Honestly, you know how some people age gracefully and truly appear more attractive as they mature?"

"Sure. Although it seems as if it happens more with men, particularly if they don't gain a lot of weight."

"I have no idea how I'm going to live without her." Denny stares at the snapshot, moves it to his other hand and miserably shakes his head from side to side. "You know, after being together for so long you develop a routine together. Sometimes just for fun we would go to Kmart and buy things for the garden. I just can't see myself going on alone."

I'm evil and unchristian to be thinking of myself at such a moment, but I decide that my life is over the day I go off to Kmart for fun. I mean, call Dr. Kevorkian. Get the razorblade or the pills, the plastic dry cleaning bag, whatever. I guess it isn't too hard to figure out what I'm thinking. I have this bad habit of wearing my expression on my sleeve, kind of like the nuns in elementary school wore their frustration on their permanently-soured faces, as if they had just smelled a rotten egg fart.

"Oh, I know that it sounds pretty pathetic to you at the age of twenty. When I was a kid I thought my parents were boring because we had chipped beef stew every Wednesday and Saturday was hamburger night. But a routine can be good—at least it can be good when you're older. It can be very soothing and provide this feeling that you have control over your life—that things makes sense."

"I don't mean to sound insensitive, because I know that right now your life probably seems like a chapter out of that book *Why Do Bad Things Happen to Good People?* But down the road you may meet someone and get another routine going. You'll be a living corollary," I joke. *Why Do Good Things Happen to Bad People?* You know, not right away or anything but maybe in a few years. I mean, Denny, you're still kind of young to completely throw in the towel."

While saying all this I am actually thinking that he is not very young at all but he would, nonetheless, look pretty good with a shave and a trim. Kind of like one of those rugged older guys pictured in a J. Crew catalogue wearing a sporty red life vest and portaging a kayak overland. Only his ears stick out a bit. Denny is far from having a large, muscular physique but he is certainly in good shape for a guy who apparently spends most of his days driving a desk.

"I can't imagine ever meeting someone else," Denny rejects my proposal. "No. It takes too long. Too much energy has to be expended in order to find and get to know a new person. Besides, I was optimistic back then and I'm not anymore. And you have to be optimistic and positive in order to develop a relationship."

Wow, that was pretty honest. Nobody had ever talked to me like that before. At least not a grown-up. I don't know quite how to respond and automatically take cover with a stupid quip. "It sounds to me like you've been in captivity too long."

"Are you kidding? I love being married." He is in the present tense again. "It was a huge relief to get out of the singles scene and I've never regretted it for an instant," Denny argues his point defensively.

"All I meant was that you're like a raccoon who has been fed by humans for so long that you've lost your instinct to hunt." I consider the parallels between Denny's current situation and my own frenetic love life. "I enjoy the comfort of having a relationship, having someone to do stuff with on Saturday night. And I definitely agree that it's a monumental undertaking to get a new one going. I mean, it's horrible to try and connect with a new person, and once you do, it's so difficult to get to the stage where you can take your clothes off and burp and floss in front of him. Gosh, I'm only twenty and I don't think I can face going through it again. Why can't relationships just start in the third trimester? Dating is the worst."

"Oh no. I could never go on a date again." Denny resolutely shakes his head from side to side and puts up both his hands as if to stop a medicine ball from hitting him in the chest. "I can't imagine taking some woman to a movie and having to find out where she likes to sit, if she likes butter on the popcorn, and then driving her home and wondering if I should kiss her, all the while worrying that she thinks I'm a total jerk or that I have bad breath."

I can't help but giggle when Denny finishes clarifying his thoughts on dating. "What's so funny?" He sounds offended. "You just said pretty much the same thing."

"I know. I'm sorry. But I just can't help thinking that if you worked with my dad he would organize a high self-esteem week for you."

"What's that?"

"Well, everyone would make a point of commenting on the good things about your work or the way you look, you know; a bang-up idea, a nice tie."

"You mean everyone would lie to me?"

"No, no. Well, yeah. Basically. It's just that, well, according to Gene anyway, people tend to make remarks only when they don't like something. You know, when everything goes wrong. So he encourages people to speak up and give credit when things go smoothly or someone makes a contribution, even if it doesn't work out. He believes that communication of the positive and the negative is the hallmark of skillful management."

"It sounds good in principle. Maybe I could use a high self-esteem week. In the meantime," Denny announces as he rises from behind the coffee table, "I'm taking my low self-esteem to bed. I'm tired and I believe I'm intoxicated."

"And you have bad breath."

"I do not," objects Denny. "Do I?" He does a self-breath test by covering his mouth and nose with his hand and then exhales. "It's actually pretty good, smells like strawberry ice cream. Want to smell?" Denny inquires as he walked towards me.

I make a cross out of my two forefingers as if I'm trying to ward off a vampire. "No way!"

He turns to go and walks toward the stairwell.

"Wait a second," I say. "I want to ask you something. Come back and sit down for a minute."

Denny retraces his steps and sinks back down onto the couch. "I'm not in shape for anymore of your serious discussions," he protests.

"You're a scientist, right?"

"Yes. Though more specifically a chemist or climatologist. And I used to do some aviation forecasting. Why?"

"A scientist slash climatologist. Does that make you a Scientologist?"

"I'm going to bed." Denny yawns and again begins to rise.

"No wait. I want to ask what you think about AIDS. You know, it's very scary to be dating nowadays. I mean, what do you do, go get tested for HIV together as a first date? What do you think? You know, what have you told your daughters to do?"

"Nothing—we never discuss stuff like that—that's what mothers are for. Does your dad talk to you about sex?"

"Oh God no. My parents are Catholic. Well, my mother was Protestant but she had to convert and learn to cook roast beef and cabbage in order to marry my father. So sex basically doesn't exist around here. Babies, you know, they come from the supermarket."

"I'm sure it's incredibly difficult for young people today," Denny says thoughtfully. "When I was eighteen, safe sex meant knowing what time your parents would be home on bowling night. You fooled around on the living room couch while they were out gutterballing. I honestly don't think that I can tell you anything you don't already know, Jess. You just have to be incredibly careful. You know, use protection and all that. Actually, I can't imagine being young and single right now. I worry about my daughters all the time. And in twelve or thirteen years, if I'm still alive and they haven't found a cure for AIDS, I'll worry about my grandchildren."

Denny pauses for a second before asking, "Do you have any idea what it's like living with five women?" You worry about all that stuff; including toxic shock syndrome, hormone-related mood swings and everyone ingesting their daily allowance of iron."

"Wait a second, I thought you had a wife and three daughters?"

"For eleven years we had a cocker spaniel named Susie Q," Denny says. "And for twenty years all I did was put the seat down and plunge toilets—tissues, wads of toilet paper, cotton balls, sanitary pads—you'd think that they'd never heard of a garbage can. I still keep a plunger in every bathroom. You can't be too careful when it comes to plumbing."

"You sound like my father talking about his beloved lawn. I feel so sorry for you—having to put up with all those women," I say sarcastically. "Just try having cramps for three days a month and having your emotions so out of whack that you kick in the television set when the program you want to watch has been preempted by a basketball playoff game that went into overtime."

"Speaking of your lawn, why on Earth do you have spray-painted croquet wickets all over the front yard?"

"That's one of my dad's highly effective systems for managing the lawn. White means extra watering, red is for soil nutrient deficiencies, yellow depicts insect/aphid damage and green is for gopher tracks."

"Gophers get their very own wicket, huh?"

"Yeah, don't you have gophers ruining your lawn?"

"I can't say that I've ever noticed any."

"My dad's at war with the gophers, mortal combat, kind of sees himself as a modern day St. Patrick, except instead of leading the snakes out of Ireland he's going to rid Stuttaford of gophers."

"Now that you mention it, Walt Sutherland is always muttering about a gopher scourge."

"Gophers are the basis of my dad's friendship with Mr. Sutherland. Those two can talk vermin for hours." I lean back in the La-Z-Boy. "So does your grandson Timmy understand that Sarah is dead?"

"I don't really know. We told him the truth." Denny yawns. "There should be a children's book or some type of interactive teaching toy for when your grandmother dies."

"What would you call it? *Death Comes to the Grandma*?" I laugh halfheartedly at my own joke. It wasn't bad for having consumed almost three-quarters of a bottle of rum.

"No, c'mon, I'm serious," he says. "A book would help children to understand the death of a relative."

"There probably is one. There are kids books about everything these days. My roommate has a stepbrother in second grade in San Francisco and they read this book called *Heather Has Two Mommies* in school. It's about growing up in an alternative life-style family."

"Let's write one and call it *Look Homeward, Grandma*," Denny suggests.

I'm inspired to try and top him but I'm also not so drunk that I don't wonder if this isn't such a good game, seeing as how his wife, who really was a grandmother, really did just die, and I know that he's hurting. Then again, maybe joking around a bit is a way to relieve some of the anguish. Hadn't Gilda Radner written a book saying that you should have a sense of humor about cancer—that laughing helps to heal? What the hell.

"*Gramalot!*" I propose enthusiastically.

Denny begins to sing: *"The rain will never fall 'til after sundown. At eight the morning fog must disappear, Da-da-da-da-da-da."*

"Here in Gra-ma-lot!" I join in for the finale. Maybe it's his easy smile or the way he pays attention to me and actually listens to what I have to say. Possibly it's how he lifts his hands before he speaks and then places them on his knees right before beginning each sentence, as if he realizes that he doesn't have all the answers, and that my ideas and suggestions deserve equal consideration. Or perhaps it's simply that it's two in the morning and his friendly blue eyes are focused on me.

Whatever the cause, or the case, it is at exactly this moment that I realize I have a fish on my line and I might just be able to reel him in. That is, if I want to. But do I? Meanwhile, I think I can safely assume that not only is this guy not going angling in the morning, he's not going anywhere.

"How about *My Fair Grandma*?" Denny suggests. "Or even better, *A Streetcar Named Grandma*? You could play it on a gramophone."

I groan loudly at his horrific pun. "No, no, I've got it. *Grandma IV, Part 2*."

Denny rises from the couch once again and says, "Okay, I'm going to bed but first I'll announce the winner. *Grandma on the Roof!*"

"No way. That's totally lame. *Grandma IV, Part 2* is definitely the best," I argue.

"Okay, then it's a tie."

"So, where are you sleeping tonight?" I ask and try to sound as nonchalant as possible. At college friends often slept in the same bed together, even men and women who weren't interested in each other sexually. It was comforting. However, I don't believe a proposal like this will fly with Denny. He is of a different generation. My parents' generation, to be exact.

"If I can find where I slept last night, that's where you'll find me. What about you?"

"Right here." I crush out my cigarette, fling myself onto the couch and slam my eyelids shut. "Do me a favor and switch off the light. I can't move."

Denny reaches over to the wall outlet, grabs a handful of cords and yanks out all four plugs. The light goes out and then he knocks into the end table and the lamp rocks back and forth but finally steadies itself, no help from Denny. "That should do it," he says.

"I'm saying my prayers, do you want anything?"

"You really say prayers?" He sounds surprised.

"No. I e-mail them and if they're okay then God faxes back a confirmation."

"What are you going to pray for?"

"A job! If I can get a job it will make the loaves and the fishes thing look like a cheap card trick. Are you sure that you don't want anything? It never hurts to ask."

"Thanks anyway, but I'm all set. I have too much respect for the old adage 'Be careful what you wish for because you just might get it.' Goodnight." Denny sings *Gramalot* as he staggers towards the hallway.

Damn. Maybe I read him wrong and he doesn't have an agenda. Or perhaps he is just a nice guy looking to hang out for a while. Is there such a thing? I'm exhausted but now the grandma thing is spinning out of control in my brain. *The Grandma from Ipanema, Send in the Grandmas, You're a Grand Old Grandma, What Do the Simple Grandmas Do?*

"When you fell out of the ugly tree you hit every single branch on the way down."
Jack MacGuire, age 7, to Jess MacGuire, age 10.

"After you fell out of the ugly tree the entire tree fell down on top of you."
Jess's reply.

Chapter 7

Jesus Saved, Moses Invested

Wednesday Morning

At 7:35 AM the next morning I'm lying on the couch in essentially the same position Denny left me the night before and having a hell-for-leather go on the phone with Carl. Denny appears in the kitchen and quietly starts to prepare breakfast. The phone probably woke him up.

I press a couch cushion over my face in a vampirish effort to block the emerging sunlight. Then I raise my voice and angrily hurl my pillow-cum-sunshade across the room. So what if Denny is making a pot of coffee at the other end of the room. I don't feel that I have to hide my aggravation on account of his presence.

"Of course I'm sorry!" I eventually shout into the phone, as if I'm not at all sorry. "But I just can't go, Carl! The final exam is in two fucking days! And you of all people should understand how important this is!" I switch the cordless phone to my other ear, sit up straight, and speak into the receiver with extreme conviction, and also as if I'm talking to a slow learner. "Listen, Carl, it's not as if this is a total surprise, and besides, I don't even know your relatives. As terrible and heartless as this may sound, I honestly have to believe that you're just using this as an excuse for us to get back together."

I listen to all of his bullshit for a few more minutes though I think it would be better if I were just to hang up because I feel that I'm about to start saying things I will regret. The window of opportunity passes.

"Oh right! I'm sure that I'm going to just climb aboard a plane to Cincinnati in order to help you cook. You can't cook anyway. What the hell are the rest of your relatives doing? For Chrissakes Carl, if they need help then call a fucking caterer! Whatever happened to 1-800-USA HAMM? You'll get a nice honey-glazed pig's ass in a couple of hours!"

I angrily click off the phone and shout "Toad licker!" at the receiver and then hurl it onto the floor. "And of course he doesn't even offer to pay for my plane ticket." The phone nicks the corner of the coffee table in mid-flight and the plastic backing flies off in one direction and the battery in another. I flip over and bury my face in the couch.

"Um, is everything okay?" Denny calmly asks as he scrambles eggs.

"No!" I reply and stifle a sob. My eyes must be bloodshot and hideous looking. I sit up, fumble to find some matches and light a cigarette.

"Do you feel all right?" Denny inquires.

I first have a coughing fit and then clear my throat. "Very crunchy," I reply.

After inhaling on my cigarette I have another coughing fit. A full seizure can't be far behind. I wonder how much oxygen canisters cost? Odd that you never see them for sale in the stores.

"Ah, a *Days of Wine and Roses* moment. Do you want to talk about it?" he asks.

"No," I answer irritably. More hacking. "And I don't think Carl knows that rose has a plural form—that they can be purchased in quantities of more than one ."

"Well, then have a spot of coffee," Denny says with a fake but cute Irish brogue and places a mug on the kitchen table, as if I might need this extra encouragement to get up.

I can barely move. I turn and look over the back of the couch so that I face Denny. "It's just that Carl's Aunt died and he wants me to go to the funeral—which is totally stupid because I've never even met her. I barely even know his mom. I saw her once when she came up to college for parents' weekend."

"Well, lots of folks attend the funerals of people they didn't know as a way of showing respect to the family," Denny diplomatically explains. "About three years ago I went to so many funerals during a six month period that I woke up one morning thinking I was the Vice President of the United States."

I've only been awake for a few minutes and I'm already completely exhausted. "Denny, I honestly don't believe that the funeral has anything to do with it. Carl just wants me to go to Cincinnati because he thinks we'll get back together. He was my boyfriend until he didn't want to stop seeing other people and I did and so I broke up with him. Now he wants to go back out with me and promises that he won't see other people."

"I don't understand. Okay, maybe I'm just being antiquated and stupid but isn't that what you wanted in the first place?" Denny finishes laying the table.

"No. Well—yes. But, it's too late now."

"Why is it too late? Is it that you don't care for him anymore?"

"Oh God. Don't use backward talk. Please. I can't stand it," I complain crankily. "My mother does that all the time, 'Is it that you are not going out?' I mean, what the fuck is that supposed to mean? How do I answer that? 'Yes, it is that I'm not going out,' or 'Yes, it is that I'm going out?'"

"I think somebody woke up on the wrong side of the couch with a hangover," Denny responds.

"Oh, please forgive me," I say sarcastically. "What I wanted . . . " I pause, take a deep breath and think for a second before continuing. After all, what exactly is it that I want? I don't think even I know anymore. "I guess what I would have liked is for Carl to not want us to see other people instead of just offering to stop because I gave him an ultimatum and he caved in. I mean, what kind of basis for a relationship is that?"

"Are you sure that's what you wanted?" Denny asks skeptically.

"Oh, leave me alone dammit! Whose side are you on, anyway? I said I don't want to talk about it. You're much too calm and pleasant this morning. It feels like I woke up with Mister Rogers and I can't find my Prozac. You're just like all the Others after all!"

"What others?"

"You know, Others. The people who have jobs and money and have figured out their lives and are looking down their noses, or out of their tinted car windows, such as the case may be, in judgment at all the rest of us nobodies who are students or unemployed or underemployed and still pedaling bicycles. But Others can't just enjoy their success and keep quiet about it. No. Do you know why I don't go out? Because as soon as people hear that I'm jobless, whether it's at church, or at the mall or even in a lousy gin joint all I hear is: 'You should get computer training—that's the future,' and 'You should do more with your college alumni resources,' and 'You should join the Young Republicans to network for a job' and 'You should have participated in more clubs in college or run for student government since that's what they look for on a resume.'"

"Ah, yes, I'm sorry. I forgot about them—the smug and arrogant Greek Chorus of citizens who you believe to be proffering unwanted counsel in your time of transition. And I am now officially among their ranks. I suppose it serves me right." Denny theatrically raises his spatula in the air. "According to Oscar Wilde, there are only two tragedies in this world. One is not getting what one wants, and the other is getting it. And it sounds to me, at least as far as your boyfriend Carl is concerned, that you've been afflicted by both."

"Get on your fucking spatula and ride away will you? The flying monkeys await you!"

"Listen, don't think I disagree with you," Denny says. "At a certain point most serious couples want to progress from the dating stage to a one-on-one relationship. It's natural for you to want a monogamous relationship."

"Thank you. Only Carl thinks that Monogamy is a board game."

"Very funny. Now get up. There are turkey vultures circling above the couch."

"I'm waiting for the floor to come around again," I retort as I bend over and put my head between my knees before attempting to rise. What a fucking headbanger. "Christ almighty, did we land or was I shot down?"

"I don't mean to discount your DTs kiddo, but I personally believe that hangovers are wasted on the young. You have to be at least forty to appreciate a really splendid hangover."

I finally crawl off the sofa and stagger over to the pantry and retrieve my jar of Flintstone vitamins. For emergencies such as this toward the back of the pantry I have hidden a six-pack of D.O.A., an herb-based drink laced with ephedrine—an amphetamine-like stimulant that, on college campuses, is more popular than playing Ultimate Frisbee and has recently been banned by the health department, which has only added to its cachet. I quietly open a bottle, surreptitiously down the contents and then replace the empty on a back shelf.

"You don't really take Prozac, do you?" Denny inquires. "About fifty percent of what comes out of your mouth is accurate and the rest is complete crap. I just haven't known you long enough to tell which is which."

"No, I don't do prescription drugs. They're for middle-aged celebrities and empty nesters and a huge cop-out if you ask me. Not to mention that you need some serious insurance to keep a habit like that going. Besides, I'm apparently addicted to indifference. No remedy in sight." I sit down at the table and proceed with my daily vitamin ritual. "If pharmacological solutions are your answer then you may as well just go ahead and spring for the shock therapy and really deaden the pain."

Denny carefully places a mug of coffee on the table for himself along with the now familiar faux carton of chocolate milk. Then he turns back to the stove where he is in the process of frying bacon and scrambling eggs.

"I don't know how the hell you can be multitasking at eight in the morning after all that we drank last night."

"Experience," Denny retorts as he gracefully sifts a bit of salt through his fingers and onto the eggs.

"Carl's Aunt died of ovarian cancer," I state matter-of-factly. "She was fifty-two."

"Oh. I'm sorry about that."

"Man, everyone is dying. Life is just too scary," I opine and fumble to light another cigarette.

"You know, you really shouldn't smoke. It's such a bad habit."

"My whole life is a bad habit, okay?"

"Well, it'll kill you, Jess."

"That's why I do it!" I snarl. "Fuck you Denny Surgeon General! Don't hide out in my house and give me your crap! God, how I'm sick to death of people telling me what is good for me and bad for me, and to be careful, and to be nice. You all have advice but no real answers and most of all, no one ever asks why.

"Everybody is in on it. Since my dad's heart attack my mother has made it her full-time job to go around policing everyone's habits, health, level of noise production and courtesy quotient. It's as if Joan believes that my father will somehow live longer by me acting out some dutiful daughter charade."

Denny recoils from my attack but tries to uphold his position on the health front. "I realize it's none of my business but—"

"So then leave me the fuck alone!" I defiantly take a puff of my cigarette and turn towards the window and act as if my attention is fully absorbed by some drama of nature unfolding in the backyard. "Besides, every time I try to quit I gain ten pounds and look like Miss Piggy!"

"So stick with a healthy diet and exercise. That's what all the findings . . ."

"Right, Denny!" I cut him off again. "All those diet geniuses—the ones who die of cancer or heart attacks in their fifties, that is—can blow it out their barracks bags. Diets! The only way to lose weight is to arrange for an unrelated human being to see you completely naked in a potentially amorous situation. And the only way to keep the weight off, especially if the unrelated human turns out to be a complete jerk, is to smoke. Just ask Liz Taylor. Jackie Onassis was a chain smoker."

"And look what happened to her."

Although I admire his quick comeback, I ignore it. "You should have visited my apartment. We had two sections: smoking and chain-smoking." I suddenly feel bad for having snapped at him and make this joke as a sort of apology. It is also at this moment that I decide for sure that I'm suffering from a personality disorder. There are at least two people living inside my body, maybe even five or six, and personalities two and five don't even get along. God, I'm being a complete bitch.

"I'm sorry," I say. No explanation.

"That's okay," Denny says as if he understands.

Okay. Explanation. "It's just that lately I've found myself getting absolutely furious over little things like a broken fingernail or raging at God when there is a guest change on *The Tonight Show*. And all the while I'm incapable of doing anything about the consequential issues in my life such as finding a job and either making up with Carl or unloading him once and for all. Instead I just let the relationship drift and kind of look forward to our weekly phone skirmishes. And then there's the career front. I haven't been able to force myself to send out another resume for nearly a month now. The rejections have piled up and eaten away all of my confidence. What was depressing has become embarrassing and is now absolutely devastating. Did I mention hopeless?"

"I'd tell you that I'm sure something will turn up but I know it will just piss you off and you'll hurl the coffee at me so I'm not going to respond if that's okay."

He's got good intuition for a guy and a grown-up. "Whatever."

Denny opts to instead continue his anticancer crusade. "I just cannot understand why young people start smoking these days—what with all they know about carcinogens."

I suddenly feel exhausted, too tired to fight. "Stress, I guess. You don't think about doing it long-term when you start. You know, it's like, if I can just get through this exam, this semester, this boyfriend, this job interview. And then before long you're spending fifty bucks a week and hacking up a lung and then next thing you know, you're a statistic."

Denny shakes his head, indicating that he doesn't agree with my logic but now he has said his piece it's okay to let the subject drop. "Where's the sugar?" He asks while searching the usual places.

"If the jar's empty then you have to rip open some of the packets in the box below the sink."

Denny pulls out a handful of sugar packs. "But these are from restaurants."

"Pathetic isn't it? We have to steal sugar. My dad says that the two most underutilized things in America are the public library and free sugar."

"Really? What else does he say?"

"'Buy American while there's still time.' 'Analyze, don't criticize.' Oh yeah, and 'A closed mouth gathers no feet.'"

Denny carefully tears open a pack and spills it into his coffee. "Sugar?" he offers me a pack.

"No thanks." I sit at the kitchen table and continue to classify and arrange my vitamins. The ritual gives me great comfort. Today I need like four or five Bam Bams.

Denny is suddenly standing above me holding a frying pan with enough scrambled eggs and bacon to feed a Cub Scout troop. Only the eggs are blue.

I take one look at the turquoise chicken embryos and exclaim, "Denny, you've got to be kidding me!" Before the spatula leaves the pan I halt him with a Diana Ross stop-in-the-name-of-love type hand gesture. "I can't eat that. Honestly, I'll be sick."

"It's just food coloring. I thought it would make breakfast more fun. The kids absolutely loved it when I used to add food coloring; verdant green mashed potatoes, magenta corn on the cob . . . " He dutifully backs away with his creation but manages to look incredibly hurt at the same time.

"Oh God, all right. I'll eat it in the name of science. UFOs—unidentified fried objects. Actually, it's kind of hard to believe that my brothers haven't thought of this. It's right up their alley." I slump in my chair and motion towards the half dozen rashers of crisp bacon still glistening with grease. "The cluck is fine but do me a favor and lose Porky Pig," I plead. "Besides, I'm afraid you'll have some sort of a breakdown if I don't take anything. Denny, I think you should buy a dog," I add casually.

"It's just that I thought it would be a good idea if you ate something before school," he says.

I hungrily fork the eggs into my mouth while Denny pushes his around his plate. Apparently he doesn't feel so hungry anymore. "Pass the toast please," he says and methodically spreads some half-melted margarine on a slightly burnt bread triangle.

I pass him the grape jelly, which he politely takes from me but puts off to one side.

Rising from the table I catch a glimpse of myself in the little mirror underneath the phone message pad on the wall that hangs right next to Joan's shiny Apostle spoon collection. Whoops, I'd missed this looking glass in my quest to eradicate reflections. "Oh shit—look at the time—I am so late and I look like the bride of fucking Frankenstein." I groan audibly. "I've got to run upstairs and do a ten-minute American beautification program before arriving very late to class."

"Then I'm going to do a twenty-minute kitchen beautification program," he responds. Denny clears the uneaten food and prepares to soak the previous night's dishes, which are still sitting in the sink, speckled with hardened brown gravy.

While performing a lightning make-over upstairs, I realize that although I'm late for class and saddled with a serious hangover, I'm feeling better than I can remember. Talking like I did with Denny was maybe why I wanted him to stay so much. At college we bolstered each other up and joked around when the pressure was on, which was almost all the time—constantly reeling from one exam to the next. I miss that camaraderie. And there is no way I would ever expose myself like that in front of my family. I feel almost optimistic, like someone who gets back an x-ray to find out it was just a sprain and not the multiple fracture they had imagined.

I find myself smiling as I run downstairs, hastily grab my books, stuff them into my backpack and head toward the front door. "So, uh, what do you want to do tonight?" I inquire of my new found friend.

"Don't you have people to see and places to go? I'm sure that Walt is home by now. Or, if you don't mind, I can just watch TV here. You don't have to baby-sit me. I *can* be alone with sharp objects."

"Yeah, well I don't really have friends around here anymore. Everyone has either found a job and moved away or else they've started hanging out at 7-Elevens and convenience stores in more exciting locales." I look up at him expectantly.

"Oh." Denny says. "Well then—"

"I thought that maybe we could make Jiffy pop, drink Tang and then make some prank phone calls," I helpfully suggest.

Denny stares at me for a second and then says, "I guess we could rent a movie."

"Sounds good. I've gotta go."

"See you later then."

"Yeah, see you around campus." Denny pulls the yellow and white-checked hand towel off his shoulder and turns to wipe off the countertop as I rush out the door.

"You will grow up, get married, have children and live happily ever after—in that order."
Aunt Ida. Valentine's Day card.

*"Grant me, O Lord, a steady hand and watchful eye,
That no one shall be hurt as I pass by."*
Gene MacGuire reciting "The Motorist's Prayer" before leaving on a family vacation.

Chapter 8
Just A Bug On The Windshield Of Life
Wednesday Afternoon

My calculus professor is God-awful boring, as usual. There wasn't time to hit the math clinic before class and so I go for a three-hour marathon session afterward. Chuck Benson, my tutor, lets out this huge sigh as I blithely waltz in the door. One gets to know Chuck's *sigh-language* fairly quickly. This particular one is intended to show a combination of exasperation and contempt because I missed our early morning appointment. Chuck is the graduate assistant to my calculus professor and getting his Ph.D. in thermonuclear dynamics. He works in the math clinic to pick up some extra dough. I guess it beats cleaning rat cages down in the science labs. Chuck has the sense of humor of a meat thermometer. I waste half my time trying to get him to laugh. He never does. He just sits in stony silence, without any trace of a smile, and then lets out a huge sigh like a whale exhaling after an hour underwater and finally says, "You won't think it's funny when you've got that blue exam book staring you in the face."

However, when he checks through what I'd done the previous afternoon, his whole attitude changes.

"Ahhh." Chuck releases one of his rare, at least for me, happy sighs. Then he says the magic words. "That's the end. It's time to review for the exam." We spend the rest of the session hashing through the areas in which he decides I need practice and are most likely to appear on the test. Chuck happily snaps his fingers when I get the right answer and says, "Great, great, great," and sighs heavily when things go awry.

When I arrive home at half past four Denny is sitting in the family room and reading the newspaper while the Fishing Channel blares in the background. "So how was school?" he asks as he turns down the volume on the TV and politely stands up to greet me.

"It's going to be a photo finish, Denny. But I'm going to make it. Hopefully. At least a couple of days ago I was a ten to one outsider and now the odds are even and I'm actually gaining ground."

"Oh, that's great. Good for you." Denny says this cheerily enough but doesn't look all that pleased for me. He appears distracted. Maybe someone just let the Big One get away on the Fishing Channel.

So what. Why should he care? It's not his life anyway. I shake my head and drop a thick, beat up spiral notebook onto the coffee table. It looks pretty much the way my head is starting to feel. The hot August sun was pounding down on me all the way home. I wish they would hold this stupid class at night.

"Are you free for a minute?" He asks seriously. "I want to ask you something."

"Not free," I quip. "Never free. But I'm very reasonable. Bordering on cheap, these days." Denny sits in the armchair and I plop down on the couch across from him and close my eyes. "Sounds serious. What's up?"

"Maybe it's none of my business but I was straightening up the kitchen this morning and I came across this letter."

Opening my eyes I see that Denny has a sheet of cream-colored Erie National Bank office stationery that he is holding at arms length and scrutinizing with puckered eyes and a scrunched forehead, as if he's misplaced his glasses.

"What is it?" Standing up I take the letter from his hand and can already tell that it has to be at least a year old since it is typed on pre-merger bank stationery.

"Well, this note, this letter, says that your dad has cancer and that he has to return early from a business trip to undergo chemotherapy." I begin reading the mysterious missive but Denny anxiously elaborates on the contents before I can even get through the first line.

After he finishes reciting the letter, practically verbatim, I sit back down on the couch, drop the piece of paper into my lap and start chuckling. "You mean, you thought . . . "

"Of course I did." Denny is obviously annoyed by my reaction. "What's so funny?"

"It's a fake," I announce and continue to smile. But he's still not convinced. Or if he is, he certainly doesn't see the humor in the situation. "Denny, my dad has a ton of these things. He gets his secretary to write them," I explain. "See, whenever he goes out of town on a business trip he gets the el cheapo airline tickets with the Saturday night stay-over but then he wriggles out of it with these letters and comes home early. That way he doesn't have to pay the full fare. See?"

"Oh."

"Well then what's wrong? You still look worried."

"It's my own fault. I wasted the past couple of hours worrying about it. But I shouldn't have been looking at the papers on your counter in the first place. I am not normally a nosy person, for the record."

I feel bad that Denny has been upset. "It really pisses my mom off when he uses those letters," I say in a conciliatory tone. "Joan's kind of superstitious. You know, don't lie and say your grandmother is dead because then she'll really croak and it'll be your fault. She worries that because he lies about it all the time my dad really might get cancer. Years back Gene would just make up some excuse at the gate about needing to get home but nowadays the airlines want some sort of proof.

So my dad has all these fake excuses saying he's being confirmed by a Priest or receiving radiation the next morning. I suppose that I'm more like my mom, a bit superstitious. For instance, if I want to get out of taking a test, I'll only kill off relatives who are already dead."

"But doesn't the bank pay for his travel? They must. He's an executive."

"Oh sure. You don't understand—capturing value is the essence of Gene's life. For instance, he doesn't mind paying for an upgrade on the airline because he receives what he deems 'added value'. But he can't see paying more for the exact same seat and class just because he's not staying the weekend. Get it?"

"I guess so," Denny mutters, almost as if he is angry or disappointed.

"He's cheap. It runs in the family. My grandfather, Gene's father, died of cheapness."

"And how, pray tell, does one die of cheapness?" Denny inquires, his voice indicating disbelief.

"He was having chest pains and so he went to the doctor and the doctor prescribed some medication that would have solved the whole problem. It was a minor thing, really. But Grandpa Eugene was too cheap to buy the pills and didn't even tell Grandma Maggie about the prescription and then he died two weeks later for lack of treatment."

"That might actually be funny if it weren't true," Denny says thoughtfully.

"I guess it's better than dying of a broken heart," I declare and head off in the direction of the kitchen. I take out a box of raspberry Jell-O and a rectangular Pyrex dish, normally Joan's brownie pan.

"Bartender!" I bark towards Denny, who is still sitting in the family room, and apparently recovering from the letter incident. "Do me a favor and get me a bottle of vodka from the remedy chest in there please?"

"Sure. Why not? How about some Lydia Pinkham Tonic?" he asks.

"Just bring me some cheap cooking vodka."

Denny removes a three-quarters full bottle of Smirnoff from the liquor cabinet and carefully places it on the kitchen counter, right next to where I'm standing. I make a mental note to stop at the liquor store the next day and pick up a replacement for it along with rum and gin. Gene has a keen eye for inventory discrepancies. "Now what are you doing?" he asks.

"What am I doing?" I reply seriously. "I'm cooking. Can't you tell? I'm preparing dinner for us."

"Jell-O. We're having Jell-O for dinner? Shouldn't we at least add some fruit salad or marshmallows? Or maybe carrots?"

"No. These are Jell-O shots. Haven't you ever had them?"

"Not that I'm aware of. But then I never tried hashish brownies in the seventies and I was still able to grasp the underlying principle," Denny retorts. He stares dubiously at the dusty pink powder as I put the kettle on to boil. "They don't look very nutritional."

"They're not. The real beauty of Jell-O shots lies in the fact that they look pretty much the same going down as they do coming up."

"I was thinking more along the lines of taking my car and going out for an early dinner. Maybe to that art deco diner in Westerley. The one with the old-fashioned soda fountain. What do you think? We'd be home in plenty of time for you to study."

"Okay, okay, one thing at a time. I wouldn't mind going out. But what if someone spots you? After all, you're still on the lam."

"I'll wear a baseball cap. Besides, I don't think there's an actual posse out there trying to hunt me down."

"But I just spent all this time and energy getting ready to make Jell-O," I complain and point at the kettle which is about to start whistling.

"Don't worry, we'll have them for dessert—or I'll be Joan Crawford, Denny Dearest, and serve them to you for breakfast tomorrow morning," he offers.

I liberally interpret his remark to mean that he is again planning to spend the night. And this time I haven't even asked him. "Oh, all right. Just give me a minute to change my clothes." I'm wearing a navy T-shirt from a Nine Inch Nails concert with black jeans and black Doc Marten work boots. Using a black magic marker I had carefully inked out the thick bright yellow thread that runs above the soles. After all, I didn't want to glow in the dark.

"Don't get all dressed up," Denny replies. "You look just fine."

"Don't worry, I wasn't planning on it. I just want to change into a pair of shorts."

"Oh."

"It's hot as Hades out there," I gripe.

"It is rather torporific," says Denny.

I have no idea what this word means and frankly, I'm too debilitated to bother asking and so I just pretend like I know. "Yeah. Would you mind looking at that stupid air-conditioner? Is it even turned on? Is it even trying? That's all my parents ask for around here, just that everyone try their best."

Denny experiments with the control panel but can't get seem to get it to blow anything other than moist, warm air. After a few minutes of tinkering he just switches it off.

* * *

Outside the atmosphere has turned into a wool blanket of humidity. Denny backs his dark green Volvo wagon out of the garage and picks me up at the end of the driveway, where I stand posing with my thumb extended and my right leg balanced on the curb at what I believe to be a sexy angle.

"Okay, jump in. Let's get out of here. And don't even joke about hitchhiking."

"Yes, Mother." My first instinct is to turn on the tape player. I scrutinize the empty cassette cases lying on the dashboard: *The Merry Peasant* by Schumann with Evelyne Dubourg on piano, Mozart's *Flute Quartet in G major* and Pinchas Zuckerman and the English Chamber Orchestra playing *Bach's Concerto in A Minor*. Gross.

"Do you mind if I put on the radio?" I ask as a preemptive strike against Pinky Z.

"Go ahead," he answers and turns the knob. I quickly locate my favorite rock station. At the end of the next street there aren't any cars in sight and so Denny makes a left turn on red.

"Excuse me, but are you trying to get the attention of the local constabulary? There's probably already a warrant out for your arrest."

"They just put up that stupid light. I've been driving this way for over twenty years."

"So?"

"Sooo—so I only stop if cars are coming, just like when there was only a stop sign."

"Let me get this straight," I ask in an amused tone of voice, "You think the traffic light has a grandfather clause?"

"Okay, forget about it. Listen, I paid for your mother's Girl Scout cookies today." Denny turns into the main drag and then reduces the radio volume so that his eardrums won't burst.

"Oh thanks. How much Scot Tea stock did she invest in this year? I'll give you the cash."

"No, that's okay. I didn't mean for it to sound like I wanted the money."

"Of course I'll pay you for the cookies. My parents left a bunch of cash for stuff like that."

"No, no. Just consider it rent. Besides, I ate most of the mint ones while I was watching TV. They were very dry, by the way. Did I tell you that I've become a news junkie? After reading the sports section and the obituaries in the morning paper I check CNN for updates on all the latest African and Balkan civil wars. After that becomes repetitive I tune into the History Channel and watch Poland being perpetually invaded throughout the centuries; Swedes, Turks, Prussians, Russians. Did I forget anyone? Oh, Germans, of course. It's no wonder why everyone there smokes. The anxiety of it all—just waiting for the next battalion of tanks to roll in. Finally I finish off with the stock market wrap on CNBC. I can tell you where soybean meal futures and the barge freight index closed on the Chicago Board of Trade and I don't even know what a soybean future or a barge freight index is."

I'm only half listening to this description of a typical day in the life of Denny Sinclair as I stare out the window at the neat front yards and the wind chimes that hang above all the porch railings. In the distance stands a solitary water tower painted powder blue to match the sky. As a kid I had always dreamed about climbing to the top of it. I used to imagine that I would be able to see the ocean from up there.

Denny drives cautiously and stays in the slow lane while I watch the matching front lawns pass by, one after another, blending, almost blurring into the next. If there is one redeeming feature about my side of town it's that there aren't too many lawn statues. I'd recently read about some college students who had stolen an ornamental plastic pig from a front porch and took it on a trip around the world. A picture postcard would arrive at the owner's home every so often showing the pig bungee jumping in Australia or vacationing in some other exotic location like Tahiti. All were signed *Pig*. Eventually, after a year of sight-seeing, the pig mysteriously reappeared. I fantasize pulling a similar stunt, only my traveling companion is going to be Mr. McKenna's three-foot plaster of paris Madonna statue. Maybe I could even get her a frequent flyer card with her name, *Mary, The Virgin*, printed on the front of it.

"I wish that my parents were rich and could send me on a trip around the world. Two of my friends invited me to backpack across Europe with them this summer. But even that costs two thousand dollars."

"Ah, the Grand Tour. Well, flights to England aren't all that expensive, especially off-peak. Maybe you can go there for your first vacation."

"Maybe next week I'll apply for a job on board one of those cruise ships that are always being advertised on TV."

"What kind of a job?"

"I haven't the slightest idea. Anything; washing dishes, teaching shuffleboard or the cha-cha."

My eyes settle on the *objects in mirror may seem closer than they appear* sticker on the passenger side rearview mirror. "When you consider that scientists have put people on the moon and figured out how to develop film in an hour you would think that they'd have found a way to fine tune car mirrors so as not to require these dumb warning labels."

"Uh, I believe they construct them that way on purpose so that you don't get blindsided by a Mack truck."

I don't answer and go back to gazing out at the tree-lined, aluminum-sided suburban sprawl. We pass Dora's Delectable Bakery, Harriet's Browsing Barn and the Quikcutz unisex hair salon. There are modest red brick houses which sport shingles for various entrepreneurs like Joseph Swanson, D.D.S. and C.P.A. Marilyn Greer, all of whom probably pay dues to the Stuttaford Chamber of Commerce. "I wish that asshole Chamber of Commerce would stop running that damned ad campaign, you know, the one trying to market Stuttaford as The Hurtleberry Capital of the Midwest. When I was in high school my friends and I considered putting up our own posters underneath their signs: *That's why Stuttaford is the pits!* Why can't my town be the birthplace of someone famous like Bay City has Madonna or at least be known for some useful invention like the breakfast burrito."

"What's wrong with being famous for Hurtleberries?" Denny asks.

"Hurtleberries! Who has even heard of a fucking hurtleberry? I mean, what is a hurtleberry? I've lived here my entire life and even I don't know."

"They're a distant cousin of the huckleberry. Back at the turn of the century a farmer brought some vines with him from Europe, put a few in his backyard, then sold the plants and within a matter of ten years they'd spread throughout the area."

"Like a bad case of poison ivy," I add. My college friends had arrived for a visit over winter break only to be greeted by the grotesque berry-shaped billboard on the edge of town with the bloated letters intended to be a purplish-maroon, but on the grayish-white background appearing more the color of dried blood, violently proclaiming:

Welcome to friendly Stuttaford—home of the hurtleberry!

I had felt so humiliated, so mortified, as if it had been discovered that my father was a folk singer or that my mother consulted a psychic before making my brothers' lunches in the morning—not that my parents actually did either of those things, at least that I knew of. "The last thing I'm going to do on my way out of Stuttaford is to tear down that horrendous sign and save future generations the awful embarrassment of it all."

"Forget the sign, kid. You've got bigger fish to fry."

"I'm not a kid."

"I know," he says.

"But doesn't it drive you crazy that all the houses and all the people here are exactly the same?" I say. "I mean, Stuttaford could be a movie set for the suburbs. The Chamber of Commerce should rent it out to Hollywood for those slasher movies featuring a couple of cheerleaders, axe murdering twins and a chainsaw-wielding maniac. Those films always take place in tranquil little towns just like this."

"I certainly don't find that the people here are all the same, but you can't expect much more from the houses. One German immigrant built most of the subdivisions in this area during a two-year blitz in the early seventies. Sarah and I bought our house from him, Werner Burvenich, a sixty-something contractor complete with lots of burly relatives from Bavaria working for him. I think he only had three sets of plans, all drawn up by his wife, a sausage-maker and part-time glockenspiel player named Gerta." Denny looks out the window and adds, "I suppose if one is into architecture it is kind of boring. What do they call them? Cookie-cutters. They're all made out of ticky-tacky and they all look just the same."

"What's Tricky-tacky?"

"Ticky-tacky. It's from an old Pete Seeger song called *Little Boxes*."

"Whatever," I reply absentmindedly, as if I'm listening to a half senile grandfather recount how candy bars and movies used to cost a nickel—and that was for a bigger candy bar than you get today and a double feature film.

"Oh, I almost forgot, after the Girl Scouts some kids came by collecting donations for luminarias, but I was running low on cash by then. I wasn't aware that it can cost upwards of fifty dollars just to spend the day at home in your neighborhood. And I felt bad because I like to give money for diseases and scientific research and . . . "

"Luminarias!" I laugh at him.

"Yeah, what's so . . . "

"Luminarias are those candles in the brown paper bags with the sand in the bottom that the kids make for the fall carnival."

"Oh." Denny chuckles at his own error. "Well then I think they should come up with a different name for them."

I continue to give him a hard time. "Next time I'm sick I'm going to limp over to my professor's office and tell him that it's a bad case of the luminarias." I say this last word in a sickly-sounding croaky voice.

"All right, just forget about it," Denny says tersely.

"I've finally figured it out," I announce conclusively as I look out the window. "Do you know what's wrong with this picture?"

"No. What?"

"If this were ten years ago on a hot summer afternoon the week before school started there'd be tons of kids outside playing hopscotch on the sidewalks, kickball in the empty lot, girls jumping rope on blacktop driveways and boys trading baseball cards on front porches! But now, rain or shine, everyone stays inside and plays those stupid video games like Quake and Virtual Fighter. My little brothers have never even heard of Mother May I? Red Rover, or Red Light, Green Light. It's: Nintendo, Gameboy, Sega, Playstation."

"You're only twenty and you already sound like an old fart," Denny observes and smiles slightly.

"Yeah, I suppose so. My children will think I'm a total asshole when I start droning: 'When I was a kid we used to play outside and get sunburn and mosquito bites and we were happy! We liked it! VCR's came in only two colors—coal black and an ugly battleship gray—weighed almost twelve pounds and when the power went out we had to reset the clock. And no one over forty knew how to work them. And we were thankful!'"

"And then you'll forget why you started telling them all that in the first place and they'll roll their eyes up into their heads and remind you that they had asked you for money."

"Would you mind stopping here for a minute?" I ask as we round the corner and approach the little cluster of shops with the color-coordinated gingerbread trim that comprise the Stuttaford Village Square Shopping Center. "I need to buy a calculus review book."

For no apparent reason I have a vivid memory of how, when I was a little girl, I believed that the woman who operated the steamer in the back of the dress shop was actually the witch from *Hansel and Gretel* and that she would press children who got separated from their mothers in her steam machine.

"Anything for the great middle-class God education," Denny cheerfully announces as he turns the steering wheel to the left and easily glides the car into the only empty parking spot, which happens to be directly in front of the stationery store. The windows are chockfull of back-to-school-ads. Smiling down at us is a life-size cardboard cutout of a flaxen-haired girl in a frilly pink dress carrying a red lunchbox in one hand and a brand new pencil case and notebook in the other. I can only assume her euphoria is intended to be a direct result of having just acquired new school supplies.

While sliding the gearshift into "Park" Denny spots her. Helene, his seventy-five year-old mother is exiting the narrow Hallmark shop, clutching her purse in one hand and a diminutive, neatly folded brown paper bag in the other.

"Code Blue Hair!" Denny whispers harshly and slides down in the driver's seat. "It's my mother!"

I look at the spry elderly woman in the lavender housedress with the single strand of pearls and white Reebok sneakers who is just two feet in front of the car. Unless Denny completely scrunches down below the dashboard, a feat that he is surely too tall to accomplish, or unless he has a second career as contortionist that I'm not aware of, he'll most certainly be recognized.

I jump into action. After all, I hadn't worked as a lifeguard down on the floating dock at Lake Agnes for two summers only to stand silently on the sidelines and observe as disaster strikes. Hurling myself across Denny's chest I wrap my arms around him and completely obscure his face by kissing him on the lips.

Barely a nanosecond later Helene glares directly at us as she darts between Denny's car and the white Taurus in the next spot and then looks away with a scowl and a shrug of her shoulders that, in body language, says something to the effect of, "These kids today! They have no sense of decorum."

However, I don't stop. At first Denny's lips are pressed together like a kid trying to avoid taking cough syrup. I find this pretty insulting and then for some reason I don't have time to think about, it suddenly becomes a life or death challenge to get the most reaction I can out of this male creature.

Removing my hand from the back of his headrest I use it to pull his face closer to mine. Then I shut my eyes and psyche myself up to make him the object of every erotic thought I've ever had. Pressing my mouth against his I use my tongue to gently persuade his lips to part. They do. I want or need, I don't know which or why, some real response from him. I use every muscle of my body with a determination and abandon I've never experienced.

It works. Denny answers. I feel his shoulders sort of spasm, his hands find my hair and back and I recognize that wonderful urgency that tells me he doesn't want to stop. I finally pull away. As I do so I let my hand brush across his lap and silently smile an exultant gotcha!

Helene is now purposefully marching off across the parking lot and still shaking her head disapprovingly. "Mission accomplished," I report nonchalantly, now safely back on the passenger side. I push open the car door and casually remark, "We've not only succeeded in avoiding her but I think we've grossed her out to boot."

Denny opens his mouth, apparently to say something—but nothing emerges.

I smile, all happy and innocent, hop out of the car and head off in the direction of the bookstore, leaving Denny to wait and wonder.

After about ten minutes I emerge waving a paperback book with a teal and white cover at him. "Fourteen dollars and ninety-five cents for a skimpy little review book," I complain as I clamber back into the Volvo. "Can you believe it?" I can tell Denny is still discombobulated, especially when he drives the car into the curb after putting the gearshift into "Forward" instead of "Reverse."

"Slipped out of gear," he mumbles and then backs out with a slight jerkiness.

At least I can still kiss. They can't take that away from me. Maybe the next stop in my search for gainful employment should be an escort service. No, I despise pantyhose. Though I'd once met a woman who had earned her entire college tuition by working as a hooker in Saudi Arabia during the Gulf War.

Well, if there is going to be any action tonight, I had certainly laid the groundwork. But the rest will have to be up to Denny, I resolve. I'm not about to throw myself at any guy, although I guess that's what I just did. Well I'm not going to do it again—particularly a guy whose idea of an exciting Friday night is cruising the hose, nozzle and sprinkler aisle of the local Kmart Garden Center.

The song *It's The End of the World As We Know It* by R.E.M. starts to play on the radio and I turn up the volume to a level where someone who can bury a tune can safely sing along:

That's great it starts with an earthquake, birds and snakes, an airplane. And Lenny Bruce is not afraid. Eye of a hurricane listen to yourself churn world serves its own needs dummies serve your own needs. Beat it up a notch speed.

With the next chorus I begin flopping all over the passenger seat like a freshly caught fish trying to escape from the bottom of a rowboat.

Denny inquires as to whether I'm having an epileptic fit. "Then what the heck are you doing?" he asks and reaches to turn down the volume.

His voice has a new edge to it. I'm pretty sure he's mad at me. I don't care what he thinks. Right now I don't care what anyone thinks. "I'm playing zero gravity," I explain. "You pretend that you are completely weightless and just let yourself go wherever the motion takes you."

Denny gives me a withering nod of the sort that first grade teachers normally reserve for their more recalcitrant charges. "We need to stop and get gas," he announces soberly.

At the self-serve pump Denny methodically removes the cap on the gas tank and fills it with premium unleaded gasoline, unaware that I'm watching him from the car. When the pump clicks and the tank will hold no more he removes the nozzle, shakes the handle and replaces it. The meter reads $9.02.

I lean my head out the window and ask, "Hey, why do guys always shake the nozzle before putting it back?"

"I don't know. Why do women always ask such ridiculous questions?" he counters.

"Well," I fold my arms on top of the rolled down window, casually rest my chin on them and thoughtfully reply, "I think it's a penis thing. You don't see women going around and shaking gas nozzles." I've embarrassed him. There is no end to my wickedness today.

Denny's cheeks go slightly crimson as he casts his eyes around to see if anyone else is in earshot. The only other human being in sight, if you can even call him that, is a sulky looking teenager wearing a Detroit Lions baseball cap pulled low over his face and headphones, from which the pounding and hissing of acid rock music can be heard twenty feet away. The disaffected youth is perched next to his narrow Plexiglas candy and cigarette hut in a beat up lawn chair and hasn't looked up from his comic book even once to acknowledge our presence.

"Furthermore," I add, "My fourth grade teacher said that there is no such thing as a stupid question."

Denny just looks at me as if he suspects that I played with mercury as a child and instinctively reaches for his wallet, which turns out to be empty save for some singles. "Damn," he utters, apparently suddenly recalling that earlier in the day an adorable little pony-tailed pixie of a girl wearing a green and orange uniform had made off with most of his cash in exchange for parched cookies. "Do you have a five I can borrow?" he asks me.

"Oh sure, you had to be a big shot and pay for the cookies and now you don't have any money for gas," I tease him and pull a fistful of crumpled ones out of my pocket, which I proceed to unfurl and then count. "For your information, there's a shortage of five dollar bills," I tell him.

Denny ignores this remark until I've straightened out the money and he's taken five singles from me. "Thanks," he says. "And honestly, where do you get this stuff? Is this what they're teaching in college these days? A shortage of fives!"

"No, it's true. My roommate Colleen first noticed it last semester. You hardly ever see fives any more." I glance down at the money before handing it to Denny. "Do you think that when Abraham Lincoln went to a bar and was asked for identification he just showed them a five dollar bill?"

"No. And now that you mention it, I think that he probably showed them a penny."

I laugh at Denny's clever retort. Things seem to be back to normal between us. I resolve to try and be good from now on.

Just before Denny turns to go and settle up with the malcontent petrol attendant, an olive and white squad car comes around the corner and pulls into the gas station. "Oh shit," he says to me, "Don't look now but there's a Tijuana taxi at six o'clock."

"Just act natural. I'm sure they're not looking for us," I state with the clear conscience and confidence of an upstanding citizen.

"Then why are they pulling up behind us?" he sarcastically counters.

"Somehow I doubt it's for coffee and donuts," I reply and slouch down in my seat.

An amiable looking policeman with a square build and a black name tag embossed with the white block letters OFFICER J. BARNES approaches Denny and carefully scrutinizes the scene, as if we are Bonnie and Clyde having just performed a heist and the Volvo is our getaway car. He glances in the backseat before speaking, as if to check for contraband. "Excuse me, but this vehicle has been reported as stolen by a Mrs. Lori Hartman at 101 Chicory Lane."

"Grand theft auto," I whisper up at Denny. "Five years with possible parole after twenty-six months. Don't let them convert you to Islam while you're in the Big House."

"Aha. They didn't report me missing, they reported the car stolen. Very clever," Denny says quietly to me. "One round to the girls."

"I need to buy some cigarettes." I jump out of the car and dart off just as the officer is asking to see Denny's identification.

"Your freckles are God's kisses."
Aunt Ida. Before the Easter Pageant.

"A new bike! When I was your age we didn't even have any animals so all of us children were yoked to plow the field—barefoot."
Grandpa Chester. Jess's thirteenth birthday party.

Chapter 9
Misery Loves Company
Wednesday Evening

By the time we arrive back at the house the late afternoon is curving toward twilight. I put in another hour with the new calculus review book. If this miracle manual comes anywhere close to living up to the guarantees on its front cover then I'll be receiving a scholarship to work at the Aerospace Center based on my exam grade alone. While desperately searching for common denominators, I can hear the hose hitting the back of the house every once in awhile and assume Denny is futzing around in the yard. Shit! I forgot to water the garden. If Joan's plants are all dead she's going to bury me right alongside them. Next to the watermelon patch there will be a little picture of me on a stick, just like the ones she uses to remember where she planted her carrots and green peppers.

When he comes back into the living room Denny goes to the bar and pours himself a very tall gin on the rocks.

"You want to know what I think is the criminal justice system's greatest contribution to our culture?" I ask him as I hunker down on the couch and put my feet up on the coffee table, boots and all.

"Sure, why not?"

"The richness of its language. For example, the phrase, 'You've been released on your own recognizance.'"

"What's so great about that?"

"It just sounds really cool, that's all."

"Bambaduza," Denny says.

"What?"

"I've always thought it was the best word in the world."

"I've never heard of it? Bombadoozle?"

"Bambaduza. I learned some Zulu when I was working in Africa. It means to hold one close."

"Oh. Bambaduza. Yeah, that's cool, I guess."

"You know," Denny leans forward conspiratorially, "I'm just fortunate that I had all the necessary documentation to prove that I own that car. The good thing about being over twenty-one is that they can't make you go home—even if your mother is offering a cash reward and in the process of having one of your school photos printed on the back of milk cartons along with all the other missing children."

"Oh please. You make it sound like you outsmarted everybody. As if!"

"I did," he smugly insists, not willing to have his victory spoiled.

Denny, my captive grown-up, is starting to sound more like my brothers with every word he says. Behaviorally speaking his whole *escape* fantasy lands squarely in the realm of seventh grade shenanigans. And yet Denny rather pictures himself a sophisticated jewel thief on the Riviera, his getaway bordering on the heroic. I'm tempted to remind him that if it weren't for me, he'd be right back home with Mom and the rest of the entourage. However, I don't say this as I'm afraid we'll have a real fight and he would leave. And I know that's the one thing I don't want.

"Right this minute that cop is reporting back to your mother and your kids that he found you, you're fine, and you'll be home on Sunday!" I say matter-of-factly. "Some great escape, Houdini. Not to mention the fact that you didn't even manage to finagle an ice cream cone out of that nice police officer. All missing children get ice cream cones. It's the law."

"I still won. I'm here and I have my car."

"You won? Denny, you didn't even have your damned driver's

license with you. *I* had to drive us home!"

"And now that Officer Burns guy thinks that we're having an affair," Denny complains.

"So what's wrong with that?" I narrow my eyes at Denny, effectively daring him.

"It's—it's crazy, that's all," he replies and turns away from my gaze.

"Not really. Tony Randall was in his seventies when he married some young babe in her twenties. And what about Anthony Quinn and Pavarotti?"

"I didn't know that Pavarotti and Anthony Quinn had a May-December romance," Denny quips. "So what are you saying? That we should have an affair?" He looks at me.

It isn't that I believe that either one of us is dying to sleep with the other. Actually, I had thought that I wanted to sleep with him, but now I'm not so sure. I know—maybe I just wanted to determine whether he would sleep with me. On the other hand, getting drunk every night just isn't taking the edge off. For me anyway. And it has crossed my mind that maybe if we were both bored enough it would be something to do.

"No, I don't think we should have an affair," I flatly respond to his inquiry.

"Of course not." Denny sounds disinterested and appears to scramble to fill the dead air with words. "I was just wondering if that's what you were saying. That's all."

Gosh, it was awfully safe to kiss him in the car. It didn't occur to me that we'd come back and he'd expect stuff to happen and that I might chicken out, or perhaps wasn't sure what I had been doing in the first place.

"I just meant that it happens, that's all," I reply casually but realize my voice is tinged with adolescent shakiness. "Besides, I always thought that the term affair was reserved for married couples cheating on their spouses."

Sitting in front of the television I use two VCRs to finish editing videotape I'm patching together and pretend to suddenly become very involved in what I'm doing. As if it's going to be narrated by Barbara Walters and run on *60 Minutes* this very night.

"May I buy you a rum and Coke?" he asks, sounding rather vague, like a guy who has just struck out and wishes to move on.

"Actually, I would rather just have the money. But if you really feel the urge to tend bar then please pour me something that starts with an A."

"A what?"

"An A, you know, A—B—C—D—E—F—G," I begin singing the Sesame Street alphabet song. "I want to drink the alphabet."

"Oh. That sounds like a sensible plan," Denny sardonically retorts and attempts to alphabetically reorganize the scores of liquor bottles as he searches for an alcoholic beverage that begins with an A. "How about Amaretto?"

"What's that?"

"An Italian after dinner liqueur."

"Isn't there anything else?"

"Not for A I don't think."

"Try B then."

"Sure, okay."

It's at this moment that I decide Denny is not really an Other. He is acting as if my request to find a drink that begins with an A is as reasonable as asking for two aspirin. I honestly believe he will offer to get in the car and go to the store if he has to. Anyone else would have by now told me to F-off already and stop wasting their time. Probably even Carl. Especially Carl. And I also feel safe. Denny's not going to keep hitting on me. I am relieved, I think. I assume it would be bad form to decide whether or not to sleep with someone based on a coin toss—but that's kind of what I feel like doing.

"Is Bacardi considered R for rum or B for Bacardi?" Denny asks after a few more minutes, his voice hollow-sounding as it echoes from inside of the liquor cabinet.

"It's an R," I call back. Though it's really a B. But I'm now curious to see just how long he'll put up with my shit.

"Okay," he says and goes right back to searching for the Holy Grail. "There's a lot of stuff in here. Maybe I'll luck out and find some Phenobarbital to make a little cocktail for myself."

"Save whatever that is for when we get to F."

"Actually it's a Ph, and I'm not sure you would want to end the game like that anyway."

"Why don't you make me that rum and Coke after all. We'll just say it's a B for tonight." I add another short clip to the video that I'm editing. Then I rewind the tape and play the results with the volume turned low.

"One Cuba libre coming up," announces Denny.

"One Cuba liver?" I look at him quizzically.

"Cuba libre. It's what they called rum and Cokes when I was a kid. Though sometimes we used club soda instead of Coke and added a little lime juice."

"Oh, that sounds kind of cool."

"Do kids still play a lot of drinking games in college?" he inquires.

"I guess so. We played War, Suicide, Up River-Down River. And of course the old standard, Quarters."

"That's still around?"

"Yeah. But I learned how to play drinking games from my Uncle Grady, Dad's brother. Only he's been officially banned from the house for years now. Uncle Grady is the black sheep in the family."

"Do I dare ask what he did to get permanently uninvited?"

"Gene and Joan went to Orlando, Florida, for a bank conference, and our baby-sitter got the mumps so Grady spent a rainy weekend with us playing combat-level paintball inside the house and then Beer Hunter."

"Deer Hunter?"

"No Beer Hunter. It's his version of the movie. Remember the part where they play Russian roulette by passing around a handgun loaded with only one bullet and after betting each player takes a turn putting the gun to his head and pulling the trigger until one person blows his brains out?"

"Yes," says Denny.

"Well in Beer Hunter a six-pack is substituted for a six chamber pistol and one can is shaken up beforehand so that it's ready to explode. Then each player takes his turn by holding a can up to his ear and pulling the tab until eventually one detonates. If it doesn't explode you have to drink the whole can. My little brothers were wild for it. Actually, we all had a great time. I was fifteen and Jack was around twelve. We thought Grady was the coolest uncle in the world."

"Your little brothers drank beer?"

"Oh, no. Grady substituted Sprite for Brendan, Roger and Katie, but Jack and I managed to get really drunk and sick. And then there was the paint all over the house. My mom almost killed him."

"I'm not surprised."

"My dad likes to pretend that being in the Vietnam War messed Grady up but he was in the Navy and basically spent two years scuba diving and chasing bikinis in Hawaii. Please hand me the detachable penis." I just can't resist trying to make him blush again. I tap a few more buttons on the VCR.

"What?!" Denny looks up, suddenly alarmed.

"The remote."

"Oh, the remote. Have you been studying Freud in college? I may be mistaken but I think that I've been hearing a lot of symbolism."

"As a matter of fact, I did take a psychology class this past spring. How'd you know? My final project was *The Perfume Bottle as a Phallic Object*."

"For some reason that doesn't surprise me. Only remember that sometimes a remote control is just a remote control." Denny watches me as I insert another videotape into the VCR. "What are you doing with all of those tapes?" he finally asks.

"I'm transferring recent episodes of *Primetime* and *Dateline* onto one tape for my grandmother. She goes to bed early and so when I'm in Stuttaford I record the shows for her. It started when she was in the hospital for a hip operation two summers ago and had to share a TV with a woman who had bypass surgery. Grandma always let her roommate monopolize their viewing schedule, even if there was something on that she really wanted to watch. I guess that I come from a long line of subjugated females."

Denny watches closely as my fingers quickly dart from button to button across the different machines. "I wish I could get one of those things to work properly."

"Are you one of those adults who is technologically stuck in the '80s? The revolution that started with the microwave oven and ended in ATM cards."

"Hardly. I use three computers to sort data at work and I'm competent at word processing, despite being a hunt and peck typist. And one of the summer interns even taught me how to play the deluxe CD-ROM version of *Where in the World is Carmen Sandiego?*"

"Very impressive! Do you have a telephone calling card?"

"Yes. And a debit card. I'm ready and waiting for electronic cash."

"So what's the VCR problem?" I ask.

"It's just so unforgiving. Once you punch the wrong button it's all over—you have to start again from the beginning. It's too much like launching the missiles that will start a nuclear war. One blink and kaboom!"

"Sounds like you have an old VCR. Buy one of the new ones with VCR Plus pre-installed."

"What's that other stuff you're taping?" Denny changes the subject and points at the cassettes I've been sliding in and out of the top VCR.

"Bad news depresses Grandma so I just cut it out and put in footage of wild animals cavorting in the Serengeti from the Discovery channel or some cute stuff from a morning show. You know, human-interest stories. For instance, there was a Granny dumping segment on one of the news programs I taped so I just cut it out and substituted a piece about the resurgence of quilting bees. I also delete medical fraud, unnecessary hysterectomies, terrorism, plane crashes, presidential dalliances and basically anything else that I think will upset her."

"And she doesn't realize that you do this?" Denny asks doubtfully.

"I'm not sure. Actually, I think she knows but she just likes my shows better. For instance, today I'm editing out a segment about a club of perverts that specializes in exposing themselves in front of national monuments and replacing it with a charming story about the swallows returning to San Juan Capistrano in Southern California. Those old Charles Kuralt programs make for great filler! We have a whole collection of them on video. Grandma also likes anything on gardening or history."

"You are really too much." Denny deposits my rum and Coke onto a nearby coaster on the coffee table.

"I'll tell you something else. This piece on perverts—one thing you never see is a woman running around and exposing herself in public places. It's always guys. Have you ever noticed that?"

"Either way I still say it's censorship," Denny jokes. "And besides, exhibitionism is just one of the many little differences between men and women that exist for a reason. For instance, you never see a guy calling all his friends before a basketball game and quizzing them about what they're going to wear."

"So?"

"So if we didn't have different behaviors then we'd all be the same and procreation of the species wouldn't work—which is basically why we're here to begin with. For instance, I'll bet your mother planted all those sunflowers in the backyard."

"Wrong!" I cheerfully correct him. "My dad did. He plants about fifty sunflowers along the fence every spring. When I was little he used to let me help him. It was really fun. We'd spend an entire weekend digging and planting and marking exactly where we put each little seed."

"Okay, so much for that theory."

"I'll bet you didn't know that baby sunflowers follow the sun across the sky with their faces from morning until night," I explain knowingly. "The necks all slowly bend to allow them to follow the sun, so all day they are looking directly at it."

"Is that a fact?"

"Yeah. My dad knows everything about sunflowers. You see, what happens is that they eventually grow so large that their necks become too rigid to move and so then their faces have to stay wherever they are. When I was little my father and I used to go out in the backyard together almost every night after dinner and water the sunflowers." I think back to those long, lazy summer evenings when I was a little girl and time passed more slowly than a tortoise crossing the road on a hot day. My six-foot-five father would gingerly bend down on one knee and tell me the names of all the different trees and flowers in our backyard and then together we'd search the early evening sky for the first star and he'd always let me find it and then together we'd recite:

Starlight, starbright,
First star I see tonight.
I wish I may, I wish I might,
Have this wish I wish tonight.

Afterward my mother would give me a Ball canning jar in which to collect fireflies and within an hour I'd have gathered enough to see in the dark.

"In fact," I add, "My dad used to make it into a sort of game to try and pinpoint the last day that the flowers would be able to follow the sun, before their heads became permanently bowed."

"Well that's fascinating, I never knew that about sunflowers." Denny sounds pleased to have learned something new. I suspect he's one of these people who gleefully pounce on a dictionary every time he comes across a word he's not familiar with.

"I used to love to plant with him every spring. I felt as if it was such a big honor. Especially because Jack wanted to help but he was too little and clumsy and my father wouldn't let him."

"So why'd you stop? Were you fired? Did he have to downsize? From the looks of the backyard he's still in the sunflower business."

"I don't know exactly," I say wistfully. "You grow up and your friends come over and say that it's stupid and so you tell your parents that it's stupid and then you don't do it anymore even if you want to. You know how it is."

"Yes, I know how it is," Denny says. "And then you think your parents are stupid too. So were you ever able to pinpoint the last day that they were able to follow the sun?"

"No," I say regretfully and light up another cigarette. "I think that it's like trying to catch the car odometer just as it crosses the 100,000 mile mark. You pay close attention starting at 99,985 and then one day you rush to the mall to buy a pair of jeans and forget all about it. And then the next thing you know, the dial reads 100,004 miles and you've totally missed it and all of that anticipation goes unfulfilled."

I glance at my half-eaten slice of pizza on the coffee table and dreamily remark, "I wish I had some Pringles potato chips. I'm dying for barbecued Pringles. I've been having all these weird cravings lately."

"So let's go and get Pringles," Denny says gamely. "I'll go to the 7-Eleven and get them for you," he volunteers.

He can be awfully sweet, this guy. What a nice thing to offer to do. When pigs fly is when one of my folks would offer to drive to the store for a can of potato chips. "Thanks, but we actually have a ton of potato chips in the basement. It's just that I miss Pringles. Over Easter vacation my brother Roger put one of his hamsters in a Pringles can while he was cleaning the cage and smothered it. Now we can't buy Pringles anymore. If Roger so much as glimpses one of those red and yellow cylinders or even a perfectly machine-formed potato chip, for that matter, he bursts into tears and is just inconsolable and we have to take him out to the backyard to visit the grave for, like, half an hour."

"That reminds me of the time that Katrina made the entire family squeeze around the toilet bowl to attend a fish funeral in the upstairs bathroom. She was about eight-years-old and insisted that I do some sort of a ceremony. I couldn't find any eulogies or dirges pertaining specifically to fish so I ended up reciting *Eulogy on the Death of a Mad Dog* by Oliver Goldsmith. It was actually very moving at one point. I still remember a stanza:

This dog and man at first were friends;
But when a pique began,
The dog, to gain some private ends,
Went mad and bit the man."

"There's a money-making idea right there, Denny!"

"What?"

"Pet funerals. Seriously, we could write a book of memorial services for all types of pets; frogs, birds, horses, everything! Maybe even do some merchandising. You know, little pet caskets, urns, incense and even Mass cards. A commemorative T-shirt with your pet's photo on the front!"

"Not a bad idea Miss Marketing Major. I can tell you this, I would have paid at least twenty bucks for a good tropical fish prayer or hymn, although I think they already have pet cemeteries in the big cities," he says. "But seriously, if you still want Pringles, I'll go to the corner store and get them and then we'll just throw away the can. Or we'll peel off the label and eat it so that no one will ever know."

"That's okay. What I really need right now is to pass this math exam. The stress makes me want to eat salt and sugar all day long. I need miracles, not Pringles—the one would just be a saturated fat pseudo-carbohydrate substitute for the other. A sort of snack food transubstantiation."

Denny picks up the cardboard pizza box that had acted as the serving platter for our dinner and takes it, along with the salad bowls, oregano and my half-chewed crusts, into the kitchen.

"Just leave everything." I wave my hand towards the mess as if I'm in possession of a wand that will make it all magically disappear. "I'll clean it up later."

"That's what you said last night. We're now operating on a clean-as-you-go policy."

"Says who?"

"Says me."

"I should listen to a guy who just got pulled over by the cops? Your anti-vice crusade is going really well."

"I'll have you know that up until tonight, the last time I had an encounter with a police officer was twelve years ago when Henry Kissinger came to speak at the Garrison Town Hall and my company volunteered me to head up security for the reception."

"Oh, that sounds like a wild party," I respond sarcastically.

"So let me see if I have this right, anything that doesn't interest you or isn't a creation of your generation is stupid, right?" Denny says somewhat angrily.

I know that his point is a good one and Denny has summed me up fairly accurately. Or if I were to adopt a phrase from my dad's steady cascade of corporate lingo, I would perhaps say that Denny has just offered me constructive feedback. I sit quietly for a moment before replying and concentrate instead on peeling a section of the remaining chipped purplish-black polish on my chewed-down-to-the-quick thumbnail. I also realize that he is still pissed at me for leading him on. And if I don't want to sleep with him then why did I ask about having an affair in the first place?

"Right?" Denny goads me for an answer.

"Okay, okay, don't go postal. Point taken." I look at him and contritely reply, "I'm immature for my age."

"No, your behavior is perfectly fine. I mean, you have an irreverent sense of humor, but it's childish to assume that your tastes are the only ones that aren't stupid. People were lined up around the block to get into that Kissinger lecture. I was thrilled just to meet him. Whether you agree with what Henry Kissinger has accomplished or has to say or you don't, the guy is still a genius and was Secretary of State during a momentous time. He's a very important part of American history." Denny takes a breath and continues his mini-rant, "That's why there are different radio stations playing all different types of music and Baskin-Robbins has thirty-three flavors. It doesn't mean—"

"Okay, okay, I get your point." I don't want to hear anymore of his grown-up shit. I change my mind again. He is one of them after all. "You sound just like my parents."

"Then maybe you should listen to your parents once in awhile. God, I can't believe that I offered to sleep with someone who was born during the Carter administration. Do you know what your problem is?"

"No," I say rudely. "Why don't you tell me, Mister Sinclair. What is my problem?"

"You can't decide what side of the fence you're on—child or adult—you can't figure out who the enemy is and so you act as if you're surrounded by a confederacy of dunces. That's why grandparents and grandkids get along so well—they have a common enemy, parents."

"Did you make that up?"

"What?"

"About kids and grandparents?"

"No. I read it somewhere. I've been pretty much incapable of original thought since my dissertation on latent volcanic activity in the South Seas."

"It's good. I mean, it's true."

"Thanks. Don't throw me away yet. I'm like a broken clock—I'm right twice a day." He pauses for a second. "But I'm sorry. I didn't mean to be so condescending and pedantic."

"That's okay, I deserved it," I say in a resigned tone of voice. "What's pedantic?" I'm hoping to get on a different track.

"Pedantic? It's like your parents when they're yelling at you. No, that's wrong. More like a book smart show-off."

"Even so, my parents rarely offer to sleep with me. You know, unless it's really cold." I didn't mean to say that. I thought it in my head and didn't mean to say it but then somehow it slipped out. When am I going to drop the whole subject?

"I should hope not," he feebly jokes.

"So, you offered to sleep with me before?" I ask him. "Where was I?"

"C'mon, don't embarrass me. Let's just drop it, okay?"

"No, seriously. I think I need to know if people are offering to sleep with me. What if I order a shamrock shake at McDonald's and the guy says 'That will be $1.98,' but he's actually asking me to sleep with him and yet I don't pick up on it? Or worse, what if I accidentally offer to sleep with him and I don't realize it?"

"Are you being a tease? You said what would be wrong with it—I mean, well, first I said the police officer thought we were having an affair and then you said what's wrong with that and then . . . "

"All right already. I was kidding. I remember what happened. I'm sorry."

"Dammit, you *are* a little vixen!"

If it's possible, I think that perhaps he sounds annoyed and amused at the same time.

"Stop making me look like a fool," Denny finally says.

"Oh, since when am I making a fool out of you?"

"Well somebody is. You know, there are unspoken rules about passes."

"Passes to what?" I say.

"Don't play dumb because it doesn't suit you Jess," he says seriously. "You know, if you make a pass at me and I acknowledge that I understand your pass but I reject it then I'm certainly not going to try to make you feel like a jerk about having made it in the first place. I mean, if I liked you as a friend, and I do, I wouldn't purposely try to embarrass you."

"I said I was sorry."

"It's not that. It's a rule. Every adult knows it. You should be aware of it."

"The Rule of Passes?"

"Yes. The Rule of Passes. And another thing, which is probably more important, you'd better be careful what you say and how you act around men or God forbid, you may find yourself in a lot of trouble one of these days."

This time I know exactly what he means and, of course, he is right. "I'm sorry," I say honestly. I feel like a total jerk.

Denny suddenly glances up as if he's Rip Van Winkle awakening from his two-decade slumber and seeing his surroundings for the first time. "What time is it?" he asks.

I look at the mantel clock. "It's exactly twelve," I reply. "Not AM or PM. Just M."

"What am I doing here? What am I talking about? I've gotta go. Besides, I feel like an idiot now. You're just a mixed-up kid."

That really pisses me off. "I am not! I know the Rule of Passes. And I'm not a tease, I've—I've knocked off a couple of pieces of ass, for your information."

"I don't doubt that you have. It's a free country. But then why did you say 'so what's wrong with having an affair?'"

It is by now almost definite that this is the line that will be chiseled on my tombstone. "I didn't—I mean, I did but I changed my mind."

"Oh, great."

I just stare at him, unsure of what to say next. Why doesn't he do something? How come the ball keeps landing squarely back on my side of the court? How did I screw this thing up? I had imagined that maybe he would simply kiss me and I would kiss him back and if that was okay, then well, whatever. Isn't that the way it's supposed to work? How is it that since graduation life has suddenly become so complicated? So far, this is for sure not at all how I had imagined adult life would be.

"What do you mean you changed your mind?" Denny asks me, only he no longer sounds ticked off. "Tell me what you're thinking right this second."

I hesitate. God, I can't tell him the truth—that I want him to want me, but I'm scared that he doesn't find me attractive or experienced enough to be with him. "I thought women were supposed to ask men that question." I try to buy some time.

"Quit trying to buy time. I'm just curious. Tell me what you were just thinking."

"I was—I was, uh, just thinking that if all of the animals in the country find out that they're adopted on the same day, that the crisis hotlines will be overloaded."

"Yeah, right. And I was thinking about writing out a health care proxy to make sure that someone pulls the plug before I'm hooked up to life support. What were you really thinking?"

"You won't like it."

"I can take it." He gives me a nice relaxed smile, as if to prove that he is sincere in his request for further information.

"I was thinking that you drive very slowly," I reply cheerfully, as I always do when lying to my mother.

"That's really what you were thinking?" he says, sounding convinced this time.

"Yeah." All of the Presidents must know the lie-with-a-smile trick. In fact, that's probably how they got to be President in the first place. And oncology doctors must use it all the time.

"You're not alone. My daughters claim that I'm overcautious."

"Overcautious? You should try driving with my grandmother. I don't think the car has ever gone faster than twenty-five miles an hour. She's still on her first tank of gas. Wouldn't it make more sense if, as they got older, people drove faster instead of slower, since they don't have as long to live?"

"I suppose it works in theory. But people usually become circumspect as they get closer to collecting social security for good reason. Metal crunches pretty easily. I've been in two car accidents and now my wife has died in one. It makes you stop and think that it doesn't really matter in the long run if it takes an extra five or ten minutes to get where you're going. Put young people behind a steering wheel and they get crazy—it's a power trip. We used to have a sailboat and the other boaters were very cordial to one another—always waving, stopping to see if you had trouble, giving directions. What is it about cars that the other driver is immediately an enemy? Bikers wave to one another, walkers pause to chat about the weather. I wonder about skiers?"

I am relieved that we are once again talking drivel. Inane babble seems to be the *spécialité du maison* this week.

"All right, all right already." But now that I consider it, who wouldn't drive slowly after having had their wife just die in an automobile accident? I had always thought that it was so stupid when my parents said the Catholic Motorist's Prayer before they embarked on any sort of major trip. But maybe it wasn't so dumb after all. It makes you think for a minute. Or, as the Department of Motor Vehicle so eloquently put it when suspending my license for six months after I got three speeding tickets in a row. *Driving is a privilege, not a right.*

"I don't think you drive too slowly," I remark. "I mean, if dogs start peeing on the hubcaps then you'll know you're going too slowly. Not to change the subject or anything, but why do you think old people like my grandmother insist on getting their toenails cut at the foot doctor?" I ask.

"Well, nails tend to get brittle with age, like bones. Lack of calcium. Or maybe some seniors just can't bend over to do it themselves. I don't know. Why are we talking about this? Ask me in a year or two."

"You're not that old."

"Compared to what? The Taj Mahal, maybe. So what will it be? I'm tending bar." Denny walks over and pours himself a scotch. The gin had finally run out. "White Russian, Old Fashioned, Tom Collins, Zombie, Long Island Iced Tea?"

"Make me an exciting drink; a frosty, end-of-summer blender drink with a paper umbrella, maraschino cherries, salt around the rim, plenty of vodka and a killer blast of red food coloring."

"A blender drink? C'mon Jessica . . . " Denny complains and then moans audibly.

"That's what I want. And for calling me Jessica I demand two orange slices and a swizzle stick in there." Demanding things of Denny is rather fun. I think he's one of those people pleasers, always trying to make everyone happy and smoothing things over.

"Ugh," Denny groans, goes to the freezer and dutifully starts to empty ice trays. "Okay, show me where the damn blender is."

"Did you know," I say as I glance at Denny's drink, "That Scotch Whiskey and double-entry bookkeeping were both invented in 1494?"

"No I didn't. And which, in your opinion, has caused more headaches?"

"You tell me," I retort.

After twenty minutes of Denny clanging and banging around the kitchen I happily sit down at the table and inhale the first glassful of his delicious concoction, which is heavy on fresh peaches and vanilla ice cream. With the humidity now hovering at what must be ninety-percent, the cool sweetness tastes refreshing. Denny refills the ice trays and leaves the blender plugged in. When my drink drops below the halfway mark, which it does rather rapidly, he brings over more of the pale yellow-orange slush and tops off the plastic child's sipper cup I'm using, a lavender rendition of the Kool-Aid monster with big yellow feet on the bottom, intended to prevent unsteady little fingers from toppling it over.

As Denny returns to his favorite seat in the family room I scrutinize his hair and face. He'd obviously decided against borrowing my dad's razor, since he now sports an uneven salt and pepper stubble that resembles a satellite picture of the surface of the moon. And tufts of hair stick out on the sides of his head no matter how many times he smoothes them over with the palms of his hands.

"Huh? Now what are you staring at? Did I spill something?" He checks the front of the shirt that I had borrowed for him from my dad's bureau.

"You know, you really look like shit," I reply and take another long swallow from my perspiring cup. "You're a dead ringer for a derelict beachcomber. Or maybe a milkman who was caught in the crossfire."

"Well, what do you expect?" Denny replies and again glances down to crosscheck his attire. "These aren't my clothes." Denny puts his hand up to his face and gently rubs his thumb and forefinger across his whiskers.

"You've got five o'clock shadow plus about two days."

"You think I look old?" he asks.

"No. But I loved you in *Grumpy Old Men Go to Stuttaford*," I retort and wink at him.

"Ha, ha!" Denny is clearly not amused but does proceed to examine his hands as if he is checking for liver spots, wrinkles, dryness or other related signs of aging. "I feel like a human advertisement for planned obsolescence," he eventually concludes.

"Seriously, would you like me to cut your hair?"

"Sure, why not." He pauses for a second. "In fact, it's probably a good idea. I have to be back at work on Tuesday—my company's bereavement allotment ends this Friday—and I don't want to appear so disheveled that everyone in the office feels sorry for me." He pauses briefly. "On the other hand, I don't want to arrive back looking so recovered that invitations to Friday night bridge games and Sunday brunches where they serve mimosa, start to arrive by fax and e-mail."

"Bridge games and brunches, huh?"

"Yeah, which in my book are right up there with pestilence and the green house effect. You can't be too careful. That's what happened to Harvey Richardson, the head of human resources, after he lost his wife to leukemia last fall. Exactly two months after the funeral all the awful single guy invitations started to roll in. I'm planning to avoid those at all costs, even if it means moving back in with my mother so that people will think something is really wrong with me."

I open the door to the laundry room and switch on the light but it only fizzles slightly before the room goes black again. The story of my life. I fetch a new bulb, climb onto the rickety old stepstool and unsuccessfully try to unscrew the old one. "It won't come out," I complain to Denny while tottering a few feet above him.

"Get down and let me do it," Denny says while he stands by, ready with the new bulb.

"I can do it," I stubbornly insist. "It's just stuck, that's all."

"You're probably twisting it the wrong way," he advises authoritatively.

I turn the bulb in the opposite direction and it easily unscrews. "Oh well." Taking the new one from him, I quickly install it.

"Just remember lefty-loosy, righty-tighty."

"Whatever," I reply in my rules-are-for-fools tone of voice and then carefully step down.

When I switch on the light Denny looks surprised to see such a well-organized laundry room. Joan had outfitted her main field of battle with every type of fabric softener, bleach and stain remover known to textile manufacturers; her very own weapons of mass purgation, plus enough drying racks for a swim team. The Shroud of Turin wouldn't stand a chance in this factory.

"Wow, you have a lot of laundry detergent in here," Denny remarks.

"Joan is secretly developing a process for Scotchguarding children. But until it's perfected she's just keeping their outer garments as clean as possible. It's the next best thing." Laundry is a great source of pride for my mother. She takes the extra time to separately wash delicates in Woolite, iron cotton T-shirts, lightly starch bed linens, and lay wool sweaters out flat to dry so that they don't stretch or shrink.

I nod to Denny, indicating that he should sit atop the stepstool in front of the slop sink and drape a pillowcase over his shoulders.

"And she hasn't any interest in people who put their sheets in the dryer. She says that it turns them into cleaning rags faster than you can say 'spic and span.' Colors wouldn't dare bleed on Joan MacGuire's wash watch. What Paul Prudhomme is to cooking, Joan is to dirty clothes. It is her area of expertise and she loves nothing more than sending her young charges out into the world every morning wearing perfectly-pressed whites and cheerful brights. In fact, when Roger was doing his science homework and asked Joan what the universal solvent was, she had immediately answered Clorox. Much to Roger and Joan's dismay, his teacher insisted that the correct response was water."

"Wow. Maybe I can start paying your mom to do my laundry."

I get down the red and white polka dot contact paper-covered coffee container in which my mother keeps a couple pairs of different-sized scissors, combs and a hand mirror.

"I don't mean this as a criticism, but I've noticed that almost every otherwise unfinished surface in your house has been covered in contact paper. Like that can, for instance."

"During her last pregnancy Joan enveloped the entire house with contact paper; every shelf, flat surface and canister. Around that time it was not impossible to wake up and find contact paper wrapped around the lace tips of your basketball sneakers. And when Joan had finished her mission and there was still a month to go before the baby, she went back over her work and applied contact paper borders and then lined all of our drawers with oil cloth."

"Does your mother cut your hair?" Denny asks.

"She wishes she did." Joan would like nothing more than to cut some short Catholic schoolgirl bangs onto me right this very minute.

"Then why does she keep barber shears in here?"

"Joan cuts our hair until we're about ten and then mercifully sends us off to the local barber or hairdresser. I guess I should be grateful that she's not too out of touch to know that home haircuts are about as popular with adolescents as clothes made from burlap flour sacks and being dropped off at school by a mother in hair curlers, a pink poodle bathrobe and fuzzy slippers. Gene, on the other hand, is too cheap to waste twelve bucks on a barber every month and so she cuts his hair. Not that my mother can't be cheap too—if only one leg of her pantyhose has a run in it then she'll cut off the defective side and combine the serviceable part with another good leg orphan, thereby creating a new pair, albeit one with two waistbands."

"Waist not, want not," Denny retorts.

The light in the laundry room isn't as bright I thought it would be. No wonder my mother always drags Gene into the kitchen or out to the backyard when she cuts his hair. On a nearby shelf I spot a miner's light with an attached headband and strap it around my forehead.

"Where'd you get that thing?" Denny asks. "You look like you're about to perform brain surgery."

"Jack used it at summer camp to sneak into the girls' cabins and do God knows what." I start combing his hair. Denny closes his eyes. I feel sort of weird. It's one thing to have some guy I hardly even know staying over here, it's quite another to be combing his hair in the laundry room.

"Ever since the kids started high school Sarah and I have been planning for our retirement. You know, telling each other about all the things we dreamed of eventually doing."

I busily snip away for a while before stepping back a few feet to make a critical inspection of the job in progress. Something is uneven but I can't quite put my shears on what it is or how to fix it. I anxiously chew on my fingernails for a moment.

"What's wrong?" Denny asks, as if he senses my uncertainty. "Are you sure that you've done this before?"

"Of course," I lie enthusiastically. "Millions of times. In fact, I used to groom our dogs." I pull some worn photos of two handsome giant schnauzers off a shelf and pass them to Denny. "See? Benny is the black one and Maxi is apricot-colored."

Denny inspects the photos. "Yeah, okay, this Maxy guy has a certain *je ne sais quoi*. Make me look like him."

I lean over and glance at the photograph that he likes. "Maxine is a her—but you're the boss."

"Hey, I think I remember these dogs," Denny says after studying all the photos. This one had only three legs, right?" He points to Benny.

"Yeah, that was my dog. He died last summer."

"Oh, sorry."

"It's okay. He was almost fourteen." Therein lies the great flaw with the entire get-the-child-a-dog philosophy. Basically, childhood ends and the dog dies right around the same time. The two become eternally linked and there's no going back. The only living thing that had loved me completely and unconditionally is now gone forever.

"You know, I saw him running around on your block once and wondered what happened to his leg."

"Yeah, those were the good old days when our street didn't act as a shortcut to the mall so there weren't cars whizzing by every fifteen seconds."

"Oh. Did your dog get hit by a car?"

"No, he was born like that."

"So how did you end up with a three-legged dog?"

"I don't know." I didn't feel like talking about Benny. God how I missed that dog. If only I were half as good a person as Benny had thought I was.

I trim the hair around Denny's crown. "Are you clearing a spot up here for a new face?" I ask him and mischievously reach for the container of lawn makeup that my dad has squirreled away behind the large clothes dryer. I shake the aerosol spray container behind Denny's head so the little metal ball makes an annoying clinking sound as it rolls around inside the can. "I could dust the top with Palm Green," I joke.

"Cut it out." Denny jerks his head around to see what's making the racket. "Put that down. I'm sensitive about losing my hair. I don't want to go bald. What is that? Spray paint?"

"Lawn makeup. It's Gene's secret weapon. Mail-order aerosol for concealing patches of brown grass. Like pornography, it comes in a discreet brown box without any labels so the neighbors can't find out how perverted we are. He's also got Cedar Green, Spring Green and Kentucky Blue. He can mix and match if he needs to. You know, desperate circumstances often require desperate measures."

"He actually spray paints the brown spots on your lawn?" Denny asks incredulously.

"Sure. Though usually only if we're having people over, you know, visiting relatives, barbecues, graduation parties. But Gene would never go so far as to try and fool Mr. Sutherland with something like that."

As I make the finishing snips Denny imparts more of his dashed hopes and plans for the future and for the first time I genuinely feel sorry for him. I mean, of course right from the start I had felt awful that his wife had died, but for the first time I consider what the death of a spouse really means to the person who has to stay behind and pick up the pieces.

"In five years we were both planning to retire," he says. "Sarah wanted to take a driving trip to visit some of the New England Coastal towns—Cape Ann and Martha's Vineyard. We were going to eat lobster fresh from the Atlantic Ocean every night for a week. And after that we were considering flying to Athens and perhaps even taking a cruise through the Greek Islands. For some reason I've always wanted to visit Mikonos. And Sarah was anxious to see the Parthenon since she'd studied a lot of Greek mythology in college. But now I just feel so empty, like there's no meaning to life anymore." His voice starts to tremble and then cracks. "I don't care about planning anything ever . . . "

Shit. I'm afraid he's going to cry. And then I know I'll start going as well. A regular sobfest. "Here." I shove the small mirror into Denny's hand so he can view the finished product. "Check it out."

"Hey, that's pretty good. Thanks a lot."

Leaning against the oversized front-load dryer, and taking a good look at him, even I must admit that this haircut is a pretty decent job. "I kind of know what you mean about your plans getting all screwed up. That's how it was a few months ago when my dad had a heart attack. It's like you have your own personal 'To Do' list and you're not thinking about anything else except getting through it and then WHAM! Suddenly death, or the possibility of death, enters into the picture and everything else seems so ridiculously unimportant. I can't even imagine what life would be like if my dad had died. Especially considering that with all the aggravation I've caused him over the past year or so I can definitely take responsibility for at least one-fifth of his heart attack. His left ventricle probably has my initials etched onto it."

"Wham is right," Denny concurs. "Only I feel as if I've been run over by a Caterpillar tractor. Did you notice any tread marks on my scalp while you were trimming up there?" Denny again checks himself in the mirror, runs his fingertips through his hair and then smoothes out the sides with the palms of his hands. "I'm sorry. I'm very maudlin tonight. Melo-traumatic. You probably shouldn't hang around with me. You're young and you should be out having fun at a football game or a dance or on a hayride."

I notice that he's staring but not seeing and remove the mirror from Denny's hand. I easily recognize this gaze since it is basically the way I'd gone through nine years of Sunday school classes. "A hayride! Are you kidding me? Where do you get this stuff? Besides, it's a hundred degrees out." Deciding that I enjoy playing beauty parlor, so much in fact that I may just scrap the calculus all together and inquire about getting a cosmetology license, I'm hesitant to let Denny out of the salon.

"Okay, how would you like to be a truly extinguished gentleman? Let's give you a shave." I announce this more than ask or suggest.

"Do you know how to shave?"

"Of course I know how to shave. Duh. Women have more territory to clear than men. Sometime, just for fun, you should try shaving your legs in a dark, slippery bathtub. It's more like landscaping."

"Okay, let's go for it."

"Great, I'll get my dad's shaving kit. I'll only take a second."

Taking my time since I haven't, in fact, ever before shaved anyone's face, I carefully apply the shaving cream. The idea of doing this has always appealed to me. Once my father was attacked by a deerfly while using his weed whacker to trim around the base of an oak tree in the backyard and accidentally swung it full throttle into the trunk as if the machine were a nine iron and ended up with a broken wrist. For six weeks afterwards, until the cast came off, Joan had to shave his face before work each morning. I always thought it looked like a really cool thing to do.

"You know," I remark somewhat wistfully, and for once, totally honestly, "I wish that I was like you."

"Like me? Jess, you've got to be joking. I'm a fifty-year-old widower, a few years away from retirement, and that's only if I don't get some sort of early dismissal package. If they find out that you don't have a web browser at home then you're fair game for downsizing."

"That's exactly what I mean. Your career is almost over."

"Thanks a lot."

"I don't mean it like that. It's just that no matter what happens, you'll have a good pension and so now all that you have to concern yourself with is what to do in retirement. You'll never have to worry about spending two years learning how to do a job and then a computer takes it away overnight and you're left doing oil changes at Jiffy Lube. You and my dad are the last generation to work at the same place, to know where you're heading every morning and go to sleep at night assured that you have medical insurance. Look at what my life will be like after next week. I can't even get sick unless I have a job with benefits. Hello diploma and good-bye health care. And even if I find a real job they don't usually offer any medical coverage until at least after the first six months. And small companies normally don't have any benefits. The way I see it, in the '80s you married for love, in the '90s for money and in the millennium for health insurance."

"I think that prisoners get free health care," Denny idly remarks.

"Great. If I need an appendectomy I'll pack an overnight bag, rob a convenience store and then stand in front of the video camera and wait for an ambulance. That 'three strikes and you're out law' should be called 'three strikes and you're covered'."

"I always assumed that I'd die before Sarah. I guess that every partner in a marriage must think like that."

This conversation is getting heavy again. I never know quite what to say when he talks about his wife, or even if there is anything to say. "Will you quit yammering for a minute?" I carefully slide the razor across his cheek.

"Finished?" He asks when I go to rinse my hands in the sink.

"All done. Rinse your face over here." I grab a towel and wipe the remaining shaving cream from my fingers.

"Thanks." Denny stands up and pats his face with both hands. "That's great." Then he pulls the pillowcase from around his neck and shakes his head. "Sorry, I've been such a drag. I'll shut up now."

"Don't worry," I joke. "I haven't really been listening."

"I don't blame you. You know what they say, if you want sympathy then look in the dictionary between shit and syphilis."

"I'm not that good a speller anymore."

"I don't care what your parents and teachers say, no one ever remembers how you played the game. They only remember who won."
Mr. Heffley, Jess's softball coach.

"Offer it up."
Grandma Maggie's advice to Jess after fracturing her arm playing softball.

Chapter 10

Games People Play

Wednesday Night

It's almost midnight by the time we sluggishly reenter the family room. As usual, Denny plays bartender. "Rum and Coke?"

"It's not like that Bacardi is going to drink itself now, is it? Let's have a little help here."

Then I put on some music while he digs a board game out of the storage closet.

"You've got to be kidding me!" I say in mock horror when I spy the ominous brown cardboard Scrabble box with the bright gold lettering.

"No, this will be really fun," Denny enthuses. "C'mon. Get the biggest dictionary you can find."

I acquiesce only because I rationalize that this will at least take Denny's mind off his misery. I'm half right. After about twenty minutes of just missing double and triple word spaces and staring at letters whose only apparent purpose is to form new names for Baltic Republics, Denny tips over his wooden letter stand and asks, "Did I say this would be fun?"

"You did indeed." I slide my letter tray off the edge of the coffee table and then dump the entire board so that most of the remaining letters fall back into the box.

"At least now I know why so many suburbanites got into wife swapping in the '70s," Denny comments as he goes to refill our drinks. "They got bored with Scrabble and Bingo."

"Well, what did you and Sarah used to do for fun at night?"

"Simple. We worked during the day and slept at night. But I don't sleep very well anymore and I've been off work for over a month. Sometimes I used to mow the lawn around that really nice time in the evening, you know, just about a half an hour before sunset."

"Yeah, when I was little that's exactly the time when my dad and I would go out and water the garden and the sunflowers. Sometimes we'd even measure them to see how much they had grown."

"It's hard for me to believe that I actually used to care about such mundane things as ridding the yard of crabgrass and dandelions or if the shutters needed painting."

"God, I hope that Mr. Sutherland and my dad never hear you say anything so heretical," I chastise him. "You'd be excommunicated from their weekly Lawn Talk sessions and maybe even from the suburbs altogether. They'd have to send you out to the turf farms in Westerley for nine months of grass reeducation."

"No, I'm serious. Now I honestly don't give a damn if it all burns down; the house, the shed, the portico . . . "

"Wouldn't matter," I argue. "The insurance company will just show up with a check and buy you new ones."

"Maybe I should take Mother's advice and just sell it all, the house, the pool, Sarah's car, all the furniture that we picked out together—and start fresh somewhere else," he suggests, not without a certain amount of resignation in his voice.

It sounds as if he's soliciting advice but I have none to give. What do most people in his situation do? I assume that they either scale down, remarry or just try to carry on alone, pretty much as they had lived before.

"At least it would be something to do."

"What is that supposed to mean? That I should sell the house and move just to keep busy?"

"It's just an expression I've been using when I decide it doesn't really matter one way or the other. Because in the end, nothing really matters."

"What do you mean, nothing matters? Of course things matter. And people matter too."

"I guess it depends on how you choose to look at life. You see, this past spring I was feeling particularly despondent after the college career fair. All the computer majors received, like, twenty-five job offers apiece with starting salaries of 40K and higher. So afterwards I asked a perpetually cheerful theology graduate student, the boyfriend of one of my roommates, if there is a meaning to life."

"This should be good," Denny remarks with counterfeit expectation.

"'Living is just something to do . . . ' he told me and all the while he had this stupid grin on his face and the glassy-eyed stare of a spiritually preoccupied poppy-carrying cult member. '. . . every activity you can think of; going to class, getting married, having kids, going to a movie, it's all just something to do to pass the time.' I had wanted to punch that big fucking toothy half-moon smile right off his face with a good left hook. Pass the time until what? Until death? The apocalypse? What? At the time I'd wondered how this philosophy had the ability to make someone happy. But now I'm beginning to like it."

"I can see where it could certainly make one feel better about having a lack of control over one's life. But I think it's a copout," Denny observes. "Besides, there's no way you really believe that."

"How do *you* know what I believe?"

"Jess, you wouldn't be studying your ass off and fretting the entire time about this exam if nothing mattered and you didn't care about anything."

"I guess you're right. But I'm keeping the idea as a backup in case I flunk."

"Okay. I won't dispute that strategy."

I decide to try and change the subject because when it comes right down to it, I know as much about life and death as Denny knows about the rock group Nirvana and I don't want to be entering into any heavy duty philosophical discussions in which I'll look like a dumbbell.

I begin to lob the wooden Scrabble letters into a nearby magazine rack. "I've got a better game than Scrabble," I announce while tearing a page off the scoring pad. "You get the number of points on the letter for tossing it into the rack."

Denny sits back down and gamely chucks a few of the little squares into the magazine rack, which is about ten feet away. "You know, Scrabble used to be the bomb shelter game of choice back in the fifties," he says and leans his back against the couch. "You stacked it on the shelf right next to the shortwave radio, canned peas, Hershey bars and Parcheesi. I remember being a kid and worrying: What if I'm stuck in this metal box eating chocolate bars and playing board games with my family for the next twenty years?"

"I've seen a few really decrepit signs for bomb shelters in some of the buildings at college. When I was in elementary school we used to have duck-and-cover nuclear war drills. It was incredibly stupid, fifteen first graders with their heads between their knees, all crouched underneath the hall coat rack."

"I'm sure that the coat rack would have saved you in the event that Khrushchev had pushed the button," Denny remarks sarcastically.

"If it had, I'm not so sure I would have wanted to spend the next thirty years in school while they tried to eliminate all the radioactive debris. As I recall, just attending the morning session of kindergarten class was toxic enough." I pause for a moment and think about all those years of my life spent dutifully marching off to school every morning. "What a waste of life it all is; first kindergarten, then elementary school, middle school, high school and finally college. If I die tomorrow it will all have been such a disgusting waste of time. Not to mention Sunday school."

"One can get that feeling after awhile. I remember the week after I received my graduate degree I was convinced that I was going to be hit by a bus and never get to use any of what I'd learned."

"God, how I used to pray for snow days back in high school," I say.

"Were you still here when those three prisoners escaped and everyone got to stay home from school?" Denny asks.

"Yeah, sure I remember. I was a junior at Stuttaford High school. The next time I had a chemistry test I considered throwing a rope ladder over the prison wall in order to give an ambitious con a solid head start. I'll never forget that prisoner's name: Ramone Ramone. I mean, why would you give your kid the same first and last name?"

"Just like that guy who shot Kennedy: Sirhan Sirhan. Maybe there's a psychological profile for people with identical first and last names who eventually go berserk."

"I thought Oswald was the name of the guy who shot Kennedy," I say.

"He shot John F. Kennedy. Sirhan assassinated Bobby Kennedy in 1968."

"Oh, that Kennedy." This leads me to thinking about names. "What nationality is Sinclair, anyway. Are you English?"

"Polish."

"Get out. Since when is Denis Sinclair a Polish name?"

"Our last name was Bradwaszynski. My parents were born in Galicia. It's a section of Poland that used to be the largest province in Austria. My father saw Sinclair painted on an ice cream truck in Chicago in the late 1940s and changed our surname."

"Oh. I guess you're lucky he didn't see a diaper truck. You might have been Denny Pampers. So, if you could choose another name what would it be?"

"I don't know. Maybe something Italian, like Donaldo Victoriello Morietti, something that sounds as if I come from a long line of opera singers or spaghetti manufacturers. Or maybe one of those triple barrel Wasp numbers with three first names in a row and 'the third' at the end like the ones you see on white shoe law firms, to make it sound as if my family was on the Mayflower."

"But isn't Denis an Irish name?"

"It's actually French, mine has only one N. My mother the

Francophile was going through a Charles de Gaulle phase at the time. He'd recently headed the liberation force into Paris. Meanwhile, the Poles could only dream of fighting off their enemies while they either fled or succumbed. And so she decided to name me after St. Denis of Paris. For some reason I don't think Mother was aware that his proper name was Dionysius. But I guess I should count myself lucky. My older brother Nathan was named for the hot dog stand on Coney Island where my parents went on their first wedding anniversary."

"I would choose Ruby. I think that's the most beautiful name in the world. You, on the other hand, look more like a Roscoe to me."

"Roscoe is a stupid name. It sounds like the guy who runs the Ferris Wheel at the carnival. You, however, look more like a Hattie, Eulalie, or Beulah to me. Ruby MacGuire sounds like an old stripper. And it reminds me of *Ruby, Don't Take Your Love to Town*, that Kenny Rogers song from the early seventies."

Denny sings a few bars:

"You've painted up your lips and rolled and curled your tinted hair.
Ruby are you contemplating going out somewhere?
The shadow on the wall tells me the sun is going down.
Oh Ruby, don't take your love to town."

"What's the rest of it?" I inquire. "The melody isn't so bad." This is kind of fun, a little late night concert. I enjoy the way Denny acts like a normal person around me. Occasionally I see my parents with other adults, acting completely differently than they do when they're around us kids. It always makes me wonder which are the real mom and dad?

"Forget it, it's too depressing. And besides, I'm not going to sit here and sing. I feel stupid."

"You shouldn't. You have a nice voice. Although you've ruined my favorite name for all eternity. I hope that you're happy," I say sarcastically and pause to light another cigarette. "Forget names. Which one of the *Brady Bunch* would you want to be?"

"I'm too old for that show. I'd be Ozzie in *Ozzie and Harriet* or maybe Henry Blake in *M*A*S*H*. I love fishing. I can't wait to teach my grandson how to bait a hook and fish for trout. My daughter Lori won't let me take him until he's four or five. Mothers! They're all alike."

"I'd be Lori Partridge. She had all the fun of being in a band but then became a smart lawyer with expensive clothes on that show *L.A. Law*."

Denny once again smoothes over his hair with his hands. "Thanks again for the trim. You did a nice job. I apologize if I sounded worried for a second there. But you really knew what you were doing."

"All's well that ends well."

"I'm a new man," he proclaims. "Sarah would always say how young I looked after getting a haircut."

"I guess it wouldn't be the same if I said it," I offer halfheartedly.

"No, that's not true."

I set down my glass, look directly at Denny and with exaggerated sincerity proclaim, "My Denny, how handsome and youthful you look with that fabulous coiffure."

"Thank you," Denny replies in similarly polite fashion. "Do you really think so?"

"Yes, you look positively exhumed. Now don't push it," I warn playfully. "Denny, I don't mean to sound unsympathetic or anything but could we talk about something other than Sarah."

"Sorry . . . I know I go on too much. Let's change the subject to whatever you want. How about peace in Northern Ireland? Now that's an interesting situa—"

I cut him off. "Denny, I'm drunk and it's one o'clock," I hold up my watch and squint at it. "Make that two o'clock in the morning. Let's just talk."

"Okay. We'll just talk." He pauses. "Uh, talk about what?"

"Whatever people talk about at two o'clock in the morning."

"I can't remember the last time I was up talking at two in the morning." He thinks for a second. "Actually it was last summer and I had a stomach flu."

More adept at the art of conversational slumming, I report the next thing that enters my head. "Did you know that at my college you automatically get a 4.0 average for the semester if your dorm roommate commits suicide?"

"Really?"

"Yeah," I confirm. "That could make it pretty tough to talk someone off the ledge, huh?"

"That could also generate some different permutations. Now, what if you have two roommates and they both commit suicide?" he inquires. "Or three roommates and only two commit suicide."

"I dunno. I guess you get the 4.0 and then no one else wants to be your roommate." I take a sip of my drink. "Your turn."

Denny takes a lame stab at pulling any piece of trivia out of the recesses of his alcohol-clouded mind. "Did you know that lightning kills more people every year than any other weather force?"

"Try again," I reply dryly.

"Okay. I read that in the 1800s a squirrel could travel from here to Milwaukee over the treetops without ever touching the ground."

"You are frightening," I say and laugh. "I'm trapped with a scientist who has a subscription to *The Reader's Digest*. This is definitely my worst nightmare."

"Well, I just did what you suggested and blurted out whatever came to mind," he says defensively. "Besides, that's the problem with you kids today, you only want to think about the future. The past is of no use to you. Don't you ever consider what it was like three hundred years ago when this entire area was inhabited by Indians?"

"First, I told you that I'm not a kid," I curtly reply. "And duh, of course I know that Indians lived here. They still do. There's a big bingo game on the reservation every Thursday night and you can get cheap gas and smokes there." I wave my cigarette at him as if for proof.

"Well, can I help it if I find it fascinating to imagine what a day in the life of an Indian on this very same ground was like three centuries ago? Going out hunting, preparing for winter . . . "

I love this. I can't find a job and now I'm supposed to be worrying about Indians in the 1690s. “Do you think there were any gay Indians?” I ask.

“I don’t know. I’ve never really thought about it.”

“I mean, what if a gaysexual Indian was artistically inclined and just didn’t feel like going hunting. Maybe he was even a vegetarian, or he just wanted to paint murals all day, or choreograph new rain dances and do beadwork?”

Denny appears to seriously consider this historical proposition for a moment before answering. “Actually, I do remember reading something in *National Geographic* about the Aztec having a third sex category for transvestites. I imagine that being homosexual was probably okay as long as you didn’t sit around all day. I’m of the opinion that lazy Indians weren’t easily tolerated by their colleagues.”

We sit in silence for a few minutes but it’s not an awkward silence. I use this opportunity to try and blow the perfect smoke ring while picturing a Liberace-type Indian with silver and turquoise sequined moccasins who is constantly wanting to play the drums, redecorate his teepee and grows up very compassionate, as a result of knowing the humiliation of always being picked last for bow and arrow competitions.

“I think about stuff like that,” I say defensively, not really wanting him to think that I’m an idiot, or worse, a child. “One thing is for sure, the Indians had the right idea about land, that you shouldn’t be able to own it. I mean, if someone just wants a place to live why does it have to cost, like, $80,000? The Indians just used the land for free. It should be free.”

“Well God didn’t hold 30-year fixed mortgages at 71/4% with 11/4% points back then. He should have never privatized the land use business and given it to bankers and realtors.”

“So, have you ever done it with a hooker?” I blurt out.

Startled, Denny knocks his glass off the coffee table. Fortunately it’s empty, save for some half-melted ice cubes that vanish into the shag carpeting.

“Jess! Why would you even ask something like that?” Denny tries to retrieve the ice cubes but realizes that it's a lost cause. It's so hot that they've already liquefied. "I mean, honestly, what do I look like to you?"

"You look like a warm autumn to me," I shoot back. "You know, lots of earth tones, rusty reds, rich shades of brown. But it's possible you're a winter. I'd have to check with my roommate Michelle—she majored in fashion merchandising and was very good at doing peoples' colors. Sometimes she even operated a little booth at the mall to pick up extra cash on the weekends."

"What the hell are you talking about?"

"So you have been with a hooker, haven't you?"

"No! I haven't." He appears flustered. "And anyway—it's, it's none of your business."

"C'mon, didn't you read that Albert Camus book, *The Fall*? Everyone is supposed to want to confess. Besides, this is what people talk about at two o'clock in the morning."

"Well I've never read it and I'm not Catholic anymore and so I don't do confessions."

"Not religious confessions. Confessions to strangers."

"Confessions about what?" Denny sounds completely confused.

"I'm not exactly sure. I only read the *Cliffs* notes." I think for a second. "Like the stuff you would tell a psychiatrist. You know, people go and confide to a shrink what they can't say to their families or best friends. That way there aren't any consequences. It's like having anonymous sex."

"Hold on just a minute." Denny sits up straight. "How did sex get involved in this?"

"Well if a person has sex with someone he or she doesn't know and never plans on seeing again then there aren't really any emotional consequences. See?"

"I've always been mystified by people who want to have casual sex with complete strangers," Denny mumbles, more to himself.

But I hear him. "You mean anonymous sex," I correct him.

"What's the difference?"

"If it's casual sex then you may know the person really well but the sex isn't for love, it's just convenient. You know, it doesn't matter."

"No, I don't see. All sex matters."

"Well it's mutual using then. So the next morning you just grab your purse or whatever and do the walk of shame in last night's clothing and hope that no one from the office sees you." I take a sip from my drink. "But anonymous sex would be with someone you had never met before and didn't plan on seeing again."

"So would a prostitute be considered casual sex?" he asks, apparently in an effort to firmly categorize things.

"No, anonymous," I state matter-of-factly. "Unless of course you visited this prostitute on a regular basis. Then I guess it could be considered casual sex."

"Okay, I think I get it now."

"So stop trying to change the subject." I revert back to my original question. "Have you been with a hooker?"

"No. I haven't," Denny answers, but sounds as if he rather wishes that he had.

"Oh." I'm disappointed.

"I had a stripper at my bachelor party." He seems to proffer this piece of information as a weak substitute.

"Ohhh how *risqué*," I sarcastically reply.

"I guess I should have just lied and said yes."

"Why would you lie about not being with a prostitute. It's the other way around—if you had been then you should want to lie and say that you hadn't."

"I had an affair once," he blurts out. "Does that count?"

"You did!" I respond as if I'm a talk show host interviewing a guest who suddenly admits to some horrendous incestuous sexual encounter that not even the producers had dredged up during the pre-interview. Suddenly his ratings are going up. Ad dollars are rolling in and the audience is wide-eyed and wanting more, more, more.

"Shit!" Denny barks out loud.

"What? What's wrong?"

"I'm definitely drunk. Why did I say that?" Then he chuckles.

"You said it so that I'd wouldn't think that you were old-fashioned and boring."

He eyes me cautiously, as if he is just at this moment realizing that I'm more aware of what's going on inside of his head than he originally thought. And he's not sure that he likes it. "*Touché.* Well, just don't ever tell my daughters."

I decide that Denny sounds more smug than concerned about word of his infidelity getting out.

"Besides, it was over twenty years ago," he adds.

"Wait right there for a second." I slowly drag myself up by grabbing onto the armrest. "I need a refill for this." I pour another rum and Coke for myself, only without much Coke, and a scotch on the rocks for Denny.

"Okay." I slump down in front of the couch, light a cigarette, balance the ashtray on the arm of the couch and lean my head back. "I'm ready. Now tell me everything."

"Okay, let's see," he begins haltingly. "After Lori was born everything was going fine. I mean, Sarah and I were happy together and Lori was a good baby, slept through the night and all that. I certainly wasn't shopping around or anything like that. In fact, I never even considered myself the kind of person who would be capable of—"

"C'mon, cut to the good part already," I chide him. I suddenly fear that he might start recounting when the baby went on solid foods or how they debated whether or not to install crib bumpers.

"You're the one who said you wanted all the details," he retorts, but seems to be enjoying himself nonetheless. "Anyway, about ten months after Lori was born Sarah announced that she was pregnant again. It was a little soon, for me at least, but we wanted more children and so I was pleased. However, in retrospect, I think that I felt overwhelmed by all the sudden responsibility. We had just bought the house and taken out a mortgage and in what seemed like no time there were all these mouths to feed."

"Denny, I'm begging you, tell me about the sex part, the encounter. Save the rationalization for St. Peter."

"Okay, okay. It started on a Friday afternoon. Back then Onyx was strictly an engineering firm. It was before consulting really came into vogue. Companies did almost everything in-house back in those days. Anyway, at the end of December we were having our office party in the cafeteria and at about three o'clock in the afternoon this big blizzard hit. I was having a drink with Frank Crumbley, a buddy of mine from the legal department, and he opened a gift from his secret Santa."

"His what?"

"You know, you get assigned a person to buy a gift for and then everyone exchanges at the party. Some of the departments did it. Mine of course didn't. The science nerds never even knew what day it was. Forget about what season."

"Right."

"So Frank opened a pair of potholders that were crocheted with a Mrs. Claus and some elves loading up a big sleigh. Then he decided that we had to find the woman who had made them so that he could thank her. Frank was still a bachelor back then so any whiff of perfume in an elevator or female handicraft got him aroused and required diligent follow-up. So before I knew it, Frank was introducing me to this incredibly beautiful young woman who had recently started working as a research assistant in the legal department. I quickly unloaded Frank on Elliott Brack, the head of Human Resources—Frank was always such a corporate climber—poured two glasses of punch and invited her up to my office under the pretense that we could listen to news of the storm on the radio and that she could explain the finer points of crocheting elves to me. Back then I had this huge ham radio that took up most of my desk."

"Man, what a geek you must have been."

"Yeah, that's what all you girls say until we start making the money," he shakes the ice cubes in his drink at me. "Now you made me lose my train of thought."

"I'm sure that another one will be by in a minute," I flippantly reassure him.

He scowls at me.

"All right. I'm sorry," I eventually say. "Go on. It's nice just to hear about snow and cold weather. It's so damned hot in here."

"Okay, let's see, where was I?"

"You were in your office. You had the radio on. You were discussing elves. You had a very big interest in elves as I recall."

"Ah yes. Well, I'd call it more of a consuming passion. Right. And the radio was chirping travel advisories and hypothermia warnings. I remember she commented that the disc jockey sounded a bit too perky as he announced that two men were already causalities of the storm after suffering coronaries while shoveling their driveways."

"Denny, the sex," I impatiently remind him.

"I'm setting the mood. And quit rushing me. This is the only story I have. After this it's straight back to childhood rubella and my mother comes off as the big hero." He suddenly sits bolt upright. "Do you know what? I just realized that I've never before told this story to anyone. It sounds so strange to hear it."

"I'm honored. But can we at least skim over the weather report and the exact dimensions of your desk?" I plead with him. Although I'm actually enjoying myself. "There will be plenty of space for all of those colorful little details in your memoirs."

"All right. Then they played holiday music like *I'm Dreaming Of A White Christmas, Let it Snow! Let it Snow! Let it Snow!* And, of course, that old Great Lakes regional standard *The Wreck of the Edmund Fitzgerald.* He drunkenly sings an excerpt for me.

> *"Lake Huron rolls, Superior sings*
> *In the rooms of her ice water mansions*
> *Old Michigan steams like a young man's dreams*
> *The islands and bays are for sportsmen*
> *And farther below, Lake Ontario*

Takes in what Lake Erie can send her
And the Iron boats go as the mariners all know
With the gales of November remembered."

"Okay, you're really drunk," I say to him.

"I know. But that was quite good, don't you think?"

"It's right up there with the *Pennsylvania Polka.*"

"So anyway, from out of my window on the sixth floor we spy Bart Gibson, who has apparently decided to brave the storm, struggling with the frozen door lock of his Chevy. It certainly would have been easy enough to come back inside and borrow some lock deicer—almost everyone kept a supply in his briefcase or desk drawer—but in his haste to get on the road old Bart had opted for natural de-icer. After a quick glance around the parking lot to make sure that no one was looking, he peed into the lock." It makes Denny laugh just to reminisce about the incident. He pounds his hand on the coffee table for emphasis. "Jess, it was just so funny! Here I am having a drink with this gorgeous woman and the snow is falling in big beautiful flakes that cling to the window for an instant before they melt and old Bartholomew Gibson is pissing against his car door down in the parking lot. We laughed so hard. And then I just kissed her. It was crazy. Something just totally clicked for us."

"Is that it?" I demand. "Is that your idea of a torrid affair?"

"No, no. It was a real affair. We saw each other for about six months after that."

"So what happened after you kissed her?"

"Well," Denny says slowly and furrows his brow as if deep in thought. "At about half past five the Mayor declared a town emergency so no vehicles were permitted on the roads unless the drivers were involved in medical service or snow removal. And an announcement came over the p.a. system saying that the canteen would reopen for dinner and that they were currently accepting food service volunteers. So we eventually went back downstairs to get something to eat and there was this outrageous party going on. I mean, it's amazing how much booze can be rounded up in an emergency. I'll never forget it. We all got terrifically drunk and after dinner, Larry O'Shea, a mining engineer who'd spent most of his career working on the Alaskan pipeline, recited what must have been the complete works of Robert W. Service. Those pipeline guys were crazy. He went on for well over an hour."

"Who the hell is Robert W. Service, another engineer?"

"No. A poet." Denny attempts to give me a sampling:

> *"There are strange things done in the midnight sun*
> *By the men who moil for gold;*
> *The Arctic trails have their secret tales*
> *That would make your blood run cold;*
> *The Northern Lights have seen queer sights,*
> *But the queerest they ever did see*
> *Was that night on the marge of Lake LeBarge*
> *I cremated Sam McGee."*

"I can't believe you chose a career in science over the stage," I declare and proceed to raise a toast with the remainder of my drink.

Denny sits up slightly, before continuing somewhat conspiratorially, as if he is finally going to tell me the good part. "So there was music playing and some people were dancing and the power went out right at the end of the song *Dream A Little Dream of Me* by Mama Cass Elliot."

"I hate that stupid song," I interject. "My mother plays it like three times every Saturday morning while she's sorting the laundry. Whenever I hear it I automatically start stripping my bed. And then every April she whips the entire family into a spring cleaning frenzy on the Saturday before Easter Sunday, by the end of which, every comforter, dust ruffle, afghan and throw rug in the house has been beaten, washed and fluff dried. I automatically rise at six and shout from my bedroom, 'Siblings, stations of the Clorox!' and then cross myself and genuflect before ripping the sheets off the mattress."

"Well I guess it's possible that the words aren't all that insightful. But they're better than *Hang On Sloopy*. The early seventies, in my opinion, was not an inspired time for lyricists, with the possible exception of *Does Your Chewing Gum Lose Its Flavor On The Bedpost Overnight* by Lonnie Donegan."

"Okay, so the lights went out and then what happened? Let me guess, someone was murdered."

"Wrong. I took out my lighter and we crept up the emergency stairs and went back to my office."

"Wait a second, why did you have a lighter in your pocket?" I inquisitively demand to know.

"What are you now, a detective?"

"Aha! I knew it. Reformed smokers are always the worst. Sneaking around stealing the ashtrays and preaching to everyone who smokes."

"Jess, I'm a scientist," Denny replies solemnly, as if this explains everything.

"You were a smoker!" I say. "I knew it!"

He ignores my accusations. "Anyway, I fell head over heels in love. She was perfection in every way." He smiles at the memory.

"So what happened after the storm? I thought you said this was an affair. All I've heard so far is some Harlequin romance crap."

"I kept finding excuses to work late and it became a marathon for us to get together whenever possible."

"Get together? You mean meet to have sex, right?"

"Yes. I suppose so. Maybe I'm kidding myself but I do like to think there was a bit more to it than that."

"Didn't this woman mind that you were already married?" I ask.

"Well, she certainly wasn't crazy about the idea, but she was also involved in another relationship. We were both sneaking around. It was the '70s. It may sound hard to believe but I think more people were having affairs back then than are now. Or on second thought, maybe I just no longer know people who are having affairs. My circle has grown smaller and more republican."

"Did Sarah find out?" I inquire.

"Oh *yeah*. But it was just about over by the time she did. In a way, I guess I was relieved. I'm not cut out for that kind of deception—it was just a once in a lifetime thing."

"Why'd it end?"

"Well, she had . . . she was engaged to this other guy and," he paused as if it hurt him just to think about it, "and they got married. Meanwhile, I told Sarah that the affair was a mistake and that it was over and I apologized ad nauseam and I think that I bought her a diamond necklace or a bracelet and possibly even a new car. But she never asked anything about the actual affair or the woman."

"How did Sarah find out? Did you come home with lipstick on your collar or perfume in your hair? Did she find earrings in the backseat of the car?"

"No, no. Nothing like that. In retrospect I was pretty unsophisticated about the whole business and Sarah eventually became suspicious. She phoned the office a few times when I claimed to be working late and of course I wasn't there. Finally she just confronted me when I arrived home one night."

"I think Sarah let you off easy." I pause for effect and to take a drag on my cigarette. "'Cause I would've kicked your sorry ass to Detroit and back."

"Yes, well, it's easy to say that. But sometimes stuff happens in relationships, Jess. When you see people that have been married forty or fifty years do you honestly think that they've never cheated on each other? I mean, I'm sure a lot of them haven't but . . . "

"Get off the cross," I say dispassionately. "We may need the wood for a fire this winter."

"Okay, I'm not saying that it wasn't wrong," he backpedals. "Believe me, what I did was absolutely and definitely a mistake. But I've turned fifty now and well, you'll see, it's not as black and white as you think when you're young and single. Either way, it's not really fair to women. I mean, a pregnant woman with a toddler is in a pretty vulnerable position no matter how you want to look at it."

"So Sarah didn't even break a vase or threaten you with a divorce?"

"Nope," he says and starts to smile.

"You're lying."

"How can you tell?"

"You're smiling like a goofball."

"Okay, well there was just the cooking thing," he adds quietly.

"What cooking thing?" I'm lynx-eyed.

He coughs and clears his throat. "Sarah said that if I wanted to come home and ever live with my two children again then I had to start doing all of the cooking." Denny laughs as he explains the cooking-for-offspring deal he had negotiated so long ago. "Believe me, it was a small price to pay."

I laugh along with Denny, then yell "Incoming!" and begin hurling all of Joan's decorative needlepoint couch pillows at him. One says *Age is not important unless you're a cheese.* Another has an octopus saying to a fish, *Frankly Miss Scarlett I don't give a clam.*

"You jerk!" I shout at him. "I thought you were this sensitive liberated husband who wanted to help out around the house."

"I am sensitive. And liberated." Denny sets his drink down on the floor so it won't get bombarded and defends himself against the pillows before gently lobbing them back. "You should meet my brother Nate. He says stuff like, 'If you can't eat it, fuck it or make money off it then it's not worth bothering with.' I'm pretty sure that Nate thought that there was going to be a recipe book at the end of that movie *The Silence of the Lambs.*"

"Charming," I say as I lean back on the couch and stare up at the ceiling.

"Well I'm telling you the truth when I say that I ended up enjoying cooking. But I've got to hand it to Sarah. It was a brilliant idea. Just think about it, every time I switched on that stove or took a can of creamed corn out of the cupboard I had the opportunity to recall my sins. And I did, too. I still do."

"Women are great with guilt, huh?" I agree.

"Oh, they've got the guilt market cornered. Men just aren't that gifted. In fact, I think you Catholics are crazy not to allow women into the priesthood. They've elevated guilt to an art form."

"I say we drink a toast to Sarah," I propose and raise my glass. "To Sarah Sinclair, a wronged woman who never had to work in the kitchen again." Denny amiably staggers over to the couch and clinks his glass with mine.

"To Sarah!" he says. Denny glances back at the armchair where he had been sitting as if he doesn't remember it being quite so far away. Instead of making the long return journey he sits down next to me on the couch.

"I still can't believe that you cheated on her."

"It was over twenty years ago." Twenty years ago. That's when it hits me. The trove of love letters I'd stumbled across during my senior year of high school. All from someone who signed himself D, a guy who apparently worked as a scientist.

"And ye shall know the truth, and the truth shall make you free." John 8:32
Bookmark given to Jess by Joan for her first (and only)
straight A report card.

"Someday you'll thank me for this."
Mr. Chambers, Disciplinarian at Stuttaford High School.

Chapter 11
Breakdown or Breakthrough?
Late Wednesday Night

"What was her name?" I ask and try to sound as nonchalant as possible.

"Huh?"

"What was the woman's name?" I suddenly don't feel that drunk anymore.

"Oh," Denny hesitates. "Uh, it was Jo, uh—JoAnn," he replies reluctantly. "Her name was JoAnn."

I'll bet it was. I can't fucking believe this! Denny Sinclair had an affair with my mother. I feel like winding up and smacking him across the face. How dare he fool around with my mom? Actually, I can believe that about Denny. The question is more like, what the hell was my mother thinking fooling around with a married guy? Does Dad know about this? He couldn't possibly know. Hoping that maybe I've got it all wrong, I try to think of a way to find out for sure, short of coming right out and asking.

"So just tell me what happened to her," I continue. "To JoAnn."

"Uh, well, she married that guy she was seeing, she was engaged to him actually, and then they had a passel of kids."

"What's a passel of kids?"

"A litter. A brood. A family."

"How do you know? Do you stay in touch?"

"Not really. I've seen her around every once in awhile."

"How many kids?"

"I don't know exactly." Denny looks away from me and shifts in his seat.

I can tell that he is uncomfortable and wants to change the subject. But I suddenly realize that I don't want him to know that I know and so I stop digging. "Oh. Well that was a most excellent story." I set down my glass and give him a sloppy round of applause. "So now it's your turn to ask me a question."

"Maybe I had my mid-life crisis early," Denny suggests, ignoring my request. "I remember waking up early one morning and experiencing a tightness in my chest, like I couldn't breath. I was frightened, or maybe I just felt trapped. It was as if one day I was single and carefree and only a few years later the honeymoon was over and there were kids, insurance premiums—oh never mind."

I acknowledge his explanation with a nod and a weak smile. He certainly isn't going to find absolution with me, if that's what's he after. On one hand I all of the sudden feel like throwing him out of my house. And yet, maybe there is more information that I will find out if I wait with spider-like patience and act as if I don't know anything.

"So ask me a question," I repeat.

"Oh, okay. A question. Give me a second, my brain is moving about as fast as a street sweeper." Denny glances around the room as if the furnishings may unlock an idea. "Okay," he finally says. "Did you ever want to run away from home?"

"No, Denny. A real question. One that I wouldn't necessarily want to answer." For instance, how do I feel about you having an affair with my mother, I think to myself.

For a few seconds Denny strains to come up with something else. "Don't you have any of those little paperback books with questions already written out? My daughters used to read from them at parties."

"No, not one out of a book. This isn't like *Mad Libs*," I chastise him. "For instance, ask if I've ever cheated on an exam? Wait a second, forget that. I know, ask if I've ever had a homosexual experience."

"You mean with a gay man?" he asks with obvious alarm.

"No. Earth to Denny. Ask if I've ever slept with a woman."

"Have you slept with a woman?" Denny appears stunned.

"Yup!" I respond smugly. "Sophomore year in college." I don't know why I enjoy shocking him but I do. Maybe I believe that this will force him to regard me as an adult and not a child.

"Wow," Denny mouths incredulously. He stares at me, mouth agape. "So are you a lesbian? I don't think that I know any gay women. Well, actually Aunt Sabina got divorced after three months of marriage and cohabited with Clara for the next thirty years, but the family referred to Clara as Sabina's roommate or her 'special friend.' And eventually we all just called her Aunt Clara."

"No, I'm not a lesbian." I shrug off his sudden surprise. "C'mon, everyone experiments in college."

"Not like *that*, they don't." He shakes his head from side to side for emphasis.

"Well, then with drugs or Shintoism or something." I avert my eyes from his intense gaze and decide that introducing this particular topic may have been a mistake.

Denny's face has turned pink by the time I look at him again. "What's wrong? Are you embarrassed?" I ask.

"I'm just not used to talking to people about their private sexual forays."

"You just did."

"Yeah, but that was a normal affair."

"Well so was this."

"No, I mean, you're right. What's the big deal? My company just announced that they're offering spousal benefits to the same sex partners of employees." Denny takes a long pull of gin and probably believes he's sounding nonchalant. "So—uh—what was it—uh—like?"

"What was what like?" I ask him innocently. "Sleeping with a woman?"

"Yes. Unless you don't want to—"

"Why, haven't you ever done it?" I giggle at my own joke.

"No, I mean—yes, of course." Denny is tongue-tied now. "You know what I mean."

"It was okay," I say thoughtfully. "For one thing, it takes twice as long. And then—"

"Wait a minute," Denny interrupts me. "Why would it take longer?"

"Well, because—you can't really . . . you know, at the same time. Uh, just do the math Denny, okay?"

He thinks for a second and then a look of comprehension slowly spreads across his face. "Right, I get it. Well this is certainly interesting information. You don't come across facts like these in scientific journals."

"I guess the part that really stood out was that I didn't feel nervous. I thought I'd be really uneasy. You know, because my parents would consider it to be major deviant behavior. Like, they'd probably prefer to have me busted for shoplifting or dealing crack cocaine rather than discover that a blood member of the family had consciously flirted with homosexuality."

I think back to my one night stand with Amanda from my public speaking class. Amanda, who was so beautiful that she could have had any guy she wanted, had chosen me. Boy, were those football players surprised when she turned down all of their propositions and announced that she was *into chicks* in that incredibly confident yet *blasé* way that she had. I start to laugh at the memory.

"What's so funny?" Denny asks.

"Well, in retrospect, I think the most interesting part of the whole encounter was that I didn't know exactly how to make love with a woman. I mean, with men and women there are so many books and movies with couples kissing and having sex that everyone basically knows the ropes by the time they're eight-years-old."

"Yes, that makes sense," Denny replies. "I never thought of that.

Sort of preconditioning."

"And of course, being a vagatarian eliminates that sticky issue of whether to spit or swallow," I add with mock seriousness.

"Oh God!" Denny says and puts his hand up to his forehead. "Please don't go there! I'm begging you."

I just laugh at him. "All right, all right."

"So whose team are you on now?" He asks seriously. "Would you do it again?"

"That's a real gender bender. I don't know. No, I mean I'm on your team . . . no, I don't mean your team specifically. I mean . . ." I burst out giggling again. "I like guys."

"Oh," he says and appears relieved.

"But you never know. I guess that it really depends on the person," I say slowly and thoughtfully. "Yeah, for the right person, I guess I would. This girl I slept with—"

"Name please," Denny interjects.

"Amanda . . . incredibly sexy but she turned out to be a real flake."

"How did you initially know that she was attracted to you? Did she give you some sort of a signal?"

"No, not really. She was more straightforward than that. She just asked me out on a date. Amanda says that lesbians have *gaydar* and so they can easily identify other lesbians."

"How's that? Some sort of an atmospheric phenomenon like static electricity?"

"I don't know exactly. By certain signs I guess."

"But wait a second." Denny sounds confused. "I thought that you said that you aren't a lesbian."

"I did. I'm not. But Amanda decided that I was a LUG."

"Here we go again," Denny says and collapses onto the couch cushions. "Okay, what's a lug?"

"Lesbian until graduation."

"I'm too old. Forget it. I was born before radar, credit cards, and ballpoint pens. The kids laugh at me when I shout into the Burger

King drive-thru speakerphone—I never believe that they can actually hear me inside there. I don't think that my generation can realistically be expected to go any further than being open about alcoholism, drug addiction and depression. Not that Oprah hasn't taught us a lot, mind you, but there are still things that just don't make sense. For instance, I can't for the life of me figure out why people need to carry around individual bottles of water. When I was a kid we just had a drink before we left the house, or if we became thirsty while we were out, we just found a water fountain or bought a cherry Coke at the soda counter."

Denny goes over to the bar and opens a fresh bottle of vodka. The scotch had by this time run dry and I had polished off the previous bottle of Smirnoff with my blender drinks and eighty-proof Jell-O shots. He mixes a vodka and tonic. "What will you have?" he asks.

"Give me a Valium colada."

"I'm no pharmacist but I know enough to prescribe uppers for you, not downers." He pours me another rum and Coke. "Okay, serious question coming. Maraschino cherry?"

"Two," I say as I struggle to open a family-sized bag of Reese's Pieces. It is either sealed with super glue or the rum and humidity have sapped all of my strength. Finally, after an enormous two-handed pull, the plastic bag bursts open and little brown, green, yellow and orange candies rocket across the room. It sounds like a round of fire from a toy machine gun as some of the more ambitious Reese's Pieces ricochet off the ceramic lamp bases and spray against the wood paneling. The family room now resembles an Easter egg hunt for mice.

Upon hearing the blast, Denny turns and stares at me. I'm sitting in the middle of the floor, laughing my head off and holding up the ripped orange plastic bag by way of explanation. "I can't believe they put an expiration date on these," I say as I crawl around on my hands and knees, trying to collect whatever peanut butter and chocolate bits of shrapnel I can locate. Because if these things melt into the carpet Joan is for certain going to threaten that after having given me life, she is entitled to take it away.

"Everything has an expiration date these days," he says. "If you want, you can even request your own expiration date from an insurance company."

"Who keeps candy around long enough to need an expiration date? And how does an insurance company know when you're going to die?"

"They have actuaries—people who specialize in measuring mortality. They plug your age, sex, medical history, vital signs and whether or not you smoke into a computer and then tell you how old you'll be when you strike bedrock."

"Yuck," I say.

"Yeah, it's kind of morbid, I agree. I'm supposed to go 'til I'm seventy-six and a half or somewhere around there."

"But what if you get killed in a plane crash or a tsunami?" I purposely avoid saying car crash.

"They insure a pool of people and know that statistically some will die before their number is up on the charts and likewise, some will live considerably longer. So in the end it all averages out. But I don't think they take tsunamis into account for Midwesterners."

"And how long do you think I'm supposed to live according to these charts?"

"Oh, you women carry on forever. At least that's the way it's supposed to be," he adds thoughtfully. "Right now you'd probably be in their computers for eighty-something."

"Why do women live longer?"

"Because they don't have to worry about crabgrass and they're not married to women."

"Unless they're lesbians."

"Right. Unless they're lesbians."

Denny stumbles over a pile of newspapers as he threads his way back to the couch. "Maybe I'm gay," he says seriously. "Now they say it's in the genetic code, just like having red hair. Maybe that's why I can't get it right with women, you know, get inside their heads and figure out what they really want." He clumsily sits down on the floor next to me, sets the drinks on the coffee table, and leans his back up against the couch.

"Why? Are you attracted to men?" I thought that this could be really interesting. Outing Denny.

"No. But I enjoy cooking. And I like to make jam from fresh berries and also to can vegetables, though I think of it more as chemical engineering. In fact, tomorrow I was going to ask if I could make sauce out of some of those tomatoes in your garden. They're falling off the vines and will just rot if you don't pick them soon."

"Sure. Simmer your heart out. Though I don't really care if they rot. In fact, it's probably good fertilizer. We're all decaying and we're all eventually going to be fertilizer. Why should the tomatoes be treated any differently?"

"So maybe that's why it bothers us to watch things ripen and then rot," he adds.

"Maybe. But let's get back to you joining a musical touring company of *Cats*. A lot of guys cook these days. And aren't all the great chefs men?"

"No. There's Julia Child."

"Debatable. Have you ever had a crush on a man or thought that a guy in a movie was attractive?" I quiz him. And though at the time my suspicions hadn't been aroused by the food coloring that Denny had added to the scrambled eggs, I can't help but think back to it.

"No." Denny thinks for another second. "But I definitely fell in love with Kathleen Turner after seeing that movie *Romancing The Stone*. Boy, she was great in that; snakes, explosions, crawling through caves!"

"I don't think you're gay. But here's the final test. Have you ever used the words greige, aubergine or chartreuse when describing the furnishings in your home or wardrobe?"

"Never. I don't even know what they mean, although I think chartreuse is a vile shade of green."

"You're definitely not gay."

"I guess not, but thanks for the quiz and confirmation," Denny says, not altogether happily.

"So you think all of your problems will be solved if you can find out what women want. Is this right?"

"It sure would help to have a baseline."

"Well then, I'll tell you what women want."

Denny looks at me as if this is just another one of my jokes.

"No. I'm serious. This is your prize for being on the show. Are you ready?"

"Yes," he says curiously.

"Denny, women want relationships."

"Don't we all?"

"No, not in the same way. Women need relationships in their lives. Not just with men. With their children, their cars, their pets, their banks, their work, their toasters, the stores where they shop and so on and so forth. It's just the way we're built. We come pre-programmed, like lemmings."

"But men wouldn't get married if they didn't want relationships."

"Denny, go to a porno shop. There aren't many women in there. Even the lesbian orgy smut is rented by men. We don't like to admit it but a woman's idea of an erotic chick flick is *The Bridges of Madison County*. Get it?"

Denny sits stock still after I explain this. He opens his mouth to say something and then closes it again. Finally he says, "You know, I believe what you've just said is worth some serious consideration."

"Listen, don't think that I'm happy about this discovery or anything like that. In fact, I wish it weren't so. It makes women too dependent on random outside forces and events for their own happiness and well being and frankly, this can really ruin an otherwise good day."

"And that's different from what men want?"

"Of course. A man wants a challenge—a woman who says she's a lesbian and has only two weeks to live. That's how to get a man to fall in love with you."

"I'm having a Weltanschauung moment."

"Well put your head between your knees and maybe it will pass. It's probably just the humidity. Now, getting back to the truth game, it's my turn to ask you a question."

"Fire away," Denny says.

"I went to the school psychiatrist this spring," I suddenly announce. Where did that come from, I wonder. "Well it was actually a therapist. They first have to decide if you're crazy enough to qualify for a session with an actual MD."

"Why did you go?" Denny queries.

"At school it's free, at least the first ten sessions are free, and then it's only five bucks per visit. So I wanted to have my dreams analyzed, exorcise any demons, cure any separation anxieties and dredge up any childhood traumas on a budget—you know, before graduation and the real world," I explain and wave my cigarette through the air with a flourish.

"Don't tell me that you went to a shrink and then become flip about it. Why did you go?"

"I went mostly because I wasn't happy," I reply seriously. "I can't remember the last time I was truly happy. And I don't think I know anyone, aside from my parents, that is, who is happy. Are you happy?"

"You must be kidding. No, I'm not happy. I'm miserable, bordering on suicidal," Denny replies seriously. He pauses for a second, brightens a little and adds, "However, I know a few people who are happy, or at least they appear to be cheerful and coping fairly well. And I'm happy about my haircut."

"C'mon be serious. What about before this summer? Were you happy then?"

"Of course. Sure. I mean, life's never perfect," Denny answers unconvincingly. He pauses but I wait for him to continue. "No. Not really. But then I don't think I'm what one would consider, generally speaking, a happy person. I've actually given this quite a bit of thought and I honestly don't believe that I have the capacity for large amounts of joy." He looks up to see if I'm following this logic.

"That's not to say that I haven't had moments of genuine happiness.

Because I definitely have. For instance, I had a pretty good time in college. I was in a fraternity and all that. And of course I used to enjoy a lot of things about the kids when they were little. Silly stuff they said or did. And I think that I was happy during the beginning of Nixon's second term. What a landslide!" He sighs, leans back and stares up at the track lighting. "I mean, who's truly happy?"

"That's exactly what I think," I excitedly reply. "That nobody's really happy! Actually, it's much worse. I'm completely unraveling. As a matter of fact, I'm not even trying to create a promising future for myself anymore. No, I'm just trying to prevent a really bad one from happening. You know, I'm totally in a damage control phase at this point in the low-budget indie film noir that has become my life."

"Whew!" Denny says after I conclude my lament of a suburban life lost. "So what'd he say, the therapist?" Denny asks, sounding genuinely concerned, like maybe he should be ordering purple magic markers from the Staples Office Supply catalogue so that when they chuck me into the padded room I can at least have the luxury of being able to scribble on the white walls with my toes.

"She," I correct him. "She said that most people aren't happy and that I should just peruse a few issues of *People* magazine and read about all the famous movie actors and rock stars. Their lives are almost always totally screwed up and supposedly they have everything; money, success, the adulation of the public. She said that I should just do the things that I think will make me happy and that's usually about as good as it gets."

"Oh, really? That's depressing."

"Yeah, I know. It's like saying that if you're always disappointed then you should probably just lower your expectations. I sure wouldn't mind being a therapist and getting a hundred bucks an hour for suggesting to someone who's nutty as a squirrel's dowry that the first step towards finding a cure is a subscription to *People* magazine."

"Amen. If we can simplify the definition of happiness to the presence of pleasure and the absence of pain then I could occasionally participate.

Maybe we should both move to India. Perhaps monotheism just isn't offering us enough options," he suggests.

"Thanks, but I've already got more religion than I can handle. I don't think an ashram is the answer. For me, anyway. Dr. Goodman, the therapist, she also said I'm living in the present and the future simultaneously and that it's wearing me out."

"What is *that* supposed to mean?"

"Other than the fact that I'm angry most of the time and I can't sleep very well, I'm not really sure. I guess it means I'm just stressed about everything, you know, my future."

Denny suddenly looks like he's experiencing a brilliant thought. "Maybe that's why I can't sleep, because I'm living in the past and the present at the same time."

"Great. I'm glad we can overlap in at least one time zone. That way we can get our mail and wave to each other."

"I can tell you one thing that would have made me incredibly happy. But it didn't happen. And now it will never happen. In fact, it's been one of my greatest disappointments," Denny wistfully remarks.

"Yeah. What was that?"

"Do you remember when we were supposed to switch to the metric system and finally use the same measuring criteria as Canada, Europe and the rest of the modern world?"

"Not really." I think back to my science classes. "I vaguely remember learning how to add nine-fifths to convert pounds and degrees and quarts. Or was it multiply by five-ninths?"

"Right, that's it!" he says excitedly. "The entire United States was gearing up to go metric. It was all planned. And then suddenly the government chickened out. How can they just suddenly decide not to go metric?"

"You should meet Derek. He was my roommate Jill's boyfriend and could do all kinds of metric conversions really fast in his head, sometimes to the second decimal place."

"Really? Was he a chemistry major?"

"No. The campus heroin dealer."

"Oh."

"So let me get this straight," I say quizzically, "This not going metric thing was one of your biggest disappointments in life?"

"Jess, you have to understand how idealistic a time it was before Vietnam and Watergate. And then how the government screwed up so many of the great opportunities for this country all because of greedy, power hungry politicians." In his voice is all the frustration of someone who goes souvenir shopping during a vacation in Dublin and comes back with a bunch of tchotchkes only to find they all have labels saying Made in the USA on the bottom. "It was just the last in a long string of letdowns for me. After that I just couldn't be optimistic anymore. It's as if I can pinpoint the year I grew old to when we didn't go metric."

"If it's any consolation I also wish we had," I concur.

"You do?" Denny sounds pleased to have a measurement ally.

"Yeah, I can never figure out the speed limit when I'm driving through Canada," I remark. "My high school chemistry teacher was a born again Christian and said that if we were meant to go metric then Jesus would have summoned ten disciples to teach the Gospel and not twelve."

"You're joking, right?"

"No. Serious as cancer. But then Mr. Caldwell won't drive with other people in his car, either. He's afraid that the Rapture—you know, when all the faithful get lifted to heaven right before the Second Coming—will occur while he's behind the wheel and that he'll be spirited up to heaven, thereby leaving his passengers to crash into the guardrail in a heap of twisted metal. Of course, they'd be left to face the Antichrist anyway, according to Mr. Caldwell's calculations, so I don't know what the big deal is." I realize it hadn't taken me long to get back on the subject of car accidents. Damn.

"I suppose the sciences attract all kinds."

"I guess. So would you be suicidal if I told you that pizza doesn't come from Italy?" I tease him. "Or that danish wasn't invented in Denmark?"

"Cut it out. There's absolutely nothing funny about not going metric. Our measuring system is just plain stupid, archaic and prehistoric!"

"But how do you really feel?" I jibe him.

Denny returns to the subject at hand. "Okay, so we've established that most people aren't happy, present company included," he recaps. "Now ask me another question. This game isn't as bad as I thought it was going to be."

"All right." I lean over and dramatically cup my hands over his ear and whisper, "Tell me your biggest, deepest, darkest secret. The skeleton in your closet. Something that no one else in the world knows."

After absorbing this directive, Denny looks worried and uneasily shifts his body, as if there is something that he wants to say but decides that it's too risky. "Uh, that's a hard one. I don't know. I have a secret barbecue recipe."

"Oh great," I say sarcastically and roll my eyes the way I used to when my father would appear at high school swim meets wearing shorts and black ribbed nylon businessman socks with brand X white tennis sneakers. "C'mon, I haven't got all minute. Think of something because I've got a good one to tell you."

"So then tell yours," he proposes drowsily.

"No way. It's your turn to sing." I can see that Denny is drifting away and I suddenly fear losing his interest. "But I'll tell you this much, it involves you." I can stand it no longer. I have to know for sure whether Denny is the D at the bottom of those love letters, if the man sitting in front of me has carnal knowledge of my own mother.

That does the trick. Denny perks up and suddenly becomes very attentive.

"What? C'mon. Tell me," he insists in a voice that indicates he doesn't know if the information he wants to hear is good or bad.

"What will you give me in return?" I demand. I need to buy a little time here since I really don't know what I'm going to do if it turns out to be true, which I'm almost sure that it is. Throw him out?

"Ten bucks."

"Sure you will. Duh. You don't have any money."

"I have plenty of money. It's just not here." He starts to tick off his assets on the fingers of his left hand, "I have IRA accounts, a life insurance policy, a real estate investment trust and pre-refunded triple A municipal bonds. In fact, I'll give you twenty bucks—all in fives. Four fives will be worth considerably more than twenty dollars when this shortage of yours arrives."

"Okay. But you have to pay up front."

"Jess, I can't. C'mon you know I'm good for it, I've even got stock options. I'm vested, woman! I can buy and sell you thousands of times over."

"Yeah, you're half right about that—you can buy me easily enough. But you're going to have a hell of a time selling me. Because believe me, I've tried."

"Very funny. How about I write out an IOU?"

"Okay." Out of the coffee table drawer I pull a crayon labeled burnt sienna and hand it to Denny along with a magazine on which to write.

"I can't believe you're making me do this." Denny ruefully takes the crayon from me. "You're actually going to collect the money, aren't you?"

"Double duh! You bet I am. You think that maybe I don't want some mutual funds too? Now write! Do you wanna hear the gossip or not? 'Cause it's going to cost fifty real soon."

"All right already." He quickly scrawls an IOU on the back of a *Time* magazine subscription card, signs it and hands it back to me. "Now tell me before my clothes go out of style."

"Okay, okay," I say and edge closer to him. "First I'll give you a hint and you have to try and guess."

"I didn't pay twenty bucks to play twenty questions. 'Fess up."

I pretend to totally ignore his urging and purposely take my sweet time. "Hint number one," I say deliberately: "The song *I Saw Mommy*

Kissing Santa Claus."

Denny looks alternately confused and worried. "Jess, what on earth are you talking about?"

I disregard his question and continue. "Hint number two," I recite, "Dear Joan, I mean JoAnn," I glance at him slyly, "Without you near me each second is like an unbonded atom. The minutes until I see you add up to the chaos of so many frantic electrons and protons, taking forever to unite and form an hour."

"Oh shit!" Denny shrinks into the sofa and puts his hands over his ears.

"Daddy?" I rise to my knees and stretch my arms out towards him like a toddler learning to walk.

"No! Oh God, no! They weren't even married, Jess! You weren't even born yet. I, I mean you weren't born for months after—no, I mean many, *many* months!"

"Then why else would you be spying on my house?" I ask matter-of-factly.

"I don't know, I just—I mean, I wanted to see—I guess I just thought that if I could see her, that it would somehow help. Or if I might see what could have been, then I would stop feeling so awful."

"But you got me instead of her. Or rather you didn't get me but you tried."

"I'm so mortified." Denny's face had drained of color despite the substantial heat and consumption of alcohol.

Sitting and staring at him I attempt to makes sense of it all. I can't.

"Choose one of the above: electron, proton, neutron, moron," I say instead.

Denny appears too humiliated to find anything funny, even what I consider to be a very good joke, especially under the circumstances. But then I'm drunk, too. And I suppose we're both in shock.

Denny briefly looks up at me but he doesn't say anything and then he looks back down and studies his knees.

"Cute yarn about running away and looking for Mr. Sutherland's house, by the way," I goad him.

Denny takes a deep breath before looking up again. "The running away part is true. Honest. But no, I wasn't planning on going to Walt's. I honestly don't know what I was going to do. I guess—I suppose I would have just gone home, that is, if you hadn't opened the door. But I didn't know what to say. You shocked the hell out of me! People must tell you that you look just like her."

"When they want to annoy me."

"What do you mean? Jess, your mother is lovely; beautiful green eyes, just like yours."

"I don't think that anyone enjoys being compared to her mother," I state objectively.

"So uh, how did you come to read that letter? Joan didn't show it to you, did she? My God, it must be at least twenty-two years old."

"Letter? *Letters* my friend." As I say this I take great pleasure in emphasizing the plural. "They were on the top shelf in the back of the linen closet," I explain. "Senior year in high school I was doing a project for Social Studies class on our family history and needed my mother's old college yearbook and there they were. It was so cool, they were all tied up in a faded pink ribbon, just like in a romance novel."

"Joan kept all of my letters?" he asks with what appears to be more than just a passing interest and leans forward, toward me, the fount of this incredible information.

"When I found them, of course I looked at them, I figured that they were from my father. But then I noticed they were signed with a D at the bottom, which I assumed could be for 'darling' or some cutesy nickname. But after reading a few I knew that they definitely weren't from my dad. I mean, Gene writes all of Joan's anniversary cards in bullet points. And the science references were a bit heavy, though maybe chemistry allusions were all the rage twenty years ago, what with astronauts heading off to the moon every week and people wearing mood rings. If I recall correctly, you even managed to work the metric system into a little poem. I don't know, it was hard enough to picture my sensible mother receiving gooey love letters but knowing her, it was just on this side of being believable. Gene, on the other hand, is just not a love letter type of guy. To him a piece of writing paper represents execution, you know; a requisition form, a memo, filling out the warranty on his new power mower. So I just read them and put them back and took the photos and stuff that I needed for my project."

"I'm sorry," Denny finally says after he apparently realizes I've finished my explanation. "I shouldn't have told you that story about having an affair. It was really inappropriate." He pauses for a second. "The affair? What am I saying? I shouldn't have come to your house in the first place."

"I might have figured it out all the same. But I think that you subconsciously wanted me to know."

"Jess!" He sounds shocked, or at least he pretends to. "Why would I do a dumb thing like that?"

"I told you. Everybody wants a chance to confess."

"Are you angry?"

"Me? No," I say slowly. "I mean, why would I be mad? I wasn't even born yet, as you have been so quick to point out. And if what you say is true, then my parents weren't even married when you were banging my mom." It might not be very fair to Mom but I had to put it that way. That's what happened. I want Denny to know that is how I view it.

"Of course it's true. But they were engaged. And I prefer the term *affair*, if you don't mind. Not so much for me, but your mother is a lady, after all."

"I guess I'm just surprised that my mom would have screw— sorry, had an affair with a married man at all," I say thoughtfully. "And while she was pledged to another! Perfect little Joan. In school she wouldn't even let me forge her name on a field trip permission slip. And she's always bitching that I treat Carl badly when we talk on the phone, you know, as if he's got her on the payroll to get us back together.

And well, now it turns out she's not so, I don't know . . . "

"If it helps at all, I clearly remember that, at least at the time, she was very conflicted about getting married and not pursuing a career."

"It's just that I've always pictured my mom as being so together. The happy homemaker. You know, the parent with all the answers. Christ, I've never known her to be wrong about anything or even to make a mistake, grammatical or otherwise."

"I'm sure you're aware that your mother was really quite a good catch back in those days; smart, witty, beautiful. Of course I'm sure that she still is all of those things. She had wanted to go to law school at the University of Michigan."

"Law school! My mother? Get out! She never told me that. Are you sure?"

"Quite sure. In fact, she'd applied and been accepted and everything. It was a tough call. I'm surprised that she never told you about it. Getting into the U of M program was quite a feather in her cap. Back then not nearly as many women went to law school as do today."

"My mother at the University of Michigan Law School! Are you being serious or is this just another one of your bizarre what-ifs?"

"Jess, your mother is a very bright woman. And for your information, she wouldn't have had any trouble tackling graduate school in almost any area. Furthermore, she would have made a damn good lawyer. If I remember correctly, she was particularly interested in constitutional law. But why listen to me anyway? Just ask her."

I am absolutely struck dumb by the law school thing. It's even harder to believe that Joan ever had any interest in democracy, particularly upon reviewing her autocratic running of the household. I couldn't be more shocked than if Denny had just informed me that Joan was scheduled to be an astronaut on the next space shuttle. Finally I regain my capacity for speech. "I don't get it? Why didn't she go?"

He shrugs. "Lots of reasons I guess. Your dad had come back from the army and found a job and wanted to settle down. That's just how it was back then. And right after they married she became pregnant."

"Yeah, she got pregnant with me. So it's all my fault that my mother is a housewife making Pocahontas centerpieces out of Styrofoam balls, corn husks and rust-colored yarn and she's not Sandra Day O'Connor, sitting on the Supreme Court in a pair of sensible shoes and a crisp ivory linen suit."

"Be serious Jess. It had absolutely nothing to do with you," Denny emphatically informs me. "I know for a fact that your mother wanted a family as much as your dad. And if ever there was a child who was not an accident, it's you, Miss MacGuire."

"Depends on how you define the word accident," I shoot back.

"Seriously, how was Joan supposed to raise five children and go to school or work as a lawyer? It just wasn't practical."

"Yeah," I say excitedly, "But if she'd gotten her degree and passed the bar then she could have gone back to work after we started elementary school. My mom's only forty-five right now and she's going to have the whole empty-nest syndrome thing happening in a few more years and will probably end up operating the gift cart at the local hospital or making a colossal rubber band ball just so that she doesn't lose her mind. She definitely should have gone to law school. And now that I think of it, she can lay down laws like fucking Hammurabi."

"Jess, think about it. Can you honestly picture your father having a working wife?"

But I hardly hear what Denny is saying. I suddenly feel so guilty for all the awful things I've said to her, the way I've treated her. My subconscious has somehow gone into Hail Mary overdrive. All I can hear inside my head is a pounding: *Holy Mary, Mother of God, pray for us sinners, now and at the hour of our death. Amen.*

"Not to mention a wife with more education than he has," Denny adds. "If I recall correctly, Joan mentioned that it bothered your father that he had only a two-year college degree."

When the Hail Marys finally recede to a quiet background murmur, like bad elevator music, I try to sort out what is and what could have been. Gene, who doesn't know where socks and ties come from is married to my mother, who diligently gives dinner parties for his colleagues and clients, which have in no uncertain terms aided his climb up the corporate ladder. Joan shops and cooks and holds the family firmly together during good times and bad, crisis and celebration. And somehow, deep down, I know that Denny is right. I can't envision my mother leaving at the crack of dawn each day for work in a Talbot's outfit and Manolo Blahnik heels and missing all the mind-numbing school pageants and Eagle Scout moving-up ceremonies; her latchkey kids left to purchase school lunches and eat frozen Swanson TV dinners, in the care of baby-sitters who prattle on the phone to their bass guitar-playing boyfriends all afternoon, not noticing that the children aren't wearing their jackets or wiping their noses. Whooping cough eventually settles in and along with it the slow but sure demise of an American family.

"No, I suppose you're right." I am suddenly overcome by an inexplicable wave of kindness toward my fellow man and decide that Denny, mainly since he is the only one around, will be the recipient of my unforeseen mood change. "And not for nothing, but it was pretty obvious that my mom thought that you were something special as well. I mean, it's not as if I found piles of letters from a whole lacrosse team and prison pen-pals or anything like that. My mother certainly wasn't mattress-back Joan."

"Oh, I know that," he says quietly, almost shyly. "We just really hit it off. She's a fine girl, I mean woman, a really wonderful woman. But I'm sure that I don't have to tell you that."

"No, of course you don't have to tell me that," I reply pensively and gradually lower my drink onto the coffee table, careful to set it down on a coaster so it won't leave a ring on the glass top. "And it appears that you were very accomplished at kissing," I add somewhat playfully.

"What do you mean?" Denny says with great curiosity, but also sounding as if there may be cause for alarm.

"I probably shouldn't tell you this, but, oh, what the hell. In that little bundle there was a letter addressed to D, which we can now safely say was you, that she apparently never sent. And I remember the good part in it was about kissing you." My God, I wonder, have I suddenly become my mother's secret little collaborator in Dennygate.

"Oh please! You're making this up now. Why don't you just have a full go? First my wife dies. Then I come over here to see Joan, not even to talk with her, perhaps just catch sight of her as she's closing the living room curtains in the evening, so the morning sun doesn't fade her furniture the next day, and I end up blowing the whole thing. Honest, I wasn't planning on interfering in your lives. I was just hoping to catch a glimpse of her. That's all, just to put my soul at ease and . . . "

"Why don't you get out your violin for the finale?" I interject flippantly. "You're so full of shit—catch a glimpse of her my ass!"

"What was in the letter Jess? Please, this sounds crazy but I really need to know," he practically pleads with me.

He is now truly pathetic, sounding like a man desperate to make a phone call by the side of the highway only to find he's at one of those strange boxy, brown payphones in the middle of nowhere that won't accept a calling card.

"It ended so abruptly. I mean, we never talked it out. You know what I'm saying?"

"No closure."

"Yes, exactly. That's it exactly. We never had that luxury."

I instantly feel like the goose that lays the golden eggs. I feel powerful. Should I tell him the truth? That I only read the letters on the lookout for juicy parts, as one goes through *The Canterbury Tales* in high school searching for the salacious dealings of the Wife of Bath. Or better, I could make up something that would hurt him. After all, he shouldn't have seduced my mother in the first place, only to dump her after he got caught. Then twenty years later, with his dead wife's body not yet cold in its grave, he feels perfectly justified prowling around the neighborhood still lusting after his old flame. Am I experiencing a change of heart? It was all quite sickening, the more I thought about it.

But oddly enough, after taking inventory of all my emotions, I decide that I'm basically left feeling horrendously sorry for him. He's as fucked up as I am. Bottom line: Under these circumstances, I feel inclined to provide him with the truth, so long as I'm sure it won't provide restored hope or anything like that. And as he says, maybe it will help to put some of his demons to rest. Yes, that's what I'd do. How can it hurt? My mother is obviously a happily married woman with no regrets. Isn't she?

"The letter said . . . " I start to say, because he's so strung out now I can't help myself but to goof around with him, "Or maybe it would just be better if I showed it to you."

Denny jumps up and practically spills his drink. "Would you!" Then he composes himself. "I mean, would you mind?"

Climbing the stepstool and digging through the back of the closet is not my first choice of activity, considering that I've had either way too much or not enough to drink, and my legs are so unsteady that I must look like a dolphin struggling to get out of a tuna net. "All right," I acquiesce, "But you'd better hope I don't fall and break my neck."

"I really appreciate this Jess," Denny earnestly declares his thanks in advance. "It's not like I'm trying to win her back or stalking her or something crazy like that. I—I would just like to put the memory to rest. And I know about the letter that you're referring to because I tried to call Joan and she wouldn't talk to me except to say that she had sent a letter to me at work. But it never arrived. I had always wondered if maybe it got lost. You may as well know that Joan was the one who broke it off. It's true that Sarah eventually found out, but that was after Joan had called it quits. She—she loved your dad. She really did."

"She *does* love my dad," I quickly correct him.

This is certainly news—that Joan had ended their relationship. For some reason I had automatically assumed that Denny had been trifling with my mother's affections and then got caught or he just grew tired of the whole thing and used being found out as an excuse to dump her.

"All right. All right." I heave all the linen tablecloths off the top shelf of the closet and onto the floor and dig out the box containing the letters. "What in the name of God is Mom saving all these old dishtowels for? On the other hand, if you add some plastic picnic forks and spoons, all this crap is probably the makings of my dowry."

Denny swiftly flips through the pile of letters like a casting agent who knows exactly what he wants, choosing from a thousand head shots. He hastily puts aside the correspondence in his own handwriting while searching for the final, un-mailed Dear D letter from Mom.

When he has the missive firmly in hand Denny slowly takes a sip of his drink and then a deep breath and begins to silently read, his lips moving over the words like a second grader reading *Go Dog, Go*.

I don't know why I feel nervous as he reads and rereads the letter. What could possibly happen? And besides, I had read it myself. I can't remember how it was worded exactly, but the general idea was that even though they could no longer see each other, that what they had was very special, blah blah blah. Usual breakup stuff. And that she would always have a place for him in her heart. Typical Joan. Polite. Always sending thank-you notes. Even after a love affair.

Denny seems to absorb his twenty-something year-old letter languidly, like he's swirling an exquisite glass of port of the same age in his mouth and letting the very essence of what he's read gradually, delicately, permeate his taste buds.

"Why do you think she never sent it?" he finally asks me. "There's nothing incendiary in here." Denny still looks a bit moony as he clutches the paper to his lap.

"I don't remember exactly how she put it, but that part about her really liking the way you kissed. Maybe that's why. It's probably not a good thing to say to a guy who, oh excuse me, with whom, you're trying to break up. Right?"

"I suppose." I wait some more while Denny reads the letter again.

"And what exactly do you think this last line means?" he asks. "It seems like some sort of code."

Thinking back to the letter I can't remember any last lines.

"What does it say?"

"It's enough to have someone to love," he reads. "You don't always have to win."

"What?" I'm pretty polluted.

"It's enough to have someone to love. You don't always have to win." He repeats the words as if tasting them. "That is the last line of her letter."

"Really?"

"That's exactly what she wrote. What do you think it means? That she loved me? Or that she loved Gene?"

"Maybe she meant that you loved Sarah."

"Why would Joan write about me and Sarah?"

"Your guess is as good as mine. Maybe she was afraid your marriage would fall apart because of her and she didn't want that responsibility," I suggest. I know my mother well enough to feel confident that she probably could not have lived with a weight like that on her conscience.

"Or maybe she meant that she knew that I loved her, even though we couldn't be together," Denny suggests.

"Wow, it's amazing how this could mean so many different things," I say.

"Yeah. I wish there was some way to call her and get a little clarification."

I look up to make sure that he's not serious.

"No, I don't mean that it would change anything," he states. "It's just sort of an unsolved mystery, isn't it?"

"But I don't think it was written to be a riddle Denny. Joan is not one for playing mind games. I think you're just supposed to decide in your heart what it means to you and that's that. Did you ever stop to think what would have happened to your children if you'd pursued the relationship with my mother?"

"I've tried not to because that's what makes me realize that leaving Sarah would have hurt so many people. And what has really kept me going all these years are my kids. Sarah was a great mother. And even if I didn't win any awards on the marriage front, I think that I am a pretty decent dad. Sarah always says that I make a lot of time for the children, and I have plenty of patience."

I ignore the fact that Denny is again speaking of his wife in the present tense. All I seem to be thinking now is, *What the hell, if he was good enough for Mom, he's good enough for me.*

"And now since it's your turn to tell me something, I'd be interested in hearing more about the kissing part," I say.

"Huh. What do you mean?" he asks as if he does indeed know what I mean.

"Now that we've got your checkered past out of the way, how about a demonstration?"

"My gosh, you've got a lot of chutzpah, asking a guy to kiss you," Denny manages to draw back from me slightly, even though he's seated in the armchair which is a good four feet away.

I'm nonplused by his reaction, or non-reaction, such as it is. "Nah, not really," I reply, as casually as if I've just asked if he wants milk in his coffee, and then I lean back against the couch cushions. "First, I'm more than slightly drunk. And second, since nowadays you have to ask before you touch someone, if a woman waits for the guy to ask, she'll be in the throes of menopause by the time he gets up the courage to initiate anything."

"What do you mean you have to ask?" Denny says, obviously intrigued by the word choice.

"Where have you been Denny? You have to get verbal permission before making any type of romantic overtures. It's even in our college rulebook. Otherwise it can be considered sexual harassment, especially for a guy."

"So, let me get this straight. If I want to hold a woman's hand, I have to ask her in advance?"

"Yup. The only exception is if you receive specific body language signaling her approval. But the sexual harassment lecturers all agree that you're a lot safer asking."

"Why don't they just require a statement in writing on letterhead stationary and then have it notarized?" he quips. "Or install video cameras in the dorm rooms?"

"It's not a joke," I say seriously. "I'm sure that my brother Jack is going to wind up in jail for sexual assault. He plays tonsil hockey with his dates, wrestles them into a half nelson and then whispers 'Fuck or Fight' into their quadruple-pierced ears."

"A true romantic," Denny suggests.

"Yeah, and if the girl gets close enough to Jack's head, she can usually hear the ocean. I don't think he's recovered from the fact that my parents took thousands of baby pictures and home movies of me and they were basically burned out with toddler documentary-making by the time he arrived on the scene. Jack needs a lot of validation. And of course I've purposely hidden every picture of him I've been able to find."

"Excuse me, but could we please back up for a second? You just asked me to kiss you, is that correct?"

"Yes. And then you started a fucking conversation."

"But it's all right if I kiss you, right?"

"Now I'll have talk to my lawyer and get back to you in the morning," I tease him. He walks over to the couch and kisses me on the mouth. It's a short kiss. Denny quickly withdraws and looks into my eyes as if he is performing a climatology experiment and needs to check the temperature.

"So that's the kiss that launched a thousand paper clips?" I ask with mock seriousness.

"Bad?"

"Short."

Denny takes a deep breath as if he's preparing to make a high dive into the deep end of a swimming pool. Then he leans over and gently kisses me again.

Only this time it is a real kiss. I slide back into the couch under the weight of Denny's chest. In the process my foot tips over a big wooden bowl full of Chee-tos so that it makes a loud crash on the coffee table and the flame-orange cheese curls scatter across the shag carpeting. Our hearts beat loudly, like Jack's basketball sneakers thumping round and round in the clothes dryer. Denny kisses softly and smoothly, not like some of the guys my age who think it's a real turn on to try and suck your face off. Instead of becoming more forceful, he becomes less so, but it feels even better that way, and makes me want more. All the while I wonder what's going to happen next. Should I move my hands? Should I wait?

It turns out that I don't have to decide what the next step is because Denny suddenly jerks his body away from mine and staggers up from the couch. Chee-tos crunch and crackle as he presses them into the carpet with the soles of his shoes.

Startled, I remain where I am and silently observe as Denny goes into full panic mode and lurches towards the half bathroom in the front hall.

I decide that maybe he is sick and so I stumble after him. But then it hits me. Oh God, what if I really am his daughter? Hadn't Anaïs Nin tracked down the father she had never known and seduced him, just for kicks? Or maybe she did it for closure? Why else would it freak him out? It must be incest. For sure *The National Enquirer* will be phoning tomorrow morning.

From the other side of the bathroom door I can hear Denny running the water full-blast in the sink. What the hell is he doing? Is he puking?

"What's wrong?!" I bang on the bathroom door but the only reply I receive is that of the toilet flushing.

I try to turn the doorknob but it's locked. "Oh shit," I say softly, more to myself. "Denny, what's wrong? C'mon, open the damn door." I bang my fists on the door and my ringed fingers make a hollow clunking sound on the pressboard.

There's still no answer. "Okay, stand back," I yell, "I'm coming in with the jaws of life! We're landing a med-evac chopper on the roof. Your mother will meet us at the emergency room."

"It's not your fault. I . . . I just—" is all that he finally manages to say.

"Denny, I've got to know. Don't make me pay six hundred dollars for a paternity test. I have no money. Am I your love child?"

"NO!" he says with forced energy. "Believe me Jess. Over a year after your mother and I broke up I saw her in the cereal aisle at the grocery store buying Special K and she was pregnant with you," he responds wearily from the other side of the door, as if it takes all of his remaining strength to retell this chance encounter.

"How do you know that she wasn't pregnant with Jack and that I wasn't already born?" I say this even though I believe his response, mostly because Special K with sliced banana is the only thing my father ever eats for breakfast, so it is doubtful he could have invented this detail.

I hear him let out a Chuck-the-math-tutor sized sigh. "Jess," he says slowly and enunciates each word, "Because you would have been two years old at their wedding and the entire Catholic side of the Church would have needed smelling salts. As you're so fond of saying, do the math. C'mon, you know when your folks married and when you were born."

So if I'm not his child, then what is he doing in there? "So if I'm not your child then what are you doing in there?" I ask.

No answer.

I can no longer stand up without feeling like I'm on the deck of a sailboat during a tidal wave. I lean my entire body up against the doorframe for support. "Why are you freaking out on me? Is it because I made a pass at you? I'm sorry. I drank too much . . . and I thought it'd be funny. But it was stupid—your wife having just died and my mom and everything. Denny . . . "

"Yeah?"

"It was a joke . . . Denny . . . okay. I'm sorry."

"It's my fault. You didn't make a pass at me."

"Were we on the same date? I asked you to kiss me."

"Please, I've been thinking about kissing you since the minute I saw you on Monday night."

"Denny, c'mon out. I've gotta use the bathroom."

"You do?"

"Yeah, suddenly I don't feel so good," I truthfully acknowledge.

I hear a loud thud as if he's accidentally kicked the cabinet underneath the sink.

"Can't you go upstairs?" He pleads.

"Are you sick? Are you having an acid flashback or something?" I ask this as I slump to the floor on my side of the door, not feeling so seaworthy anymore myself.

"Acid? No. I feel more like I'm suddenly trapped inside an M.C. Escher lithograph and I'm slowly metamorphosing into a Gecko lizard."

"Just tell me what's wrong?" I say to the wooden door.

"Well, I just, what if we had?"

"Denny . . . "

"Hmm?"

"Did you puke on my dad's shirt?" I inquire.

I don't hear anything for a minute.

"Uh . . . no," he answers. "I don't believe so."

"Party on then!" I cheerfully announce.

No reply.

"Denny?" I say.

"Huh?"

"I really did want to kiss you. I don't know. What's wrong with that? You're a nice guy."

"Oh God. I'm not nice, Jess. I'm a terrible person. Just look at tonight. It's not even six weeks since my wife died and I'm making a pass at a teenager whose mother I had an affair with twenty-something years ago. I'd be lucky if they let me do a call-in radio show segment before hauling me off to jail, purgatory, hell, Washington,

D.C., the John Birch Society headquarters or wherever people like me are sent."

I sprawl out on the floor and try to peer through the crack between the bottom of the door and the linoleum floor. "I'm not a teenager, dammit!" I shout under the door. God, I hate it when people refer to me as a child.

"And it's not like we're in love or anything," I say quietly to the shaft of light coming from under the door. "Can't people who like one another just sometimes . . . you know, without a commitment or reason or anything?"

"This is what it must have been like to be single in the seventies," Denny laments.

"What did you say?" My voice sounds tired.

"I was reminiscing. Nothing, never mind."

"Denny, please come out," I implore.

"I can't. I can't deal with anything anymore. Honestly, I think I'm having a nervous collapse. Is there an over-the-counter remedy for dizziness and tightness in one's chest?"

I decide that although Denny may be depressed—and for good reason, having just lost his wife, and may be even slightly confused, he isn't in the throes of any psychiatric breakdown. And quite frankly, I'm getting sick of all the melodrama. After all, I have enough of my own shit to figure out. If anyone in this house is going to have a fucking breakdown, it's going to be me. I've earned it.

Rising to my feet I lean my arms against the wooden door. "You don't have to deal with it. There's nothing to deal with," I angrily say to him, or rather the door. "What are you worried about anyway? That I feel rejected or something? Just forget about it, okay? You're not as big a catch as you may think!" I bang on the door with my fist a few times to emphasize my point. "And open the goddamn door. I promise I won't attack you! We'll go into couple's therapy." For chrissakes, lifeguarding special-ed campers had never been this complicated.

"I'll go home, all right?" Denny says.

"Fine! Whatever you say." Exhausted by that previous outburst I crumple back onto the floor into a ball and hug my knees to my chest. I'm too tired to care about anything, most of all him. In fact, I'm almost asleep when I hear Denny's voice drift quietly under the door.

"Jess?" he asks hesitantly, as if he suspects that I have abandoned my post on the opposite side of the door.

"What?" I groan and don't bother to open my eyes.

"Jess, I wanted to make love to you," he finally answers in a hushed tone, barely audible, as if he is speaking from the inside of a confessional. "I became worried because that's what I wanted."

"Well, how am I supposed to deal with that?" I reply slowly but sarcastically.

"Don't. Please don't kid around. I don't know."

"Denny, just unlock the fucking door, *now*." I try to sound like Joan when she really means business. But, of course, Joan would never say fuck. At least not the Joan that I know. However, there is always the new Joan, or rather the old Joan, the writer of impassioned love letters, the engaged-to-be-married-Joan who had an affair with another woman's husband. Then there was the unrealized Joan, the Joan who'd been accepted to the University of Michigan Law school and not only didn't go, but decided not to burden her offspring with her castles in the air, under which she'd never had the opportunity to erect the foundations.

"Okay," he mumbles. "In a little while."

A lengthy pause ensues. Meanwhile I close my eyes and hope that if God is watching all this on His *All Creatures Great and Small* all-the-time video network he will hopefully decide to treat me as a long-term investment. Or at the very least, think of me as a work in progress.

"Jess?" Denny whispers.

"Huh?"

"Are you still there?"

"Yes," I reply tiredly. "I'm still here. Why?"

"Nothing."

Nothing says the man I met three days ago who has now locked himself in my bathroom.

"What are you doing?" asks Denny.

"I'm reloading Denny." I vaguely wonder if his phone number is in the book just in case I have to orchestrate an intervention before my parents get home.

I decide the floor outside the bathroom is not very comfortable and so go back to the family room and crash on the couch. A moment later I hear the bathroom door creak on its hinges followed by the sound of footsteps slowly trudging up the stairs.

"A diet at your age is ridiculous. That's just baby fat."
Aunt Ida. Thanksgiving.

"A college degree is your ticket to success."
Gene MacGuire remarking on Jess's acceptance to college.

Chapter 12
The Descent of Woman
Thursday Morning

I wake up on the couch a few minutes before seven the next morning. My mouth feels like the bottom of a fucking birdcage. The sun is already blinding me and I assume it's going to be another scorcher. I hear music. Beautiful music. Maybe I'm dead. But then I should be hearing harp music and this sounds more like a violin. I've had hangovers accompanied by ringing in the ears, but never violin concertos. I crawl off the couch, stumble to the window and look out in the backyard. The dew has already burned off the grass and there is no sign of a breeze. Denny Sinclair is standing on the back steps of the porch, looking bedraggled in his clothing from the night before, and playing some kind of classical music on his violin.

As the notes jump perfectly formed from his bow I suddenly feel ill. I grab my cigarettes and run to the bathroom and hurl a cat. Resting my face against the cool ceramic wall tiles I strike a match to a Marlboro Light. Following a long drag on my cigarette I listen to Denny play in the distance. At least he is feeling better.

After I lean over the toilet and throw up again I decide that the cigarette may not be such a good idea after all. I pitch it into the bowl and watch it swirl around and then downwards and think how fortunate I am to have a mother who regularly inserts blue Tidy Bowl cubes into all of our toilet tanks.

Mr. Edwards, the burly next door neighbor, starts shouting in a menacing, earsplitting voice, "HEY! SHUT THE HELL UP!" Mr. Edwards works a swing shift at the nearby steel plant, Russo Steel, which most locals refer to as Rustco Steel, since it polluted Lake Agnes with toxic chemicals in the early eighties. He is the self-appointed disturbing the peace police and has made a hobby of leaning out his second-story window in his ribbed undershirt and hollering a few denigrating observations about the democrats and the moral decline of America in general.

The violin music ceases and the screen door slams.

By the time Denny enters the family room I have emerged from the bathroom and concealed my eyes behind black-rimmed Revos with mirrored lenses, my all-time favorite hangover sunglasses, since they wrap around my face and cut out any light from the sides. I'm smoking another cigarette and trying to vacuum up colorful 3D pukelets—a combination of Chex Mix, Reese's Pieces, and Chee-tos—with the Dustbuster. It doesn't take long to realize that for a small household appliance, this Dustbuster makes a disproportionate amount of noise. More than I remember. After expertly knocking the ashes off the end of my cigarette I run the nozzle over them only to get lots of racket but no suction, the sound and the fury signifying nothing. I figure that Roger must have once again commandeered the portable vacuum to remove the sawdust from the bottom of his hamster cage. Mom is going to kill him.

"What's with the dawn patrol?" Denny asks over the cacophony, holding his violin in one hand and bow in the other. "What are you doing?"

"I was sleeping on the couch and I puked," I answer truthfully and switch off the annoying appliance.

"Oh. Are you ill?" He looks concerned.

"Let's just say that the wheel is spinning but the hamster is blowing her breakfast. But the question is more like, what are you doing?" I motion towards his violin.

"Nothing really. I was just waiting for you to wake up so I could say good-bye. I'm going to pack my stuff and leave."

No longer do I feel inclined to try and keep Denny captive here. Maybe it was last night or maybe it's my hangover. But I just don't give a shit.

"You've pretty much reached the point of being decorative around here, unless you know someone who can give me a job. And by the way, you don't have any stuff," I casually remind him. I lift up some dirty tumblers and carry them through to the kitchen. "You're pretty good on that ukulele."

"Runs in the family. My Uncle Mitch, my mother's brother, was a cellist with the Chicago Symphony Orchestra for twenty-three years. It broke her heart when I turned down a scholarship from the music department at Oberlin College in order to study 'compounds and clouds,' as my mother calls chemistry and climatology."

Denny follows me into the kitchen and silently watches as I lean over the sink and methodically rinse the glasses. Eventually I stop what I'm doing and turn to face him. "Listen Denny, I'm sorry. What happened last night was really stupid. Let's just forget about it. Okay?" No harm in clearing the air before he leaves. No guilt or blame on either side.

"No. Please." He waves his hands as if he's refereeing a ball game and motions for me to stop speaking. "Please. Don't say another word. It was my fault completely. I don't know what's wrong—I—"

At exactly that moment the phone rings. This sudden pealing startles me so much that I drop the glass I've been washing. It shatters loudly against the bottom of the white porcelain sink and makes me jump. "Shit!" I exclaim loudly.

"Gravity, it's a law, not just a good idea," Denny wryly observes.

I shrug my shoulders in resignation and finally pick up the handset. "Hello," I croak into the receiver.

"Good morning, Merry Sunshine! It's Mom, honey," Joan identifies herself as if I routinely mistake her for an aluminum siding saleswoman. She sounds much too loud and cheerful for my current state of mind. Not to mention that I now know about Joan's *other* life and haven't had time to think through how this has changed our relationship. I cringe and hold the phone as far away from my ear as possible.

"Who is it?" Denny whispers. A worried look crosses his face.

Covering the mouthpiece I whisper to him. "It's my mother!"

"Oh," mouths Denny, who appears as if he is not sure whether or not this should concern him.

"How are you honey?" Joan launches into her routine out-of-town inquisition. "Is everything all right? Is anything the matter?"

I sit down at the kitchen table and squeeze my eyelids tightly shut as I listen. Even this small motion launches a sharp pain in my sinus cavity. As I brush my bangs from my face I'm convinced that even my hair hurts. "I'm okay," I clear my throat and rasp in reply. "No, nothing's wrong. I mean, I sprained my wrist from carrying the family Bible around and so I haven't been able to pray or cook as much as I'd like, but otherwise everything's fine."

Denny silently observes as I try to respond to my mother's inquest.

"Don't be smart Jessica," Joan admonishes. "You sound stuffed up. Are you catching an end of summer cold, dear?"

"No. Just allergies." I shuffle some more phlegm around in my throat in an effort to prove my point.

"I just called to tell you that we're having fun and that we all miss you. How is school going?" I can hear my little brothers shouting in the background. They must have all made the journey to a payphone in order to call me. Gene is too cheap to buy a cellular phone.

"Fine. It's okay." I can't hang on much longer.

"And what else is going on?" Joan continues the interrogation in her chirpy morning voice.

"Nothing's going on Mom," I tiredly reply into the phone and then turn to Denny and slyly whisper, "I've been getting drunk with your old lover."

"What's that dear?" Joan asks, since I haven't bothered to cover the mouthpiece.

I panic and glance around the kitchen for some ideas when my eye catches the cover of the *TV Guide*. "I said I'm watching *New York Undercover*, it's a television show." Joan doesn't reply so I add, "You know, they follow the police around with a video camera. It's very real. *Cinéma vérité* I think they call it." I realize that I'm sounding desperate.

"It's awfully early to be watching a movie, Jessica. Have you had some breakfast? There's some nice bread in the freezer that you could use to whip up some French toast with maple syrup."

It was just like Joan to suggest *whipping up* some complex carbohydrate and covering it with sugar and saturated fat-based liquids when I'm fighting the worst hangover of my life. Just envisioning melted butter and gooey golden-brown syrup makes me want to barf all over again.

Meanwhile, Denny has wandered into the other room where he absentmindedly picks up the Dustbuster and begins vacuuming where I left off.

"Cut it out asshole!" I quickly bark at him. How in the hell to explain a Dustbuster running in the background when I'm supposedly the only one at home?

Denny immediately realizes his error and switches it off.

"WHAT?" Joan raises her voice, not sure if she has heard me correctly.

"CASSEROLE," I quickly yell into the receiver. "Uh, for breakfast—I'm having bacon and egg casserole. Listen, Mom, I've really gotta go. I'm going to be late."

But Joan isn't finished. "Jessica, I had to phone Barb Greenan about switching the carpool and she said that Kay Miller saw the police at the house."

"The police?" I ask very innocently, all the while picturing the uniformed officer standing in our driveway at dusk the other night and copying down the information on Denny's driver's license.

I'd worried about the neighborhood busybodies. Some of the widows on my street had added new meaning to the concept of a community watch, which, in theory, is supposed to be dedicated to crime prevention. Mrs. Miller, for one, is always spying on people and then relaying her findings to the rest of the block faster than if she shared a party phone line. "No . . . Mrs. Miller can't see very well. No wait . . . " I change my mind. "Actually, they had a lost dog."

The Spanish Imposition proceeds. "Jessica, don't take in any strays," Joan sternly warns me. Her voice rises an octave. "It could—"

"It could have rabies." Ha, I beat my mother to the punch on that old chestnut. I was down but not out. "Don't worry, no strays." I begin frantically pushing the pound sign on the phone so that it makes a beeping sound. "It's call waiting, Mom. I've gotta go. Grandma's supposed to call."

"We don't have call waiting dear," Joan mindfully points out.

"Yeah, we didn't but I signed up for a one week trial period." I cradle my perspiring forehead in my hand and briefly toy with the idea of dropping the phone down the disposal in order to bring the cross-examination to an abrupt halt. "The phone company had a special," I enthusiastically fib.

"All right then, Honey. We'll see you on Sunday afternoon, God willing. And don't forget to go to church. I love you. And so does Daddy. And remember Jess, the best sleep is the sleep you get before midnight."

"I love you too, Mom. And how could I possibly forget to go to church?" I'm about to click off when I hear my mother's voice calling out to me.

"Jessica, hang on a second. Brendan wants to say hello."

I can hear the small shrill voice spewing the eminently recognizable verse of Dr. Seuss before his mouth even reaches the receiver.

"My New Zoo, MacGuire Zoo, will make people talk.
My New Zoo, MacGuire Zoo, will make people gawk

At the strangest odd creatures that ever did walk.
I'll get, for my zoo, a new sort-of-a-hen
Who roosts in another hen's topknot, and then,—"

I hang up on him. It's one of Brendan's favorites, he changes the name McGrew to MacGuire in *If I Ran the Zoo.* My mother will be pissed that I ditched him. The psychologist said to humor Brendan's need for positive reinforcement. Too bad. I tend to agree with my Grandma Maggie, who privately believes that Brendan's "speaking in tongues" may be a sign that the last-born child is wrestling with demonic possession.

I carelessly toss the cordless phone onto the table in front of me and then drop my head down onto my folded arms. "There is no rest for the wicked," I state wearily. "My mother knows." Logic tells me she couldn't possibly know, but I often feel from the tone of her voice that she's observing me on a hidden camera.

"What do you mean she knows?" he asks with wide-eyed alarm. "What did she say?"

"Nothing. She just knows everything. Her maiden name is Polly Graph."

"You're being paranoid," Denny firmly replies.

"I suppose so."

"But I'll tell you one thing—I've been trying to persuade my company to install video telephones and I can finally see why they may not be such a good idea."

"Amen," I concur.

"Do you go to church every week?" Denny inquires.

"Only when I have to," I say. I lift my head slightly, bend my elbows and rest my chin in my palms so that I can see him. "It's not that I mind going so much as that it's just so inconvenient. I mean, in Sunday school they teach you that God is everywhere, and so why isn't it okay to worship privately, like in my bed, with the covers pulled up over my head. Besides, it pisses me off that I have to go to church and

Jack doesn't. You wouldn't believe the double standards that go on in this house. No matter if it's about curfews or keeping commitments, the boys always either make out better or catch less flak when they screw up."

"How do you mean? Why do you have to go to church and not Jack?"

"It's my father's brilliant theory that since Jack has basketball games on Saturday nights, it's too much for him to get up early for church on Sunday morning so he's allowed to attend mass on Saturday afternoon. At least he's supposed to. My brother claims that he goes to five o'clock mass with his buddies."

"That sounds fair," Denny says.

"Only on Saturday afternoons I usually run into him having a Heavenly hamburger in place of a Communion wafer at St. Burger King. Even though Jack blatantly disregards Gene's rigid 'No Church, No Allowance, No Kidding' policy, I suppose I have to give him credit for at least getting one of his friends to pick up an order of service which he turns in as proof of religious indoctrination."

I stand up and glance at the clock. "Listen Denny, I have to get an early start for once. I mean, you're just a suburban househusband and so I know that you don't understand these things, but the final exam is tomorrow and, as you've probably figured out, I'm not exactly a quick study when it comes to word problems. If I leave here in exactly twenty-five minutes then I can put in some time at the math clinic before class. After school I should stop by my grandmother's, drop the tape, write letters disputing her Medicare bills and then bank her pension check. She doesn't trust direct deposit. Then it's off to the mall for a job interview. I'm really sorry about last night and if you want to, stay here today and we can talk about it later. But only if you want to. Okay?"

Denny slowly rises from the table and looks like he is preparing to leave for good. "Thanks for everything. Um, you've been a great sport about all of this." Denny walks toward the front door. "I'm going to take off, okay?"

"Sure, whatever you say. See you around then."

Denny gingerly picks up his violin, gives me a halfhearted wave with his free hand, walks out and gently closes the front door behind him.

I am too tired and too numb to feel anything right away. Sluggishly I rise and remove an industrial-sized jar of Brand X aspirin tablets from the cabinet above the kitchen sink. At times like this I'm grateful to my father for purchasing over-the-counter medicines in bulk. I shake a handful of the aquamarine-coated pills onto the counter and select four and then chase them down with a big swig of cola. Yuck. I hate swallowing pills.

Did the last few days really happen, I wonder, or was it all a dream? I'm barely finished drinking my soda when the doorbell rings. The jarring *brrriiinngg* makes me cringe and squeeze my eyelids shut. It feels as if an airplane is taking off inside my head. If it's one of the nosy neighbors coming to borrow a cup of sugar or some shit like that I'm going to hit her really hard because I'm just not in the mood.

The front door isn't locked. It swings open and Denny reenters the house.

"Do me a big favor and clean up this broken glass, will you?" I gesture towards the sink and say this as if nothing at all has happened between the two of us. I scoop my books and shades up off the counter and head towards the entrance hall.

"Hey!" Denny yells after me, also as if nothing at all has happened, "What time will you be home?"

"About five," I call to him over my shoulder. In the driveway I try and steady myself on the bicycle. "I've got an interview at the High Seas Seafood buffet restaurant at the mall. I've been so excited about it that last night I could hardly sleep a wink. High diddily dee, it's a pirate's life for me," I deadpan.

"Congratulations. That's great. I'm sure you'll get it."

"Congratulations? Are you fucking kidding me? I have a four-year college degree in marketing and I'm being offered a lousy six-dollar an hour hostess job where I read the menu aloud for senior citizens who dodder in for the early-bird special, all in the comfort of my very own pirate costume—the Tartar Saucebuckling Queen! This is my great reward for fifteen, no sixteen years of being a good girl and going to school and believing the teachers when they said that I could be anything I wanted and that I could accomplish anything that I set my mind to!"

"Oh. Well maybe you can just view it as a career steppingstone."

"Maybe I can do some rum-running on the side and maybe you can shove a stuffed green parrot up your ass." I give him the finger and leave.

Halfway down the street I turn and glance back at my house. It stands solid on its one-third acre square lot in the middle of the block, the white aluminum siding absorbing the rays of the morning sun.

"Jesus Christ loves you and wants to help."
Father Francis O'Flaherty, Catholic Youth Organization.

"That's a good school, and then you can transfer later."
Mrs. Tidwell, high school guidance counselor.

Chapter 13
The High Cost Of Low Living
Thursday Evening

When I arrive home that evening Denny is wearing my father's blue and white-checked cotton sports jacket with the sleeves folded up about two inches. I'm tired and sullen and cranky is just around the corner and I have nothing much to say aside from, "Hey, what's up?"

"Ah, MacGuire. Party of one?" Denny has prepared a cold meal of sliced turkey breast, lettuce, tomato, potato salad and corn which, between the heat and our respective medical conditions, I regard as a very prudent culinary selection.

"Yeah, smoking." We both solemnly sit down and begin to eat.

After awhile I try to think of a way to break the awkward silence between us. "Nice jacket." It's way too hot for a jacket but I don't say so.

"Thanks, it's actually your dad's," Denny replies.

"No shit Sherlock. It looked better on the horse," I quip in an unsuccessful attempt to lighten the mood.

"Would you rather I borrow your mother's clothes?" Denny asks.

"They'd fit a lot better," I reply quite seriously.

"So what's wrong with you?" he finally asks. "Is this about last night?"

"No."

"Is it about that hostess job? I was afraid to ask. Did you get it?"

"Yes and no."

"Meaning?"

"I got the job but I was too tall for the regulation High Seas pirate costume and it costs too much to buy another one and so the manager is giving the job to a guy who is three inches shorter than I am. Can you believe that they had almost fifty applicants for this job? Most of them college grads; liberal arts, except for two water colorists and one Jungian psychology student. Meanwhile, I thought that the economy was supposed to be so good."

"Unfortunately I think that small town Michigan is still lagging behind the rest of the nation as far as employment goes. But it says something that you were chosen over so many other qualified people."

"Yeah, it says that I have a certain flair for handing out menus, setting up highchairs and tying lobster bibs around drooling adults whose arteries are erupting with cholesterol," I retort disgustedly. "Just think, my family could have gotten a ten percent discount on the Friday night fish fry. Not to mention that tempting Employee of the Month plaque hanging behind the cash register. That's a pretty big carrot to keep in mind while scrawling out the daily special in sea foam green-colored chalk."

"I'm sure that something better will turn up."

"I just thought that as long as I'm going to be stuck here for awhile, I could at least start saving some money for a car."

Actually I'm secretly relieved not to have landed the job. While filling out the application I heard Butch, the asswipe twenty-something manager, torturing an employee my mom's age: *Now Virginia, if you can lean then you can clean. And if you sit then you can quit.* I could already hear myself joining in the rhyming: *Hey Butch, if you think my work sucked, you can go and get* . . . Well, I didn't get the job so there's no point fantasizing.

"Okay, so what else is wrong? You obviously didn't have your heart set on this job. Are you mad at me? Because if you are, I wouldn't blame you for one second."

I simply shrug my shoulders and take another bite of potato salad.

"You really hit a nerve last night." He looks down at the floor and then up at the ceiling. "I do have a dirty little secret." Denny suddenly appears to be exhausted by everything that has happened. "Jess," he takes a deep breath and quickly states, "Sarah was in the process of divorcing me."

I stop eating mid-chew and look at him with an expression of such astonishment that he may as well have just announced that Puerto Rico has declared war on the United States. "You what! I mean, here I am hanging on by a thread of sanity for the past three days and giving you my very best sympathy because I think you've just lost your lifelong companion. And you're laying it on thick the entire time about fucking trips to Cape Cod and shopping at the Kmart Garden Center. And that's without even getting into this whole affair thing with my mother. Damn! You've totally used me Denny!"

The color drains from Denny's face as I rant at him. Good, it serves the lying son-of-a-bitch right. But then I suddenly realize, as he takes a deep breath and his nostrils flair, that he's not white with shame but mad as all get out.

"Shut the fuck up!" he says, or rather shouts, at me. He raises his right arm and for a second I almost think he's going to wallop me one but he slams his hand down on the table, hard.

"I've been to two funerals this year. One was for twenty-five years of marriage and the other was for my wife. And I made the Godawful mistake of telling you about it because I credited you with some maturity and intelligence, Jess. And you repay me by trying to fucking bury me! Have you heard anything I've said to you?"

This was not adult yelling at foolish child. This was adult yelling at adult. I don't know what to say. I hang my head and look down at my plate like a contrite ten-year-old. "I'm sorry. I'm so sorry, Denny. I've been listening, honest I have."

Denny exhales as he puts his other hand down on the tabletop, as if for ballast, and I can hear him sigh.

"Why don't you tell me what happened," I quietly say.

Denny takes a long look out the window. I follow his gaze to the birdfeeder. There are no seeds left. Yet two vesper sparrows tilt towards one another on the narrow aluminum perch, as if hoping that some food might miraculously appear. But it doesn't and so the sparrows seem to instead settle for a discussion on the merits of migrating to St. Petersburg versus Miami.

"About two years ago Sarah fell in love with this guy named Joe while volunteering at the Red Cross," Denny finally says.

"You mean Joe Carter who drives The Bloodmobile? The guy with the major league comb-over?" I can't help but blurt out. "He came to my high school once and gave an educational presentation about the Red Cross, after which we all tested our blood types and filled out little cards for our wallets in case we're in an accident."

"Yes, I guess so. I only met him once, at the funeral. But it wasn't just Joe." He pauses. "It was other stuff."

I realize that it's definitely none of my business but at the same time I really need to know what kind of other stuff makes a guidance counselor at my old middle school suddenly run off with The Bloodmobile guy. Sarah Sinclair had seemed like such a nice lady.

"What kind of stuff?" I ask, "I mean, if you don't mind my asking."

"We were stale. The marriage was finished. In fact, at Easter we were going to tell the kids that we were divorcing only we couldn't get everyone together and we didn't want to do it over the phone." Denny sighs. "Then the next time we were all gathered was for Sarah's funeral."

"Oh shit," I say.

"Oh shit is right," Denny responds dismally.

"Does anyone else know this?" I ask. And though I can't help but feel sorry for him, I'm still mad at him for lying the entire time. What else has he been lying about, I wonder.

"No." Denny bites down on his lower lip and shakes his head from side to side. Neither Denny nor I say anything for almost a full minute. "Just our lawyers . . . . And of course Joe. And now you."

I don't know what to say so instead I just go on automatic pilot and make the international sign that says my lips are sealed—my thumb and forefinger pressed together as I run them across my mouth in a zippering motion. A very childish thing to do I realize immediately afterwards.

"Are you going to tell your kids?" I can't help but think how awful it would be to go around believing that your parents are happily married and then suddenly finding out that it is all a lie. And why is there this conspiracy among parents to treat their children like half-wits?

"I don't know. I guess the reason that I've been so upset is that I just don't know what to do—if I should tell the kids or not. At this point what they don't know won't hurt them, but on the other hand, I feel like it's disrespectful to their memory of us as a couple not to do so. I just don't know. Right now I can barely look at them. I feel like I'm living a lie. You're smart, Jess. Should I tell them the truth?"

I prop my elbows up on the kitchen table and rest my head in my hands. I didn't think that today could possibly get any worse than having to solve third degree polynomial curves. One thing you could say about grown-ups is that once they start to self-destruct, they can produce bigger and more expensive problems than any twenty-year-old.

"I dunno Denny," I reply. "That's a tough call. I mean, nobody wants to think that their parents weren't happy together. Especially now that Sarah . . . " I think for a second and then add, "But you have to be careful. Because secrets tend to have quite a few properties in common with nuclear waste."

"What is that supposed to mean?" he asks, apparently confused by my remark or possibly thinking that I'm making some sort of indecipherable stab at humor.

"It's a lose–lose–lose situation," I say and explain my theory. "See, if you tell your family the truth then you will look like an asshole. And if you don't tell them, the information just seeps into the soil and gives everyone cancer. Or they find out about it some other way and once again, you look like an asshole."

"You're talking crap now."

"You don't believe me? Okay, here's an example: You start dating someone new and before it gets too serious the inevitable questions come up like 'Who have you slept with?' You know, 'Have you ever been in love with anyone before?' It all sounds harmless at the beginning, right? But it's death in disguise. For the rest of the relationship, every time the name of your ex comes up, or God forbid, you still run into him or her occasionally at work or social functions, it's good for a fight every time. Don't you see? You're damned if you do and damned if you don't. That's all I'm saying."

"Maybe you're right. Remember what Haldeman said? 'Once the toothpaste is out of the tube, it's hard to get it back in.'"

"Who's Haldeman?" I'm thinking that perhaps he's a fancy scientist like Madame Curie or Louis Pasteur.

"H.R. Haldeman was Richard Nixon's Chief of Staff." Denny squints over at my wrinkle-free face as if he has just been reminded that he is a redundant, prehistoric creature. Or alternatively, that I am a child.

"Oh. Well he sounds like a smart guy," I say.

"Yeah, he was. Except that he went to jail."

I pick up my fork and take a couple bites of turkey. Christ, what a day.

"Don't look so worried," Denny says. "I appreciate your concern but it's my problem. Like I said, I just felt I owed you the truth."

"Actually I had kind of a bad day," I say despondently. "I found out that I got a D on the calculus quiz we had last week. And so now if I don't get at least a C on the final exam tomorrow I'm going to fail once again and I won't get my diploma. No degree, no job, no money. The circle of life."

"I see," he replies evenly and appears to be somewhat relieved that I'm not ticked off at him.

"Why can't I be really smart, Denny?" My voice starts to break and I suddenly feel as if I'm going to cry. "I was smart once. I actually skipped the second grade. Can you believe it? Oh, I was a whiz back then, telling time like a bank clock and correctly spelling words like 'mosquito' and 'tomatoes'. I don't understand what happened. I wish that I could get good grades, not have to study and just sail into some high-paying cushy career. There are people like that, you know. I see them at school—just breezing through life and partying until they're ready to join Daddy's law firm."

"Aw, Jess. Don't put so much pressure on yourself," Denny says in a tone that I think makes my worries sound trivial or worse, inconsequential.

"Don't patronize me just because I don't have any of your grown-up problems," I angrily shoot back at him. "There's a lot of pressure on me! And it just so happens that I didn't put any of it there. It's this whole stupid system of school and grades. And you know, it's not as if anyone ever asks me what's best for me! Nobody understands me! All I have ever wanted is to get the hell out of this stupid, jerkwater, rustbelt, mistake-on-the-lake place of my birth for good. The only reason to stay here is if you're a fucking hurtleberry!"

"You forgot Podunk, parish-pump and bush league," he chimes in.

"Those too! And college is a lot more expensive than when you went. A lot more! Tuition is almost $25,000 a year, though my dad likes to refer to it as a 'sunk cost which will be the foundation of future opportunities.' That's about two hundred and ten bucks every time you put your fucking butt down in a chair in a lecture hall. I figured it out once. I feel guilty taking that kind of money from my parents. But you know, they expect you to go, they insist that you go. And so, of course, it's a lot of money, their money, and then you feel tremendous pressure to succeed. Do you have any idea how awful I felt asking them to pay again for the two classes I flunked? Even though I worked almost full-time during the school year, my seven-dollar and fifty-cents an hour job didn't even make a dent in books. A frigging accounting book costs eighty bucks and then three months later you go to turn it in, unused, unopened even, and they give you nine dollars back. My roommate donated her eggs just to pick up some cash for the phone bill and a pizza every once in awhile."

Denny appears startled, almost frightened, by this diatribe. "Listen, I know what college costs these days." He seems to struggle to make amends for his initial lack of concern.

"I . . . What do you mean she donated eggs?" Denny is apparently sidetracked as the last part of my statement sinks in.

"Not eggs. *Her* eggs. She answered an ad in the college paper and got two thousand dollars for donating her eggs so that some woman can be artificially inseminated or a gynecologist can mix up an embryo in a petri dish. Virtual reality babies."

"Wow . . . Is that legal?" Denny stares at me wide-eyed.

"I don't know." I'm annoyed by this change in subject. "I suppose so. It's advertised in all of the campus newspapers," I reply, exasperated. "What's the difference? I know a girl who works at an escort service just so she doesn't have to sling hash at some shitty fast food joint or take out millions of dollars in loans. It's a lot easier for guys to make money. They can load trucks down at the mill for twenty bucks an hour or participate in medical research. Carl earned thirty-five hundred dollars just for doing a hypertension experiment."

"Really?" Denny says, sounding astounded. "Can't women do that?"

"No. If you must know, they're afraid it will interfere with our reproduction capabilities so they rarely let us do anything unless it's specifically about women. Once I got paid to do a sleep experiment."

"What the hell is going on at these schools?" Denny angrily asks. "They're using the students as guinea pigs?"

I glare at him. Then he seems to realize that he has lost track of the problem at hand.

"Okay, okay, forgot about eggs and experiments." Denny takes a deep breath and begins to address my concerns calmly and seriously, in the manner one would approach a crisis at work or the way Planned Parenthood might explain your options right after informing you that the pregnancy test came back positive. "Okay, just hang on a second now. I put two kids through college so far and believe me, I know that it costs an arm and a leg. I remember years back when people actually hoped that their children would be smart. But nowadays, if you have an eight-year-old with good grades and medical ambitions, just thinking about the high cost of tuition is enough to make you start encouraging her not to study so much and lower her sights to pharmacy school."

"I know," I say. "My cousin has been giving her two-year-old son swimming lessons at the YMCA in the hopes that he can eventually pick up a sports scholarship."

"However I'm going to let you in on a secret," Denny says, almost conspiratorially. "Parents want to spend money on educating their kids."

By twisting my mouth into a frown I demonstrate that he's preaching to the obstreperous and inconvertible. It's just one more ring of smoke being blown at me by a grown-up as far as I'm concerned.

"Honestly. It's like spending money on yourself," Denny reasons. "There's nothing of greater value in life. Especially for a talented, good kid. And you are one." For emphasis he points his finger at the silver and black "Y" shaped chain hanging around my neck.

"Wrong Denny. For your information, I'm not a good kid. First, I'm cranky and sarcastic, chiefly to my mother. Second, I'm rebellious and I have two juvenile delinquent cards on file down at the courthouse. And most of all, I resent the fact that everything was easier for my parents. I mean, they of course don't think that. According to them, we kids today are leading the absolute life of fucking Riley. And I'm furious that I'm indebted to them because they paid for my education. Then they have four more kids who will probably go to college. Over one hundred thousand dollars for each of us to go to college! I can't make that kind of money in my first four years of working full-time. Meanwhile, this past spring I sent out over two hundred resumes, fifty-two cover letters, went on twenty-six interviews and still couldn't find a job. Just thinking about the torture and humiliation of the past six months makes me want to start the car, close the garage door and go to sleep for good. Too bad I don't even own a car in which I can commit suicide. It would probably be a challenge to kill myself by inhaling the burned rubber fumes from the tires of a ten-speed bicycle. And I just love these interviews where some gum-chewing pompous thirty-year-old in a double-breasted Italian suit yawns in my face and asks, 'So, where do you see yourself in five years?' What am I supposed to say? 'I see you being shit-canned and me in your job' or 'I'll probably be crocheting pot holders in a booby hatch somewhere if my life is still this degrading.'"

"Don't worry," Denny says reassuringly. "You'll find a job. And well, with all that money your dad saves by bulk shopping, he can afford to send his children to college!" Denny jokes.

"I'm being serious," I gripe and give him a death stare in return, "Just for a change."

"Sorry. That was stupid. Okay Jess, joking aside, your dad has a very good job, right? Your parents can afford to send you and your siblings to college."

The distraught look on my face surely makes it apparent that this logic is not working either. But Denny seems determined to say something in order to buck me up.

He takes a deep breath before offering up a fresh angle. "Okay, I'm speaking as a father now. Your parents had a family because they wanted children." He pauses for a second to work on his line of reasoning, which appears to be progressing only as he speaks. "They didn't have children so that you could make them proud and fulfill their dreams. Believe it or not, children fill voids in our lives, egos, and relationships. Gosh, I think back to all the trouble we had with our daughter Zoë. Not only did she rebel the entire time but she also had bulimia all through high school. However Sarah and I certainly didn't resent the fact that we had to try and help her to work through the problems, even when they involved her relationship with us. If anything, we felt guilty, as if we'd done something terribly wrong. You're not a burden, Jess, you—"

"You still don't get it. I can never pay them back. And I'm angry that I need their money rather than just being grateful that they're still willing to support me. And the worst part of it all is that they have total control over my life. You know what I've learned from going to college? Money means control."

"It's just nature saying that you should be out on your own but the system won't let you go quite yet," says the confident voice of experience. "I think it took a lot of courage to change your major and then go to summer school. You're the one taking the risks and doing all the work. And once you have this degree, you'll have the control. And you'll have opportunities and earning power. No one will ever be able to take all that away from you."

"Yo Ho Ho and a bottle of rum," I chant, alluding to my recent brush with Buccaneerhood. "I wish it were only that easy. Try getting a decent job with a bachelor's degree and no experience. Every place I go they want experience, but how can I gain experience if no one will give me a job? It's an impossible infinite loop," I argue. "What do you have? A master's degree?"

"Uh, actually a Ph.D."

"Wow. Really? Well your secret is safe with me. But don't you see? These days you need an MBA or a law degree. The only undergraduate major that's worth anything in the real world is computers. Even if you want to be a teacher you've only got five years after graduation to produce a master's degree. A liberal arts graduate can't even start a damn bookstore in Ann Arbor anymore and hope to eke out a meager existence."

"Why not?"

"Because people either go to those big chain superstores or buy books off the Internet. And in another ten minutes they'll be purchasing them along with everything else off interactive TV. I feel as if it's pre-WW 2 and I'm going to have to marry some guy just to get out of my parents' house. We've come full circle. The technological revolution has landed women back in the home, right where we started."

"Believe me when I tell you that having a Ph.D. has definitely not made me rich. You know what it stands for? Piled high and deep. It's the top executives in my company who rake in all of the money. And if I've learned one thing over the past thirty years, it's that you're absolutely right—money matters. And the people who say that it doesn't either weren't born with any or don't stand a chance in hell of ever making any. Money may not buy happiness but it sure can buy opportunity. Or as Lou Fisk, the head of our finance department, likes to say, 'Money is the loudest sound in any room.'"

I smile. Not my wise-ass smile but my pleasant smile. And Denny looks relieved to see it. He obviously doesn't think that anyone so young and with such a bright future should be so anxiety-ridden. And although he can't help me I really do feel that he genuinely cares.

"They should print that on the cover of the course book instead of instructions for getting beer and crepe-paper stains out of your pajamas. That way you'd see it the first day of school and could save a lot of time," I suggest. "I guess I have this inherent disgust for myself because all I want right now is MONEY! And in Sunday school they pound into you that money is the root of all evil."

"Aha, that's where you're wrong!"

"What do you mean I'm wrong? Denny, that's exactly what it says in the Bible."

Denny suddenly looks excited. "Okay, are you ready? Because I'm going to change your whole life with one piece of information."

"I can't wait," I reply glibly.

"The exact words in the Bible, Timothy 6:10, are: *For the love of money is a root of all kinds of evil.*"

"So."

"So it's not money that is the root of all evil, it's the *love* of money. Greed, in other words. Money itself is wonderful. Consider all the problems that can be solved with money, all the charities that help people through donations of money."

"Is that a fact? So you think it's okay to just want my fair share?"

"Of course. What kind of a God wouldn't want you to be able to provide for yourself and your family."

"You know what the career counselor told me?"

"What?"

"That I should rebalance my strengths."

"What does that mean?"

"He said that I was a laugh a minute and a thought an hour. And that companies prefer it the other way around."

"Yeah, well I have to agree that most companies don't have a very good sense of humor. Um, so what was your job at school?"

I give him a suspicious look, as if he may already know something about my part-time employment. "Never mind," I brush him off. "It was stupid."

"C'mon, what did you do? It's only fair. I've imparted enough secrets in the past twenty-four hours for you to ruin my entire life—not that you actually could, since I've pretty much already taken the liberty of doing so myself. But either way, it's time for a little quid pro quo here."

"Oh, all right. I worked in a back rub clinic."

Denny appears startled and I defensively jump in, "No, it's not a massage parlor. It's a legitimate back rub business."

"I didn't say anything!" Denny argues.

"Yeah, well you were thinking it. We don't give blowjobs on the side. People—a lot of students and even professors—come in and get a fifteen-minute massage for $14.95. Plus I get tips."

"Okay, okay, it's a legitimate vocation." Denny backs off.

"Why?" I taunt him. I'm starting to feel like my old self again. "You don't think I could work at a massage parlor or an escort service? I'm not pretty enough, or sufficiently endowed, perhaps?"

"I'm not getting involved in that conversation again." Denny rises from the table and starts clearing the dishes. "Just forget it. Let's talk about something else."

"Yeah, well I'd appreciate it if you didn't say anything to my parents about the back rub thing." I rise and open the freezer, allowing the cool air to wash over my face. "They wouldn't understand."

"Deal. Besides, I have no intention of speaking to your parents, ever. And I'm quite certain that the feeling is mutual."

"Thanks for dinner. Where'd you get that corn on the cob? It was really good."

"'Duh', if I may quote you. It's from your own garden."

"How should I know? I don't go out there for anything. You're the avant gardener around here."

"Very funny. You know what my grandmother said to me just before she died?" Denny asks as he stands at the sink and loads the dishwasher.

"What?"

"She said, 'Denny, always put a spoonful of sugar in the water before boiling the corn. That's the secret to sweet corn.'"

"She did not."

"She did. Though maybe it was the second last thing she said."

"Girls do NOT wear black, except for velvet-trimmed dresses."
Joan MacGuire. Week before the Senior Prom.

"If you do what you love then the money will follow."
Dr. De Vries, Stuttaford High School Graduation Speaker.

Chapter 14
Keep The Home Fires Burning
Thursday Night

Although I had made good progress on the math front so far, aside from the bad quiz news, after dinner I settle in the family room to study one last time for the following day's final exam. I absentmindedly play with my brother Brendan's slinky while trying to concentrate on my notebook.

Denny finishes straightening up the kitchen, pours himself a beer and then wanders into the family room searching for something to do. He inspects the inside of the small closet which houses the toys and games and finally selects a two hundred and fifty piece jigsaw puzzle depicting Donald Duck and his nephews, Huey, Dewey and Louie.

Denny plays around with the pieces for about ten minutes before looking up. "This is pretty simple," he announces after finishing the entire border. "So what if the age recommendation on the front of the box suggests that this puzzle is appropriate for three to eight-year-olds?"

"Why don't I go upstairs to study so that you can turn on the TV in here?" I offer.

"No, really. This is fine." Denny locates more pieces that easily fit together. "It's very relaxing."

I am feeling anything but relaxed and vigorously bounce my knee as I study. Math has always frustrated me because it just doesn't seem to have much relevance to the real world—at least my world. I know that you need it to build bridges and airplanes but those are things I had absolutely no intention of ever doing.

"This is so stupid," I finally blurt out. "When am I ever going to use this crap? Just listen to this: A boat leaves the dock at 3:30 traveling 45 mph. Another boat leaves at 3:45 traveling 60 mph. When will they meet? Well, what if they're going in opposite directions? Am I studying to be a first mate or what?"

I make up my own word problem: "A cigarette boat leaves Grand Bahama Island at midnight traveling 110 mph with 50 kilos of cocaine hidden under the fiberglass shell. The coast guard begins pursuit at midnight.

a) When will they reach Miami?
b) When will the blow get to LA? And what will be the street price?
c) If they're busted will the cops keep the coke or turn it in?
d) If they throw the stash overboard will the fish go berserk, chase sharks and get really thin?
e) If convicted, will the dealers watch *Rescue 911* reruns from prison?"

"Math comes in handy if you're measuring for carpet," Denny helpfully suggests.

"I'll fix your carpet," I say wryly. "Ever hear of a razor blade?"

"So what's your favorite food?" Denny asks.

"Why?"

"I thought that tomorrow I'd make something special, to celebrate the end of calculus."

"Let's just hope that I pass this exam so that there is an end and there is something to celebrate."

"It's better to cheat than repeat."

I glare at him.

"Just kidding. Sorry, I won't say another word."

"Aha!" Denny exclaims upon finding the last piece of his puzzle. "Sorry," he adds.

"I'm going upstairs to study."

"Suit yourself."

"That's so parental."

I go up to the room that I still share with my younger sister Katie, stretch out on my bed, light a cigarette and spread my notes across the faded purple cotton comforter with the little white peonies on it. I'm tired after so many late nights. And the lack of air-conditioning isn't exactly helping me feel up for a marathon study session. I gaze up at the laminated fire diagram that is taped above the light switch. Gene had painstakingly drawn one, to scale, of course, for every room of the house, complete with dotted red exit arrows that indicate the path to safety in case of an emergency.

Suddenly my alarm clock is going off. I'm hot and sweaty and dreaming that my final exam requires baking oatmeal cookies and that I burn them because I don't remove the tray from the oven when the timer sounds. Next thing I know, a thickset home economics teacher with fleshy upper arms is sternly announcing my failure on the evening news and saying that now I will never get hired for any job and that my education has been a complete waste of my time and my parents' money. The alarm clock, however, won't stop ringing.

I wake up and jump off the bed just as Denny rushes into the room hollering, "Fire!"

In the spot where my cigarette has fallen out of the shallow ashtray and onto the comforter there is a crater at least eight inches in diameter that extends right down through the blanket, sheets and into the mattress. Inside I can see the springs. Flames lick out the top and speed towards the edge of the bed. They move so fast that it appears the entire room will be on fire in a matter of seconds. Above the headboard one panel of curtains quickly disappears in a blaze of shriveling pale purple cotton and flourishing blue flames.

"Call the fire department!" I jump up and shout above the shriek of the smoke alarm.

But Denny has already grabbed the matching comforter off Katie's bed and beats the curtains and then throws it over my bed. Next he runs across the hall and into the bathroom. Not knowing what to do, I run after him. With a hard tug Denny pulls a planter in a macramé holder from off its brass hook in the ceiling, rips out the dirt and foliage and tosses them into the bathtub. He dunks the green plastic container into the toilet bowl and races back to the bedroom where he pulls back Katie's comforter and hurls the water down into the smoking hole, underneath where the ashtray had been. The dousing seems to neutralize any flames that had not already been extinguished by the comforter. Denny goes back for another round of water and this time neutralizes the remnants of the curtains. He moves so fast that the water barely has time to run through the tiny drainage holes in the bottom of the planter. I stand frozen next to the dresser, useless, blankly observing his flurry of activity. Denny, the one-man bucket brigade, completes the process with two more trips—another one for the mattress and one for the valence that had not yet caught fire, but was close to where the flames had been.

Upon finishing he carefully inspects the damage. "Mattresses are big trouble," he says, feeling inside the wet cavity with his fingers. "They can smolder and reignite." Denny looks over at me but I can't respond. I'm just staring at the bed in a state of semi-shock.

Denny walks up behind me and puts his arms around my shoulders, the way you might reassure a frightened child. He hugs me tightly, leans his head down and whispers in my ear, "Hey, it's okay. It's over."

"Why aren't you yelling at me? I fell asleep with a lit cigarette! I could have burned the house down! I could have killed you!" I say in a voice still full of panic.

"Why would I yell at you?" Denny asks gently, placing his hands on my shoulders and turning me around so that I'm facing him. "It was an accident."

I start to sob and push my face into Denny's chest. He stands with his arms around me and uses one hand to smooth my hair.

After a minute Denny steps away from me and says, "C'mon, I'll feel better if we take this mattress outside, just to be safe. There's really no way to tell if there are any sparks left inside."

I nod and move aside. Denny has black smudges on the front of his shirt where my face was. I try to rub away the coal black eye makeup that I know must be smeared across my cheeks.

Working in silence, we yank off what remains of the bedclothes and drag the charred mattress down the stairs and out into the backyard. It's just after sunset but the air still feels stagnant and oppressive. I can't help but think of the fits my parents will have when they find out about the fire. Joan has laid down the law about me smoking inside the house. Gene isn't even aware that I smoke. He will be mortified when he discovers the stained, half-burned mattress in his backyard—an official sign to the neighbors that the MacGuire family has been reduced to white-cracker carnie folk.

After this task is completed, Denny pours me a glass of cold water and a vodka and tonic for himself. By the time we finally take up our posts in the family room the clock on the VCR reads 9:45 PM.

Denny is the first to speak. "So," he asks without a trace of sarcasm in his voice, as if the fire never even happened, "How's the studying going?"

"I'm so sorry, Denny. What if you weren't here? Or worse, what if you had been sleeping and the house burned down? Or what if I had killed my little brothers or . . . ?"

"Well, I wasn't sleeping and nobody got hurt," he replies reassuringly. "Besides, the smoke alarm woke you and you probably would have been able to put that fire out before it got out of control. You certainly don't have to apologize to me. Save it for your folks. That room will have to be painted. Not to mention the fact that you need a new mattress, bedding and window treatments."

"Aren't you going to say something? I mean, this is the dumbest thing

I've ever done in my life and believe me, I've done a lot of stupid stuff."

"I guess if you were my kid—I don't know. Just learn from it, okay? What do you want me to say to you? You're twenty-years-old, not twelve. We've all made mistakes. And there will be more."

"I'm quitting right now. I'm never going to smoke again."

"That's one good thing then."

"What have you ever done that's stupid?"

"Haven't I told you enough already? By now you should be worrying that I've never done anything smart."

"Please tell me something else."

"Oh, all right." He pauses for a second. "I smoked like a fiend all through my late teens and early twenties. I was so addicted to Camels that I preferred to make love after enjoying a good cigarette rather than before. Then I spent the two weeks leading up to my twenty-third birthday in bed, insisting that I had a bad chest cold. I refused to see a doctor and so my mother came over and promptly called an ambulance." He laughs at the memory of what happened next before continuing. "So I, in my infinite wisdom, refused to open the door for the medics, knowing full well that they can't just abduct patients. I had my rights! Whereupon the unsinkable Helene Sinclair simply went to the phone, called the police, and sobbed that her son had a handgun pointed at his head and was going to commit suicide. The fire department arrived and started breaking my front door down with pickaxes."

"Wow. Your mother actually called the police on you?" I say with admiration.

"True love knows no boundaries. Or maybe it's more accurate to say unconditional love."

I briefly wonder if my parents would ever make such a spectacle in front of the neighbors. "So what happened? Did you go to the hospital?"

"Go to the hospital? An ambulance deposited me in the emergency room in approximately four minutes. And an hour after that, a chest x-ray revealed acute viral pneumonia. I spent the next three weeks in the hospital. It was the biggest *I told you so* in the history of motherhood. Helene reveled in it. She had given her son life twice so far and he was only twenty-three. It was immediately reported to all of her bridge and Scrabble cronies that she had single-handedly managed to wrest her son's life back from the clutches of the grim reaper in spite of his own stupidity. To this day she gives me a new scarf and pair of gloves for every birthday. Evil little woolen reminders. Why do women always have to be so . . . so right?"

"At least you only *threatened* to harm yourself."

Denny glances at the clock and then says, "I want you to come into the living room for a second."

"Why," I query like a sulky teenager.

"Because I want to show you something. That's why." He answers back as if he's addressing a sulky teenager.

"Oh, all right." I slowly follow him into the living room, which, as a result of one of Gene's beloved automatic timers, is dimly illuminated by a table lamp.

Denny goes over and turns off the lamp. I know this will screw up Gene's timer and he'll be pissed but I don't say anything. I'll blame it on my brothers. Standing in the darkened room I suddenly realize that he must be planning to kiss me. Why else would he have decided not to go home, to stay here instead?

"The weather's changing," Denny says matter-of-factly and strides over to the big picture window. I watch his dark shadow reflected in the glass.

"Hello?" I don't understand what the hell he is talking about. "I don't get it. Does this mean that Mary Poppins should be arriving soon? Because if anyone needs a nanny right now, it's definitely . . . "

"Shh. No. The cold front is moving in. This heat wave should be over by tomorrow night."

"You wanted me to come into the living room to tell me this?" I ask suspiciously.

"Just come here and look out the window." Denny returns and takes my hand and leads me to where he had been standing in front of the window. I half expect to see a bright orange mushroom cloud on the horizon, signaling that the end has indeed arrived, and not in the form of matrix multiplication madness or a failed calculus final exam, after all. I'm still thinking that he wants to kiss me so I turn and face him, only he puts his hands on my elbows and turns me back to face the window. So much for that idea.

"Do you see it?" he quietly asks.

"Oh," I finally say. "The Aurora Borealis—or rather, the airport."

"It's so clear outside tonight that you can see the planes landing. Look, there's another one not far behind it."

"So what?" I say mournfully. "It's just bills and catalogs and stuff."

"I don't know. I guess I thought that it might cheer you up. Maybe you'd still like to make a wish."

"Make a wish on mail planes?" I ask incredulously.

"Sure, why not? Where is it written that shooting stars, fountains in Italy and facedown pennies have the wish market cornered?"

"Okay." I close my eyes for a second and wish that I have so much money in the bank that I can live off of the interest for the rest of my life and not ever have to touch the principal.

I look back up at the night sky. "What's that cloudy patch over there? UPS?" I point to a section of the Heavens to the far left.

"Actually that's all the lost luggage from Northwest Airlines," he deadpans.

I giggle. Shit. I wish my parents were funny like Denny. But then maybe he's not funny with his kids. Maybe he's always asking if they have a calling card and reminding them to pump the brakes if the car goes into a skid and crap like that.

"That's the nebula that makes up the sword-handle of Orion's belt." He points skyward. "You see those three bright stars in a line? That's the belt of the great hunter and above them are Betelgeuse and Bellatrix, the shoulder stars."

"You know so much, Denny," I say, truly admiringly.

"Not really. And it's mostly just stuff out of books, not very useful. Orion is associated with stormy weather, by the way."

When we go back into the family room I finish my ice water and curl up on the couch. Denny sits down in the armchair and picks up the newspaper.

"Denny," I say languidly.

"Uh-huh," he replies without looking up.

"Tell me a story."

"What?"

"You know, a story. A bedtime story."

"Uh Jess, I'm not good at making up stories. How about I read aloud from the newspaper? There's a very good op-ed piece on government vouchers for school choice."

"Gross. Tell me a story that you know. You don't have to make it up."

He sighs and rests the paper on his lap. "All right. A story. Like *The Three Little Pigs*? Is that the kind of thing you're looking for?"

"I don't like that one. Too much violence."

"Then I guess *Goldilocks and the Three Bears* is out, too."

"Yeah. Nothing with three in it. Bad things happen in threes."

He reflects for another moment. "Okay. Once upon a time in a land far away there was a bat that lived in the jungle and—"

"Hold on a second. What's the name of the story?"

"The name? It's a fable. It's called *The Birds, The Beasts and The Bat*. So one day it comes to pass that there is going to be a war between the birds and—"

"Denny," I interrupt him again, "Come sit over here and tell it to me." Story time is probably the only thing I miss after a lifetime of going to school, and that ended in the second grade. I used to love returning from lunch and the teacher would have us all sit around her in a circle and she would read aloud to us from *The Tale of Peter Rabbit* or *Make Way for Ducklings*.

Denny carefully refolds the newspaper and tucks it beside the armchair and then moves across the room where he arranges himself on the edge of the couch, next to my folded knees. I lay my head on the cushion I use as a pillow and close my eyes.

"There was going to be a war between The Birds and The Beasts and so all the animals started to get organized."

"Why were they going to war?" I ask.

"I'm not sure. It was probably over oil, assisted suicide, God, taxes or something like that, the usual reasons. Anyway, when the birds asked the bat, which had some characteristics of both bird and beast, to fight on their side, the bat declined. You see, he insisted to them that he was not really a bird and therefore couldn't become involved with defending their positions. And when the beasts attempted to recruit the bat for their army, he insisted that he was not entirely a beast and so was unable to offer any assistance. So eventually the conflict was resolved and the birds—"

"How was it resolved?" I ask sleepily.

"How? I don't remember exactly. The ambassadors figured something out and probably the beasts were allowed to export more automobile parts to the birds or vice-versa. Anyway, after the war, the birds condemned the bat for having remained aloof throughout the battle and likewise, the beasts rejected the bat for not having taken a stand."

"Denny, you're a jerk."

"I know. But don't you want to know what happened to the bat?"

"No. Go and read the fucking newspaper."

"He was forced to live in dark corners and not show his little bat face until dusk."

I stretch my legs out in order to push him off of the sofa. And after about one minute I easily fall asleep.

"Of course I love you. It's just that I think we should see other people."
Carl Boyd, Jess's boyfriend. College Homecoming Dance.

"The answer to my prayer may require a miracle, even so, you are the Saint of miracles."
Jess MacGuire, before calculus exam. From *Prayer to St. Anthony.*

Chapter 15
I Don't Know Whether To Kill Myself Or Go Bowling
Friday Evening

The following evening I waltz through the front door and head directly to the kitchen, where I can hear all the familiar banging and clanking noises that ordinarily indicate the preparation of dinner. Denny is standing alongside the stove and wearing Joan's vermilion-colored apron with the green leaves appliqued onto the pocket.

"That's a very brave use of the color red," I tease him.

"It's ridiculous, I know. But I didn't want to spill anything on your dad's clothes. He was so kind to let me borrow them." Denny says this as he lifts a wooden spoon from a pot of boiling broccoli. "Well, did you get your grade?"

"Yup." I smile. "That's why I'm late. I waited for the grades to be posted. C plus! I passed. Not great, but it'll transfer. And even better, you're looking at a college graduate! It's official." I walk over to the white rectangular Rubbermaid garbage can and ceremoniously drop in my thick Calculus book.

"Congratulations!" he practically shouts. "Wow. It's hard to believe that you can get your mark back on the same day as the test."

"They run most of the answer sheets through an electronic grading machine. It's not the final grade, just the exam grade. But I already knew that I had a C average in the class and the exam counts for a third of the final grade. So I'll get a C, or if everybody does really lousy, the professor said there might be a curve, in which case, there's a chance I could even land a B."

"Well, congratulations again then." Denny gives me a big smile. "I knew you could do it. I'm so proud of you Jess." He pats me on the back as if together we've just succeeded in executing a big football play. And in a way, I know we have done something together because without Denny showing up when he did I'm not entirely sure that I would have gotten through this ordeal.

"I attempted to fix the air-conditioning—to no avail. I think that your dad had better call the repair company," he says.

"Thanks for trying. It's not as hot today, anyway."

"No problem. I guess I just thought that after putting out the fire I was on a roll."

"Can you just imagine if a couple of fire trucks roared up in front of the house—complete with old Mrs. Miller peering down the street with her binoculars and Mrs. Butler waiting with her B-B gun, preparing to shoot on sight if the smoke were to send any rats fleeing in her direction? Speaking of fire, my dad says that one of these days, her house, Mrs. Butler's that is, is going to get struck by lightning because she belongs to some kind of wacky religion."

"What is she? A Christian Scientist?"

"No. Something where you have to go around and get petitions signed."

"Petitions for what? What religion makes you do that? Is she a Seventh-day Adventist? Or maybe a Mormon?"

"I think they're trying to remove drunk drivers, save the ozone layer and stuff like that. I don't really know what church it is. Oh, and my dad says that they act as bodyguards for the doctors and nurses who work at the abortion clinic." I shrug my shoulders. "She hasn't come over very much since my dad put pro-life bumper stickers on all of the cars and had our priest bless the tool shed with a prayer and a splash of holy water."

"Maybe it's not a religion but a political party that she belongs to," Denny suggests as he finishes preparing dinner. "Maybe she's just a liberal democrat."

"No. It's definitely a religion. But it sounds more like an infectious disease." I think for a second. "I remember. She's Urinarian! And get this—the church closes in the summer, just like school. Can you believe it? They must believe that God goes on vacation."

Denny laughs so hard that he almost burns his hand on the stove. "I think you mean Unitarian."

And for once I'm not pissed off to be made to look stupid. I know that it's nothing personal and Denny's not trying to be patronizing. "Whatever. They're pretty wacky. Last year a whole group of Units, or whatever they're called, held a demonstration and threw charred and deformed baby dolls all over the empty lot. They were supposed to represent children who had been exposed to radiation from accidents caused by leaky nuclear reactors which they claim should be decommissioned. Then they declared the block a nuclear-free zone. The local news did a big story about it. My mother says that Mrs. Butler's daughter got divorced and came to live with her last summer and that they bonded over advocating disarmament."

"Now that you mention it, a few years ago I think I gave a donation to one of their members for interracial day camp scholarships. It was such a bizarre request, at least for around here."

Looking in the kitchen I notice that Denny has made all sorts of elaborate dinner preparations. I peek into his steaming pots. "Well aren't you Holly fucking Housewife! I can't believe you bought lobster and shrimp."

"On the fifth day, Denny created shrimp scampi and lobster gumbo," he announces with a flourish of the saltshaker. "And that's not all." Denny opens the freezer door and pulls out an ice-cream cake. "Meet Fudgie the Sperm."

"Are you trying to torture me about the High Seas job?" I respond and then drink cola directly out of the plastic jug. "Weren't you worried about being spotted at the supermarket?"

Denny whips a pair of sunglasses out of his pocket, puts them on and then pulls one of Gene's fishing hats off of the kitchen table, plunks it on his head and models for me. "Ta-da! Polish movie star."

"Yeah, right. More like Norman from *On Golden Pond*," I tease him.

"I guess that's better than Norman from the Bates Motel."

"I can't believe you actually touched that disgusting hat."

"What do you mean?" Denny asks with mock disdain. "This is a manly hat. And for your information, the art of fishing is a true calling." He gingerly removes the hat and places it back on the counter.

"If you're such an expert fisherman than tell me something."

"What?"

"Fish live in the water, right?"

"Uh-huh," he says as he takes a loaf of garlic bread out of the oven.

"And worms live on land, right?"

"Yeah, of course."

"So how do fish know about worms?"

"Simple. It's in the genetic code. Just like women are born knowing how to match clothes and men wear brown socks with a blue suit. Now, do you have any cocktail sauce for the shrimp?"

"I don't think so. Jack's allergic to shellfish so we never have it. Can't you make it by mixing ketchup and vinegar or something like that?"

"Yes, I think so. But with what?" Denny searches the shelves on the inside door of the refrigerator.

"I don't know. Maybe Tabasco sauce. Call and ask the operator. They know everything."

"Do they have a cooking hotline?" Denny inquires seriously.

"No. Just the regular operator. I do it all the time. Especially when I used to baby-sit. They know how to heat bottles, change diapers, cut cantaloupe, everything." I demonstrate by picking up the phone and pushing zero.

"But what if you get someone who doesn't know the answer?" Denny asks dubiously.

"They sit close together and you can just ask the next one. That's why you always hear laughter in the background." When my call is answered I say, "Hello, I'm sorry to bother you, but does anyone there know how to make shrimp cocktail sauce? —Sure, thanks," I reply into the mouthpiece. Then to Denny I report, "She's asking."

When another woman's voice comes on the line I recognize it immediately. "Hi Debbie." I wait for a response and say, "Yeah, I'm fine. I've been away at school." Debbie gives me the information while Denny stares at me in disbelief. I get a kick out of being able to solve problems and surprise him at the same time. "Yeah, we've got the ketchup. No kidding? Horseradish!" I continue out loud. "Great. Okay, you too. Bye-bye."

"I don't believe this," Denny says. "You missed your calling as a researcher."

"If it's free then it's for me," I reply and go to get the horseradish from the refrigerator. "Horseradish. Whodathunkit?"

Denny dumps the shrimp into the stainless steel colander that he's placed in the sink. "Oh bash!" he exclaims as a few shrimp slip out of the pot and into the drain.

"What's bash?" I ask.

"I don't know." Denny retrieves the escaped shrimp and rinses them off. "I made it up so that I wouldn't swear in front of the kids when they were little. I think my father used to say it when I was a kid. Maybe it's Polish. Do me a favor and take the salad out of the fridge."

I remove a glass bowl filled with lettuce, tomato, and cucumber and topped with radishes that resemble little flowers. "Wow. How did you make those radishes?" I am impressed.

"Didn't they teach you anything in home economics?" Denny asks.

"Home-ec? They haven't taught *that* since Domino's Pizza began delivering to Stuttaford in the late eighties. Also, it became kind of redundant to learn how to sew clothes when workers in Thailand started cranking out the same stuff for ninety-nine cents. I took shop. We rebuilt the engine of a Ford Thunderbird."

"Really. So are you a good mechanic as a result of this?"

"Oh no. But I adored Mr. Lloyd, my shop teacher. He gave me an A even though I mostly sat around painting my nails and letting the knuckle-draggers do all the work. Besides, an industrial arts teacher with two fingers missing off his left hand and only half a thumb on the right isn't exactly in a position to be critical of how other people learn shop."

"Shop, huh? I think my daughters took shopping." Denny finishes putting the food on the table. "Wash your hands and sit down for dinner."

"Okay," I say, bypassing the sink for the table, too ecstatic to even take offense at being talked to like a five-year-old. "What's going on?" I finally ask him. "You've got the biggest grin on your face."

"All right, I can't stand it anymore," he says. "There's a message for you on the answering machine."

"A message from who?"

"Whom," Denny corrects me. "Go and listen."

I rewind the message tape. I hear a male voice come on: "Tell me, you who my soul loves, where do you pasture your flock, where do you make it lie down at noon; for why should I be like one who wanders beside the flocks of your companions?"

Before the message concludes I turn to Denny, tilt my head slightly and ask in disbelief, "You wanted me to hear this shit?"

"No. Next one. What is that anyway?" Denny asks curiously. "I think that maybe a tele-marketer found God during his long distance pitch."

The evangelical voice continues: "If you do not know, O fairest among women, follow in the tracks of the flock, and pasture your kids beside the shepherd's tents."

I hit the pause button. "It's Carl," I say and can't help but smile ever so slightly. "Song of Solomon. He's never been the same since this Bible as Literature class we took last fall," I explain. "It's mandatory at most Jesuit schools."

"Well then please tell Carl that it's 'you *whom* my soul loves.' Doesn't anyone know the difference between who and whom anymore?"

I ignore his grammar lesson. "Damn, I wish that you'd picked up and said that you were my fiancé," I say wishfully. "That would have made him completely crazy," I add while forwarding through to the next message.

"When I first heard it I thought that maybe you'd applied for a job as a shepherd or . . . " Denny stops as the tape begins again. "This is it," he says and nods towards the black box.

"Hello there. This is Judd Walker calling from the personnel department at the Geller Soup Company in Oak Park, Illinois, for Miss Jessica MacGuire. I apologize for getting back to you so late but a couple of decision-makers integral to the process were on vacation. However, we'd like to offer you the position for which you interviewed. I hope we haven't lost you to any of our competitors (totally fake Ha-Ha) but the job is yours if you still want it. Unfortunately we're running a bit behind here and so it would be best if you could start the Wednesday after Labor Day. Please let me know your plans. Thank you."

I can't believe my ears. The Geller Soup Company in Chicago is offering me a job as a marketing trainee in their tomato paste division.

"A job," I shriek and hop around the room. "I've got a job and it's in Chicago and it starts on Wednesday. Can you believe it?"

"Applause, applause," Denny says and hugs me. "And it doesn't sound like they require you to dress up as a tomato."

"And they don't pay much either, five hundred dollars a week. I'll probably have to fold jeans at The Gap on the weekends just to eat."

"Five hundred dollars before taxes?"

"Unfortunately."

"Oh well. I'm sure you'll quickly double the amount of tomato paste they're selling and get a raise and eventually be running the entire tomato paste division. Then look out ketchup!"

"So why do you still look like the cat who swallowed the canary?" I eventually ask him. This is one of my mother's favorite expressions.

"What do you mean?" he says with mock surprise.

"I mean that you look smug."

"I'm just happy for you, that's all. You know, pleased that you got a job."

"Is it about Carl?"

"No. Well yes, kind of. This is going to sound stupid, but I was glad to be here when you landed your first real job."

"You mean, that you were here and not Carl."

"I guess so. Say, when did you get so smart?"

After dinner I sit at the table and light up a cigarette. This is, without a doubt, the best day of my life and I'm determined to celebrate, even if it's only with small pleasures. I'd graduated from college and found a job, all within the short space of six hours.

"Excuse me?" Denny says in an accusatory tone of voice. "But I thought that you quit smoking after our little one-alarm blaze."

"Well, I decided to quit either smoking or drinking, since I think it's only dangerous if you combine the two," I explain.

"But you are drinking." He nods towards my rum and Coke.

"Yeah, well except at meals. I can't very easily set the Formica-topped table on fire now, can I?"

Denny gives me a look of disapproval.

"Oh all right." I put out my cigarette by tossing it into the ice cubes at the bottom of my glass. "Nag nag nag."

"You just don't get it, do you?" he asks.

"What? I put it out."

Denny pushes his chair back from the table, marches over to the counter, and grabs his car keys off the counter.

"What are you doing?"

"I'm going to visit someone," he announces mysteriously.

"Huh? Since when do you go and visit people? You're in the Stuttaford Witness Protection Program. Are you coming back? Why are you acting so weird all of a sudden?" To disguise my concern for his sudden strange behavior I get up from the table and start clearing the dishes.

"I'll be back in forty-five minutes. But I'd really prefer it if you came with me."

"Oh-kay," I say hesitantly. "But at least tell me where we're going."

"It's a surprise," Denny replies.

"I hate surprises," I firmly respond. "My brother Brendan was a surprise and I had to start sharing a bedroom after he was born. Failing calculus last semester was a surprise and I had to go to summer school. I've been on the roller coaster of life; I laughed, yelled, threw up my arms and then puked. Ride over. No more surprises."

"Oh, I think you'll like this one," Denny says slyly.

"Sure, why not?" I say though I can't imagine what he's up to. "Can we get fro-yo on the way home?"

"I guess so. What is it? Where do you get it?"

"Frozen yogurt. Dairy Queen."

Within five minutes Denny is ushering me out the door to the garage and in less than fifteen minutes we're entering the tree-lined driveway that leads to the Elmhurst Retirement and Rehabilitation Center. Denny reaches over and removes a small brown bag from the glove compartment.

Once inside the main building, Denny takes my hand and, after signing us in at the front desk, leads me down a series of clean, white, fluorescent-lit hallways. It isn't by any means a romantic type of handholding. I feel more as if I'm a toddler being pulled along through the Eden Center Mall by my mother.

Denny stops at room 172 and taps lightly on the half open door, directly below two copper-colored nameplates. The bottom one reads: Jerome A. Sinclair. Without waiting for a reply Denny pushes open the door and announces, "Hi Dad! It's me, Denny."

I follow Denny into what looks like a hospital room with its breathing apparatus, metal bed tray and charts on the walls. Denny steers me towards his father, who appears smallish slouched in the shiny chrome wheelchair and has a plastic tracheotomy tube extending from his throat. Suddenly I realize that I didn't even know that Denny had a father. It is so easy to think of older people as parents and not as someone else's children.

Denny politely introduces me to Mr. Sinclair Senior and I'm surprised when the wizened old man slowly puts a cord with a microphone up to his neck and speaks through a vibration amplification device. His voice sounds as if a computer is synthesizing it. I say a polite hello to Denny's dad, as I've been trained to do, no matter what the circumstances of the introduction, whether I'm meeting someone's grandmother or Stalin. I can hardly make out the words that follow but it is obvious that Denny understands his father's awkward, burpy-sounding speech. They talk like this for a few minutes and I remain silent and try not to stare too long at anything in particular, including out the window.

Denny eventually regains my attention by saying, "Dad, Jess has brought you a cigarette." The old man's dull gray eyes suddenly light up. Denny slips me a cigarette and motions for me to hand it to his father and then he closes the door to the room, opens up the window and rolls his father's wheelchair up alongside it.

His father's hand trembles as it reaches for the white coffin nail. He holds it lovingly for a few seconds before Denny takes the cigarette, expertly lights the end, and then passes it back to his father, who greedily sucks in the smoke via a clear plastic aperture in his throat.

I watch this drama unfold with morose fascination. The scene reminds me of the cable channel that specializes in showing up-close open-heart surgeries and magnified retina reattachments. I have to peek at the screen through my fingers, mesmerized, unable to look, yet unable to turn away. All of the sudden I feel sick and think that I'm going to throw up. But Denny just smiles and observes the dying man's eyes close as he savors the nicotine.

As we get back in the car Denny considerately asks me where the nearest Dairy Queen is to be found.

"Fuck you," I say softly. "Just take me home, thanks." I want more than ever to hate him, to hit him. Denny is just another self-righteous grown-up trying to control my life. And just when I thought he was treating me as an equal. But why should that surprise me? There are lots of exceptions to the rules when it comes to calculus and grammar, so why not when it comes to life.

"He would have liked you more if it wasn't filtered." Denny carefully maneuvers the car around the Elmhurst circular driveway and heads back in the direction of my house.

I roll down the window and lean my head back. We ride in silence for several minutes.

"Won't he tell your mother that you miraculously appeared from the wilds of the Yukon?" I finally ask.

"Not a chance," replies Denny. "I go over there and sneak him a cigarette almost every day. And sometimes a Limburger cheese and onion sandwich. Though I can't decide which is more lethal—nicotine or Limburger. Anyway, he never mentions my visits to Mother. At this point, a cigarette fix is the highlight of his life."

"But you're just making him worse!" I argue. "He shouldn't be smoking at all."

"Jess. Think about it. He's got lung cancer and emphysema and probably Anthracosis."

"Isn't that a continent?"

"It's long for black lung. If you put a parakeet next to his Pall Mall polluted body it would probably gasp and then keel over. Really, what's the difference? Would you deprive a dying eighty-seven-year-old alcoholic with cirrhosis of the liver from taking a drink? Besides, I honestly believe that anticipating his next smoke is the only thing keeping him alive. There's nothing else in Dad's life. One time we brought my grandson there to visit him and when Timmy saw Dad attached to all those tubes and machines he screamed bloody murder and then started to cry uncontrollably."

We ride the rest of the way home in silence. Denny looks as if he might be feeling a twinge of guilt.

* * *

When we arrive back at 42 Ferndale Drive the house is stale with the smell of cooked broccoli and old heat.

I drag a faded blue plastic baby pool from the garage and arrange it in the middle of the family room. Then I run the garden hose inside the house and begin to fill it. "I'm going swimming," I announce, feeling the need to do something liberating. "Could be my last chance for the season. My country club membership expires on Tuesday. Thank God."

"Great," Denny says as he watches me. "We've had a death, a fire, and now we'll have a flood. Then all we need is a swarm of locusts. You might want to warn everyone to keep their first born inside this weekend."

"Oh shut-up. If you were a real man you'd have fixed the air-conditioner by now."

"Please, it's at least ten degrees cooler than it was last night."

"Yeah, and last night it was ninety-five."

"I only know how to fix window units. Besides, if your father is so cheap what's he doing with central air-conditioning anyway? Talk about a waste of money."

"That was his punishment for being away on a business trip when Brendan was born. Joan hadn't wanted my dad to go in the first place. She said that she had a presentiment that the baby was going to come early but Gene sided with the doctor. And everyone knows that Joan's presentiments are not to be trifled with. Sure enough, Gene was closing a deal in Duluth and the baby was two weeks early."

"Expectant mothers must have a newsletter or something. Sarah went out and ordered new furniture for the family room after I pulled a similar stunt." Denny sighs a *Women: can't live with 'em can't live without 'em* sigh. "I'm going to have a look at the evening paper. Do me a favor and turn on the hi-fi before you start doing your laps."

"The hi-fi?" I mock him. "How totally antediluvian."

"Okay then, the stereo," Denny corrects himself.

"No. Play me something on that fiddle of yours."

Denny appears to weigh this proposition for a few seconds before deciding against it. "No. You'll just make stupid jokes."

"I promise that I won't. I heard you playing the other morning. It was lovely. Please."

"Okay. But only if you're serious."

"Of course I am. You're amazing with that thing. I mean, just don't play a funeral dirge or something depressing like that."

"And it's not a thing. It's a violin."

I go upstairs and put on my bathing suit. My room smells awful, like a combination of a forest fire and a flooded basement. I try to air it out by opening the window, the window that had recently been covered with starched cotton curtains, protecting me all my life from the morning sunlight and the glare of nosy neighbors. Now a singed shade is all that remains.

Before heading back downstairs I go into my mother's room and check myself in the full-length mirror just to make sure my straps are all lined up and so forth. Ugh. I look like a boy. I consider going back and changing into the one-piece suit. Even if it flattens out my chest it doesn't make my ass look like a weather balloon, the way this one does. I try slouching but it only makes me look worse, like a question mark. How empty life would be without appearance anxiety. I decide changing will not improve matters and stay with the two-piece.

When I return to the family room Denny is carefully tuning his violin. While the pool fills I take out the blender and mix in vanilla ice cream, a can of frozen orange juice, some ice cubes and half a bottle of vodka. I pull the coffee table up next to the pool and rest my drink on top of it. For the finishing touches I locate some of Roger and Brendan's plastic flotilla from the closet and launch it in the kiddie pool.

Just as I'm about to step into my plastic natatorium the doorbell rings. Denny drops the newspaper and rockets off the couch as if it is a launching pad. "Who is it?" he asks me.

"How do I know?" I say and throw my bathrobe on over my bikini.

"So far my mother is the only family member with ESP," I reply.

From the safety of the family room I peep around the corner and glance toward the screen door. Through the gray steel mesh I can see the outline of yet another uniformed authority figure. "Oh Jesus, it's the cops again! You'd better hide upstairs."

Absolutely unbelievable. I walk to the door and say "Hi" with a certain amount of trepidation in my voice. At least it's a different policeman.

"Good evening," says the officer, somewhat suspiciously, I think, all the while glancing down at a clipboard and then peering over my shoulder. "Forty-two Ferndale is on my list of families on vacation. I was under the impression that no one was at home."

"Well, you see, I was supposed to go on vacation with my family but my math class ended a week later than was originally on the schedule and so I couldn't go." I spread my arms in the doorjamb like a human cross and keep shifting my shoulders from side to side in an attempt to block his view of the interior. In a counter-effort to see past me the officer keeps bobbing slightly to the left and then back to the right as if he is watching a tennis match at Wimbledon. If this continues much longer we will appear to be jitterbugging together in the doorway. "I'm staying here by myself," I add.

Either his calves give out or he finally decides that everything is okay. "Then if everything's all right, have a good weekend. You can't be too careful on a Friday night, that's usually when the kids get up to all of their mischief."

"Those crazy kids," I say knowingly. "So long then." I decide to close the heavy oak front door, heat be damned.

"You can come out," I yell towards the stairs.

"What's going on?" Denny shouts back. "Do they know I'm here?"

"Well, it seems that earlier today a man about your age and who fits your description molested some Girl Scouts at a fish market."

"Cut it out. Did my mother find out that I'm here?"

"No. Gene gives a donation to the Policemans' Benevolent Association and in return he always asks to have the house watched while we're on vacation."

I walk around the family room and draw all the window shades. Then I remove my robe and step into the shallow pool. I catch Denny stealing a glance at me in my yellow and white-striped swimsuit. I wish I could tell what he's thinking. Is he thinking that I have a good body or is he wondering who left the giraffe carcass in the family room?

"Police scare me," I add. "I always worry they know about something else I did." I sit back in the cool water, close my eyes and make like I'm very relaxed.

"What else have you done?"

"Nothing too horrendous," I reply languorously. "A few illegal, late-night pet burials in the public park."

"Is that how you got the juvenile delinquent cards?"

"No. C'mon now, play some music. I'm tired of talking."

"Only if you tell me why you got arrested."

"I didn't get arrested. They were just warnings."

"Warnings about what?"

"Fine. Toilet papering. Okay?"

He looks at me quizzically.

"You know," I explain, "We put toilet paper all over the houses of some of the teachers we didn't like."

"Oh. That's not so bad."

"It is when it rains. Now play something!"

With a shrug that says *If you insist* he stands next to the small blue plastic pool and asks if I have any requests.

"Yeah, *Turkey in the Straw*."

"Forget it." Denny puts the violin down and starts walking back to the couch.

"No, wait. I'm sorry. Play something by Hootie and the Blowfish."

"What?"

"Just kidding. Play something baroque," I say with the air of a connoisseur. The only reason that I even know the word baroque is because Carl dragged me to a medieval madrigal performed by the school drama department the previous fall.

"Something baroque, huh?" Denny says in an amused tone of voice.

He slips the violin under his chin and begins playing.

I lean my head back on the thin inflatable slide and shut my eyes. The music is enchanting.

When Denny finishes the piece and removes his bow with a flourish I give him an enthusiastic round of applause. "Denny, you should be cutting CDs or something. You're incredible."

"Thanks, but if you heard Itzhak Perlman tune his violin you wouldn't think so." He delicately settles the instrument back in its case.

"No," I protest. "Encore."

"Maybe later. It is still kind of warm, isn't it?" He looks up from the case. "So uh, what is Carl like?" I think Denny is trying to sound nonchalant. He doesn't look at me for a reply and instead busies himself with browsing through a stack of videotapes piled next to the VCR. "Perhaps a callow, pimply youth with a sparse goatee, majoring in comparative literature?"

"I don't know," I reply absentmindedly. "Tall, dark brown hair. Pretty smart. Kind of good-looking, I guess. Bio-Chem major. Premed. Why do you suddenly want to know so much about Carl?" My pulse quickens a little as I sense that Denny views Carl as somewhat of a rival.

"So are you saying that Mr. Right doesn't exist?" I ask.

"No," Denny replies thoughtfully. "I'm saying that for most people there's a Mr. or Mrs. Okay and you turn him into Mr. or Mrs. Good Enough."

"That's totally depressing." I go underwater and pretend to drown myself. Then I climb out of the pool, put my robe back on and sit down across from him on the couch.

"I become depressed when I think about the divorce rate being stuck at fifty percent. It's like you said, what are the chances of meeting that one special person? How do I know if Carl is the right one for me?"

"I don't think the risk is that you'll never meet that one special person. It's just that the chances of finding him or her a week or a month or a year after you've already walked down the aisle with someone else are awfully high," Denny says. "Like they say, it's all in the timing."

"So, uh, if you don't mind my asking, how'd you find out that Sarah was in love with Joe?"

Denny glances up at me as if he's just seen a ghost.

"Sorry, never mind," I say.

"No, that's okay," Denny says hesitantly. He takes a sip of vodka, leans back in the armchair and appears pensive. "One night," he begins slowly and quietly, "Sarah invited me out to dinner at my favorite restaurant, Bondi's—you know, about twenty miles Southwest of here." He points in the general direction of a little town called Monument.

I give a little nod to indicate that I understand the geography. Although I've never been to this Italian hotspot, I've heard that the restaurant, which is run by Sicilian immigrants, serves excellent food. My parents once went there for their anniversary celebration, only my father wasn't too pleased that they didn't serve meatballs with the spaghetti.

"And then, over a magnificent plate of veal Parmesan, and a superb bottle of red Chianti, Sarah announces, 'Denny, I'm in love with another man and I want a divorce.'"

He sips his drink and takes a deep breath before continuing. "I said, 'I don't understand,' and Sarah asked what part I didn't understand—the being in love with Joe part or the wanting a divorce part? The problem was that I did understand, both. I just—I had known for a long time that the marriage was slipping away but it was like watching a cup of coffee fall off a countertop. You see it, you think that maybe you can even catch it, but in reality you can't do a damn thing about it except clean up the mess afterwards and contemplate the brown stain on the white tiles for the rest of your life. Or maybe I didn't really want to do anything to save it. And I was just too chicken to make the first move to split up."

"You had no idea that she was seeing someone?" I ask, surprised.

"No. But I was so dumb. During the year leading up to that unenchanted evening, which I just recounted to you in its shortened form, Sarah had undergone a complete transformation. Her skin radiated the way it had when she was pregnant and she lost a little weight—I mean, she didn't need to, she was in good shape—but clothes started looking terrific on her. The jewelry she wore was flashier and there were new, brightly colored silk scarves in her wardrobe, which she draped attractively over her blouses. I assumed that it had something to do with menopause. What do I know? Jesus, it never occurred to me that Sarah had fallen in love!"

"So what happened after she told you? What did you say?" Meanwhile I'm trying to picture Denny sitting at an Italian restaurant while his marriage unravels right before his eyes.

"I asked Sarah if she wanted to marry Joe, but I was actually contemplating charging out of the restaurant, hunting Joe down and killing him for stealing my beautiful wife away from me."

"Did she want to marry Joe?"

"Sarah said that she wasn't exactly sure what would happen. But that she had decided that it was unfair to me to stay in the marriage any longer because," Denny pauses for a second and takes a deep breath before continuing, "because maybe there was still a chance for both of us—not just for her—to find relationships that could bring us happiness. Then she started to cry and apologized for not having been able to make me happy."

"Ouch," I said without meaning to. I couldn't decide whom I felt worse for; Sarah, Joe or Denny.

"We'd both known for over a decade that it wasn't working. At least Sarah had the courage to do something about it. I give her credit for having the sense to say what should have been said years earlier."

"I've never even considered the possibility of my parents falling in love with other people. It's like the idea of them having sex. It's totally yucky!" I glance up at him. I decide that this is not a very mature observation to make when someone is describing the demise of his marriage. "Although I guess my mother was in love with you. Was she?" I had to know. It was all that I had been thinking about since Denny had spilled the beans about his affair with her.

"You can imagine that I'd like to think so. But it was a long time ago and there were a lot of circumstances. It was complicated, as these things tend to be."

"Yeah, but how do you make yourself stop loving someone? Did Joan just decide that she was going to love Gene instead and forget about you? How does it work? Or did you stop loving her and that made it possible for her to stop loving you?"

"I wish I knew the answers Jess, but I don't."

"Denny, this is serious. Do you still love my mother?"

"Jess, it's not serious." He finally lets out a little chuckle, as if amused by my wide-eyed innocence, looking at life's little situations as if they are TV dramas which always have cataclysmic problems followed by commercials and definitive conclusions. "There are a lot of individuals wandering around this earth in a daze or a permanently distraught state because they're in love with a person they'll never be able to have for one reason or another. And besides, how could I possibly know how I feel about Joan? I haven't so much as spoken to her in over twenty years. We're totally different people now."

"Then why did you come here?"

"I don't know. I don't know, okay?" he says almost irritably. "I don't have all the answers you're looking for. Unfortunately being fifty only teaches you what you've screwed up in the past, Jess, not how to do it right in the future."

I'm skeptical. You could never tell with grown-ups. Sometimes they pretend to know more than they actually do and try to impress you with all of their years of experience and so-called wisdom and yet, at other times, they hold back information that you could really use, assuming that you aren't competent enough to handle it. Particularly the truth.

"Listen, want to hear something really bizarre?" Denny asks me. "After Sarah told me that she wanted to get divorced I kept thinking of that Gershwin song, *How long has this been going on*? Do you know it?"

"Is this it?" I sing, "*Kiss me once, then once more. Da Da Da . . . How long has this been going on . . .* "

"Yes, that's it. Well, I always thought the song was about some poor schmuck who finds out that his wife has been cheating on him. And then I really listened to the words for the first time just few weeks ago: *'Now I find out I was blind and oh lady, how I've lost out. I could cry salty tears. Where have I been all these years? Little wow tell me now, how long has this been goin' on?'*"

I look puzzled.

"Don't you see? It's about me. Sleepwalking through life while other people are living it." He pauses and takes another sip of his drink. "Let me tell you, I wept when I listened to those words for the first time and really heard them. I keep thinking that somehow I could have made our marriage work if only I hadn't been so oblivious to Sarah's needs."

"Denny, you can't force yourself to love someone if you don't love them anymore."

"But do you have any idea how painful it is to want to love someone and you can't?"

"If that's supposed to make me feel sorry for you, forget it."

"But Jess, I was in love with Sarah, I just didn't love her. At least I was in love when we got married. But it just sort of—oh, I don't know. I didn't do the right things, I guess. It wasn't that Sarah didn't want to have sex—she just didn't want to have sex with me. I'm telling you that I know for a fact that she and Joe were having great sex!"

"C'mon. You don't know that," I chide him and then am forced to laugh at such a ridiculous statement. At the same time I can't believe a fifty-year-old is telling me about his sex life. What would it be like if my dad sat down at the kitchen table, winked at my mom and said, "So, what about last night, huh?"

"Like hell I don't," he insists. "The woman walked around my house for almost an entire year with that look."

"What look?" I ask.

"Oh please, you know the look."

I knew the look. "Yeah. The just-fucked-look."

"Yes."

"The drink-champagne-out-of-my-high-heels-just-fucked-look."

"That's the one."

"The toesucking . . . "

"All right already."

"Sorry. I just wanted to be sure that I was following the story correctly."

"I don't think it was just sex. Sarah always complained that I wasn't a spontaneous person and that I didn't pay enough attention to the relationship."

"You mean you took it for granted?" I ask.

"Yes, I suppose so. And now I just feel so incredibly guilty. I made Sarah unhappy. I made her a prisoner in a dead marriage and then well, then she died—just when she had found a way out. Don't get me wrong, I was extremely angry that night when she first told me. But, it's important that you believe me when I say that after I realized that things were never going to click for us again, I honestly wanted Sarah to be happy. Even if that meant her marrying Joe. I contacted a lawyer to get the divorce going and I had no intention of making things difficult for her. On a piece of paper I split our assets fifty-fifty and said, 'That's your half. Take it.' And I certainly never wished for anything bad to happen to her."

"Denny, it's not your fault that Sarah died. She was in a car accident. Please, you can't take responsibility for everything."

"I know, I know." Denny slumps back in his chair. "But what should I do? What do I do now?"

"Gosh, I don't know. I mean, there's really nothing that you can do."

"This may sound crazy Jess, but I want to change. Maybe that's the one thing I can still do for Sarah. I don't want to be the old me anymore, the person who ruined her life."

"Well, you should talk to my dad about that. He'll have you at a Dale Carnegie course in ten seconds flat. Seriously, self-improvement is his drug of choice. At the end of every school year my sister Katie and I have to change the grades on our report cards to make it appear as if we didn't do very well at the beginning of the school year but pulled ahead by the final exams. You see, he prefers it if you started with a D and brought it up to an A rather than if you got straight As the entire time. I guess it shows more determination or something. Gene calls it a turnaround story and it really makes him ecstatic. He loves those sagas about Olympic gold medallists who overcome polio or kayaking accidents and go on to make tremendous comebacks."

"Well it might be worth looking into because I'm serious," Denny says. "I really want to change and I'm going to make it happen. I just finished reading a book on psychotherapy and it says that the definition of a mentally healthy person is one who is flexible and spontaneous. Are you a flexible and spontaneous person Jess?"

"I'm a little lazy but yeah, I guess so." I slowly walk over to the bar and refill both of our glasses. "I'm game for anything most of the time. And schedule changes don't bother me. Plus I can still do a handspring. At age twenty I guess that counts as being flexible."

"So how do you think I should go about doing it?" Denny asks. "Become more spontaneous, that is."

"Are you sure this isn't some sort of a mid-life crisis? Maybe it's time for the white convertible and some gold chains."

"It's funny you should say that because I do believe in the mid-life crisis. I just don't think that's my problem. It's all this other shit that's been piling up."

"So you want to change, even though you're not having a

mid-life crisis?"

"Right. In fact, I'm thinking of becoming a vegetarian."

"I don't think that's what your self-help books meant by change."

"Then what would you suggest?"

"Personally, I think that you have to throw caution to the wind and start doing things on the spur of the moment, activities that you wouldn't normally undertake. For instance, why don't we go bowling?" I suggest this even though the thought of standing in the middle of the loud bowling alley and smelling grease-soaked burgers makes me want to puke. But I want to see how he reacts.

"Bowling? You mean now?" Denny looks at me and then glances at the clock. It reads 12:35 AM.

"Yeah, c'mon. We've been drinking too much to drive. I'll call a cab." I get up off the couch and sway towards the phone.

"Jess, it's after midnight. This is crazy."

This is getting to be hard work. "So what? The bowling alley is open until 4:00 AM on Fridays and Saturdays. Denny, you said that you wanted to become spontaneous." I hold the cordless phone in my hand. "And this is how to do it. You know those old Nike commercials?"

"Yeah, yeah, 'Just do it,'" he crossly repeats the sneaker maker's slogan. "Okay, bowling it is." Denny sighs reluctantly, as if the matter is completely out of his control.

"If you want to be spontaneous then you can't act like you're being dragged along," I criticize him. "Or it'll piss off everyone else."

"Okay," Denny says with mock cheerfulness, "Let's go bowling! At least it will be air-conditioned!" He drags himself up from the armchair. "Do we need anything? I haven't been bowling in years. I don't even remember how to keep score."

"It's all done electronically now. Do you mind if we don't go?" I wonder if my voice sounds as tired as I feel. "I'm not really in the mood for bowling."

"But wait a second—you just said," Denny protests.

"Yeah, I know. But that was to get you into a spontaneous frame of mind. And it worked." I sit back down in the family room. "So we don't really have to go after all. See?"

"Oh, okay. I guess that's a relief." Denny slumps down next to me on the couch and picks up his drink from the coffee table.

"Anyway, don't try and change too much. I have this strange feeling that your daughters love you the way you are. And besides, nobody expects his or her father to be spontaneous. Dads are supposed to be stable, boring, dependable creatures of habit."

"My marriage was a mistake."

"Maybe so, but why keep insisting that you were in love with Sarah. Forgive me if I'm talking out of turn here, I don't mean any disrespect towards you or even Sarah, but if you weren't in love with your wife then you weren't in love. Just be honest about it. Why keep lying about it or trying to achieve posthumous passion. It's like you're trying to talk yourself into it. Or worse, experimenting on me to see if you can make the story sound plausible enough so that you can give yourself permission to start believing it."

"What do you mean, an experiment? That's ridiculous."

"Don't you see, if you can convince me of your love for Sarah then it must be true, right? Denny, it's not anybody's fault. It was a mismatch."

"A mismatch, that's what you think, huh? If my life were a scientific experiment I'm operating with an error margin of plus or minus 100%."

"Mismatches happen all the time, it's not anybody's fault; between brothers and sisters, parents and children, coworkers, roommates. And husbands and wives. God, look at me and my brother Jack. We can't stand one another."

"That'll change."

"I doubt it. Jack's a prime candidate for natural de-selection. At the beginning of the summer he and some friends drank a bottle of vodka that was in our freezer, refilled it with water, and then put it back in the freezer. It exploded in the middle of the night."

"My brother and I fought like cats and dogs until we were in our twenties. It's normal," Denny says. "You know what I sometimes think happened? Sarah was in love with me and I only thought that I was in love with her. I didn't even know what love was when I was in my early twenties. So I've spent the rest of my life wondering what it would have been like for me and someone else. And in the process I ruined any chance Sarah and I ever had for a healthy marriage."

"But Denny, how do you know that life with someone else would have been so great?"

"That's the problem. I'll never know how anything else would have worked out. Besides, I don't believe in second chances."

"I do. That's what summer school specializes in, those of us who didn't get it right the first time around. And let me tell you, they're doing a damn good business. Therefore, I don't think we're the only two screw-ups in the world."

"It's just too bad that when relationships don't work it seems they usually aren't evenly distributed lose–lose situations. You know what I mean? It just seems that one person loses worse than the other."

"It's the same when they're win–win," I say. "One person usually wins more."

"And the girls—I think they truly enjoy spending time with me. But," he sighs, "I think if they were aware of the pending divorce they'd hate me, or at least blame me. In so many ways I've ruined our lives with all of my stupid regrets."

"I think you'd better tell them the truth sooner or later, at least the part about you guys planning on getting divorced. Maybe not right away, but otherwise you're just going to torture yourself to death."

Denny doesn't respond to this right away. He stares over my head at the brick fireplace.

"Besides, kids usually know more than people think they do," I add.

"Funny you should say that. I was just thinking about the girls when they were young. You know, I used to love watching those Christmas specials with them. Especially that one about the Grinch, *The Grinch Who Stole Christmas*."

"It's actually called *How The Grinch Stole Christmas*," I correct Denny and then treat him to the first several verses. I burst out laughing when I see the look of astonishment on his face.

"Wow," he remarks, "You remembered all that?"

"I told you the other day, Dr. Seuss is very popular in the MacGuire house."

During the past hour or so as we talked together I made up my mind that I really do want to sleep with Denny. I'm so thrilled that my life seems to be back on course and I finally have a shot at a future. It's as if the black cloud that has been hanging over my head the past nine months has finally lifted and I can see a shaft of sunshine breaking through. Denny didn't really do anything specific to change things and yet everything started to get righted after he arrived on the scene. He's very sexy, in that rumpled sort of way. I can definitely see what attracted my mom to him. I wonder if Denny wants to make love with me, too. There should be some set of signals when one reaches this point—like holding up one finger for yes and two for no. Something to avoid that moment where you have to throw your cards on the table.

"Okay, I've got another idea for spontaneity," I announce.

"What?" Denny asks.

"Why don't we sleep together?"

Denny stops smiling and looks down intently at his bare feet, as if he's just noticed that someone has stolen his shoes. "Uh, no . . . I don't know . . . "

"What's not to know. Unless of course you don't want to. Then just say so." Though I wonder how he could have kissed me like that if that's not what he wanted.

"It's not that Jess. It's just that . . . there are so many people."

"There aren't any other people here. Only you and me. C'mon, it'll be fine." I take him by the hand and pull him up.

"Well . . . I guess. Okay," he mutters.

I'm going to lose my nerve if he keeps acting like I'm dragging him off to the dentist for a root canal. "Do you have anything?"

"No, I mean, I had a cold last week. But, uh, it's fine now. The doctor said it was from stress. I didn't even need antibiotics."

If I weren't so nervous I would laugh. "Uh, that's not exactly what I meant Denny. Do you have anything so that I don't become a single mother? Not that my parents wouldn't love grandchildren, eventually . . . "

"Oh, of course. Right! I mean no. I don't. I was going fishing."

"What does fishing have to do with it?"

"I don't know. Nothing, I guess. It just came out. I uh, I thought you modern women were on top of all this sort of stuff."

"I'll check upstairs. If my brother Jack doesn't have a few condoms lying around then I'll send him to see a shrink when he gets home." I head toward the stairs. "Hang on, I'll be right back." It's obvious that I'm going to have to do all the work if this thing is ever going to happen.

After a few minutes I reenter the family room carrying an old stamp album with condoms inserted into each of the small, square plastic compartments.

Denny hesitantly flips through the yellowing plastic inserts. "Wow, this looks like a stamp collection."

"It used to be. I think Jack switched hobbies sometime during the eighth grade."

Denny seems astonished that condoms are now available in so many varieties. He carefully selects one, examines the package and asks, "Why is this one labeled '7- Eleven, summer '00'?"

"Maybe it's his lucky rubber. I haven't a clue, Denny. Teenage boys are frightening. Jack's got a telescope in his bedroom so that he can watch Jennifer Edwards undress. Remind your daughters to always close their bedroom shades at night." But he isn't paying attention. "Hello, did you hear anything I just said?"

"Yeah, something about the Hubble telescope," he nervously mumbles. "Uh, Jess, I haven't used one of these in . . . "

"Well they haven't changed—just check the date. It's not impossible that he acquired some of them back in middle school. Condoms are the wave of the future Denny. Buy stock if you don't already have it in your pension fund. Most are made by Carter-Wallace. It trades on the New York Stock Exchange and they have sixty-percent of the market."

"I think you'll do just fine in business and marketing," Denny says.

"Trojans come in all colors so that you can too," I add.

Denny selects another condom and then hesitates. "Jess . . . I'm not sure. It's been years since I . . . with someone else . . . "

"Well how do you think I feel sleeping with a man who's wearing my father's shorts? An analyst would surely have something to say about that."

I take the condom out of his hand and examine it. "Definitely not purple. Try again."

"You do it." Denny turns away and heads to refill his glass.

"Better pay up your bar tab before you get whiskey dick," I playfully warn him.

"Jess!"

"Maybe this isn't such a good idea," I say doubtfully.

"I didn't say that I didn't want to. I just said that I wasn't sure."

He has apparently changed his mind about another drink and returns to where I'm standing by the stairs. "Maybe we should do an environmental impact study first," he suggests with apparent seriousness.

"Denny, we don't have to." I set Jack's safe-sex binder down on the coffee table. Honestly. I'll ask someone to bed. I'll get drunk and go to bed with someone that I don't care about all that much. I'll even lead someone to bed. But I won't drag someone to bed. I do have standards, low as they may be.

"No, we don't." He takes me into his arms and kisses me softly on the mouth. I love the way Denny doesn't jam his tongue down my throat like Carl does. For some reason guys my age seem to think that the tongue jam thing is really erotic, when in actuality it's one step worse than a culture for strep throat. Denny's kisses are gentle and soft and yet they grow more sensual, making me want more.

We kiss again and then we pause to take deep breaths. Denny seems unsteady.

"What's wrong?" I ask.

"I feel kind of dizzy. It must be the heat."

"Then I think you'd better come lie down in my parents' bedroom. They have a ceiling fan in there." I grab two condoms, take Denny's hand and lead him up the stairs.

I dread the idea of using my parents' bedroom but what else is there—the linoleum kitchen floor. In movies I see people making love all over the place—counters, couches, cars—but as far as I'm concerned a double bed is about the best you can do. My parents, unfortunately, have the only double bed in the house.

"I'm worried about the technology Jess. I'm not up-to-date."

"No electronic devices or marital aids, I promise. And no toegasms. Old-fashioned. Just like those Katherine Hepburn and Spencer Tracy movies that my folks love to watch. Or rather, my mom likes to watch while my father refolds all his road maps and writes out lists of the core competencies of each child in preparation for our annual allowance reviews."

"Which movie?" Denny asks.

"What's the difference Denny? They never actually showed anything back then."

"Then how do you know if they did anything?"

"Actually, I don't think they did. Number one, Katherine Hepburn's hair never fell out of that washerwoman bun and number two, wasn't Spencer Tracy a Catholic?"

We walk to the bedroom in silence. At the doorway I stop, and trying to sound very serious, I ask him, "You don't mind if I videotape us?"

"Only if you make a copy for your grandmother," Denny retorts. "What in the hell am I doing?" he mutters.

On my dad's nightstand is his battery-operated flashlight in case the power goes out. A small paperback entitled *Meditations for Daily Family Life* is perched on Mom's side with a slim leather bookmark peeking out of the top. I've never before fooled around in my parents' bedroom. This is for sure going to lead to a confession and a half. The priest will probably jump through the screen of the confessional with a camera and then add my picture to a *10 Catholics Most Likely To Be Struck By Lightning* poster over at the Vatican.

"Don't get sucked down the toilet of life and drown."
Grandpa Chester to all Jess's friends. High School Graduation.

"Life isn't fair."
Butch Wallen, manager of The High Seas Seafood Restaurant at Stuttaford Mall.

Chapter 16
Sex And The Suburban Girl
Friday Night

Just after we enter the marital bedroom the phone on the night table starts ringing.

"Shouldn't you field that call?" Denny suggests and glances suspiciously at the pealing telephone.

"Ignore it," I advise. "The machine will pick it up. It's probably a wrong number or," I joke, "my mother reminding me not to drink directly out of the milk carton."

"Just in case, maybe you should answer it," Denny calls out as he detours from the path to the bed and ducks into my parents' bathroom.

"It's probably a telemarketer offering to come over and paint the house if we'll switch our long distance carrier."

"After midnight? Seriously, who would be calling at this hour?"

"It's probably Carl," I say. The ringing finally halts as the answering machine downstairs clicks on.

I hear Denny slamming all the drawers and cabinets in the bathroom and surmise that he is frantically searching for a toothbrush or toothpaste. Well there's one for the books. I ask a guy to make love to me and the first thing he wants to do is brush his teeth. If I was in my forties or fifties I suppose I would be flattered by such a selfless act of personal hygiene. After all, it's not like he said, *Why don't we go and brush our teeth?* Still, I don't exactly relish the thought of kissing someone who tastes of mint-flavored toothpaste.

"What the fuck are you doing in there?" I yell out from a sitting position on the edge of my parents' bed. God, I'm about to back out if something doesn't happen soon. I'm starting to feel very edgy. What am I trying to prove and to who? Or rather, to whom. Haven't I accomplished what I wanted? It isn't necessary to follow through. Or is it?

"Nothing," Denny says and sounds as if he has a mouthful of toothpaste. I can only pray that my dad doesn't decide to dust for fingerprints.

"I'm going to kill you if you're brushing your teeth in there!" I holler towards the bathroom. "Get out here now."

I hear him spit. "When you're half a century old we'll see what kind of breath you have. People rot from the inside out, you know," he shouts back through the door.

The next time I hear his voice it's very soft. "Uh Jess, there's a . . . a snake in the bathtub."

"Oh shit," I say as I march into the bathroom and look into the tub.

"At first I thought it was one of those vinyl nonskid patterns which prevent people from slipping in the shower and breaking a hip," Denny explains in a whisper, as if the snake is listening, "But then I thought, who in their right mind would glue a three-dimensional five-foot boa constrictor onto their bathtub enamel? Especially one so lifelike."

Denny stands stock still, balancing himself by placing both of his hands on the edge of the sink counter and stammers, "That's an awfully big snake. Is it yours?"

I slide the glass shower door open the rest of the way and glare at the shimmering beast. "Noose," I address the snake by name, "Jack forgot to feed you again, didn't he?"

"It's my brother's," I offhandedly explain. "Noose gets hungry and then breaks out of the aquarium. Do me a favor and get him out of there. I hate touching that slimy thing."

"Uh, Jess, to tell you the truth, I don't really like snakes either, particularly hungry ones. I had a rather close call with a black mamba when I was working in Rhodesia and well, let's just say that it left a bad taste in my mouth for reptiles."

"Well I'm certainly not about to feed it any of those live mice he's got caged up in the garage," I say indignantly. "It's inhumane. However, I don't particularly like the idea of waking up with a boa constrictor around my neck either," I declare and release an involuntary shiver. "It travels through the house behind the walls and pops out in weird places. It's not exactly as if he glides through doorways with a bell around his neck."

"Great," he says.

"So what should we do?" I defer to Denny.

"You wouldn't happen to have a mongoose lying around, would you?"

"Roger has a guinea pig named Tootsie but I don't think he'd be very happy if we fed it to Noose."

"Wrong end of the food chain. I was thinking more along the lines of something that would eat a snake," Denny says as he stares into Noose's dark, beady eyes. "I've got an idea. Let's get a chicken out of the freezer, thaw it out in the microwave and then throw it in the tub and close the bathroom door. I think that generally speaking boas like to kill their food, but if he's really hungry then it should do the trick."

"Good idea," I say and skeptically eye the errant family pet that is apparently in search of a late night snack or an early-bird special, whichever comes first.

After tossing Noose a raw Perdue oven roaster chicken we sit next to each other on the edge of the bed. I think that Denny is perhaps somewhat preoccupied with the idea of a famished, carnivorous reptile on the other side of the door, one that isn't in the habit of knocking before entering a room. But I gamely proceed to kiss his cheek and start to unbutton his shirt.

Denny hastily reaches over and turns off the lamp on the night table.

"You think I've never seen gray hair before?" I inquire.

"Why waste the money?" Denny leans back onto the bed and promptly jumps up. "OUCH!" he yelps. "That snake bit me! Quick!

Turn on the light!"

I switch on the lamp closest to my side of the bed and Denny proceeds to extract a metal eyelash curler from between the sheets, right where his back had just been. He appears worried, as if he's discovered some strange sex toy. "What is this?" he asks, holding the small gleaming instrument up to the light for further scrutiny.

"It's only an eyelash curler. It's my mom's." I drop it onto the night table and once again turn off the light. We resume kissing. But this time I press myself against him and Denny starts to caress my back with his fingertips. With his left hand he gingerly slides a bathing suit strap off my shoulder.

Denny abruptly stops kissing me. Damn, just when the toothpaste was starting to fade.

"Does she sleep with it on?" he asks.

"No. It probably fell out when she was packing," I reply. "Now shut up."

"It looks like some medieval torture device."

I pull away from him and turn the light back on. "It is. Try it sometime. Listen, Denny, I get the feeling that you aren't really into this. And that's okay. But . . . "

"No, I am! I'm—I'm just thinking that . . . I was just thinking . . . "

"Thinking what?" I ask crossly.

"Thinking that uh, that well, that maybe we're consuming too much fuel as a nation."

"Lie face down on the bed," I instruct him as I pull up the strap to my bathing suit top.

"Why?" he nervously asks.

"Trust me. Just do it."

Denny looks at me warily but finally acquiesces and flops down on the bed with his face turned sideways on the pillow. I switch off the lights for the third time.

"What are we doing?" Denny whispers tensely. "I hope that whatever it is, it doesn't have to do with role playing."

"With *what?*"

"You know, pretending we're different people. I have to do it at corporate management seminars and it's really stupid."

After removing his shirt I straddle Denny with one knee on each side of his waist and begin to massage his back and shoulders.

"Oh, God." He shudders slightly. "That feels so good."

"Just relax. You're way too tense."

"I know. Why do you think I drink so much? It's strictly medicinal."

"Shut-up. Has anyone ever told you that you talk way too much in bed?"

"No. Ouch," Denny cries out as I knead his back with my hands.

"Sorry, I slipped. You're sweaty from the heat," I explain. For some reason I'm reminded of my first frat party freshman year of college when this really handsome basketball player asked me back to his dorm and I wound up getting so drunk that I passed out and never ended up sleeping with him. At least I don't think that I did. Maybe this thing with Denny and me just isn't meant to be. Some folks are married and divorced in less time than we've been circling each other.

"You have knots in your muscles that feel like cement pilings," I add.

"Is that bad?"

"You should probably do relaxation therapy. You know, yoga or meditation or something like that." I continue to give him my best back massage, the $15.00 one. My mind wanders to the exciting prospect of informing my parents that I've landed a job marketing tomato paste, or more likely, making photocopies for the people who market tomato paste. But no matter, after twenty years I'm finally off the MacGuire family payroll. Gene will be especially thrilled that he need no longer regard me as a 'non-performing asset.' Sure, it isn't tomato sauce or tomato soup or even ketchup, but it's a start. And as far as Gene is concerned, joining the ranks of Corporate America is the ultimate victory. I wish there were some way I could call them. Oh well, they'd be home the day after tomorrow. Soon enough, I suppose. My mind wanders some more. I'll move away and get a studio apartment.

Katie can have my bicycle. I'll take the El in Chicago. In my little fantasy I'll come home for holidays with an armful of great presents for all the members of my family. And Jack will either be pumping gas or clerking at the convenience store and have to give everyone candy bars or magazines as gifts.

I slowly and precisely massage Denny's muscles all the way up to his neck. "Okay, get ready," I finally announce. "This is it!" I'm breathing hard as I lightly pummel my fists all over his back for the finale. Afterwards I collapse on the bed next to him in a mock state of exhaustion.

Denny rolls onto his side and faces me. My body is slick with perspiration. "Aren't you tired after all that?" He asks.

"Not really. At work I used to do eight or sometimes ten a day."

"Well, thanks," he says and exhales loudly. "I feel much better."

"Yeah, that's because now all of your bad energy is pulsing through my veins."

"But that was really incredible," Denny enthuses. "Did they teach you how to do that at work?"

"Sort of. The manager gives a two-day training class at the start of every month and then you just figure out what works and what doesn't along the way—it's kind of like learning how to drive. But the manager is a licensed massage therapist. The rest of us are just hacks. Do you really feel more relaxed?"

"Definitely. Actually, I feel kind of worn out."

Figures. I must have that effect on people. "I noticed that you don't breathe very much," I say seriously. "You should try to take deeper breaths. Maybe that's why you get dizzy. But you have great muscle tone. You're really strong."

"You sound surprised."

"Well, I've done a lot of backs and, unless they work out regularly, most people get flabby. Do you exercise?"

"Kind of. At work we have sample cases of rocks and I lift out the biggest ones and put them in my head."

"That explains a lot." I make idle chatter while trying to figure out how to revitalize the sex thing.

"Actually, I used to be a boxer."

"Oh."

Our bodies glisten with sweat and our faces are only inches apart from one another. Suddenly the phone on the night table starts ringing again. Simultaneously, lime-green bolts of heat lightning flash outside, momentarily illuminating an endless grid of fenced-in backyards. Denny is startled by the noise and jumps slightly. I lean over and unplug the phone. I'm sure it's the Vatican calling to confirm whether or not the lightning was on target. They've probably got me on speed dial by now.

"That phone is spooking me," he says in a hushed voice. "It knows something."

"Forget about it. Jack's drinking buddies are always calling on Friday and Saturday nights." I inch a little closer. He doesn't move away. "Are you sure that you brushed those choppers?" I tease him.

"Yeah, why?" Denny looks away from me. "Do I have harmful breath?"

Why did I say such a dumb thing? He's probably going to run back into the bathroom. I put my hand up to his chin and turn his face to mine. "Let me see." I lean closer and press my mouth against his warm lips. Denny responds by pulling my body closer and running his hands up and down the backs of my legs. Something about caressing my thighs seems to wake him the fuck up and he begins to breathe deeply and lightly runs his mouth across my chest and shoulders—just barely leaving a trail of kisses as a bumblebee ever-so-briefly alights on a flower.

I rub my hand against the front of the khaki shorts that he'd borrowed from Gene's closet and whisper, "Shouldn't you put it on?"

"In a minute. Jesus, slow down a little."

Without removing my bikini bottom Denny slips one hand inside the front of it and gently feels his way around. I take a sharp breath and tense my entire body.

"What's wrong. Is that okay?" Denny asks as he continues to move his finger inside of me and delicately kisses my neck.

"Um, yeah." I writhe ever so slightly beneath his touch. I feel way self-conscious, bordering on embarrassment. The hot-blooded, young Lotharios in my crowd can't climb on top of their coed girlfriends fast enough. Never before have I experienced the full attention of a man concentrating solely on giving me pleasure. My legs are modestly close together. Using his free hand Denny reaches down and gently nudges the insides of my knees in order to move my thighs slightly further apart. I'm suddenly nervous. I seriously consider bailing out or passing out or something that ends in the word *out*.

But Denny starts to create an incredible sensation within me. I arch my back slightly and place my palm across my face, as if I'm shielding my eyes from the sun. Denny moves more vigorously until I feel a tingling sensation from my waist all the way up to my shoulders. And when the final jolt of electricity is imminent, I'm torn between simultaneously fending off and welcoming my body's response. When the moment arrives I just close my eyes and let out a huge sigh of relief. Never before have I had an orgasm without intercourse and certainly never one of such intensity.

Without saying a word, Denny quickly removes the rest of his clothes and puts on the condom.

"This is kind of a weird order of doing things isn't it?" I ask him.

"Climax insurance. This way, no matter what happens, you don't go away empty-handed. And I don't have to list my age group as nostalgic during the next census." He gently removes my bikini bottoms, which slide off easily down my straight legs.

Once more Denny leans down and tenderly overlaps my parted lips with his. And then he expertly enters me and sets a rhythm that I easily emulate. I wrap my arms tightly above his waist and draw his body even closer to mine.

In the small beam of moonlight that is peeking through the white lace curtains we can just barely make out the curious expressions on each other's faces.

"I'm not hurting you am I?" he leans forward and whispers.

"No," I answer softly. I can feel his heart beating as he presses against me. Or maybe that's my heart. Although I'm pretty sure my heart stopped for good about three minutes ago. "I'm sorry," he says.

"Why?" I ask.

But Denny doesn't respond. After another minute he lowers his face and manages to say, "I can't last . . . " before exploding inside of me.

Denny deftly shifts his body and carefully removes the condom to make sure there won't be any telltale signs of our liaison. He turns on the light and then returns to a sitting position next to me in the bed. "I'm afraid that last part wasn't very good for you. Sorry."

"Mmm," I say. "No. It was. I—I never quite bounced back from the first part. Most of the guys I've slept with—it's more like slam-bam-thank-you-ma'am."

"Oh. Don't you ever masturbate?" Denny asks me.

"Denny . . . " I look away from him. I feel myself blush and tug the sheet up over my head.

"I can't believe it. I've actually embarrassed you! Miss-ask-me-anything." Denny pulls himself up and leans against the headboard and delightedly laughs out loud. "Well do you or don't you?"

"I am not embarrassed," I reply indignantly and move the sheet back down to neck level. "You just caught me off guard, that's all. Why? Do you?"

"Oh, please," Denny replies, still chuckling, "Any guy who says he doesn't is lying. I mean—not so much now as when I was a younger," he adds. "But I asked you the question, didn't I? And I have no intention of letting you off the hook."

"Well sort of. I mean, I guess," I answer evasively.

"That's like being sort of pregnant. The judges will put that down as a yes."

"Well," I say and stall for a few seconds. "I've started but never really finished."

"That's fair," Denny says. "The judges will leave that as a 'sort of.'"

"I have roommates," I say defensively. "And I always got the impression that the Sunday school teachers had something against it."

"You don't have to make excuses," he says.

"Do you think that's unnatural?" I ask shyly.

"No, of course not. The whole point of sex is to do what feels right. That's the only way it can ever feel good."

"It's obvious that you don't go to church. If you did, then you might not think so. Do you talk to your kids like this?"

"Are you kidding me? It's different when it's your own daughters—you don't ever want them to have sex and you worry that every guy is just after one thing. Besides, I really can't imagine sitting around the dinner table, buttering my roll, and asking the girls if they've tried any good contraceptive foams lately. Just like I'm sure that you can't picture talking to your dad about sex."

"Definitely not," I agree. "My dad won't even go in the laundry room if there's a bra hanging in there to dry."

"He doesn't know what he's missing. Lingerie hanging out to dry is the eighth wonder of the world. On second thought, make the dangling brassiere the seventh and put the Lighthouse on the Isle of Pharos down as eight. I think I can safely say that I'm speaking for all of mankind on this one. I mean, how many lighthouses has Victoria's Secret sold this year?"

"Don't make fun of lighthouses. Being a lighthouse keeper is still my backup career."

"So, uh, how many guys have you slept with?" Denny asks offhandedly.

But I sense a feigned indifference. "Why? Are you jealous?" I counter.

"No, just curious."

"One, two, three," I hastily tick them off on my fingers. I pause at three, roll my eyes up towards the ceiling and grimace. "That one was so stupid. The things we do when there's nothing on TV." Then I briskly continue, "Four, five—does Amanda the lesbian thespian count?"

"No," Denny quickly replies. As the count increases I think that maybe he is starting to look concerned, as if he is secretly hoping for a low number.

"Now it's just the number of different guys. Not number of times with each one," he carefully restates the contest guidelines.

"Duh! Okay, without Amanda it's five. Wait a second, should I include you?"

"No," he officiates with conviction.

"Well, then it's five."

"Oh." Denny exhales. "Five, that's not too bad."

"Why do you want to know? For some reason it seems like every guy I go out with asks this question. Did you think I was some sort of professional mattress tester, the town nympho perhaps? Please. Give me a break!"

"How the hell do I know? You sure talk an awfully good game."

"Yeah, I guess I do. Lightly armored, heavily armed. That's me." I giggle. "What about you?"

"Me?"

"Yeah, you. Is there anyone else here?" I add sarcastically and pretend to look around the room.

"Yeah," Denny replies more to himself, "There are probably about five people here."

"C'mon, tell me how many people you've bedded," I persist.

"Women, not people," Denny corrects me. "I've only slept with women."

"Ugh, that's *so* hetero," I say and start to count for him. "There's Sarah and Joan. Ha! I just realized that my mother got you stuck on permanent K.P. That's two right there."

"Okay," Denny says seriously. "We're going back a long way here, about three decades. But let me see." Denny thinks for a moment before completing his list. "Well, Evelyn was the first and then there was Robin in the Peace Corps."

"Robin could be the name of a guy. You know, Batman and Robin."

But I don't really care how many women Denny has slept with, I just pretend to. What I really want to know is if the sex was good for Denny. He didn't say anything afterwards. Maybe I was the only one who enjoyed it.

"Well it wasn't a guy," he says. "I can't really remember if that was it. Sarah and I actually had this conversation right after we were married."

"So it's four then?" I ask.

Denny considers the question once more and finally says, "No. There was Marsha. I was so nervous about getting engaged to Sarah that I had sex with Marsha the week before I bought the ring, just to make sure. So she's five and you make six."

"I'm not even going to bother asking you how sleeping with Marsha could have possibly helped you decide whether or not to marry someone else. Because I don't have to ask you. It sounds exactly like the kind of thing that Carl and every other guy I know would do."

"Then I'm glad that you're not going to ask," he says. "It's good not to be too judgmental, especially at your age."

"That's not so many. I mean, for a guy your age."

"That's not fair. First, I've been married the past quarter century and second, it was different back when I was single," Denny says defensively. "In the sixties nice girls didn't go all the way. And The Pill was barely out of the research pipeline. Besides, I was a shy kind of guy. I didn't meet a lot of women. And in the program for climaxology—whoops, I mean climatology . . . "

We both laugh at his slip.

"In the sciences there weren't any women. Well, there were the odd ones but then they really were odd ones," he finishes.

"So then where'd you meet Sarah?"

"At a hootenanny."

"A what?" I smile at the silliness of the word.

"A hootenanny. You know, a songfest. A lot of young people getting together to hear popular music."

"Oh, you mean like a rave?"

"Sort of. We'd sing *If I Had a Hammer*, *Kumbaya*, *Where Have All the Flowers Gone*, and other songs about peace and creating labor unions. A guy would set fire to his draft card, a few women would burn their bras and then we'd go home to our white, middle-class suburban families in segregated neighborhoods. In fact, I still remember the first time Sarah and I held hands. A Peter, Paul and Mary style folk group called the Rainbow Combination was singing *Puff the Magic Dragon* down at Birchfield Park and we sat down by the creek together, just the two of us, and she took my hand. After that Puff was our song. We even had the band play it at our wedding."

"My parents probably loved Peter, Paul and Mary. Three Saints in one band. A Biblical tri-fecta!" I decide it's probably best not to dwell on Sarah. "Hey, I know *Kumbaya*, I announce.

"How many verses?"

After quickly running through the words in my head I reply, "I didn't know there were any other verses."

"Four. See, if you had gone to Bible camp then you'd know them all."

"Anyway, you're number six for me too," I say. "Not counting Amanda."

"She definitely doesn't count," Denny reiterates.

"Why not?" I appeal this decision.

"Six is lucky," he says illogically. "I'd like it if we were both on six."

"Six isn't lucky. It's the number for the devil."

"But only if you have three sixes."

I can't stand it anymore. "So what did you think?" I ask tentatively.

"What did I think about what? Uh-oh. You're asking what I thought about the lovemaking aren't you?"

"Of course."

"Jess, it's not some sort of test."

"Then why did you need to take out insurance?"

"That's different."

"How's that?"

"Right now, this is the reason for smoking. After sex you're just supposed to light up and think nice thoughts."

"Oh," I reply somewhat dejectedly. I guess this means it wasn't that good. Denny sees my expression and appears concerned.

"Jess, I know you're not inexperienced so please don't take this the wrong way."

Oh boy, I think. It must have really been bad.

"Making love with you was wonderful. You're a fantastic lover."

I'm relieved. I also like the way he says *making love* and *lover*. It sounds very sophisticated.

"But well, let's see, how best to explain this. Okay, two things. First, good sex is kind of like having your hair on fire; just in that it is or it isn't. No one goes around asking, 'Can you just look in the back there and tell me if my hair is on fire?'"

"And the second thing?" I ask.

"Ah yes, the second thing." Denny leans over and gently brushes my hair off my face and kisses me lightly on the cheek. "You're beautiful."

"That's the second thing?" I ask, confused.

"No. The second thing is don't ever ask a guy what he thinks of you because you're great and that's all you need to know and if he doesn't like you then he should just get lost. Because good sex, just like a good relationship, should make you feel good about yourself."

"Oh."

"So don't make me send you for a high self-esteem week with your dad," he adds impishly and rests his palm on my bare thigh.

"Got it. Don't you want to know how you were?"

"Sure, but I'd rather you fill out my survey card at the end and mail it in so I can make sure I have the proper professionals standing by."

"You've got a lot of wind for an old bag," I say.

"You're too kind."

"So now I understand the mystery of the older, experienced lover."

"Yeah, well I was a lot more, I don't know, a lot more impatient when I was younger," Denny admits. "And believe it or not, sex can get boring after twenty or so years with the same person if you don't experiment a bit. I don't mean anything kinky—just exploring some different possibilities. For instance, when your wife is seven months pregnant, you have to be rather creative."

Talk of pregnant women makes me think of ice cream. "Want some ice cream?" I say and get up and pull on my mom's robe, which is conveniently hanging on one of the bedposts.

"You want ice cream?" Denny asks, sounding surprised.

"Yeah. It's either that or light up a smoke." I glance at him hopefully.

"Ice cream it is!" He also starts to rise.

"Stay here. I'll bring it up." I head towards the hallway.

By the time I reenter the bedroom carrying a quart of ice cream and two spoons, Denny has propped the pillows up against the headboard so that we can comfortably sit up in bed. "Flavor?" he inquires.

"Choc-van-straw. It's the only kind we carry. Otherwise there's a family feud. All the J's in the family like vanilla, while my dad and Katie insist upon strawberry and my little brothers only eat chocolate—which happens to be about the only thing in the entire world which they agree on aside from the joys of worms."

"What are the J's?"

"Joan, Jessica, and Jack. And Gene sounds like a J." My mother thought it would be cute to name all of her kids starting with the letter J."

We sit in bed and attempt to spoon down some ice cream before it melts. Condensation slowly drips from the carton and trickles onto the starched white cotton sheets. I accidentally drop the lid onto the bed, sticky side down. "Oh Harold!" I declare as someone might say, "Oh shit."

"Who is Harold? Did you sleep with a Harold?"

"No. I never slept with a Harold. It's just a word. You know, like Bash. My parents take away money from our allowances if we say 'Oh, Hell' or 'Goddamn.'"

"But why Harold?"

"You know, Our Father who art in heaven, Harold be thy name."

"So why didn't your mother finish with the J's? You said that you have a brother named Brendan?"

"Yeah. And Roger. But Katie's name is actually Justine, Justine Katherine. You see, my mom was home from the hospital for about three days after Katie was born when my dad developed a stammer every time he tried to talk to or about any member of the family. Then my grandmother became so addled that when she went to buy us savings bonds she screwed up all the names on them. She said it would have been easier if my mother had named us after the Seven Dwarfs. That was essentially the end of the J concept, aside from a goldfish named Jeremiah. And I had a twin brother named James. But he died a few minutes after being born."

"Oh! I'm sorry." Denny looks up, startled. "I didn't know that."

"That's okay. Obviously it was a long time ago—twenty years. I guess it shouldn't really affect me," I say thoughtfully. "But I can't help thinking that James would have been the golden child. You know, a great student, terrific athlete, altar boy, polite, all that stuff. And I'm the evil twin. The immaculate misconception." I have given this theory some serious consideration over the years.

"Wow Jess. That's pretty heavy penance just for being born." Denny passes the ice cream carton back to me.

"You remember my dog Benny, the one in the picture?"

"Y-es," he says slowly as if he doesn't quite grasp the connection to the dead brother.

"Well, when we went to get the dogs," I explain, "I was six and Jack was about three and we were each allowed to pick one dog from a litter of seven. Benny was walking towards the corner of the yard and I could see right away that he was lame. He was staying away from the rest of the puppies, like Rudolph at the beginning of *Rudolph the Red-Nosed Reindeer*, when he isn't allowed to join in any of the reindeer games. Anyway, Jack picked out Maxy and when it was my turn I told my father that I wanted the three-legged puppy. But he said to pick out another one so I went over to Benny and started to cry until my mom talked him into it."

"This sounds like one of those tearjerker animal movies for children like *Benji The Hunted.*"

"Yeah, well when I was around five-years-old, my mother—she would always sob after my birthday parties—explained to me that James died because if God sees that you're going to be born all wrong and live in pain then He sometimes decides it's better to take you to heaven right away. So I thought . . . "

"You thought you could save Benny before God took him away."

"Something like that. I was only six. Anyway, I don't want to talk about it. I really miss that stupid dog." Scraping out the inside of the container with my spoon I decide to change the subject because I'm feeling soggy and otherwise I think I may start to cry. "Say that you killed someone and had to get rid of the body. How would you do it?"

"That's a horrible thought," Denny says and grimaces.

"Okay, well say you didn't murder the person but that you had to get rid of a dead body so that no one would find it. Like, maybe it's for a friend or something."

"Is this a problem you're currently facing?" Denny inquires.

"No, but I think it's good exercise for the mind to consider hypothetical situations, so you're prepared in case one ever comes up for real."

"Oh. Kind of like a premature extrapolation?"

I ignore his remark and enthusiastically explain my thinking on this subject. "You know what I'd do? If I were near a college I'd take the body and dump it outside of the medical school late at night. I've heard that they're always on the lookout for fresh cadavers to dissect. And that some even give kickbacks to nursing homes in order to line up more stiffs."

"Are you sure this is legal?" Denny asks distractedly.

"Selling corpses?" I wave my hand in the air. "No, of course not, but if you . . . "

"No, not that. Us. Is this illegal? How old are you again?"

"Are you kidding? I'm twenty—almost twenty-one. Besides, I think you only have to be fifteen in this state to get married, even if it's to your second cousin."

"I'd feel better about twenty-one. It sounds much more lawful."

"Twenty is legal. I mean, at least as long as you don't pay me then it's legal. It's perfectly legitimate to give sex away. You just can't sell it. Then it's illegal."

"So what happens on Monday?" Denny asks somberly, as if he knows full well what the answer is going to be.

"I leave for Chicago, I guess," I reply. "This job starts on Wednesday, in five days, and I don't even have a place to stay yet."

"And on Tuesday I go back to work," Denny says rhetorically.

"So?"

"Nothing. Some of the best trout streams in the world are catch and release. It doesn't diminish the fishing experience."

"What kind of fish am I, Denny?" I ask. Although what I really want to know is, how exactly was the fishing experience.

"You're, let's see . . . that's a difficult one." Denny stares at me for a long moment as if he is trying to drink me all in at once.

"And it better not be some frigging bottom fish such as a halibut or something gross-looking like a dirty old catfish."

"Your eyes have a way of changing from green to gray, like breakers on a beach running from sunlight to shade. Therefore I picture you as an ocean fish. No rivers or small ponds for you, positively not a perch or a striped bass," he says decidedly.

"Well thank God for small favors."

"How about a mullet?" He suggests.

"I don't even know what a mullet is but it sounds disgusting."

"It is. Gray, cylindrical, your basic suckerfish. Definitely not you. Just some angler humor."

Denny pretends he is a medium receiving a vision and for some reason this makes me giggle. With his eyes tightly shut and his fingers pressed to his temples he continues, "Let's see, there's fluke, flounder and sturgeon . . ."

"Sturgeon sounds yucky."

"Don't be so fast to judge, sturgeon can have lovely caviar inside."

"No sturgeon."

"Possibly an angelfish? No, too much preening. Maybe striped bass, zebrafish, bluefish, sunfish."

"Sunfish sounds nice."

"No. Too fat. You wouldn't like that. I know, you like to wear black. How about a blackfish?"

"No, I've decided to move out of my black phase."

"Codfish?" he asks teasingly and opens his eyes.

"Cut it out." I push on his shoulders with both of my hands but he grabs my arms and pretends to fall backwards on the bed with me on top of him. We both laugh.

Denny kisses me on the mouth. "Hmm. You're a tasty fish. Perhaps a pompano?"

"That sounds like a Mardi Gras float. Now be serious. What fish am I?"

"Okay. You're broad and shiny and beautiful to gaze upon; perhaps a flying fish, a sailfish or a even swordfish, but you're very difficult to catch."

"How's that?" I ask. "You caught me."

"Ha!" He rolls us over so that he is squatting above me, straddling my waist but with his weight on his knees, and looks into my eyes. "Hardly! I saw you break up through the waves for a tiny instant while the sun broke above the horizon. I touched your dorsal fin as it sparkled through the spray—that's it! You're a blue marlin! A blue marlin in the Gulf Stream, genus Makaira."

"That's nice." I clap my hands above my chest.

"Or how about a mermaid?"

"No way. Mermaids are neither here nor there. They can't live on land and yet they don't entirely belong with the other sea creatures and so have to hang out on rocks in the middle of nowhere pining away. And besides, whom do they date? I mean, you never see any guy mermaids. The blue marlin idea is much better. A fish that can drag a boat with a couple of beer-swilling guys in it. Now that's a fish!"

"Blue marlin it is then!" He pauses for a few seconds. "So I guess we're not going to have a song, other than *Fish gotta swim birds gotta fly*," Denny surmises and sounds vaguely disappointed.

"Uh, no. I guess not."

"So why are we doing this?" he inquires.

I desperately want to smoke a cigarette. Why hadn't I picked up some chewing gum on the way home from school? You can't quit smoking without gum. "I don't know. Because we're in the 'burbs and there's nothing on TV and so eventually you sleep with everyone."

"C'mon Jess, seriously," he says.

"Well," I think for a second and then continue, "you'd probably agree that everyone does things for his or her own reasons and sometimes they're entirely different reasons. Mine is this: I find you to be an interesting, attractive man. And, you know, there's kind of a mystique about older men, particularly ones who have slept with my mom. How often in this life do you get a chance to share boyfriends with your mother? Or maybe it's a father figure thing. I don't know for sure. I haven't read enough Greek literature." I abruptly stop talking but then quickly begin again. "But, I mean, I think it's important to understand that we're not in love or anything like that. It was just a once off kind of thing." I look at Denny for confirmation.

"Sure, of course." Denny climbs off of me and gets up out of the bed. "Just a once in a lifetime thing. A one night stand, that's all," he explains unconvincingly. Denny leans over to pick up his clothes.

"So then what was in it for you?" I inquire. I start to think that maybe this whole thing was a mistake, after all.

"Me? I was just following nature's path. That ache, that sensation, that longing which completely obliterates any thought of dirty diapers, 2:00 AM feedings and the high cost of basketball sneakers. The primordial urge to continue the species. How else would there be a next generation, for *Star Trek* or anybody?"

"How romantic," I reply. "I'm dating Darwin."

Denny sits on the side of the bed and begins to pull on his clothes.

"Where are you going?" I ask.

"Well, you know . . . "

"I didn't mean that you couldn't stay. It's only Friday night and my parents aren't coming home until Sunday."

"Oh." He drops Gene's shorts back onto the floor. "Do you want me to stay?"

"Of course, if you want to."

"Yeah, okay, a two night stand. That could work. A meaningful half hour relationship." Denny climbs back into the bed next to me and says, "I knew that. Of course I'm not Mr. Right. I mean, I never even entertained the thought that . . . "

"It's more like you're Mr. Right Now. How's that?"

"That is . . . " Denny starts to chuckle. "That reminds me of a Crosby, Stills and Nash song that was popular in the late sixties, *Love the One You're With*."

Denny softly sings a few lines: "*Don't be angry, don't be sad. And don't sit cryin' over good times you've had. There's a girl right next to you and she's waitin' for something to do.*"

"I like that. You know, when you say stuff like that I can't decide if it's your mind or your body that I'm after," I tease him. "So why don't we make that our song?"

"Great idea. I'd like it if we at least had a song. It's much more civilized, don't you agree?"

"Just promise me that you won't get crazy and spray paint our names on an overpass or call the local radio station and have them wish me a happy birthday during morning drive time."

"I promise," Denny replies and slides his hand underneath the terrycloth robe I'm wearing and caresses my stomach. "But seriously, I was thinking that we could move to Vermont and, well, perhaps open an Inn together. My house would sell for a lot of money. And then, I mean, with your marketing degree I could take early retirement and . . . "

"An Inn in Vermont?" I ask skeptically, not knowing whether or not his offer is meant to be sincerely entertained, although it sounds very romantic and all.

"Sure. You know, a Bed and Breakfast," he continues. "But if you don't like Vermont we could go to Massachusetts or even New Hampshire. I really like their license plates in New Hampshire: 'Live Free Or Die.'"

"Only they're probably painted by guys in prison," I suggest.

"C'mon, it would be great up there; ski trails, hot apple cider with cinnamon sticks, and snowmobiles," he continues dreamily. "You could do the brochures and I'll fix things and . . . and make the breakfast, of course."

"You just want to poison people with fuchsia biscuits and tangerine omelets."

But Denny doesn't smile. He looks at me intently, earnestly. Oh, God, I've created a monster.

"Pennies in a stream, falling leaves of Sycamore, moonlight in Vermont," he sings.

"No, Denny," I interrupt him, my voice sounding firm but polite. I really don't want to hurt his feelings by explaining that it's definitely a mistake to combine the end of his life with the beginning of mine. "I'm sorry but I just don't think that an Inn in Vermont . . . "

"Like I said, it doesn't have to be Vermont. There's also Maine. Don't forget about Maine," he looks at me hopefully. "Picture a big white Victorian clapboard called The Down-Easter or The Blue Marlin."

"Let's just say New England for the purpose of this discussion," I say gently, but matter-of-factly, still trying my best not to demolish his charming fantasy. "It's a sweet idea and everything but I really think that uh . . . "

But before I can find the right words he leans over and whispers in my ear, "I was only kidding," and then smiles at me.

"You're an asshole!" I holler at him. "Why do I even listen to you?"

He gently moves his hand up and across to my breast, lingering for a second when he brushes against my nipple. Denny leans over and places his mouth where his hand was and slides the robe off my shoulders.

Determined not to lose control of our lovemaking session for a second time, I deftly slide down so that I can perform oral sex on him.

Denny leans his back against the headboard and watches me slide my mouth up and down on him. As I hasten my rhythm Denny suddenly stops me. He quickly reaches over to the night table, seizes the remaining condom and hastily slips it on.

As Denny starts to position himself above me, I press down on his shoulders so that instead he slides down underneath me. And once I maneuver to get on top of him, he either remains still or gingerly moves to try and keep my pace. Denny seems to know when I'm about to finish and he makes a few deliberate thrusts and we simultaneously reach a climax.

Denny looks very serious right up until the final second and then a little smile pulls on the corners of his mouth. And though I feel a hot rush of pleasure course through my arteries I imagine that whatever expression is on my face is probably one of complete idiocy.

Afterwards, my body feels totally relaxed, my spirit at peace with the world and yet my mind starts to race. I instantly understand how so many successful careers have been ruined by plain old-fashioned friction. And how so many lives have spun out of control as a result of a twenty-minute illicit sexual encounter. It's no wonder the Catholic Church is so worried about young people discovering orgasms. No one would show up for Friday night Vespers anymore. Or if they did, it would be with a partner and a blanket and they'd light some candles and cuddle in the back pew. But the Church is actually missing out on a big marketing opportunity. Because I suddenly feel a lot nicer. Like, if my family were home I could easily see myself clearing the table, weeding the garden and reading bedtime horror stories to my little brothers. There is just something incredibly exciting and satisfying about sex that you can't find in *Jeopardy* reruns or even in a good job offer, for that matter.

But most of all I wonder why, for the past two years, I'd defined myself by the way Carl felt about me. Denny is right. It's about the way the other person makes me feel about myself

We remain silent for almost a full minute, busy sorting our individual thoughts, and, I imagine, dreaming of nicotine.

After I finally move off to one side, Denny groans and crushes a pillow over his face.

"What's wrong?" I ask.

"Jess, what if Sarah was the only thing between me and insanity, going off the deep end?"

"Denny! Please tell me you weren't thinking about Sarah while we were having sex," I demand, more than a little indignantly.

"Oh God, no. I can promise you that. I guess . . . I guess it felt so good that I just suddenly started to feel guilty."

"Are you sure?"

"I promise," Denny says, and gently kisses me on the cheek.

Okay, I'm convinced. "So you're thinking that maybe Sarah's purpose in life was to keep you away from the devil?"

"Exactly!" he replies excitedly. "You read my mind."

"Why? Would she say something bad about all this?"

"Oh God, I can't even imagine. Wait. Yes, I can. Sarah would always find some book she'd recently read which she thought explained all of my behavior. For instance, the one time that she referred to my affair with Joan, when we were arguing about what year we had sold the yellow Cutlass, Sarah said, 'I know that it was 1979 because you were going through your *Couples* phase.'"

"I don't get it. What's that supposed to mean?"

"I forgot, you weren't born yet. *Couples* was this 1960s John Updike manifesto which portrayed adultery as the opiate of the flourishing suburban masses. And then years later, when I became interested in astronomy and tried to locate a comet, she told the girls that I was going through a *Contact* phase and that it could all be traced back to Carl Sagan. So I guess right now she would have exactly two words for me: *Peyton Place*."

But I'm too exhausted to continue trying to make sense out of the constant collisions between Denny's past and present. I actually consider telling him to just go home. "Aren't you tired?" I ask him.

Denny turns towards the night table and clicks out the light. "You know what? That's the first time in about twenty years that I've had sex with the lights on."

"Trying to conserve energy?" I ask while stretching out on my side of the bed, ready to fall asleep. I am truly exhausted. But I'm also curious again as to what Denny thought about us. "So the protocol is that I'm not supposed to ask or talk about the sex, right?"

"Actually, there's a way around that."

"How's that?"

"You tell your lover how good he was and this gives him the perfect opportunity to throw you a compliment."

"Yeah, right. Dream on Gramps."

"How can your parents possibly make love with that wooden crucifix staring back at them from above the dresser?" he asks. "It interfered with my concentration."

"Then don't look at it. If you need visual aids concentrate on the gun rack instead," I sleepily suggest even though I'm not planning on having sex with him again. Gene's five hunting rifles, which the children are forbidden to touch under any circumstances, are stored in a gun rack above the dresser. Joan allows him to keep the guns there under the condition that no moose heads or other taxidermist creations are ever to be displayed in her home. She calls it his bureau of alcohol, tobacco and firearms, since it's also where he stores his pipe and miniature bottles of airplane whiskey.

"How can you help but look at it?" Denny says. When I don't respond he asks, "Jess, do you believe in God?"

"Of course I believe in God," I mumble drowsily. "Especially if I have a big exam. Why? Don't you?"

"I used to. But I don't think that I do anymore. Robert Frost wrote: 'I turned to speak to God / About the world's despair / But to make matters worse; / I found God wasn't there.'"

"Don't you believe in God if you're on a plane?" I ask in the darkness.

"Well, sometimes if there's a lot of turbulence and they interrupt the beverage service so the flight attendants can strap themselves in. I mean, I'm not crazy. Asking for heavenly protection is a hard habit to break. I've recently asked God to give me the strength to become an atheist." He turns over so that he's facing my back and puts his arm around me. Eventually we both fall asleep.

Some time later I wake and go to use the bathroom at the opposite end of the hallway, assuming, or rather, hoping, that Noose is still ensconced in the master bathroom. And if for some reason he isn't there, I decide that I really don't want to know about it.

Upon returning to the bedroom I study Denny for a few minutes in the pale moonlight and decide that he is a tidy sleeper. He certainly isn't a bed or blanket hog, and he doesn't appear to snore or make funny slurping noises the way that Carl does. He even sleeps with his hands neatly arranged by his sides and a peaceful look on his face. In fact, I decide, he could just as easily be lying in a coffin.

After that last thought, I can't expel this possibility from my mind. What if he is dead? What will I do? I briefly imagine the police making a fluorescent chalk outline on my parents' bed.

No. It's ridiculous. He's breathing—surely the sheet is moving up and down. Isn't it? I start to panic. Somehow, I have to make sure. I turn on a light and run to retrieve a small hand mirror from my dresser drawer.

Before I can place it under Denny's nose his eyelids flicker open. He stares up at me and calmly asks, "What are you doing?"

"Nothing," I reply tersely and quickly hide the mirror behind my back and turn out the light.

"You thought I was dead, didn't you?" he inquires sleepily.

"I did not." Once under the covers, I move closer to Denny and hug his broad back.

"You're as bad as my daughters. God, I feel like I'm in *The Invasion of the Body Snatchers*. Every time I close my eyes someone runs for a tape measure and embalming fluid."

"I didn't think you were dead," I insist. "All right, maybe a light coma."

"Well don't flatter yourself. Sex with you couldn't kill a guy, even one of my advanced age," he says and then yawns.

"We'll see about that," I reply. A few minutes pass.

"Jess, are you still awake?" he asks quietly.

"Hmm."

"I've been thinking and I-uh-I want you to have Sarah's car. Amazingly enough, it wasn't damaged very much in the accident and the insurance paid for what needed fixing. It's a nice blue Camry. I'm serious and I won't take no for an answer. If you want you can send me a thousand dollars after you've earned some money. But I'd rather you just take it. As I'm sure you can imagine, no one in my family wants it."

"Okay," I eventually respond. "But just tell me why."

"Why? Because I want you to have all the things you desire in life. I want you to succeed beyond your wildest dreams. And so it will help if you don't have to take public transportation everywhere when you're in Chicago or have to make a few hundred dollars in car payments every month."

"And what else?" I ask.

"I think that you already know what else."

"Tell me anyway."

"Jess, just leave it alone. Please."

"Denny?"

"Yes?"

"You knew when you came here that my dad recently had a heart attack, didn't you? Mr. Sutherland told you, right?" After all, didn't Denny even admit to me that the first thing he does every morning is to scan the obituaries. Has he been paying special attention to the M's?

"Yes. I knew."

"He's okay now," I say. "Everything is fine now."

"Apparently so."

I turn away from Denny and curl up in order to go back to sleep. But I can't sleep thinking about everything—making love, moving to Chicago, Denny and Mom. Should I be worried?

It's as if Denny reads my mind. He slides behind me and begins lightly kissing the back of my neck and breathing heavily. "Everything will be okay," he whispers in my ear.

Denny's kisses are more than the goodnight variety. I start to feel a tingling sensation wherever his hands caress my body and I rub against him like a cat that's being stroked and wanting more.

"Turn around," he says quietly.

"Should I go and get another condom?"

"No, no. Just turn around. I want to kiss you. We can just enjoy each other a little while longer."

We lie there and kiss for a long while. Denny's lips are soft and his mouth is inviting and he has the saliva thing figured out perfectly, not like some guys, where you wish there was a little dentist's vacuum running on the side. And Denny doesn't say stupid stuff while kissing me. Before he sticks his tongue in my mouth Carl always makes some idiotic football reference like, "Okay, collapse the middle." And it often seems as if guys only bother to kiss as a pit stop on the highway to the tunnel.

But Denny and I kiss just for the sake of kissing. I open my eyes ever so slightly to check and see if he's looking at me but he's not. Denny's eyes are closed and his face looks calm and lovely. I decide that from now on I'm going to kiss just like Denny, slowly and passionately and with my eyes closed.

"Goodnight stars, Goodnight air, Goodnight noises everywhere."
Jess reading *Goodnight Moon* to her little brothers.

"Sweet dreams 'til sunbeams find you.
Sweet dreams that leave all worries behind you.
But in your dreams, whatever they be, dream a little dream of me."
Dream A Little Dream of Me, Mama Cass.

Chapter 17
Two for the Road
Saturday Morning

Gene's rich tenor voice singing *Don't Fence Me In* echoes in the stairwell as he clambers through the entrance hall at ten o'clock the following morning. The words act as an alarm bell for me. Specifically, more like a death knell. Denny and I wake up at precisely the same second.

"Oh my God, my parents!" I exclaim in a stage whisper. "They're home!"

"Jessica, are you home?" Gene's voice booms from the front hall. "Why do I smell smoke? Mother, do you smell smoke?"

"Maybe something is burning," I hear my eternally sensible mother suggest. "Or maybe Jessica is grilling some burgers in the backyard."

I can hear Joan trotting up the stairs and then feel the beat of her short, quick steps treading down the hallway towards the master bedroom. Denny frantically attempts to untangle some clothes from out of the heap of blankets on the floor next to the bed.

"Jessica?" she calls. "Yoo-hoo. Are you here?"

I try to recall if I've recently killed a leprechaun. There is some serious bad luck heading towards this room in the form of Joan MacGuire, neatly dressed in J.C. Penney casual sportswear.

"But you told me they weren't coming home until tomorrow night!" Denny says accusatorily.

I wonder if by pointing this out Denny is hoping that I can somehow rescue us from the horrible reality of our situation.

"Honey, are you still sleeping? We're home!" Joan calls out as she first checks the now smoke-damaged room that I share with Katie. "Oh my goodness," she exclaims. Apparently the missing mattress and the charbroiled curtains have not gone unnoticed.

"Quick," I frantically whisper to Denny, "Hide!"

Denny panics. With one leg in Gene's khaki shorts and one free he takes a step towards the bathroom door—the only place he can possibly attempt to hide.

Before making his move he quickly grabs my hand. For only a second we squeeze each other's palms. It's just enough time for Denny to quickly say, "Bye, Darling."

"Bambaduza!" I reply as he rushes towards the bathroom door.

"Jessica, are you in my bedroom?" Joan turns the doorknob.

But Denny has already scrambled three-quarters of the way to the bathroom, as if he is competing in a three-legged race. Right before grabbing the bathroom doorknob he trips and plunges to the floor. I gasp as I see the bedroom door slowly open. Somehow he manages to drag himself the final two feet and close the bathroom door just before Joan enters the room.

"Would someone please explain what is going on here!" Joan insists. Her green eyes dart around the room and quickly register an empty ice cream carton, two dirty spoons, a panicky daughter, rumpled linens and clothes strewn across the floor.

"Mom! What are you doing home early?" My voice is trembling.

"Don't answer a question with a question young lady." Joan automatically begins to straighten up the untidy room. "Roger has tonsillitis and we have a doctor's appointment at eleven-thirty. I tried to phone you late last night but eventually decided that you must have gone to bed early." Joan looks skeptically at the men's Polo shirt that is lying on the floor.

"I can explain everything," I lie and pull the sheet up around my neck. I know that I can't explain anything. If only I had studied law. I could perhaps have argued the inherit conflict between the church doctrines *Honor thy Mother and Father* and *Thou shalt love thy neighbor.* I had taken to treating the commandments more as sound suggestions over the past few years.

"I certainly hope so." Joan heads towards the bathroom with her toiletries bag in hand.

"Don't go in there!" I shout and abruptly sit bolt upright in the bed. The final convulsion of a chicken before being butchered.

"Why not?" Joan stops briefly, doorknob in hand. If seeing the room in disarray hasn't set off her maternal radar then it is certainly notched up to red alert status by my reaction.

"Jessica, what in heaven's name is going on here?" Joan suspiciously inquires.

"Nothing. I mean the snake. Loose is noose. No, I mean Noose is loose. He's in there!" Shit! I point an accusatory finger at the closed door, desperately urging my mom to change her course.

"Ishkabibble!" Joan replies. This is part of her home economics slang that includes such daring expletives as *Holy hat racks* and *Good gravy.*

"Joanie, where are you?" Gene bellows irritably from the bottom of the stairs. "There's a mattress lying in the middle of my backyard! An entire colony of gophers is probably moving all their little gopher furniture in there right this very minute." Then he begins trudging up the stairs.

"Jesus H. Christ on rollerblades!" Gene bellows upon surveying the master bedroom. "Why don't we just take a jalopy apart on the front lawn? It looks like a band of tinkers moved in while we were away. Has Grady been over here? This house looks worse than the Donnybrook fairgrounds." Gene's face is flushed and he appears overdue for a blood pressure pill.

I realize that I may just as well start reciting the Mass for the Dead. I find myself wishfully gazing up at the miniature replica of Jesus nailed to the cross—Jesus, who died to pay for my sins—and praying for a medium to large-sized miracle. I promise God that I will never again blow off church. I make a mental list of good works which I pledge to perform each week that include everything from weeding the garden for the Nuns, to not sleeping with any of my mom's ex-boyfriends, or father's ex-girlfriends, for that matter.

My urgent prayers are suddenly answered by none other than Joan MacGuire. It is remarkable. In a real emergency, the Lord has almost zero turnaround time.

"Gene, calm down please," Joan replies curtly, but continues to eye me doubtfully. "Noose has escaped his cage again," she evenly informs her husband. "Please go downstairs and see if you can find that reptile before he goes over to the empty lot to feast on Mrs. Butler's rats. Jessica believes that he may be in the garage."

"Jesus, Mary and Joseph. Where's Jack?" bellows Gene. "I've told your son to make a new top for that aquarium at least ten times!" When Gene is displeased he automatically turns over his half ownership in the children to Joan so they become *your* sons and daughters. "And would someone mind telling me why there's a burned out mattress lying on my grass?" Gene looks directly at me as I sit leaning up against his headboard with the sheet drawn up over me.

"There was a fire," Joan calmly interjects. "Now Gene, please go and find that snake before it gives a fright to one of the neighbors. We'll deal with the mattress once Jessica has had a chance to shower and get dressed. I'm sure that she can explain everything."

"I hope so," Gene replies sternly and obediently turns to exit the room.

I'm in shock. Is my mother covering for me? After all, I'd just told her that the snake is in the bathroom. Or is this just the calm before the storm?

Joan narrows her eyes at me and sternly inquires, "All right, who pray tell is in my bathroom, Jessica? Is it Carl?"

"Uh, no." I decide that the chance of Denny having climbed out the two-by-two second-story window is slim to none and Slim just walked away. "Denny Sinclair," I whisper as softly as possible.

Joan looks startled after I report the truth but appears to quickly regain her composure. "I see," she says as she stands directly in front of the closed bathroom door. "I had a feeling he might show up—although not in my bathroom. But then the Lord works in mysterious ways." Joan takes a deep breath, pulls herself up to her full five-feet, seven inches and raps three times on the door. Then she bluntly warns of her plan to invade: "It's Joan and I'm coming in!" The door with the full-length mirror covering it opens slightly and then my mother disappears through the looking glass.

It immediately crosses my mind that I'm now faced with a golden opportunity to flee. In fact, my parents don't even know about the new job. I can move to Chicago and start a new life under an assumed name and have plastic surgery.

Joan must have telepathically tapped into what I'm thinking because at the same second the door opens a crack and she says, "Jessica, I'll see you at the kitchen table in exactly fifteen minutes. But first I want you to find out where your father is. I don't want him to see Denny leave this house. And Denny *is* leaving this house. Now."

There is a certain amount of relief to be found in no longer being in charge, I decide, despite any unpleasant consequences, particularly when circumstances become bigger than one's self.

What are they talking about in there? I wonder. The logistics of Denny's escape? Or is it more? Is he going to confess everything? Is Joan purposely using the old police trick of keeping the suspects apart so we can't collaborate on our story? And if that's the case, what exactly is our story?

Then it hits me. Joan isn't covering for me, she's protecting herself. Or possibly both of us. What can Joan possibly do to me? I haven't done anything that she hadn't herself done. I decide to go along with my mother's plan to facilitate Denny's escape.

After he's been hurriedly ushered out through the back porch and Joan has told him just to keep Gene's shorts, my mother makes a fresh pitcher of iced tea and directs me to the picnic table in the backyard, apparently so that we can have some privacy. I prepare for the worst. Joan has seemed entirely too placid up to this point.

"Have you been using some sort of contraception during this little tryst," she evenly inquires as she pours us each a tall glass of iced tea with a remarkably steady hand.

I feel my face turn scarlet. Surely it is in both Denny's and my best interest to deny that anything has taken place. I don't answer right away. Maybe my mother is bluffing.

"What do you mean?" I say evasively. "What did he tell you?"

"He didn't have to *tell* me anything. Don't take me for a fool Jessica," my mother snaps authoritatively. "Now give me an answer. I'm too young for grandchildren. I'm too old to fall for any fake story you might try to concoct. And it goes without saying that your father doesn't need another heart attack."

I gulp, look down at my full glass and murmur, "Yes."

"Are you sure?" Joan narrows her eyes so that they double as a lie detector test.

I decide that I should have followed my initial instincts and fled to the bus station. "I'm sure," I reply. I have suddenly developed laryngitis. "Mom, it's not what you think . . . " I start to explain in a voice that's barely audible and then I choke.

However, my mother takes a sip of iced tea and appears to be entirely refreshed. "So," she asks, almost too cheerfully, I decide, considering the circumstances, "Tell me how your exam went."

I clear my throat. "Fine. Fine. I got a C, maybe even a B. It'll transfer. And I—I got a job."

"Oh really?" Joan smiles approvingly at me as I share this news.

"In Chicago. I'll be an assistant to an assistant in the marketing department at the Geller Soup Company. Tomato paste."

"Now won't that please your father," Mom announces good-naturedly.

"It doesn't pay a lot. Five hundred dollars a week."

"No one earns much money in a first job, Jessica. Everybody has to start somewhere."

"I guess so."

"And what happened to your bed?" my mother continues the interrogation in an upbeat tone, as if we are discussing what tulip bulbs to plant next spring.

I'm too exhausted to lie. "I, uh, I set it on fire. I'm sorry." I cast my eyes downward and study the grass. "I'll buy a new mattress as soon as I get my first paycheck."

"I assume that you learned a lesson about careless smoking the hard way. I'm just grateful that you . . . " she pauses, apparently remembering that I was entertaining while she was away, " . . . that no one was hurt. You don't have to worry about buying a new one. Knowing your father, our insurance will cover it. He doesn't take any chances, what with five children and a septic tank. We're covered for everything, including dog bites and acts of God."

I really wish that my mother hadn't brought God into the conversation. "Uh, about what happened, I—"

"Jessica," Joan cuts me off again, but not in an unfriendly tone of voice, "If it's all right with you, I don't think there's any reason to ever discuss this matter again."

My lower jaw must drop an inch and a quarter. My mom is the last person on earth I ever expected to implement a *Don't ask, don't tell* policy around the house.

Joan breezily continues, despite my apparent surprise. "You are probably more aware than anyone that I'm not one of these modern mothers who strives to be best friends with her children. It's my philosophy that you can always find a confidante, but that you only have one mother." She takes another sip of iced tea. "And I'd like to continue on in that capacity, if it's all the same to you."

"Sure," I say. In fact, I welcome not having the dreaded Denny conversation practically as much as I was relieved to discover that sex education would be taught in school and not around our kitchen table.

"Do you understand me?"

"I think so. I just thought that I should tell you that he, that Denny, gave me one of his cars. A Toyota Camry."

"Oh. Well, that's between you and Denny. However, if you decide to pursue the relationship, I would urge you to consider it very carefully."

I gaze up at the clear blue sky. In the distance I can see the water tower with the name of the town painted on it in thick, inky black letters. From our backyard I can only see the last five, which spell out AFORD.

I turn back to my mother. "Mom, he's in love with you, not me."

She brushes some imaginary crumbs from the folds of her skirt. I wonder if she's examining the ivory-colored linen material or perhaps the gold wedding band that is fitted securely on her ring finger.

"Well, that's his problem then, isn't it?"

This is such a Joan thing to say. Like *Hand-me-downs are fun*, or *Just worry about yourself.*

"He'll get over it," Joan continues philosophically. "Men are like cats. They always manage to land on their feet. It's we women who end up bearing the burden."

I replay the words *we women* over in my mind. It is so inclusive.

Then Joan looks over her shoulder as if she's making sure that no one is in earshot. "Let me just say one more thing."

Okay, here it comes, I think. I'm about to be grounded for an eon. There will be no tricentennial party for me.

Mom leans towards me conspiratorially. "Jessica, you're a grown woman now and you have to do whatever you think is right. I wasn't a virgin when I married your father." I notice she says the V word very quietly. When Mom uses the words Virgin and Mary in a sentence it is usually one with an entirely different meaning.

She takes another cursory glance in the direction of the house. "And with your father being Catholic and all, I thought it was best not to mention that fact at first. Who knew we were going to get married?

And well, you know how secrets are—if you don't start out on the right foot then there never seems to be an appropriate time to remedy these things. Anyway, we all make mistakes, Jessica. I guess that what I'm trying to say is that you're not accountable to us anymore, just to yourself. That's all. I just want you to be careful. And of course, I want you to be happy."

I silently stare back at my mother. In the bright sunlight I notice her flashing green eyes and think that perhaps they are indeed similar to my own. And that maybe there are worse things in life than turning out to be just a little bit like her. And even though I'm positive that I don't want to be a lot like my mother, or live a life similar to hers, I think that at the very least I might no longer be embarrassed when we're in the mall together and she has on one of those plastic rain bonnets that makes it appear as if her entire skull has been engulfed in Saran Wrap. And maybe I'll no longer pretend to be with someone else in the toy store when my father totally mangles the name of whatever gift he is supposed to be buying and in his confusion asks the clerk for *Mutilated Morphin Power Teenagers.*

"Mother," Gene suddenly bellows from out of the upstairs bedroom window, "Jesus Christ on crutches. Why are my sport shirts in the laundry basket? They were clean when we left."

"What are you going to tell him?" I anxiously look up at my mother.

She calmly places her hand on top of mine. "Let me worry about that. You just go and report the good news about the math exam and your new job." Together we rise and Mom automatically straightens out the flimsy foam cushions on the painted wrought-iron chairs. "And remember, loose lips sink ships," she softly warns me.

"Right," I agree. "Case closed."

This legal reference is not lost on Joan, though she doesn't say anything. She catches my eye and gives me a subtle smile, one that speaks the world to me. It seems to say: *Now you know that it isn't necessary to spend your days in torment, desperately trying to explain who you are to your family and friends, in an effort to feel understood and therefore loved. The people who care, will, of course, understand, and maybe understand even a little better than you thought they would. And, of course, they will love you.*

But maybe I'm reading too much into it.

We head towards the house. But Mom stops. She faces me and places her hands on my shoulders. I am only about an inch taller than she is and so we basically see eye to eye and from the odd way she is looking at me I think that she is about to say something very, very profound indeed. Here comes the meaning of life. I am finally ready. The wisdom of the ages will be passed from mother to daughter, from one generation to the next. She removes her left hand from my shoulder and brushes my overgrown bangs off my face and says,

"You're so pretty Jessica. Now if only you would put a clip in your hair."

ABOUT THE AUTHOR

Laura Pedersen currently hosts her own TV show on Oxygen Media. She was the youngest person to have a seat on the floor of the American Stock Exchange and wrote her first nonfiction book, PLAY MONEY, about that experience. Her second book, STREET-SMART CAREER GUIDE is about entrepreneurship. Ms. Pedersen has a finance degree from New York University's Stern School of Business, and writes for THE NEW YORK TIMES.

In 1994, President Clinton honored her as one of Ten Outstanding Young Americans. She has appeared on shows such as "CNN," "Oprah," "Good Morning America," "Primetime Live," and "David Letterman." She has performed stand-up comedy at "The Improv," and other clubs, and writes material for several well-known comedians. GOING AWAY PARTY is her first novel.

She lives in New York City and teaches at the Booker T. Washington Learning Center in East Harlem.